REMNANTS:
SEASON OF GLORY

Other books by Lisa T. Bergren

Remnants: Season of Wonder

Remnants: Season of Fire

REMNANTS: SEASON OF GLORY

BOOK 3 IN THE REMNANTS SERIES

BY LISA T. BERGREN

BLINK

CHAPTER
1

ANDRIANA

She should have come with us," I said, looking over the farm, far below. "They're coming." My heart pounded as we watched four vehicles wind down the dirt road toward Galen's house. To the east, the sun was just beginning to warm the horizon. "She did her best to save you, Ronan." My eyes flicked from him to Niero—who had literally *breathed life* into my Knight—and back again. "And we just . . . left her."

Ronan took my hand in his. "She wanted to stay," he said. "To come with us . . ."

"Would've changed her entire life," Niero finished, brushing past us. "Come on. We need to cover more miles before dawn gives them the edge they seek." He inclined his head down the hill, as the Pacifican vehicles drew near. I swallowed hard. Had they simply guessed we were there, or had they learned of our presence by some other method? We'd escaped Palace

Pacifica and killed a number of the guards and, hopefully, Lord Maximillian Jala, if not more among Keallach's Council of Six. They'd chased us through the tunnels and now, apparently, had tracked us to Galen's farm. *Galen, oh, Galen . . .*

I stayed rooted to the spot, ignoring Vidar's empathetic pause and Bellona's gruff, "C'mon, Dri." Mom squeezed my arm as she and Dad passed. Only Ronan stayed with me, his hand moving to my lower back. "Dri?"

"I-I can't," I whispered. "I have to know . . . know that she's all right. We *owe* her, Ronan."

"We gave her the chance to come with us," he said.

"It wasn't as if she had days to think about it. She has a life here."

His breath caught and then eased out, as he decided on patience. Galen had been our savior the night before. If she hadn't taken us in, given us shelter, operated on Ronan's wound . . . would Niero have been able to save him? Angel or not, had he built on what Galen started? I wrapped my hand around Ronan's arm and rested my cheek against his shoulder, remembering how close he'd been to death, how pale he'd been after all the blood loss . . . and then the ivory tone of Niero's wings. *Wings,* I mused. *Our captain has wings.* It was at once both a surprise and yet something I'd known for a very long time. His uncanny way of knowing what I was thinking, his fierce protection, his skills in leading, and his body's ability to heal . . .

Ronan stiffened as the trucks ground to a halt. The sound of the tires against the gravel of the barnyard carried up the small canyon we'd just climbed. I reached forward and moved a branch slightly to the side so we could see Galen leave the barn, wiping her forehead with one gloved hand and carrying a pail, as if just completing her morning chores. I prayed she'd been able to clean up the bloody table and stow any evidence that we'd been there.

"Down on your knees!" the Pacifican guard growled, lifting a pistol toward her. His voice came to us, distant but startlingly clear.

Galen immediately dropped her pail and did as he asked. In the dawning light, their bodies looked like golden-edged forms, far below us.

"Hands on your head!" cried another as the first approached her. Others surrounded the barn and entered cautiously, weapons drawn. Yet more ran to her house to do the same.

"Who are you? What are you doing here?"

She faced away from us, so we couldn't make out her words.

The man reached her and circled her. It was then that I thought I recognized him as one of the men we'd battled in the palace. There were still great blotches of blood on his gray uniform.

"Fugitives were seen coming in this direction last night," he said to her. He said something else, but he'd turned again and dropped his voice, making his comments unintelligible.

I let the branch cover us as I glimpsed a Pacifican passing a window in a top-floor bedroom of the house. The last thing we needed was to be spotted. It would be hard enough to escape Pacifica without a significant head start. I could hear the low tones of continuing discussion between Galen and her captor but still couldn't decipher any words.

"Over here," Ronan said, crouching and leading me by the hand to the right. We peered out through a pine tree that had a split in the middle.

The men who had gone into the barn and house now streamed out, and two approached the one in charge to report.

"No! I swear it!" Galen cried suddenly.

The man pistol-whipped her across the cheek. "You lie! There is blood on the table! They were here. You treated their wounded!"

"I did not. I butchered a lamb yesterday," she said. "You can check my shed and see the carcass for yourself."

"Smart," hissed the man. But then I saw another man on the outskirts of their circle toss a plastic bag inward. It was the plastic bag and tubing she'd used to put blood back into Ronan.

Oh no . . . I dared to peek out farther to get a better look.

The Pacifican held the bag above Galen's head. "This is not the tool of a butcher. It is the tool of a *physician*," he said, leaning toward her, and spitting out the word as if it was foul in his mouth. "How many were here? Where are they now?" He grabbed hold of her shirt and pulled her to within inches of his face.

"Where?" the Pacifican snarled. The man shook her so hard that her head whipped back and forth. "Where did they go?"

When she remained silent, he threw her to the ground. She sprawled on her side, arms outstretched.

"Half of you search the hillside!" he commanded the others. "Move! And the other half take a Jeep and search down that road." He gestured toward a road that splintered off the main drive, to our left.

A group of Pacifican soldiers reached the bottom of the hill and fanned out, searching the foliage and ground for any sign of us. "Dri," Ronan warned in a whisper. "Now we *have* to go."

Reluctantly, I allowed him to pull me away, aware that we couldn't stay . . . couldn't be discovered. But as we entered the path behind the rest of our party, who'd gone on without us, we heard Galen scream. I froze, pulling Ronan to a stop.

Worse was how her voice cut off in a horrific, brief choking sound.

Then all was silence.

No. No, no, no . . . .

"Dri," Ronan whispered, pulling me in close as I trembled. "It's over. We can't do anything but live for the cause Galen served." My throat burned with the sobs that I desperately wanted to let loose. It was all too much. Too much. Because she'd chosen to help us, Galen was now dead.

"It's war, Dri. This is but one battle," he said. "We'll make them pay for this. But not today. If we're discovered here, now, we might never escape Pacifica again."

I nodded slightly and swallowed hard, closing my eyes and concentrating on my breathing, on Ronan's welcome warmth and scent, on the gift of his beating heart, his life, and on the hundred questions I wanted to ask Niero. Why hadn't he done something now, here, about Galen? Why hadn't he saved her, as he had saved Ronan?

But the thought only brought anger and resentment flooding through me. I needed to concentrate on what was good and right. I dug deep, thanking the Maker that Ronan was with me, alive, as were my parents. *My parents . . .* For so long I'd thought them dead. I focused on Niero finding a way out of Pacifica and across the Great Expanse, as I turned to follow my Knight.

Ronan and I settled into a jog, now bent on not letting our pursuers glimpse us as we moved deeper into the forest. We spotted the rest of our crew ahead on the next ridge, waiting, watching. I itched to be with my parents and the rest of the Ailith, fully connected again, along with those we were missing—Chaza'el, Tressa, Killian, and Kapriel.

Just as suddenly as it came, my smile faded, as my thoughts moved from Kapriel to Keallach—the emperor of Pacifica, Ailith brother, my former captor, and Kapriel's twin. My feelings were jumbled each time I thought about him. How much had Keallach known of what was to come? Of what the Council would demand of me? Had he been absent on purpose?

I lifted my face to the gently falling rain, welcoming the cooling drops and relishing the scent of ozone on the air, which reminded me of the Valley.

Home. Home was where the Maker was calling us.

"You sense that, Ronan? Where we're to go?"

"Is that our true direction? Or is it just the rain, making us homesick?" he asked. Our trail dipped, and for the moment the rest of our crew was hidden. Ronan pulled me to a stop and turned to face me.

"Maybe both," I said, pulling him closer until our foreheads touched. There was some hesitation in him, a distance I didn't care for. "Are you all right?"

"Yeah," he said, lifting his head from mine. But I definitely felt it. Irritation? Frustration? Doubt? I tried to pin it down. I'd rarely felt such things from him.

"Hey," I said. "What's wrong?"

"Dri, I . . ." He pulled his hands from mine and closed his eyes, sighing heavily. "It's nothing. We can talk about it later."

"Talk?" I said, edging closer to him again, lifting my lips toward his. "Are you sure that's what we need?"

His eyes stilled, but he did not lean down to meet me. He put his hands on my shoulders. "Yes. We need to talk. Definitely before we kiss. But now is not the time." He set off down the trail again, and I quickly followed.

"Ronan."

"Leave it alone, Dri," he said, flicking his hand out and away. "We'll talk later."

My heart clamped in fear. What was happening here? Why was I feeling a widening chasm between us, when we were finally reunited? "Why not now? Ronan!"

He turned so abruptly that I almost ran into him. "He saw you, okay? Chaza'el. He saw you kissing Keallach."

I swallowed hard. It didn't take an empath to detect the bitter pain and anger in his tone.

"Oh," I said, feeling the heat rise in my cheeks. Of all the things that Chaza'el might have seen, he had to see *that*? "Ronan, I'm sorry. Keallach—I think Sethos has some sort of spell over him. He would fade out and be distant once in a while."

"It didn't sound like he was *distant* around you."

"No, you don't understand. He'd seem distant, and then he'd compel me. Force my body to do things I didn't wish to do."

"Things?" he said, eyes narrowing.

"Kissing. Just kissing," I rushed on. "I think Sethos was behind his desire to take me as his bride. When we talked about it, he denied it. But the Council . . . they thought our union would help them bring the Trading Union into the Pacifica Empire. And our shared Ailith blood . . . they wanted to capitalize on it, as well as on my gifting. I don't think . . ." I lifted my hand and massaged my forehead. "I don't think that Keallach was fully engaged in the plan. Sethos was making him compel me into such kisses, probably hoping I'd believe I was falling for him, that there was an attraction I couldn't deny—and maybe that'd make me more amenable to their whole plan."

His green-brown eyes searched mine. "So you *don't* find him attractive?"

I hesitated, unwilling to lie but trying to find a way to spare his feelings, and that's all it took. He whirled and set off down the path again. "That's what I thought," he tossed over his shoulder.

"No! Ronan! I mean, yes, I think he's handsome. That's the honest answer. But am I more attracted to you? Yes!"

He paused again for a moment, panting, and grabbed my forearm, as if in warning. "It's all right, Dri. I know it's confusing, and you've been through a lot. Let's just let it go now, okay? Until later."

I clenched my teeth, seeing what he did—we'd nearly reached the rest of our group.

I came up beside Ronan as he told Niero and the others of what had happened. I remembered Galen's horrible last cry and wished I could forget it.

"We should go back and bury her," Bellona growled.

"She is gone," Niero grunted. "With her Maker. What remains is not worth the risk."

I frowned at him as he turned to go, and we all reluctantly followed. It was true. The eternal part of Galen, her soul, was gone. But it did seem wrong not to honor her life, her gift to us.

"Galen would understand, Dri," Vidar said, interrupting my thoughts. "We need to put more ground between us and those who hunt us."

"I know," I sighed. "I just . . . well, you know."

"I know." He looked up at the others, moving off down the trail, clearly wondering why Ronan wasn't waiting for me. But then his dark eyes shifted to Niero. "So, how did I not sense it before? I mean, he's been right there in front of us the whole time."

I smiled and shrugged, relieved that I wasn't the only one in on the secret. "Guess he wasn't ready to be revealed. Does anyone else know?" I remembered Niero's finger to his lips, silently asking me to keep his confidence as Ronan had come to and Vidar had roused. Apparently, Vidar's gifting allowed him to see beyond the veil now.

"Not yet," he said with a toothy grin, gesturing for me to go ahead of him. "And I kinda like it that way. Just our little secret—yours, mine, and Niero's. Ronan didn't suspect anything? Even with his wound?"

"No. I'm not sure he even remembers getting stabbed. He seems more preoccupied with what Chaza'el saw of me and Keallach," I groused.

"Oh, that. I wondered why you two weren't making your normal googly eyes at each other."

"We don't make googly eyes."

"Oh, yes you do."

I sighed, knowing that would be an endless argument. "So what do you think made Galen do it? Help us?"

Vidar let out a low whistle. "She was remarkable, wasn't she? All I can figure out is that she'd been touched by the Way. Somewhere, somehow. And the Maker encouraged her to help us, just when we needed her most."

I nodded, considering his words. But even as we spent hours hiking in a northeasterly direction, my mind remained on Galen, her body now likely abandoned in the dirt in front of her barn. I puzzled over the sacrifice she had made for us, which then led me to think about all the Aravanders who had died by my side, by the side of other Remnants, all because they were called to serve.

Keallach, too, had been called. And if the call was that strong for others, how could he possibly still ignore it?

CHAPTER 2

ANDRIANA

We spent the night in a cave, huddled together trying to ward off the chill. We didn't dare to light a fire, and the Knights took turns watching for the bird drones that might be searching for us. We'd learned the hard way—Pacifica's reach was long and deep. They had caught me as we fled the Aravander camp, and I had been taken to Palace Pacifica. We didn't intend to be caught again. As we hiked, my eyes moved to Niero, and I wondered why he hadn't saved me that day. He had protected me before and breathed life back into Ronan. Could he not have swept in and pulled me from Sethos's grip? Would that not have been a good time to do his angel thing? I ached to have time alone with him to ask him some of the hundreds of questions in my mind and heart.

Later that morning, we crossed through what appeared to be Pacifica's main aqueduct, a broad span of water flowing swiftly through a concrete channel. "They get their share of rain, come Hoarfrost," Niero explained as we wrung out our clothes on the far side. "But this land was once as dead and arid as the Great Expanse. Come Harvest, they need more water yet for their fields and growing city."

"It's a weakness," Bellona said, placing a boot to the lip of the duct and looking up and down the waterway, her dark eyes glinting. "This water flows from other places. Places that might find themselves dammed up on occasion."

"Or destroyed," Niero said with a single nod.

"So let me get this straight," Vidar said, crossing his arms. "You're thinking we'll not only take on the dragon, we'll make him thirsty first."

"Maybe," Bellona said, smiling.

We moved on, rarely stopping and never seeing another soul. The Pacificans really didn't live far from their cities, which seemed odd, given the protection of the Wall. Why not spread out? Settle in other places? Each family claiming land of their own? "I'm surprised we haven't come across another town or village," I said.

"My people are like bees in the hive," Lord Cyrus muttered, looking thoughtful. He had been one of Keallach's Six, and it was largely due to his betrayal of Pacifica that we were making our escape at all. "All focused on the same task. Working together. Congregating together. Moving out to work together again. It's admirable, in a way. If they weren't so sick, they could accomplish great things."

"Some would say they've already accomplished great things," I said.

Niero and Ronan looked my way first, then the others did as well. I felt the heat of a blush gathering on my neck. "Schools. Orphanages for the children."

Cyrus turned to face me. "Keallach showed you what he wants to see himself. What he wanted you to see. He didn't take you to a factory or to a mine, did he?"

"No," I said slowly, hating the tension building between my shoulders. "But he told me, Cyrus, that those children who aren't chosen for adoption are put to work. I saw it for myself. They're taught to read. Read! And—"

"They're taught to read, yes," he said gently, as if explaining hard truths to a child. "But did you see for yourself what they read?"

I stared back at him, feeling a level of agitation equal to his own. He knew I hadn't. It had to be plain on my face.

"They're given words that poison their minds," he went on, "words that will help Pacifica rule their lives forever. As it nearly did mine."

"What'd you think, Dri?" Bellona muttered, brushing past me. "That the *emperor* was handing out copies of the Sacred Words?"

My face burned. What had I thought? Was it all a lie? "B-but they're given food and shelter," I said, hating the defensiveness inside that made my voice rise. "And Keallach seemed shocked when I told him that I'd seen children stolen from families in the Trading Union. He promised me he'd put an end to—"

Cyrus stepped toward me, his face a mask of compassion and concern. "My friend Keallach has been trained by the master of lies all his life. He believes he knows the truth. But he doesn't. Trust me, Andriana. Whatever he told you, showed you, cannot be trusted."

"It's all so much," I tried again. "So much for one man our age to manage! I think . . . I think that Sethos *has* lied to him.

He's given him the information he wants and hidden the rest. How can we expect Keallach to know what he is not told?"

"How can we *expect* it of him?" Niero asked, his eyebrows lifting in exasperation. "Keallach usurped the throne. He seeks to usurp all power. To rule Pacifica, the Trading Union, and beyond. Whether that is born of his own sick need or a bowing to Sethos, it matters not. All we know is that he *is* responsible for his choices. He *chooses* who informs him. He *chooses* whether or not to ask the hard questions. He *chooses* what to believe. As do we all. Right?"

I swallowed hard, feeling contempt and concern gather in every one of the Ailith around me, as well as in my parents and Cyrus. "He is responsible, yes. *Yes*. But you have to know . . . all of you have to know that I felt the pull of the Way within him. He is our brother yet."

"That's the one brother I vote we disown," scoffed Vidar, looking around. "Am I alone in that?"

I scowled at him. "None of us is perfect, right? We are all fallible, given to choosing wrongly. At any time!"

"Well, maybe for you, but not for me," Vidar said, arching a brow and sliding his fingers down one side of his coat, as if it were fine linen.

I kept staring at him until he sobered and faced me directly. "Seriously, Dri, you sensed the Way within him? Or were you just feeling that connection we get from our shared Ailith blood?"

I shook my head slowly and rubbed my forehead. "I think . . . I think I had cause for hope. He is lost right now, yes. But doesn't that mean he could one day be found?" I dared, then, to look toward Niero, Ronan, and the others.

"Or is that exactly what he wanted you to think?" Vidar said, taking my hand in both of his. "He knows you are the empathetic one. That your gifting gives you power but also makes you vulnerable, right? He didn't capture me, who would've been able to clearly make out light from dark. Or Chaza'el, who would've been able to see the future. And while Tressa would've been handy to have on hand in case he got injured, it was you he chose. You, Andriana."

Ronan tensed beside me. "They wanted her as his bride," he spat out. "Saw her as a means to unite the Trading Union with Pacifica."

"There was that element," I said quickly. "But this wasn't just about political gain."

"No," Ronan said. "From the first time he saw you, he wanted you as his own." He stalked away from us, past my parents, and I frowned in confusion. By the heavy hurt and heightened anger I sensed in him, it was clear that he was thinking about Keallach kissing me again.

I forced myself to concentrate on Vidar. He was the only one likely to give our brother a chance, if he had the opportunity to weigh the dark—and the light—within him. "Think about it, Vid. The twins were so young when they were divided. If we each had been tutored by one such as Sethos, rather than our trainers, how might *we* have turned out?"

He stared back at me, and a furrow formed between his brows. "It's too late, Dri. Our brother chose his path long ago. He murdered his parents. *Kapriel's* parents."

"He was a child," I said sorrowfully, avoiding looking at Mom and Dad—remembering how horrible it was when I thought them dead—by watching the wind rattle drying leaves that spoke of the end of Harvest. "Think about us at that age. We were innocents, all of us. Keallach made a horrible decision."

"A horrible decision," Dad repeated, and I met his gaze then and thought about all he and Mom had endured at the hands of the Pacificans—Keallach's people. But had he even known they were there? Or was this all Sethos's doing? My head pounded with the conflicting thoughts bouncing around within.

I took a deep breath and felt the group's collective skepticism like a noxious smoke, threatening to choke me. "So you're saying it was all a ruse." I turned to stare at the water in the aqueduct, rushing past us, down, down, down toward Pacifica. "You all think he was just using me," I said dully. "Playing me."

"Yes. He's far cleverer than you can imagine," Cyrus said gently. "And even if Sethos has been behind all that has happened, Keallach allowed it. If he's trapped, it's a trap he helped build himself, one decision at a time. I was nearly trapped myself. But am I not proof that one can escape Sethos's cage?"

"You were important to Sethos, Cyrus," I said. "But I'd venture to say that his focus was on Keallach, first and foremost." I thought about Keallach in his finer moments . . . and then in other moments. I'd felt him turn on me, try and control me, his eyes cold and distant. "I do think there are spells that surround him, that compel him, in certain measure. It's as if he has power, but it isn't entirely his own—and yet it's not entirely Sethos's to use either. It wasn't an accident that he was absent when Sethos was beating me. Nor was it an accident that he was absent when the Council tried to force me to accept a betrothal. In both cases, I think—no, I *know*—he would've put a stop to it."

"Or is that what he wanted you to think?" Vidar asked, stepping up to my other side.

I sighed heavily, closed my eyes, and shook my head as I turned back to face the group. "I don't know. I don't know, I don't know, I don't know."

Niero wrapped a bracing arm across my shoulders. "Then you must concentrate on what you do know. Only Keallach can choose to free himself. None of us can reach him. Even you." He squeezed my shoulder. "From what I know of you, I'd wager you tried every which way you could, right?"

I nodded and rubbed my temples. "Again and again I tried."

His mouth tensed. "Only the Maker knows what will come of that."

"Or maybe Chaz does," Vidar quipped. "Or a certain somebody with wings . . ."

Niero ignored the baited hook, staring only at me. "Perhaps your words will echo in his mind. Perhaps a miracle is on the wind. We've seen others . . ." He glanced over to Ronan—still standing a distance off, head down—then meaningfully to Vidar, and back to me. "Until then, we must treat Keallach as both our mortal and spiritual enemy."

"It's true, Dri," Vidar said quietly, taking my hand.

I looked around at all of them and realized this would never be an argument I could win. They hadn't been there with me. They hadn't witnessed what I had. Keallach's draw to the Way had been real. True.

Or had it?

CHAPTER
3

ANDRIANA

We'd been walking for a few hours the next day when I realized we were no longer heading north and east, but north and west. Was it possible that our way through the Wall was deeper into Pacifica than I'd thought? I'd been walking and talking with my parents, telling them all that had happened to us since we had parted, and finding out what had happened to them. They'd nearly been killed that dreadful night when the Sheolites came to torture them. It was true that our enemies had used their love for each other to try and coerce information from one, then the other. "But we loved you too," Mom said with tears in her eyes as she took my hand and glanced at Dad. "We knew that no matter what it cost us, we couldn't betray you."

"You are worth everything to us, to the Community," Dad said soberly, sliding his arm around my shoulders. "I'm sorry we endangered both you and the cause we serve. If only we'd gotten away in time, Andriana . . . not allowed ourselves to be captured. There were nights, once we realized what they intended—to use us to control you . . ." His voice cracked, and he paused to wipe his eyes and then looked to the sky and over at Mom. "There were times we wished we had died that night."

"Hey," I said, pulling him closer, then Mom from my other side. "Look. Here we are. Together. It's okay. It all turned out all right."

"Thank the Maker," Dad said.

"And Ronan," Mom said, looking toward him. He was ten paces ahead of us, yet glanced back as if he'd sensed us talking about him. He'd been distant for the last two days. Physically present, once again my constant guardian, but emotionally separated from me. I didn't know if it was because my parents were around, or because the rest of the Ailith might observe something more, or because of his trauma. Or worse, that he was still jealous over Keallach. I thought I'd detected a similar distance in the rest of the Ailith too, when we'd argued over my interactions with the emperor. But while the others gradually warmed to me again, Ronan had not.

I frowned, looking at him as he talked with Niero, who tilted his face upward to the sun and then pointed to a path to the right. I had to force myself to focus back on what my parents were saying. Mom and Dad were clearly keeping a portion of their story back to protect me, but it wasn't hard to tell that they had narrowly lived through the Sheolites' torture. In hushed tones, they also told me that once they reached Pacifica, they were given dramatically different treatment. Doctors. Food. "We were still in our cells, but it was different," Dad said thoughtfully.

"Do you think Keallach intervened?"

He shrugged. "Or it was simply Sethos, or the Council," he said bitterly, "planning to use us to get you to do what they wanted."

Thoughts of Sethos and the Council and the palace took me back to Kapriel and Keallach and how it all began. "Why were the twins left in the palace at all? Where they would be such a target for manipulation?" I asked. "The rest of us were spirited away when we were born. We moved to the Valley then, right? Why weren't Kapriel and Keallach moved?"

Dad shrugged. "For the parents of most of the Ailith, like us, I'd wager it was far simpler to move, to hide you away. For royals, it would've been far more difficult. I imagine the birth of the princes would've been the cause of much excitement, what with the low birthrate among the Pacificans and all. To spirit them away might've caused rioting in the streets."

"All who expected children around that seventh month of the seventy-seventh year wondered if their children would be born with the Ailith strain," Mom said. "It was all the people of our village could talk about. Elders approached us, warned us of what we would need to do, and we made preparations, but . . ." Her voice trailed off, and her eyes were wide and watery, remembering. I felt the joy in her memories, but also the grief, like shudders racking her body.

"But you had hoped you wouldn't need to go," I finished for her, for the first time truly understanding the impact of what they had chosen to do. I remembered the searing pain of saying good-bye to them the night that Ronan came for me—the night of our Call—how much it hurt to believe we might never see one another again. Whom had they left behind? What family? Friends? "Where did you come from? Who did you lose the night I was born?"

Mom gave me a rueful smile. "It is best if we still not speak of it, Dri. In case . . ."

I swallowed hard. *In case our enemies choose to find that family too, and use them against us.* I thought of how Mom and Dad would always dodge my questions about cousins and aunts and uncles and grandparents, continually redirecting me toward those of our own tiny village. *"They're our family now. The Maker has given us a new clan."* And I'd accepted it. At least we'd had that option—to protect our greater family. Kapriel and Keallach's parents chose to hide in plain sight. "Maybe the queen and king of Pacifica thought it a divine promise. That the Maker would not make a mistake, giving them twin sons, both marked with the crescent moon that night. Maybe they thought they were in the perfect place to raise the future leaders of all those who would seek the Way."

"Or maybe they gave in to greed," Dad said gently, "refusing to leave the bounty to which they'd become accustomed."

"We should not speak ill of them," Mom said. "They paid a great price for their decision."

"As you all did," I said. I remained silent after that, my mind a whirl of conflicting thoughts. Seeming to sense my attempt to sort it out, my parents allowed me to pace ahead of them, walking on my own. In the distance, I saw Bellona and Vidar—who that morning had moved out ahead of us, scouting—emerge from the hilly woods and go directly to Ronan and Niero. Cyrus drew near, listening in and nodding. Vidar was pointing and seemed to gesture about something beyond the woods that bordered our trail. We all caught up to them, gathering in a group, but the five of them turned slightly away, speaking in hushed tones. I frowned and tried to catch Ronan's eye, but he was still ignoring me.

So were the others, I decided, looking around to each one. I moved back to my dad and touched his arm. "Do you know what's going on?"

He shook his head, confused.

It was then that I detected the collective apprehension among the others. I turned to face them as they all warily glanced my way. "There's something you need to see," Vidar said, pain etched in his voice.

Pain. And anger. Indignation. Those three emotions practically radiated from him and Bellona.

"What?" I said, trepidation flooding through me.

"Come," Niero said.

I swallowed my irritation, clearly understanding how they wanted this to play out—that they wished for me to personally see whatever was there. And if so, it had to have something to do with Keallach.

I steeled myself for what was to come, half desperate to know, half heartsick at what was ahead.

We set off at a quick pace, easily reaching the crest of the hill. From there, we slowed down, following a winding, narrow trail through thick brush on the other side. Once we reached the valley, we headed north. We paused only when we reached a well-maintained dirt and gravel road, to be certain no one approached before we crossed it, and then began climbing again. Not long after, Bellona and Vidar crouched down and led us around boulder after boulder until we could safely peer beyond them down into the canyon.

What filled my eyes made me suck in my breath. In a quarry below us—with a high fence all around—were countless children, some of them younger than their first decade, some of them closer to our age. They were in rags and emaciated. Armed guards circled constantly, barking orders. One guard carried a whip, sneering at the children he watched, taunting the older boys in particular.

The wave of collective misery that enveloped me made me want to turn and vomit. I knew what this was. It was where the unchosen children went "for meaningful work," as Keallach had put it. I swallowed back the acrid bile in my mouth and eyed Cyrus, beside me. "How many of these places are there?"

He shrugged, sharing in my misery, and then slowly nodded. "About twenty. Mines. Lumberyards. Factories. And quarries like this."

"Pacifica's hunger for labor such as this can only grow," Niero muttered, looking down upon the yard from Cyrus's other side.

Cyrus shook his head, and I could see the tears in his eyes. "This is not what the king and queen wanted for Pacifica. It's not what the Maker wants. But you have to know . . . neither Keallach nor the Council was fully informed on facilities such as these." He paused. "I mean, I knew they were out there, that it was where we sent the unclaimed children. But we thought . . ." He swallowed hard and tried to gather himself. "We thought they were more . . . humane. It was only recently that I investigated it for myself."

I swallowed hard, again, and stared at them all. Hundreds of miserable, young souls. I thought of Palace Pacifica and how Keallach was so proud of his reconstructed buildings. Had those stones been hewn by slaves such as these? How could he not have known?

Or had he?

It just wasn't possible. That he'd known. He couldn't have deceived me so.

He was imperfect, yes. But there *was* good in him, I thought.

I felt the heat of Ronan's stare and glanced his way. There was a measure of triumph in him, gloating, as well as anger that made the muscles in his jaw twitch. It made me angry in response. We had no time for petty jealousies!

I took a breath. Ronan would remember that I loved him, in time. For my own part, I needed to get over my irritation at his childishness. I focused on the workers below again.

"We need to free them," I said to Niero.

"We do," he said evenly. "But not now. If we free them now, Pacifica will know exactly where we are and will capture us within the day."

My eyes returned to the misery before us. If Kapriel and Chaza'el and Tressa were here, we'd have the collective power to level this camp, to take down the guards one by one.

A young man about our age said something to the guard I was eyeing, appearing to ask a question. The guard wheeled about and sneered at him. We all stilled as the man's hand went to his whip and casually pulled it from the strap at his belt. He ran his fingers over the coils as he circled the boy, whom another guard forced to his knees.

Dimly, I heard Niero muttering prayers to the Maker to intervene, to stop the guard, to still his hand and put the whip away. As he prayed, I felt my thumping heart slow and a peace wash over me. Below us, the guard with the whip looked up, as if he'd heard something on the breeze. He stiffened and then turned partway around, then back, as if arguing with himself about what to do next.

Niero was still praying, hands cupped open, head bowed. The guard gestured with the whip to the boy, and with eyes wide, the young man rose and walked away, looking over his shoulder with fear. The two guards exchanged heated words, nearly coming to blows for a moment, but then the second one backed away, shaking his head. He called out to the gathered kids, who were watching it all unfold, and gestured for them to disperse. But instead they formed into lines and headed toward the long, narrow buildings that I assumed were their barracks.

I turned to Niero and blinked several times, laughing under my breath. He had a slightly smug, sly smile on his face. "I think they're calling it a day," he said.

I laughed with him and shook my head. It was perfect. The only solution. *Thank you, Maker, for guiding him,* I prayed silently. *For guiding us all. Show us how we help free these children. Soon.* We wanted to get out of Pacifica alive, but I knew we couldn't forget what we'd seen.

We wound our way out of the canyon, quiet and each lost in our own thoughts. Any good humor we'd had over the guard's "intervention" was soon lost to the overwhelming burden we'd just taken on. I thought about the young man, so narrowly saved from what I assumed would have been a brutal whipping. If we hadn't been there . . .

But we had. At just the right moment. No matter how hard it was to observe, it was what I had needed, and without further word, I knew it was what my fellow Ailith had known I needed to see too.

Keallach may or may not have known that this sort of camp existed in his country. But I knew why the others found it impossible to believe that he was innocent of such knowledge. In the end, I too held him responsible.

As we hiked eastward, a rare desert goat startled from his hiding place. As he fled, Bellona swiftly took him down with a single arrow. We all cheered, as the supplies we'd taken from Galen's were long gone. That night, as we sat around a small fire cooking skewers of meat, Niero looked to each of us. "We're near the Wall. By sundown tomorrow, we'll reach the tunnel we used to enter Pacifica."

"And then what?" Vidar asked, pushing his dark hair out of his eyes and swallowing his bite of food before continuing. "You weren't serious when you mentioned Zanzibar."

I started in surprise. "Zanzibar?" Obviously they had discussed this when I wasn't around.

"I was serious," Niero returned.

"Oh, Killian is going to love that," Vidar said. Killian, a Knight, and Tressa, his Remnant, had grown up in the evil city. The rest of us had been called there earlier to find them and had barely escaped with our lives.

Niero ignored him, poking a stick in the fire and turning the embers beneath another skewer, dollops of sizzling fat dropping to the hot rocks below. Never had I tasted anything as delicious as that desert goat. I tried to concentrate on it and the present moment, even as the mention of Zanzibar in the future made my heart beat faster.

"We will face whatever comes, in whatever city we're sent to, together," Niero said with a firm nod, "trusting that the Maker is sending us there for a reason. But first, we will join the other Ailith and get Dri's parents to the Valley. I think we would benefit from the elders' counsel."

"We're going *home*?" Vidar asked, his mouth dropping open, brown eyes rounding with hope.

"To . . . the Valley?" I sputtered, glancing at Ronan. His eyes shifted to me too, and I sensed a bit of a thaw in the look he gave me.

"For a time, yes," Niero said, smiling slightly. "There we'll find strength in gathering with them, in order to face what lies ahead."

CHAPTER 4

ANDRIANA

It came as some surprise to me that a group of outlaw Pacificans were running a smuggling operation beneath the Wall. Their clothing was unmistakable, even if it was tattered and dirty. I suppose I'd thought of them all as mindless—willing to do whatever the emperor or Council told them to do. Seeing some think for themselves and act on their own impulses, even if it was to do something illegal, left me oddly spirited.

Sethos's reach was long, but it did not yet cover all.

There were only about ten of them at the Wall, with four guarding the tunnel that went below it. Many men and women came and went along the rocky path, carrying sacks or leading sturdy horses with barrels or boxes strapped across their backs. As we got closer, we saw massive bags of flour and rice go by and smelled the yeasty odor of beer from a passing barrel. Others carried boxes of fruits and vegetables. If the Hoodite farmer,

Dagan, had been with us, we would've had to physically hold him back. Even my mouth was watering. As good as the goat meat had been, it was all we'd eaten in days.

"We will gain more by befriending them than trying to deceive them and failing," Niero said as we drew nearer. "The coin I carry will ensure their willingness to aid us."

"Or I can," I said.

Niero eyed me a moment and then assented. "You're right. Come. You too, Ronan. The rest of you wait here."

We ignored the two men who closed in behind us as we climbed the rocky hill to the others who stood, gazing down at us, clearly in charge. All of them carried guns and swords at their hips. We'd seen enough open crates of bullets that we had no doubt the swords were only worn as backup.

"Why not just give them a flash of your wings?" I said under my breath to Niero. "Why bother negotiating at all? Why not just command them?"

He shifted his dark eyes to me. "Because that is not my purpose here."

I stifled a sigh. As we got closer, the man in charge looked each of us up and down, giving me an extra long look until Ronan cleared his throat. "Who are you?" grunted a smaller, broad-shouldered man in back, edging between two bigger men in front.

"We are travelers, friend," Niero said, "seeking passage beneath the Wall and across the Great Expanse. We came through here a week ago." He glanced over his shoulder. "It appears you're loading a convoy. Perhaps we can be a part of your load."

The small man's eyes narrowed, and he smirked toward his companions. "We are not operating in human cargo." His eyes moved back to me, as if thinking about the trade in women in Zanzibar, and in response, Ronan stood taller, his shoulder moving slightly in front of me.

"I'm certain you are not averse to any sort of cargo, if the price is right," Niero returned.

The man edged between me and Niero to look at the others beyond us. "You are many. You would displace much of my cargo."

I took the opportunity to touch the man's arm, willing him to feel what I felt at that moment—protection, care, generosity.

He flinched and shied away from me, back toward the other men, who had tensed at his response. "What did you just do?" He rubbed his arm as if it ached or felt strange.

"What?" I asked innocently, shaking my head in confusion. But I'd seen the momentary softening along the hard lines around his eyes and mouth. Felt a flash of warmth and goodwill.

He scowled and shook his head. "What are your names? Why are you sneaking out of Pacifica and across the Great Expanse?"

"All you need to know is that we are of the Valley and wish to return home," Niero said.

The man squinted his eyes up at Niero. "The Valley is far. My cargo train stops at Castle Vega."

"We merely ask for safe passage there," Niero said. "And a fair price for that passage."

The man crossed his arms and then cradled his chin, looking me over again. "I might be able to help," he said, and then swore, rubbing his forehead as if it ached. Even now, the seeds of compassion I'd planted were growing within him. I fought to keep a small smile of triumph from my face.

He scowled. "How did the lot of you—Valley dwellers—end up in Pacifica?"

"It's better for you not to know," Niero said. "If we could, would we not simply be riding a transport out, rather than seeking to travel with you?"

"You will tell me who you are," he sneered, "and what you were up to in Pacifica, or there will be no passage for you through the Wall."

"I think the Maker has hinted who we are," Niero said with a sigh. He jutted out his chin. "Deep within you."

The man's eyes narrowed.

"This woman is one of the prophesied Remnants," Niero said, gesturing toward me. "Andriana of the Valley. And this is her Knight of the Last Order, Ronan of the Valley. Andriana was kidnapped by the emperor of Pacifica, but we retrieved her from the palace." Niero lifted his chin as Ronan crossed his arms. "You do not really wish to come against us. Even now, you feel the call of the Way within, urging you to aid us."

The small man's eyes narrowed again, but I could feel the growing awe within him. He believed us. *Knew* it was true. He swallowed hard and then gave us a dismissive gesture. "Go. But I'll send you in a Jeep. I will not risk my entire cargo train if the Pacificans are on the hunt for you."

"But Boss—" complained one of the giant men beside him.

"Make it so!" yelled the leader, sticking out his chin. "Go and speak with Joauquin. Inform him of the change."

"Thank you," Ronan said, ignoring the disgruntled man who left us and reaching an arm toward the boss.

The smaller man pulled back, not accepting the gesture. "I don't want your friendship. I don't want your money." He leaned forward then. "But if you are who you say you are, there will come a day when I ask you to return this favor."

Ronan dropped his arm and smiled a little. "And when that day comes, I think you'll find you won't need us to grant it. You'll be seeking something greater. The Way is—"

"No, no!" said the short man, putting up his hands. "I already taunt the Pacifican guards with my trade. I don't need Sheolites breathing down my neck. Be away from here. Quickly."

Ronan and I turned to go, with Niero following. I felt an urgency to depart before the boss changed his mind. Before he thought of capturing us and trying to take us to some other location to garner favor with the Pacificans. To do so would mean exposing his whole black market trade, of course, so it wasn't likely to happen. But as we passed underneath the weight of the giant wall, through a tunnel only wide and tall enough for the horses, I knew that it was the Maker who had made this gate open to us. I only needed to trust the One who had breathed life into us and placed this call in our hearts to follow where he led.

Why was it that I so frequently gave in to doubt rather than trusting what I knew to be true?

"Doubt your doubts," Niero whispered to me as we emerged on the other side, "trust what you believe."

I blinked at him, surprised again at his seeming ability to read my mind. But now, after what I knew about him, I understood. Perhaps he could.

KEALLACH

They kept it from me until I returned. But as soon as we pulled up in front of the palace, I knew.

She was gone.

The realization stole the breath from my chest.

"Majesty?" Sethos said, leaning down to peer at me, still in the car.

"She's gone," I whispered. "Andriana." My strength returned to me in a rush, and I scrambled from the car and turned in a circle, as if I could sense which direction she'd gone. My hands went to my hair, and I turned in another slow circle. But it was no use. She was too far.

"Andriana is gone," I said, my voice high and fragile, even to my own ears.

"Come with me, Majesty," Sethos said, taking my arm and urging me up the marble steps.

"How?" I muttered. "How could she have gotten away?" Even as I said it, I hated the words. Who was I to keep a woman here against her will? Why was it that I so loved her, needed her, wanted her, that I was willing to imprison her until she felt the same for me?

"There was an attack on the palace," Sethos said as we entered through the towering doors, passing lines of bowing servants.

"Wait," I said, pulling up short. "You knew? You *knew*?" I turned toward him and took his red robe in my fists, studying his face.

He'd known.

"Leave us," I growled, power and fury surging through me. I barely had the patience to wait as the servants scrambled away and my guards closed the door before I narrowed my eyes at my trainer and shouted, "How long? How long have you known? When did it happen?"

"Three days ago."

I let out a cry of rage and slammed Sethos into the wall. Though he was larger than I, he allowed it. "Why? Why did you keep it from me?"

"Your attention was needed at the border, Majesty. And I had hoped the Council would succeed in finding Andriana and the traitor, Cyrus, and bring them here for you to consider proper retribution." He let out a small sigh. "Unfortunately, it seems my faith in them was misplaced. Lord Jala was injured in the attack, and the others—"

My anger sagged. "What? *Cyrus*? A traitor? And Maximillian. He was hurt?"

"Yes. Severely. I can take you to him now—if you would only release me, Majesty."

I loosened my hold on his cape and let my hands drop, feeling suddenly like a defeated boy caught doing something horrible. "You should have told me, Sethos." I shook my head and rubbed my temples, feeling a familiar ache return behind my eyes.

"Yes," he said. "I see that now. Forgive me."

"Take me to Max," I said, feeling lost, empty. I glanced up and around the marble foyer, sensing the structure as a cold, sterile cell, now that I knew Andriana wasn't within it. While she'd been here, I'd felt such hope, such warmth. It was if her mere presence had made it more a home than a palace.

I turned to follow Sethos, who moved down the south wing to our small palace hospital. I tried to hurry, but my legs felt like weights.

What had I been thinking, leaving her here alone? And after she and I had our . . . misunderstanding. When I'd tried to get her to acknowledge what I knew she had to be feeling, that what was between us was love. The purest understanding, the closest I'd felt to the Maker in all my life. The culmination of an ancient destiny, just as Sethos had said. All of it had been falling into place so rapidly that I'd gotten ahead of myself. Pressed her. If I'd been more patient, would she have gone? Even if they hadn't come for her? Maybe she hadn't had a choice . . .

My eyes narrowed.

Ronan.

Of course it had been Ronan. Only he would have had the power to wrench her from my home. From what we had been building together. When she had been so close to acknowledging it.

Hate lashed through me. I wanted him dead. He was a Knight, but he was no brother to me. Only the enemy. Only a barrier to what I might have with Andriana—what was meant to be.

My mind moved to the other puzzle. "Tell me what you must about Lord Cyrus," I said, trying to keep my tone light (as Sethos himself had taught me to do) as if all of this hadn't thrown me.

"Of course. It appears that he fell for a courtesan in Castle Vega, a follower of the Way."

I sniffed and frowned. Surely it had taken more than that to convince Cyrus to leave my side. To aid Andriana in escaping.

"Who else was here? Who helped her escape?"

"Ronan, her Knight. The one they call Niero," he said, with particular venom in his tone before he caught himself. "Others—Vidar and Bellona—were seen in the tunnels as they fled."

"The guards were that close to them?" I said, pausing to face him again. "Close enough to see them, and yet they still escaped?"

His nostrils flared. He didn't like it when I made him take responsibility for errors. "Yes, Majesty."

I sighed heavily and turned to walk the rest of the way to the hospital. Inside the long, cavernous room, multiple beds were occupied, but I spied my Council at the far end, loitering around a pale Max. A woman sat on Daivat's lap, kissing him as he sloppily gestured with a glass of wine. Others gathered around Fenris. I cleared my throat, and Kendric looked up. With a quiet word, all rose to their feet.

"Highness," said Kendric, nervously clearing his throat before bowing hurriedly and then glancing at Sethos and me. "You have returned. We have much to tell you."

"Get out," I said to the women. "Be gone!" I growled when they paused and looked to Fenris and Daivat before obeying. They hurried past me. But my eyes remained on my men. I wanted to yell, but I was conscious of Max and forced myself to focus on him first. I slipped past Fenris to the bed. Max was on a respirator, and he looked ghastly, like he'd faced death and only narrowly avoided succumbing. His eyes were mere slits. "How is he?" I bit out. "What is the prognosis?"

"They don't know," Sethos said, reaching out to put a hand on my shoulder. He'd known this too, then. Known that Max's life hung in the balance.

I edged out from under his hand and faced him and the others. "You have the best doctor for him?"

"Of course. We will summon him so you can speak to him yourself—"

"Not now," I interrupted. I stared at the others. "Tell me what happened!"

"It was her Knight, Majesty," Daivat growled. "The one they call Ronan. He was in our prison."

"Are you telling me," I said, walking toward Fenris until I'd backed him against the wall, "that you allowed Ronan—a Knight of the Last Order—anywhere *near* the Council chambers? In the palace at all? When and how was he even arrested?"

"He returned with Lord Cyrus after we'd departed," Sethos said, leaning against the wall with a sigh, crossing his arms. "Cyrus claimed he had captured him in the desert. That he wanted it to be a surprise for you upon your return."

I struggled to absorb this. "Regardless of Lord Cyrus's stated desire to *surprise* me," I said to Sethos, "you didn't think it wise that I know of it? And did you not think twice about bringing him here? You know what the elders say about a Remnant and Knight together. They're three times as powerful."

Sethos's eyes moved to what remained of my Council, his gaze silently reproachful. *My Council of Five,* I thought bitterly, wondering which noble would soon be vying for the coveted sixth spot that Cyrus had vacated in this treasonous act. The thought of it made me feel nauseous. Betrayed. As well as deeply hurt. Cyrus had been one of my favorites among the Council. He was far more serious and thoughtful than the rest. It dawned on me then. Only four were present. "Where is Broderick?"

Fenris stiffened, and Daivat's head slumped. "He's dead," Sethos said. "He was killed in the fight that ensued as they battled to leave the palace."

I slumped to the cot beside Maximillian. "Dead," I muttered, trying to get my head around this latest blow. *Ronan.* He had to have been the one that killed him. Surely Cyrus wouldn't have gone so far. We were like brothers, my Six and I. We had been together since the day I had to send my twin away to the Isle of Catal and Sethos realized I mourned for him in more ways than one.

I rubbed my head again. "How did Ronan escape the dungeon and make it all the way here, with so many soldiers on each level?"

They all shook their heads and looked away or to the floor.

"And Cyrus . . ." I said, repeating his name, still trying to believe that everything had transpired as they'd said. It didn't make sense. Why would Cyrus give up all he had here? And, yet, the pull of my fellow Ailith was strong. Had I not felt it myself? Did others feel that way about them too, even if they weren't of Ailith blood? Was that the key to their draw? Why so many were following them now among the Trading Union?

"Cyrus fell for that girl at Castle Vega," Kendric said. "We thought it was a fling, but when we found out she was a follower of the Way . . ."

"We thought it best if she was removed before becoming a serious . . . *distraction*," Fenris said distastefully.

I stared at him as the pieces fell into place. "So you killed her. Murdered her."

Fenris frowned at my surprise and horror. "Well, it was poison, Majesty, as we've utilized before in such circumstances."

I closed my eyes and turned slightly away from them, sickened. What if they had poisoned Dri? How might I have felt? This was what had turned Cyrus. Why he'd been willing to do what he had. "And . . .?" I asked.

"He was seen carrying her out of Castle Vega. He explained it away as too much drink to the guards and said he was taking her home."

I resumed rubbing my temples. "And returned with Ronan as his prisoner." It had been the Knight's way in—the only, desperate way in—to Palace Pacifica. I had to admire the sheer bravado of it. The risk he'd taken to get to Dri.

And now he'd stolen her away.

"It all happened so fast," Fenris said, daring to look me in the eyes. "If you'd been here, if you'd seen what they did to poor Max, how they cut him down in cold blood, you'd share our desire for retribution."

I wrenched my eyes from him to Max, my dearest friend. My most trusted confidante. It was Max I'd go to before Sethos. It was Max who advised me, protected me, and helped me sort things out when I got confused. I squeezed my eyes shut. He couldn't die. If he died . . .

On and on they went, telling me how Ronan and Cyrus and Dri broke through the Council chamber windows and ran to the forest. How others were there, ready to defend them. How they'd all but disappeared into the tunnels and then out, and later been tracked to a farm where a doctor obviously treated one who had lost a great deal of blood. After that, despite heavy searching, the trail had run cold.

I let silence fall before I dared ask what I had to.

"Did she . . . did Andriana go willingly?" I said, keeping my eyes on Max and his machine-driven, rhythmic breathing.

For a moment, I thought no one would answer me. "Yes," Kendric said at last.

I took a breath, then two, considering what it meant, to breathe within this space that I had come to associate sharing with Andriana. "Summon the doctor," I said softly. "And the rest of you, go to your quarters for the night. *Alone*," I added, knowing there was venom and disappointment dripping from my tone. "In the morning, I'll expect you to rise the moment I call."

RONAN

At the end of first watch, I continued walking the perimeter as they slept, but it was Dri I looked to, again and again, even though I could see little of her in the darkness. She was sound asleep, with her back practically against Bellona's. Vidar snored loudly, but it didn't rouse the women, Lord Cyrus, or Dri's parents. We were all exhausted. I was fighting to stay awake until Niero relieved me.

I settled on a rock near the smuggler who drove us, asleep himself. The black market boss had sent his convoy on a separate track from us, not wanting to endanger the whole shipment. Our driver had a few crates and barrels that we rode atop of, though, just in case we went undetected and he made it.

Content that we were safe here, for the moment, two-thirds across the Great Expanse, I looked up to the starry skies and then rubbed my face and eyes, feeling every ache of the battle behind us—in particular, a nagging ache at my side. I knew I'd been injured in the fight and that the Maker had somehow healed me—even without Tressa present—but not much more. I hadn't really wanted to go back to that memory. Remembering the sword piercing me. The moment I knew that it was likely a deathblow, one from which I'd die slowly. The moment I knew I had failed Dri.

Dri, I thought, staring over at her silhouette in the darkness, remembering how it felt to be leaving her as I lost consciousness, wondering if I'd ever wake. Losing her forever. Abandoning my post as her guardian, her protector. And then later, rising to consciousness, Dri and Niero hovering near.

Suddenly, there was a movement beside me, and I half rose, startled and already drawing my sword, when I realized who it was. "Ah, Niero," I whispered, relieved. "Just in time. I didn't know how much longer I'd last."

"I thought that might be the case," he said quietly, settling down on the rock and casting an eye over our sleeping companions. But when I turned to go, he gestured to me. "Sit a moment with me." He waved back to the rock.

It was the last thing I felt like doing. I wanted to unroll my blanket and settle down next to Andriana. To close my eyes for a few hours before daybreak was upon us. But I took a deep breath and returned to my seat.

"You cannot continue to hold on to your resentment with Dri," he said, without preamble.

I frowned. "Resentment?" Was that what I was feeling?

"I think you're well aware of the divide between you," he said. "And a Remnant and a Knight . . . they cannot abide by divisions. It leaves you vulnerable in a way the enemy might use."

I took a deep breath. It was true. Our trainer had drilled it into our minds from the start. Made us work out our petty grievances. Drove us to build our relationship in every permissible way.

"I thought you'd be glad for a bit of separation between us," I said, knowing there was an edge of bitterness in my tone.

He glanced at me from the side, and I knew my own shame. There was no truth to that. Not really.

"You and Andriana," he began, pausing, as if choosing his words, "are on a path that none of us had foreseen. Love blooms where it will, and with all you've built together, all you've endured, and all you will endure, it will likely deepen still. I don't sense displeasure in that from the Maker. Not now. Do you?"

I turned to face him more fully. "Wait. Are you . . . *blessing* us? Giving us permission to deepen our relationship?"

He shifted. "I'm saying it's already done. Your relationship is what it is. And now you must make the most of that, rather than allowing it to become a detriment. Let's follow where the Maker leads. Forgive as you have been forgiven. Give up this irritation, this jealousy over what happened to Andriana with Keallach, and move on. We have no time for it. You have a bigger call on your life, do you not?"

A desert breeze blew then, fanning the flames of the dying campfire and sending sparks swirling into the sky to meld with the stars. Niero's words washed over me and through me, and I felt a curious sense of healing to my heart, my ego. A renewal, of sorts.

What was it about Niero, our captain, that made me feel so at ease? How did he speak to my deepest needs and address my weaknesses, all the while calling me to more? He was like no man I'd ever met before, except maybe our trainer. Did it just come from living in Community all his life? What was it about him that made him so . . . different?

Something niggled at my memory, but then it was lost to me. I rose and clasped arms with him. "Thank you, Raniero. I'll consider your words. Keep close watch."

"I shall."

I made my way over to my bedroll, settled down beside Dri, and was just thinking that I didn't ache so much now, from any of my wounds, when I gave in to sleep's siren call.

CHAPTER 5

KEALLACH

I sat straight up in bed, just as the sun tinged the cloudy sky a deep coral. There was one thought in my mind. Why had Ronan been brought to the Council chambers at all? And why Andriana? What business had the Six had, calling her to them, there, without my permission? I threw aside my covers and strode out of my room barefoot, clad in nothing but my long nightshirt, and startled two sleepy guards outside.

"My-my lord?" stammered the first guard. But I ignored him.

I walked down the hall and turned the corner into the next, which ended in the Council chambers, a grand room with towering ceilings and paintings all about. My eyes scanned the perimeter. On the far wall, where the two-story windows were, work had already begun to replace the priceless, rare glass. Consequently, the room held the morning's chill, and I rubbed my hands together to warm them. I looked to the front of the room, where the Council chairs sat in a row, then to the guards who had followed me.

"Tell me what happened the night Lord Jala was injured."

The two looked at each other then back to me. "We were of course with you, Majesty, on your journey," said one.

"I know that," I said irritably, waving a hand. "But guards talk. What have you heard about that night from those who were here?"

The two shared a brief look of consternation and then one of them stepped forward. "The Council summoned Andriana to the chambers, here. Her Knight, Ronan, was held in the ante-chamber. As were her parents."

"Her p-parents," I sputtered. "Andriana's *parents*. They are *alive*? They were here?"

"Yes, my lord," the guard said, shifting uncomfortably in light of my apparent lack of knowledge.

My eyes tracked left and right across the fine speckles of the smooth terrazzo floor then back to my guards. "Why were they all in the Council chambers, together? Why was Andriana brought before the Council at all?"

The guard's mouth opened as if to speak then abruptly closed when he caught sight of something over my shoulder.

"Because they wished to secure Andriana's agreement to your union," Sethos said, striding through the door, fully dressed. "And offer the opportunity for her parents to bless that union, of course," he added.

My eyes narrowed. I did not appreciate him butting in. "That is false," I said. "Tell me the truth."

"It is the truth, Majesty. Wouldn't it be your heart's desire to have a woman by your side like Andriana? We knew that, given her ties to the Valley, she'd do best with some sort of familiar support, so I had them brought here."

"Without my knowledge."

"You have far too much to consider each day already, Majesty. The Council and I wished to ease your burdens. If it had all worked as we wished, wouldn't it have been the culmination of all we'd dreamed about?" He turned to the guards. "Step outside and close the door, please."

"No," I said through gritted teeth, as they turned to go. "Remain here." The two resumed their positions.

"Keallach, really," Sethos complained. "Isn't this a conversation best left for—"

"Andriana believed her parents had been killed by the Sheolites. Have you had them in custody all this time?"

"I have. I assumed that at some point they would prove useful."

"Useful. As in, you could threaten them in order to force her agreement."

"Certainly not," he sniffed. "You speak of the woman you wished to be empress. I did not wish to harm her, only help in wooing her to your side."

I swallowed, disliking the past tense of his wording. "If you did not intend to force her hand, why was Ronan brought up from the dungeon?"

Sethos was silent.

I stepped toward him. "If you intended only good for Andriana's parents, why keep them in the dungeon? And why would you not inform me? I assume they've been here ever since the night of our Call?"

His lips formed a line, his eyes moving quickly, clearly thinking. "Our entire goal was to support you, Keallach. To see your vision fulfilled. And when the Council and I knew you felt something for the girl, we wanted it all the more, and we were willing to take extraordinary measures to accomplish your union."

I shook my head and let out a long breath of exasperation. *Extraordinary measures.* I could well imagine what that meant.

"To have brought together the empire and the Trading Union through a symbolic marriage," he went on, "would have saved countless months of effort and probably many lives. There would likely have been half the conflict we expect now, what with followers of the Way daring to gather *publicly.*" He sniffed and gazed at me down his long, straight nose. "They are a rapidly growing force to be reckoned with, Majesty. And they are a closed-minded, stubborn lot," he added. "Thoroughly opposed to us ruling them. Do you not see? Your marriage to Andriana would have gone a long way to resolving all of that. We simply intended to aid you in any way we could."

I sighed and studied the floor again. I could see the wormlike marks of a recent mop, but there . . . I crouched and licked a finger and rubbed it across a dark brown spot. When I looked at my finger, what I saw was plainly blood. Out here. Far away from where Maximillian had likely been injured. I looked to my guards. "How many died here?"

"Seven guards, Majesty, and Lord Broderick, of course," one of the guards answered. "As well as Lady Andriana's father."

"No," Sethos said, shaking his head and drawing closer. "He faked his own death. Part of an elaborate scheme with Cyrus and Ronan."

"He had to fake his own death? So they *were* threatening him."

"For reasons I already described," he said with another sniff. "But then Ronan and her father came up with their clever ploy, surprised the guards and the Council, and made their escape."

I frowned. There were pieces missing to this puzzle. But Sethos hadn't been here. He'd been with me. I thought of awakening the Council and grilling them, but I didn't entirely trust them. "Did any guards survive the attack?" I asked. "Anyone who was in this room through the entire meeting?"

The guard shook his head. "No, Majesty."

I sighed, crossed my arms, and looked to the ceiling. "And Ronan. Tell me why they brought Ronan up from the dungeon."

"As a last resort," Sethos said idly. "Maximillian thought that if all else failed they could barter her agreement to your union in exchange for Ronan's freedom."

I groaned and shook my head. "Why? Why could they not allow it all to unfold as it was? I was making headway with her, Sethos. I know I was."

He stared at me sadly. "Unfortunately, we were running out of time. Their power grows, Keallach. And so does their following. Exponentially. If we do not quell their uprising soon, they will likely disrupt trade imports, and if they somehow manage to draw the Trading Union into an actual *union*, they could represent a threat to Pacifica. Your dreams of an empire? Gone."

I scoffed at the thought. I knew they were gathering followers, but none of power. "Whom have they drawn to date? Some Drifters? The northern rebels, the Aravanders?"

"So far," Sethos said, steepling his fingers and turning toward the window, thinking. "But the draw of the Way is powerful, as you know yourself. The Remnants, together . . . and now with your brother among them . . ."

His mention of my brother among the Remnants shot a dark arrow of jealousy and hatred through me. I clenched my fists. "Let us go to the war room," I said, striding toward the door. "And summon my Council," I bit out. "I want to know everything. *Now*."

ANDRIANA

We were almost across the Great Expanse when we saw the drone turn in a broad arc, as if it had caught sight of us. The

Jeep pulled to an abrupt halt. "Get out!" the driver screeched. "Out, now! Hide over there, among the boulders!"

Niero lifted his chin in agreement. "Everybody out. Fast."

As soon as the last of us were out, the Jeep surged into motion again, out across a shallow, sandy, desolate valley. We could already hear the whirr of the approaching bird's propellers.

We scrambled to find the nearest hiding places wherever we could. Vidar edged under a thorny bush. The others went for the big, round boulders and crevices. Bellona covered her exposed legs with sand.

"Dri," Ronan said from somewhere nearby. "You clear? Out of view?"

"Yes," I said, pulling my shoulder in a bit more.

"Everyone be still," Niero said.

The bird buzzed over us, circled, and then returned. It seemed to be hovering above us, searching, moving a few paces, and then scanning the ground below further. My heart pounded, remembering how close the drone had come to me at the river near the Aravander camp . . . and what followed. Would they spot some detail that would bring Pacifican soldiers after us again? I couldn't be captured again. Not after we'd come so far.

Home, I thought. *I just want to be home. In the Valley.* To rest. Recover. Before taking on the next fight. *Please, Maker,* I prayed. *Protect us. Shield us.*

After several long, agonizing moments, the bird flew off. Gradually, we all emerged. It was with some relief that we saw it followed the dusty plume of the Jeep, now in the distance, rather than returning to Pacifica. With any luck, we hadn't been discovered.

"They'll think our driver is a Drifter," Vidar said, half in admiration of the smugglers. "That's why he changed into those clothes. And with such meager cargo, even if they detain him, they'll have no reason to arrest him."

"Think he'll return for us?" Bellona asked with little hope.

"I think we're more likely in for a long walk," Niero said.

"Hey, but we're more than halfway," Vidar said cheerfully. We all turned doleful eyes toward him.

"It's better than a quarter, right?" he said.

"We'll spend the afternoon in the shade," Niero said, "preserving our energy and not getting too dehydrated. We'll walk when night falls."

CHAPTER 6

ANDRIANA

We circumvented Castle Vega by a wide margin to the north, and then Zanzibar a couple of days later. I practically started running when we crossed the river that led toward home. Recognizing it, we picked up our pace. We knew that by nightfall we'd surely reach the mouth of our valley. A fine mist had covered us since morning—and I welcomed it. After so long a time in the desert, the smell of water on my skin and leather made my heart sing. But it did make the dirt a bit heavier to plod through, which slowed our progress.

As we passed the first pines, I reached up and ran my hand through the long needles, inhaling their scent as we walked. Even that seemed to strengthen me, giving me the will to continue to put one foot in front of the other though I was so very weary. I remembered the last time we'd returned here and how I'd slept for most of two days and awakened to learn of my parents' disappearance. I glanced ahead to them, saw Dad's arm around Mom, and shivered.

Ronan edged nearer and interlaced his fingers with mine. We brought up the rear of our party, and in the gathering dark, no one was likely to see us. "Smells like home," he whispered.

I smiled at him. Between the scent of his damp coat and the trees, if I closed my eyes, we might have been three years in the past, waiting for our trainer to arrive. And in that one action—taking my hand—I felt as if he'd chosen to believe me, forgive me, trust me again, regardless of what Chaza'el had foreseen. Regardless of what I had allowed to happen with Keallach.

Ronan tightened his grip on my hand. "What is it?" he asked, pulling me closer to whisper, his dark brows knitting together.

Belatedly, I understood that, through our touch, he'd felt what I had, in thinking of Keallach. I'd cast my emotions into him. This time, guilt. "What?" I said, hoping not to get into it.

He waited me out, refusing to let me go.

"I was just thinking how good your hand felt in mine," I finally admitted, "and how I'm glad you are not Keallach."

He leaned close to whisper, "It feels good to touch you again." Then he took the lead on the narrower trail as we entered deeper forest, still holding my hand. Seconds later, he whirled and grabbed my waist, pulling me into the brush. "We're not alone," he growled to Vidar, who had paused just ahead. "Sense anything?"

"No," Vidar whispered back.

Everyone eased from the path and into the shelter of the forest, except for Niero. We could barely make out his dark form in the dim light, but I knew his tension. Worse, I felt it from others around us. *Many*, screamed my mind. *So many*.

"You're surrounded," growled a low voice. "We have ten archers with arrows pointed at your chests, plus four with guns. Raise your hands."

We all lifted our hands together. How had we not heard them?

"Who are you?" barked a low voice. "What are you doing here?"

"We are people of the Way," Niero said, striding back toward us. "Valley dwellers. Who are you?"

After a pause, I felt the easing of tension, and joy replacing it. My armband was warm. Those holding guns switched their safeties on again; those holding bows released the tension on their strings. I turned as Vidar and Bellona whooped in joy and clasped arms with the dark forms behind us. It was then I knew. *Aravanders*. The Aravanders were here. They'd formed an advance guard to the Valley.

A torch was lit, and we saw that two of them were the same women who had rescued us from the Isle of Catal—the dark-haired gunner and Aleris, the boat captain. Vidar sidled right up to the gunner, who held a fearsome weapon in her strong arms. "Have I mentioned how much I love a woman with a gun?" Vidar asked, flashing her one of his winning smiles. "I've dreamed of meeting up with you again. And now this . . ."

The girl rolled her eyes in return as she passed by him, but I felt her pleasure.

"Wait!" he cried, following after her. "What is your name? I've kicked myself a hundred times for not asking."

I grinned. How could she not be charmed? Bellona, on the other hand, just groaned and moved past them as the gunner turned to chat with Vidar. Camilla was her name.

The guards led us to their post, where we were placed on mudhorses. Wearily, gratefully, I sank onto an old mare's back. "As tired as you might be after a long day of work, girl," I said, leaning forward to stroke her mane, "I think I might have you beat."

More torches were lit to surround us, and we continued up the Valley with the Aravanders pointing out new trails to various encampments. "There are thousands here now," said Aleris. "Every day, hundreds more come. They're all under strict orders to live as we direct them—dousing campfires before nightfall, hiding their dwellings under branches. Many have taken refuge in the caves to the west side of the Valley. We don't want Pacifica to know how many are here when they come hunting."

"It's effective," Bellona said. "We had no idea upon our approach that so many had arrived. But we don't have drones."

"True. But I can tell you from experience that, even with the drones, the Pacificans are always surprised at who rises to fight them," she said with a flash in her eyes.

"Are all willing to fight for the Community if it comes to that?" Ronan asked the guard nearest him, a tall man walking beside his mudhorse in traditional Aravander skins.

"They are. There are many capable men and women among them. Better yet, there are hunters and goatherds and farmers who improve by the day in making the most of our last weeks of Harvest. You might also be surprised that your old friend Jorre moved his trading post here. After your visit, he said he couldn't ignore the desire to join you, any way he could. He found great joy in the stores that our people brought with us—salt, dried fish, and pelts—and has made good use of them in trade on behalf of the Community."

I breathed a sigh of relief. While our trader friend Tonna seemed capable of holding her own in the desert near Zanzibar, Jorre had seemed vulnerable, with his many wives and adopted children.

"His camp is just over there," he said, nodding to the right. It made sense to put a trading post near the mouth of the Valley. "While this is a boon to us, aiding us in gathering provisions for so many," the man continued, "it necessitates further guarding of the Valley's mouth. You'll see that your Valley gets far more visitors these days, and once they understand the power among the Community, many of them choose to stay."

We learned that Zulema and Ignacio, the grandmother and grandson that Tressa had healed, were up on the northern slope, among the cliffs that lined the river—which the goats loved. "They've grown fat and happy in these last weeks," Aleris said. And to the left of the trail, Dagan had cleared forest and prepared ground for next season's plantings. "We have hope that he will be successful," she said. I could hear the shrug in her voice. Our Valley was far more damp a territory than that of the Hoodites. But the idea that we might grow our own food, even in part . . . My mouth watered at the memory of berries on my tongue.

More guards met us on the path. People from Georgii Post, we realized, friends of Azarel and Asher, reached up to touch our hands, muttering their welcomes in awed tones. On and on it went as we climbed deeper into the Valley. More Aravanders, among the trees, shouted down to us in greeting. People from Chaza'el's village thronged around and greeted us with tears streaming down their faces.

"It's more a city than a forest now," Bellona muttered. "They're everywhere."

"They are!" I said, grinning from the collective joy all about. "Isn't it wonderful?"

"Wonderful," she said reluctantly. I knew she was worried about protecting them all. It was a Knight's way. But if the Maker had led them all here, we would have to rely on him to see us through. And together, were we not stronger yet?

Up and up we wound along the trail, past camps with the delicious smell of roasting meat and fish on spits. I was wondering where they had found such bounty—it couldn't all be from Jorre's trading post—when I heard a flock of geese flying above us, heading south, and then glimpsed two Aravanders raise their bows, close their eyes as if only relying upon their hearing, and manage to take down a pair with their arrows, even in the dark. We could hear the geese come crashing down through the trees and brush. I would have marveled at their prowess as archers if I hadn't been so taken with the fact that there were *birds*. Birds here, in the Valley. Geese. I hadn't seen any here since I was a little girl. The birds—so long hunted out—had returned to our Valley.

Niero looked back at me from atop his horse. "The Maker has made a way for us to feed all these new Valley dwellers, has he not?"

"It's a miracle," I said.

"Indeed," Ronan said. He grinned at me, and there was such joy and relief in his eyes it made me tear up. I realized then the weight he carried, watching over me, worrying over me. Here, at last, he could find some relief from that burden for a time.

The people seemed to seep from the forest like sap from the trees, thronging around us with so many torches that the surrounding trees glowed with their golden light. I knew that the Aravander guards behind us would send word if a drone approached. For now, it was just us—Community, gathering—and it made my heart swell with joy. Some began to sing, and the sound of their combined voices, encapsulating us when we did not have the strength to join in, nourished me from within. Vidar and I shared a look—this was good, so necessary, so vital for us. To be with others of the Way. To feel their joy from the outside in. We had been away too long.

We reached the Citadel and slipped between the edges of the deep crevasse that led into the fortress carved from rock. There were hundreds of people inside this time, and it transformed the structure from a cold cave to a comforting palisade against the dark. We were led into the hive-like meeting room, where every seat was filled and even more stood, as if they'd been awaiting us for weeks. And perhaps they had. Asher and Azarel, Chaza'el, Kapriel, Killian, and Tressa were among them, grinning and rushing to hug us.

Everyone in the room applauded, and I blushed at the attention. It was rare for praise and adulation to happen within the Community for anyone other than the Maker. But here, now, all I felt was the comfort and approval of our brothers and sisters. And it was glorious. Vidar reached out and wrapped one arm around my shoulders and the other around Bellona's waist. One by one, we interlocked, we Remnants and Knights, and grinned up and around at the people in this room. Those of the Valley, Drifters, Aravanders, people from Georgii Post, and even Castle Vega. Everywhere we'd gone, it was clear that the Maker had used our presence to call his people home.

Finally, they all grew quiet, and someone brought us chairs, as well as water and meat and even a bowl of rice. We gratefully ate and drank, taking turns sharing our story with them all. For hours, they sat, so silent and still, hanging on our every word.

"And now? Where does the Maker send you next?" asked one elder.

"To Zanzibar," an old, sightless elder said, with a mixture of distaste and wonder on her wrinkled face.

Chaza'el started in surprise. "That is right," he said firmly, with a nod.

Reluctantly, I knew it was true, deep within.

"But there are inherent dangers in going there," Niero said, "that we hope you can help us mitigate, fathers and mothers, sisters and brothers. We narrowly escaped with our lives last time."

"You'll need papers," Jorre said with his big, booming voice. He lifted a hand and twisted his lip, dismissing our worries. "I can speak to Tonna about it."

"Or simply a tattoo," added a woman, pulling down her tunic to show the mark on her shoulder that every Zanzibian was required to have.

"They will help, but we'll need more than that," Ronan said, rising to his feet. "The women among us, warriors though they may be, are in distinct danger there. Any woman who is not betrothed in the City of Men becomes ten times the target. The Lord of Zanzibar prides himself in collecting women for his harem. But I have a solution."

I held my breath as he glanced at me. I'd had no idea he planned to speak.

"I am well aware that it has been forbidden for the Ailith to love beyond the ways of kinship. I understand we must remain true to our calling and mission, first and foremost, and there has been concern among the elders that anything else would distract us from that calling and mission. But the Maker has carved something much deeper in my heart for Andriana, and I publically declare now that I intend to have her as my wife. Whether you bless our union now or in the future, we shall one day be together." He looked only at me as he said it.

I stared at him in shock. And in joy. Could it be? Was he making a way for us? Or destroying any hope we ever had?

People gasped and whispered, and there was a mixture of consternation, yet also compassion, among their faces. The elder raised his hand, and the room remained silent. "This has clearly long been on your mind, son," he said to Ronan, and Ronan turned to face him. "What has brought you to this, besides love?"

"We narrowly avoided losing Andriana to Pacifica's emperor," Ronan said, sliding his eyes toward Kapriel and then back to the elders. "Keallach's Council intended to see her wed to the emperor and were willing to put me and her parents to death in order to secure her agreement. It is my belief as Andriana's protector that if we are to enter Zanzibar and beyond she would be safest as my bride. Or at the very least, my bound bride." He waited for another moment as the room again erupted in whispers. Bindings had only occurred a couple of times in our community—usually when one was about to leave the Valley but intended to return seasons later. "But fathers and mothers, sisters and brothers, it would be my joy to have her as my wife now. I know it is our way to wait until our second decade, but that is only five seasons away. And in this time, given our extraordinary circumstances, I humbly ask that you grant us permission to share our vows on the eve of the upcoming Harvest moon."

"I, too," Killian said, rising and pulling Tressa with him, "ask for the same blessing and honor in taking Tressa as my bride."

Ronan and I shared a knowing grin. We always knew they were in love.

Vidar turned to Bellona.

"Don't even think about it," she hissed, with an eye roll and a shake of her head.

Ronan turned to me and offered his hand. Eyes on his, I took it and rose, realizing my knees were shaking. Out of weariness? Or because of what he had just suggested? Or both?

I glanced over his shoulder at our captain. Niero remained stoic, his dark eyes canvassing the room as if taking it all in at once, considering. He appeared to be waiting for the elders to take the lead on this. Ronan's proposal did make sense, as did Killian's. A marriage—or binding—would help in keeping us safe. In Zanzibar. In Pacifica. Perhaps everywhere.

Someone near the back of the room began to applaud and then another near the front, rising to his feet. Others joined in. And then still more, until the entire room was standing, other than our elders who were robed in white at the front and still sitting. Contemplating. Slowly, the elder who had given us our armbands rose and again lifted his hand until the room was silent. Then he turned to face the crowd. "We understand your enthusiasm for our beloved Ailith. We, too, want the best for them. Now, please, brothers and sisters, leave us to pray and confer with them."

Obediently, hundreds of people filed out, row by row, many of them reaching out to touch our hands or grip arms with the men as they passed. Then it was just us, and I realized that the other Ailith had also risen around me and Ronan, along with the elders and my parents. We moved into a circle.

"You should know, Father," Niero said, "that Ronan and Andriana, Tressa and Killian have done their best to avoid what has been proposed." He paused to eye each of us. "But love happens where the Maker wills it. And I, too, believe this could be the Maker's way of granting protection. Allow them to at least accept the vows of binding. If Andriana and Tressa are claimed, no other man can claim them. And taking vows now will only formalize what they already hold in their hearts."

The white-haired elder shook his head slowly and rubbed his neck—not as if he disagreed, but because he was thinking and struggling with conflicting thoughts.

The oracle reached out her bony, spotted hand toward him. "Cornelius," she said softly. I startled, realizing I had never heard his name before this.

The elder looked at her, paused, and then took her hand in his.

"They simply propose to do now," she said, "what was to come in time. Why not allow it if the Maker has made the way and it shall grant them further protection? I sense none of his displeasure in this. Do you?"

He covered her hand with his other one, then looked to the rest of the gathered elders. Each gradually gave him a single assenting nod before he turned back to us. Again, I held my breath. Could this really be happening?

"Ronan and Andriana of the Valley, Killian and Tressa of Zanzibar, your request for binding shall be granted. Upon the full moon, you shall exchange your vows and bind your hearts and lives together. To the world beyond the Valley, it shall appear as if you are fully betrothed. But you shall remain pure, leaving the intimacy reserved for those truly married until five seasons hence, when, as is our custom, you shall exchange your final vows and be bound by the Maker's blessing."

It wasn't all that Ronan had asked for, but it meant a great deal to us. It meant we no longer needed to hide how we felt for each other—or even attempt to. It meant we could be together, whenever, wherever, without question.

Killian grinned and turned to enfold Tressa in his arms. Ronan pulled me around to face him alone.

He sank to one knee with my hand between both of his. "Andriana, would you do me this honor? Would you pledge me your heart, forever, as you already hold mine?"

I glanced to my parents. Dad had his arm around Mom's shoulders. She was crying. But both were smiling, and I knew their blessing was ours.

"If you will pledge me yours," I whispered to Ronan, tears slipping down my face as such intense love from him surrounded me, enveloped me, and warmed me through. "I will certainly pledge you mine."

He rose and lifted me in his arms, grinning wider than any time I'd ever seen him grin before.

"You, Bellona, shall be handfasted to Vidar," the elder went on.

"Oh, no, Father," she protested. "We cannot. There is no need . . ."

But he was holding up both hands to her and nodding. "Yes, you shall. I know as a Knight that it seems ridiculous. But you shall draw attention to the others if you are not . . . attached. We shall break the binding upon your return."

Vidar, the scoundrel, was hiding a toothy smile behind his hand, grinning in victory at her. I knew he had no more interest in her than she had in him, but he delighted in teasing her.

"And Raniero?" the elder went on, after conferring with the oracle. "If Azarel is to go with you, you shall do the same."

Niero was visibly taken aback. Azarel wasn't even in the room with us—I'd heard him ask her to go fetch Jorre, Socorro, and Dagan to speak with us. "Azarel?" he stammered. I stared at him, eyes wide. *Now that might be a very complicated union.*

"She will be a blessing and a boon to the Ailith, just as you are," the oracle said, and there was a tiny quirk to the corner of her droopy, aged lips.

There was one thing for certain—the ceremony on the full moon would be one the Community would long remember.

CHAPTER 7

KEALLACH

W here . . . is . . . she?" I ground out, studying my fingers splayed out on the marble table before me. I was tired of it. So sick of their excuses. "Your spies told us that they have returned to the Valley. I want to know specifically where she is. Can you not activate her ID chip?"

"We can," Sethos said in a measured tone. "But we've heard that some among the Trading Union have a device to detect active chips. I thought it in our best interest to wait until we're very close to retrieving Andriana before activating it."

"I see," I said, hiding my shame at not thinking of that myself. "Surely your trackers can enter the Valley as they did before and give us some report?"

"No," Sethos said, staring at me until I looked him in the eyes. "They cannot. The Valley is far more populated now. And the team we sent in had only one survivor."

"What? How is that possible? Your Sheolite scouts are the best trained men we have."

"I am telling you, those in the Community are growing in force and daring. And now they have the valley mouth watched by guardians—those wretched rebels. The Aravanders are used to us and our methods. They have deadly aim and a decided ability to meld into the forest when pursued, picking off those who follow."

"It is time, Majesty," Kendric said, crossing his arms. "We cannot allow them to be so bold. I don't care if it's the heart of the Trading Union. Allow us to go in there and cut down every one."

"What? No," I said. "The best sort of empire is a *willing* empire. If it comes to war, so be it. But we shall try other methods first."

Daivat tucked his head and moved toward the map, pointing to where the Valley lay beyond the Great Expanse and the milder Central Desert. "They have already drawn people from west and south. If there are others beyond them, to the north and east, and they have the means to call upon their aid, they may become a more formidable enemy than we thought possible."

"They might not have been our enemy at all," I ground out, "if you had allowed me to see things through with Andriana rather than taking things into your own hands."

The remaining men of my Council and Sethos all stared back at me, silenced for the moment.

"I think we understand the price of our misjudgment," Max said from where he sat, propped up in his chair at the far end of the table, still looking thin and wan.

He and I locked eyes for a long moment, and I felt a stab of guilt before my carefully controlled rage won out. Apart from Sethos, I felt his interference most keenly. I kept renaming the act in my head. Betrayal is what I felt; interference is what I chose to call it. I constantly fought the desire to beat every one of them for possibly ruining any chance I might ever have with Andriana, and beyond that, to eventually be one of the Remnants. It had been such a tenuous hold I'd had, such a whisper of a connection. But she had felt it and allowed it. I know she had. And now that it was gone, I felt the grief of her loss just as I'd once felt it with Kapriel.

Except it was different.

Harder even than my parting from my twin, in that she held my heart as both a woman . . . and Ailith kin.

RONAN

I led Andriana to her room, and for a moment, just a moment, the hallway was empty. She peeked inside, and we saw Bellona and Tressa, each unpacking their small bags. Dri silently closed the door again and looked up at me. I grinned down at her, both of us searching the other's eyes, so much of what we had to say unspoken, and yet, in our touch, so clear. "I love you, Andriana," I whispered.

She reached up and touched my face with her long, graceful fingers. I thought I could spend days just closing my eyes and feeling her touch like that, and die a happy man. "I know," she whispered. "I love you too." And the air around us felt almost charged, as if I was supernaturally aware of every sound and smell, able to sense everything with increased acuity.

With a quick glance left and right to see that we were still miraculously, blessedly alone, I bent my head and kissed her. I thought I'd steal only one quick kiss, but when she leaned into me, her hands against my back, I leaned in as well. She tasted like the earth and sky—at once familiar and yet new too, calling me to know her more. Our kiss deepened, and I knew I should summon the strength to draw away but—

A hand on my shoulder brought my head abruptly upward.

Niero.

He was stern, yet not angry. "You are not yet bound," he said, still holding my shoulder. "And even afterward, you are to remain . . . *somewhat* chaste, yes?"

"Yes," I said, feeling the burn of embarrassment at my cheeks, as well as irritation at his interruption.

"Good night, Andriana," Niero said.

"Good night," she returned, and I thought the blush on her own cheeks made her all the more beautiful.

"Sleep well," I said, feeling a roguish grin steal across my lips. I felt jaunty. Romantically daring. And able to give into those feelings for the first time in my life, because our plans had been blessed. We were to be bound within days, and married in time.

Dri entered her room and softly closed the wooden door between us.

"Come," Niero said, already moving away. "As much as that woman is on your mind, you both are in dire need of sleep."

I tore myself from Dri's door and followed Niero down the corridor. "How did Azarel take the news?" I asked him, grinning a little to myself. Even the break in my kiss from Andriana couldn't dampen the glory of this day.

"I haven't yet spoken to her," Niero said, casting a scowl over his shoulder at me.

"Ahh," I said. "Can I be there when you do?"

"No," Niero said, his scowl now deepening. "And I'll thank you for not asking me about it again. Azarel and I have . . . other plans that do not include binding." We turned another corner and, three doors down, entered a room that we were to share with Killian and Vidar.

Killian rose and took my arm. "I owe you my thanks, brother. I had not the courage or the thought to try. But when you did . . ." He cocked his head and grinned. "Thank you."

"Yeah, thanks," Vidar said, lying back on his cot and knitting his fingers behind his head with a look of satisfaction. "I'm going to ride this train for some time with Bellona."

"Better not," I said, sitting down on my cot to yank off my boots. "Or Bellona will take apart that pretty face she's supposed to protect."

Vidar frowned. "What? No. She loves me! Well, not in the way that Dri feels for you or Tressa for Killian. But hey, maybe she'll come around and realize this stud is the best she'll ever meet."

"Even if you're three inches shorter," Killian teased, unbuttoning his shirt.

"Hey, what I lack in height, I showcase in brawn and intellect," Vidar said. He flexed his arms while pointing at his temples.

"All right, all right," Niero said. "Enough. There is time enough for such talk tomorrow. For now, we rest." He leaned toward the oil lamp on the table beside his bed and looked around to see if we were ready. Apparently satisfied that we were close enough, he turned the key, and the room was immediately encased in darkness.

Here, within the Citadel, behind so much rock, was the one place I knew I could trust that Andriana would be safe. But still, my heart longed to be at her side. To be taking her into my arms for another sweet kiss . . .

"Sleep, Ronan," Niero said, the rustling of rough woolen blankets telling me he was settling in beneath them.

I laughed under my breath. "Sure you're not a Remnant, Niero?" There was something different about him that tugged at the edge of my memory. As if I'd discovered something about him, but couldn't quite remember what it was.

"Absolutely sure," he muttered.

I took a deep breath and huffed a "good night," my cheeks hurting from all the smiling. I didn't know if I had ever smiled so much in my entire life, but this idea that I might make Dri mine, forever, was the greatest joy I'd ever felt.

I pulled off my shirt and then yanked my own blanket up to my chin, shivering a little in the chill of the granite-bound room. For a moment, I wondered if sleep was possible, but that was the last thought I had for many hours.

CHAPTER
8

ANDRIANA

We slept for the better part of three days. We'd awaken to eat and then sink back into sleep, our eyelids too heavy to stay open. On the second day, they'd kept us up long enough to receive our Zanzibian tattoos, ignoring our protests, so that there'd be enough time to heal before we entered the city gates. As the tattoo artist embedded mine with one painful prick of her needle and ink after another, her hand drifted lower, to below my scapula. "What happened to you here?" she asked, running her fingers over an old wound.

"Oh," I yawned, glancing back. "I suffered some injuries in Pacifica. I think it's been there since then." I rolled my shoulder and felt a shiver run up my neck, remembering Sethos, Maximillian Jala, and the creepy physician they sent to check me out. My back didn't hurt at all compared to the cracked ribs I'd suffered, which still hurt. My fingers moved to the place that had hurt worst, and to the odd bump there. It was like a tiny piece of bone had broken off. I could feel it just below the skin. I sighed and dropped my hand, knowing that we all now carried bruises and scars from the battles we'd endured, and there were bound to be more ahead.

She finished her work and again allowed us to return to our chambers and slumber. On the third day, I roused enough to be disgusted by my stench and the grease in my hair.

"I really need a bath," I moaned to Bellona when I saw her stir. A small gas lamp was lit in the corner—I'd dimly recognized that a woman came several times a day to refill our water pitcher and leave food, which we took turns at nibbling and drinking before falling back into our deep slumber.

"Maybe if we bathed, it would help us break out of this eternal desire for sleep," she muttered, rubbing her eyes.

On the far side of the room, Tressa sat up, her auburn hair a crazy nest of curls. "We have to *do* something," she agreed. "Do you think it's sleeping in the cave? In such darkness?"

"I think it's so many weeks of trauma," I said, forcing myself to rise too. "If you think over what we've done . . ."

"And how many miles we've covered," Bellona added.

"Yes," Tressa said, nodding while she yawned. "It makes sense. Even though I'd been resting here while you two were busy escaping Pacifica. So . . . where do we bathe?"

"I think the Citadel has its own sauna, showers, and baths near the latrines," I said. "But I'd rather show you another spot. There's a mineral spring my father used to take me to."

"Oh, up past Thumb Rock?" Bellona asked.

"Yeah! Have you been there?"

"A few times," she said. "That'd be good. Still a crop of sweet william up there to use?"

"Yes, but I have something better," I said, waggling my brows. I rose, stretched, and went to my bag. "Jorre left me a bar of lavender soap the night we returned."

Tressa clapped and looked instantly more awake. She rose and went to the corner of the room to look through a pile of clothes that the maidservant had brought for us to choose from. Underneath were several towels made from a fine, soft cloth. After Bellona and I had each chosen new leggings, shirts, and sweaters—as well as new underwear and a bra band that I was so happy to see that I nearly hugged it—we left our room and walked down the corridor and past the guards, as if we did it all the time. I felt some guilt leaving without telling Ronan where we were going, but I didn't want him to see me as I was. I wanted to surprise him tonight, looking rested and clean. Besides, Bellona was with us, and she carried her bow and quiver of arrows, as I did my sword. We weren't going far.

Outside, Bellona told the guards where we were going, in case anyone asked.

The man grinned and tucked his thumbs into his front trouser pockets. "Well, now, I think you girls might need a man to watch over you there."

Bellona didn't return his smile. "Come anywhere near us, and I'll make certain you never see a girl again," she growled. "We'll be back in an hour or two. Tell no one but Remnant or Knight where we've gone."

I smiled as the man paled in shock at her words. We turned and climbed a trail that wound through the boulders, then up through a small ravine to the left. At the top, there was a rock that resembled a fist with a crooked thumb extended, which had spawned the name. There, across a small meadow with underbrush that was becoming drier, signaling the end of Harvest, was a bubbling pool at the edge of a creek. The air was tinged with the slightly foul smell of sulphur, and I knew Tressa's worry before she looked at me.

"Don't be concerned," I said to her. "Between the creek water and the lavender soap, we won't smell like that. But the hot spring keeps it blessedly warm."

It was more than warm, I found out. With the dwindling creek stream as Harvest waned, there wasn't as much fresh water coming through. But we undressed and eased in carefully, and found the hot, steaming water soothed the remaining knots in our muscles. We lathered our hair and bodies and sank under the steaming water to rinse, then we did it again and rinsed clean in the creek, the cold doing its good work to help us feel more fully awake. "Come Hoarfrost," I said to them, "we'll return here and roll in the snow between soaks."

"That's the best," Bellona agreed.

"Or we can simply use the Citadel sauna," Tressa tried, rubbing her bare skin, which was covered in goose bumps.

I handed her the comb after I was done. "Trust me, it's worth a visit, even in snow."

"Maybe you can come with your husband," Bellona said, arching a brow. "It's long been used in the Valley as a spot for young lovers to steal away for . . . well, some bathing," she said meaningfully, an uncommon grin on her lips.

Tressa blushed. "Yes, well, we'll see," she said, wincing as she hit a particularly stubborn knot in her hair. "I still can't believe the elders approved our binding," she added. "But tell me. In Zanzibar, I've only known of betrothals, not bindings. I mean, on the streets, I heard of it. But I don't know . . . What I mean is, does it . . ." Even flushed with the heat of the spring, we could see the blush rise on her cheeks.

"You want to know how much intimacy bindings entail," I said gently.

She gave me the faintest of nods. "The elders bade us to remain chaste, but does that mean we cannot even . . . kiss?"

"It's up to the newly bound," Bellona said gruffly. "Commonly decided between them. Some decide to avoid kissing. Vidar and I will definitely be making *that* decision, of course."

I smiled with Bellona, knowing how she chafed at what was to come, then looked to the swirling steam rising above the water.

"Is it what you truly want, Tressa?" I asked her. "I've known I loved Ronan for some time. And I had the idea that you and Killian . . ."

She took a deep breath, putting her fingers to her lips, thinking. "Yes. It is what I want. I simply had not allowed my mind to go there. But the thought of ever being without Killian . . . Of bonding with another man as I have my Knight . . ." She lifted her eyes to the quaking leaves above us, most of them already umber, and shook her head. "No, the choice is simple."

"But it goes beyond a Remnant-Knight bond between you, yes?" Bellona asked, sitting down on a rock a few steps away, naked from head to toe and yet utterly at ease as her skin steamed in the relative cool. "I am bound to Vidar. I admit that. But there is no way I'd ever want to bed him." She shivered at the thought, and I laughed.

"Yes, it goes beyond our Ailith bond," I said.

"Far beyond that bond," Tressa agreed, in little more than a whisper, her big, blue eyes full of understanding, as if she were just coming to terms with it.

Bellona sighed. "I don't think I could *take* any more bonding with Vidar."

And that made the three of us laugh until we cried.

We saw Vidar and Killian sitting on the rocks outside the Citadel, keeping watch on the path we returned upon. Bellona turned at once, hand tightening on the curve of her bow, until all of us recognized it was Ronan's presence behind us. "I told the guard to tell you they were safe," she grumbled.

"Yes," he said, grabbing my hand and turning me around, looking me over from head to toe. "I just had to be certain."

"You didn't—" I started, horrified that he might have seen us.

"No, no," he said with an impish smile. "As much as I *wanted* to. I just kept watch on the far side to make sure you didn't get any *unwanted* company. When I heard your voices fade toward the Citadel, I followed behind." He reached up and pushed the hair out of my face. "You look beautiful. And clean. And rested. And . . . beautiful," he repeated.

"So do you," I said with a grin as he interlaced his fingers with mine.

"Yeah," Vidar said, jumping off the rock as he fluttered his eyelashes in Ronan's direction. "Bellisimo."

Killian was already tugging Tressa along a side path, probably intent on stealing a moment alone before supper. Bellona had continued along the trail, barely pausing, and Vidar trotted after her. "Some guardian she turned out to be," he huffed, with no real malice in his tone.

And at that moment, I realized we were alone ourselves. Ronan lifted his arm to the rock behind me and leaned in close. He closed his eyes, and let his lips drift a hair's breath away from my cheek, my nose, my other cheek, and into my hair. "Dri," he breathed. "Heavens, you smell wonderful."

He did too. I lifted my hands to his new, clean shirt and tugged him closer, kissing him then, ignoring how it reminded me of my healing ribs. His other hand pressed against my lower back, pulling me firmly against him. On and on our kiss went, and I realized that a few years from now I wouldn't blush when I thought of him seeing me naked by a pool. We could know one another fully, as husband and wife, at that time. Feeling my desire for him—along with his for me—I began to not only sense both our emotions, but I could almost see them in explosions of color. *Vermillion red. Verdant teal. Valley green . . .* I swallowed hard and edged away. "We should . . . we should go back," I said.

He nodded, his eyes full of desire, before resolutely stepping back. "We should. Because here . . . in private . . . it's hard to keep that chaste boundary firmly in place."

I smiled mischievously. "Agreed." I stepped closer and went to my tiptoes to kiss him once more, softly on the lips.

"This is going to be harder than I thought," he said softly, his voice nearly cracking from feigned strain. He closed his eyes for a moment and then looked into mine. "The Maker will give us the strength. We will figure out what we can do and what we cannot, and wait until our true betrothal."

"We will," I said, offering my hand.

He took a firm grip of my hand and matched my easy stride back toward the Citadel. "Ever think you were given the gift of sensibility over empathy?"

"Oh no," I said, letting out a deep, long breath. "Because I just felt every bit of my desire *and* yours. I'm most definitely an empath."

And that made him grin all the wider.

CHAPTER 9

ANDRIANA

On the appointed evening, everyone in the Community dressed in shades of white—a far better choice than the Pacificans' matrimonial blue, I thought—and trekked to the high meadow on a wide path that was easily lit by the massive moon above us. Mom and Dad walked beside me, arms entwined with mine, their collective emotions almost a burden, even though it was mostly joy. I knew Ronan walked directly behind us. Fear and consternation, as well as wonder and bliss, swirled like a tornado within my chest, until I concentrated on asking the Maker to show me what I felt myself. Alone. And what I discovered there was simply joy and peace.

We reached the top of the hill and gazed out at the wide meadow, full of thigh-high grass that was now brittle brown, the green of its blades long spent. Our trainer had brought us here over the years, to spar and perfect our methods of crawling through grass undetected. Even as children, we'd recognized it for what it was and avoided fully looking each other in the eye until we'd left it. But now all I wanted was to look Ronan full in the face, and have his look into mine.

Dad led us to the far side of the meadow, where the hillside fell away to a spectacular view of the mountain ranges that protected our valley and the silver, winding river at the center of it, now glittering in the moonlight. We could see all the way to where the desert sands met the first trees, and beyond that to the bumpy dunes of the Central Desert. It was a rarity, such clear skies and horizons—but as pretty as it was, I couldn't wait for what was about to unfold, right here.

Mom, Dad, and I faced Cornelius and Ronan, all of us in a fit of smiles. Another elder was on one end, and Kapriel and Azarel on the other. I didn't know how Raniero had talked the elder out of his own binding to Azarel, but there had been no further word of it. I was too focused on Ronan to think about it for more than a moment. Around us, countless other couples faced one another, each surrounded by those closest to them among the Community. Three women in long, white gowns moved to the center of the meadow, each carrying a torch and a triangular bell that dangled from their wrist. When they reached the center, they stood back to back. Together, they rang their triangles three times, and the sound stilled us all.

"Ronan of the Valley," Cornelius said, the timbre of his voice warm and joyful. "Andriana of the Valley." He nodded to each of us in turn. "Long have you both been loyal servants of the Community, and tonight you pledge to love and serve the other for life, as thoroughly as husbands and wives taking their full matrimonial vows do. Are you prepared to do so?"

"I am," Ronan said.

"I am," I repeated with a smile, looking up into his wide, kind eyes, wishing this were the night we took our full vows. At least it was a step in the right direction. Such a sweet step.

We fell into silence, waiting until the other couples and their presiders grew quiet too. At that moment, the women at the meadow's center rang their triangles three times, and then in sequence, each note a step higher.

"Ronan and Andriana," Cornelius continued, "do you pledge to love and honor each other, just as you love and honor the Maker?"

"I do," Ronan said.

"I do," I said.

Once more, we awaited silence. I knew that what was to come was where our binding vows differed from the betrothal vows that others would share. The women rang their triangles—this time, three rounds of sequential notes.

"Face each other, dear ones," Cornelius said, "and place your right hands together." I set my palm atop Ronan's wide, warm hand and smiled up into his eyes. The elder took a long, green sash from a young girl at his side and set to wrapping our hands together. Those who took their betrothal vows were wrapped in white sashes. "This agreement will hold until the time when you mutually agree to disband and come to an elder for formal unbinding or decide to take your betrothal vows after your second decade. Agreed?"

We both said yes.

The women at the center began to play their triangles, at first slowly, then building in tempo as the elder spoke and wrapped our hands in the silken cloth. "May your hearts become even more deeply entwined with each day you share," he said, making the first loop. "May you use your bodies to serve the other in protection and care," he said, making the second. He continued wrapping and speaking. "May you use your tongues to speak words of kindness and encouragement. May you choose the same path and may your paths never diverge. And may you use your lives, together, to serve the Maker," he said, tucking the end of the ribbon under the last fold.

Ronan looked into my eyes with such tenderness that it made me tear up. "May it be so," he whispered.

"May it be so," I repeated.

All around the meadow, each small gathering erupted into applause as couples completed their vows.

"These are good promises, children. Keep them sacred, and your union will be strong forever. You may kiss now. *Briefly.*" But there was an edge of indulgence to his tone, more than warning. With that, he untucked the ribbon and gently let it slide from our hands.

Ronan grinned and wrapped his fingers around the back of my head, and his other arm around my waist, pulling me close. Hovering near, he searched my eyes, clearly seeing the joy that pulsed from us both in such clear waves, I thought the emotion might actually make a sound.

And then, unable to stand it any longer, I rose up on my toes and kissed him.

From there, we returned to the Citadel, where we had a fine celebratory dinner and then were ushered to our various "matrimonial" apartments. The chamber I was to share with Ronan in the days ahead was spacious, with a tiny airshaft that brought in a hint of a breeze. But we had two separate beds, on opposite sides of the room.

"We could push them together," he said, wrapping his arms around me from behind and pulling me close, nuzzling my neck.

"Probably not the best idea," I said, turning to kiss him and then hug him close. "This is going to be challenging enough, isn't it?"

He sighed and ran a hand through his hair. "Something I'll have to pray about day and night, Wife."

"As will I, Husband," I returned, kissing his nose.

He laughed under his breath. "Maybe we should just kiss each other's noses."

I smiled. "That would probably keep the heat at bay."

"That's it," he grinned, pulling me closer. "Five seasons of nose kisses until you're mine and I'm yours, completely."

"Or … not," I said, lifting my lips to meet his.

CHAPTER
10

ANDRIANA

The days passed in a blur of activity and joy as we continued to rest and settle into our new roles as bound pairs, as well as Ailith family. Gradually, I became accustomed to this new claim I felt on Ronan, and he upon me. Somehow, it made things easier, this understanding between us. The promise. Anything that had kept us apart was gone. I'd never felt closer to him. Safer.

"We have someone we want you to meet," Niero said.

His grave tone made us all share concerned glances before rising to join him in the hallway. Moments before, we Remnants and Knights had all been sitting around a long dinner table in the hall, with hundreds of others, laughing as Vidar shared a meandering story that got progressively funnier as he went on. It was good, so good, to be back in the Community. Every one of us was showing improvement after our days among them. We all had more color in our cheeks, renewed strength in our veins. And even though six of us were now bound by our vows, never had I felt more bonded to my fellow Ailith. This was *elation*, I decided, unable to stop smiling. Even with the ongoing threat beyond our Valley, there was a collective deep, abiding joy within us that I could not ignore.

Niero led us to a large meeting room several corridors down. Inside were two Valley guards as well as an older man with olive skin and black hair streaked with gray that was tied at the nape of his neck. He wore thick furs, but they were styled differently than the Aravanders typically cut and sewed theirs. Slowly, he rose to his feet and cautiously nodded, as if in deference.

"I am Barrett of the Uintah Range, high country to the north and east of your valley," he said. "I have come to discover if the stories are true. If you are truly the foretold Remnants, gathering to lead us into a new age."

"We are," Vidar said, taking the lead, inherently telling us that we had nothing to fear from this individual.

"But if you are from the Uintah Range," Kapriel said, giving his clothing a second look, "then you have traveled a very long way indeed."

"Yes," the man said, with a sober nod, squinting at Kapriel. "You know of my land?"

"There was once an emissary in Pacifica who visited my father. I remember how excited my father was."

"Pacifica?" Barrett muttered, frowning. Almost subconsciously, his hand went to his belt, but I saw that the Valley guards had relieved him of his weapon.

"You have nothing to fear in this one," Vidar interceded. "This is Prince Kapriel of Pacifica, himself a Remnant."

The man's eyes widened, and he nodded, a half smile lacing his lips. "Kapriel," he repeated, as if wanting to make certain he'd heard correctly.

"Yes," Kapriel said.

Barrett's wondering smile widened. "I believe we've met before. I was that man who came to your father. But you and your brother couldn't have been more than a decade old."

"Just about," Kapriel said, stepping forward to take his arm. "It is good to meet you again."

"And you as well, Majesty. Your father and mother were good people," he said, a trace of sorrow passing behind his eyes.

"Indeed, they were," Kapriel said.

My mind turned then, unbidden, to Keallach. Where was he? What was happening to him? Was he still feeling the pull of the Ailith?

"Now, please," Kapriel was saying. I forced myself to focus on him, our prince . . . not the prince I had once known. "Tell us of your land. Your people."

Barrett turned and went back to the table, where he pulled a scroll out of a leather tube and spread it flat. It was a map, hand drawn, with the finest detail we'd ever seen. "I am a cartographer," he said, "and my life's mission has been to travel the land we've been left since the Great War. It's allowed me to go far," he said, "in all directions. I've traveled for an entire season northward, until snows as deep as my waist turned me back, even in the midst of Harvest. And I've traveled south, to where the ocean spreads as far as the eye can see. To the east, where mountains give way to plains, and to the west, where your brother now reigns."

"But I suspect you do more than map the lands you travel," Niero said, crossing his arms.

"Well, of course," Barrett said, his dark eyes twinkling as he raised one brow. "I, my friends, am your servant, a brother of the Way. And I can be of service to you as emissary. There are villages to your east that have long waited for the rise of the Remnants. They understand Pacifica's greedy intent, and they will back you in fighting for the Trading Union's freedom and autonomy."

Hope surged within us all. "Are there many?" I asked. "Close at hand?"

His dark eyes fell on me. "It is a struggle, survival, as you yourselves have seen in the Valley. Most tribes are not many in number. But those who remain are strong. And if we gather them all together ... It's a force of note."

I nodded, but all I could think of was Pacifica, with her well-trained—and armed—soldiers and Sheolite scouts.

"The good, Dri," Vidar whispered, squeezing my elbow. "Concentrate on the good, not the bad, in this. It's excellent news, really. The Valley couldn't sustain thousands of others. But a few hundred more? Absolutely."

"What do they trade in, these tribes?" Niero asked, waving in the direction of the Plains.

"Wheat, mostly," Barrett said with a half shrug.

"Wheat," Ronan repeated. His eyes danced. "Jorre will love hearing that."

Niero ignored him. "What about lands beyond this map?" he asked. "What do you know of the people from across the sea?"

Barrett grew more serious. "Since the Great War? There is some trade between Pacifica and those across the Sea to the West. And southward, small outposts, as I understand it. But to the Far East?" He shook his head. "No one knows if anyone lives in that territory any longer. I myself traveled eastward for months after I left the last village and never saw another soul. The elders said no one remains on what was once the eastern coast of our continent. I came to believe them."

"But you never reached the coast yourself?" Kapriel asked.

Barrett shook his head. "I had to turn back, come Hoarfrost. They may be there, but if they are, they are very far indeed."

Chaza'el said, "The elders in my village always said it was beyond that shore that the Great War began."

"As it was told in ours," Barrett said stoically. "Radicals took over. Dark souls, the forefathers of the Sheolites here in our own land. They sought to conquer every important religious site and force others to bow down to them alone. They murdered and bombed and struck out until their victims turned and attacked them as well. And then other countries entered the fray, bombing, destroying, and poisoning city after city. The scope of the Great War grew from there until there wasn't a continent untouched by bombs and poison that led to the Cancer. It was the Sheolites who slandered the faith, whispering and shouting it everywhere they went—they laid the mantle of blame for the Great War, the destruction of our world, at the Maker's feet rather than where it belonged—with humanity's own corruption."

"And through all that, any name for the Maker was banished," Killian said. "His people were hunted to extinction, the Sacred Words destroyed."

"Or so they thought," Niero said, raising his chin.

The two shared a thin-lipped smile. But the story only made me feel sick to my stomach. How close we had come, as a people, years before. To annihilation. To death. To darkness. Were we really enough to push back the darkness? We here, in the Valley, even with the reinforcements that Barrett mentioned might come to our aid?

"Do you know how many?" I asked, pausing to clear my throat when it came out warbled. "How many soldiers does Pacifica have?"

Barrett turned to look at me. "Two thousand, perhaps," he grunted. "Half again as many as we might raise. But they are unfamiliar with the terrain of your valley, which will give you an advantage. It is here, now," he said, resting his index finger on our home, nestled between mountain ranges, "that we must stand. If they take us here, if they succeed in conquering us now, the fight will likely end with us."

"So you propose that you will press along our eastern border, summoning those who might come to our aid," Kapriel said. "And we shall press west, as the Maker calls, seeking to establish increased defenses between us and Pacifica."

Barrett's bushy brows knit together. He obviously thought Kapriel was joking. "You think the Maker is calling you *west*? You really think you can turn Zanzibar or Georgii Post into friends of the Maker? Why not continue to await people to come to you here? I can tell you that word already spreads, everywhere I go." He paused to look over us. "You bring the people hope, just by living. Why not remain here, where you can be relatively safe?"

Kapriel gave him a tiny smile. "Because our Maker hasn't called us to live a safe life. He's called us to live a life of trust. If he sends us, there is a reason."

"And it will have far more impact than if we remain sheltered here," Niero said, eyeing Killian and Tressa.

"Sometimes it makes no sense to us," Vidar said, "but we understand in time."

Barrett's eyes swept over the lot of us again. "You are young, barely of age. Are you certain that this is the right time to taunt Pacifica? Why not allow a few more seasons to pass? Allow the people to hear word of you and gather to our cause?"

"Because it is *now* that he has called us," Kapriel said.

CHAPTER
11

ANDRIANA

I reached for dreams but couldn't grasp deep sleep. I tossed. I turned. And, finally, I rose.

I blinked several times, trying to get my bearings. Ronan slept in the bed on the other side of the room, as peacefully as if he hadn't a care in the world.

But I did.

I did.

I rubbed my temples, trying to wriggle out the troublesome thoughts in my brain, then eventually slid to the door—well aware of the Knight in my chambers and his otherworldly ability to sense subtle changes in me—and eased out to the hall. I counted it as a small miracle that I succeeded. Ronan's breath still was slow and deep as I gently closed the door behind me.

My heart stuttered for a second. Niero was at the end of the hall, his wings partially unfurled, a mighty, fearsome silhouette against a torch in the distance. With one glance over his shoulder at me, he turned and walked away. This was why I had awakened and couldn't go back to sleep. He'd called to me.

I followed after him, sure he'd slipped into the meeting hall, the beehive-like room where we first received word of the Call, where we received our armbands, where the Community always met. But it was empty. I had no idea where Raniero went, so I climbed the stairs to the top and sank onto the rock-hewn bench at the very back, marveling at the view from this steep angle and pondering why Niero might've called me out and then disappeared. But the space felt good to me. Like breathing space. Time to think and feel . . . and pray. I leaned against the cold wall behind me and turned my cheek to look down the line of it, to stare at the scoops in the stone and, for the first time, to contemplate what they represented. It occurred to me, for the very first time, that this hall had been carved, bit by bit, by my people. Over years. Over decades. Over . . . centuries? The Maker hadn't created it. People had. How long had it taken? How many?

And all for . . . us?

For . . . now?

I turned and looked down below to Niero, who now stood in the center of the dais, hands at his side, head bowed, as if preparing himself for what was to come. His wings had disappeared. He'd led me here then left me to contemplate, as if orchestrating my thoughts.

"Were you here?" I asked, my voice echoing eerily down to him in the cavernous hall.

"Here?"

His voice sounded hollow, distant, echoey, from just fifty paces away. And yet close. *Inside* me. I hadn't even seen his lips form the words. And yet I'd heard them.

I thought of what I had seen when Ronan almost died. When Niero brought him back to life.

How his wings stretched out . . .

"Were you here," I forced myself to repeat, feeling half fearful and half mesmerized, "when they hollowed out this room? Niero. Have you been alive . . . for a very long time? Awaiting our arrival?"

His dark eyes met mine. "No. I was not here. It was many seasons before I came to the Valley." He paused and then moved to the wall behind him, his brown, strong fingers brushing the unique, carved texture for a moment. "But the Citadel has been here for a long time, Andriana. It was always meant to be our fortress. Our shield."

I rubbed my hand across the opposite wall, thinking of all the men and women—the generations—this room had welcomed. The hundreds upon hundreds who had gathered sat on these benches, talking, praying, laughing, crying. They'd carved these halls from solid rock—not sandstone, but granite—preparing this place for us, a fortress for the faithful.

"Were you brought here to lead us?" I asked, still staring at the wall, the scoops and divots that represented so many.

"To guide and defend you," he said, climbing the steps toward me now, as if he hovered over them. And perhaps he did.

"But you did not defend us from everything," I said, meeting his gaze again. He was now just ten paces away. "From all of our enemies." Again, I thought of him with Ronan. Of watching me disappear with Keallach. Of all I'd endured within Palace Pacifica. Of all my parents had endured.

"I was sent to guide and defend," he repeated. "I cannot keep you from your own choices."

"My own choices," I choked out, rising. "My own *choices*."

I started to walk down the stairs toward him, pausing two steps away so his eyes were on my level. "You, Raniero, have the power of the *heavens*. And you allowed Keallach to take me? To Pacifica?"

His dark eyes met mine, and in them, I saw the wisdom of the ages, startling yet reassuring all at once. How had I ever—*ever*—not known this man was anything but human?

"It was your choice," he said, an edge of pain in his eyes. "To run into the woods without your Knight. You wanted to save Killian. To do it yourself. You did not wait, did not wait to seek the wisdom the Maker might give you. You simply *went*."

I winced. I wanted to deny his words, to defend myself. But I could not. What he said was the truth. I looked down. There was nothing to parse. No shred for me to argue.

Niero reached out and touched my chin, lifting it. "But it was for good in the end, yes? The Maker uses all for good, if we allow it." His hand moved to my cheek, cradling it, forcing me to think it through and giving me the rare opportunity to freely sense his intense emotions.

I searched his eyes, wondering what he wanted me to discover. But it was mainly encouragement I sensed from him. Hope. I considered why I was angry with him, why I blamed him.

"He has made you strong, Andriana," Niero said. "Soft and malleable in some ways, as an empath. But you are capable of utilizing wisdom and connection with him to make the most of that. He will mold you, if you allow it. He will use every experience in your life, good or bad, to mold you into a woman after his own heart. Which is what he wants most, Andriana," he said, taking my hand, and I felt a jolt of holy connection run through me, warming me from my head to my toes. "Not to use you, or harm you. But to bring you closer to his own heart. The closer you get, the greater your empath skills will grow, and the wiser your decisions will be."

My mind went through all I'd endured, all I'd encountered, all I'd reached for. My failures. As a Remnant. Reaching for Keallach. Trying to bring him . . . home.

And it was true. Somehow, someway, it'd all been for good. It was good that I'd tried. It was right that I had been there, trying to bridge the gap between Keallach and his brothers and sisters. It had been worth it.

All of it. Every treacherous moment with Keallach and Sethos. Those long days locked in my room. Weeks away from the Remnants, all in an effort to reach my brother, my kin, the one I had loved like a—

"Dri? Are you all right?"

Ronan's voice shocked me out of my reverie, and I glanced down the steep stairs to where he stood in the doorway. I saw at once how it might have looked, Niero holding my hand between his, me looking so intent . . . while I was now Ronan's bound bride.

Niero dropped my hand but refused to look at Ronan . . . refused to give in to guilt-by-assumption. But I wasn't as strong. And the false guilt made me blush, which made me angrier, which in turn led to more furious blushing. I brushed past Niero and went down the stairs.

"It's fine, Ronan," I muttered. "I simply couldn't sleep, and Niero was helping me think through some things. We should go back now. I'm terribly tired." I tried to edge past him, but Ronan caught my wrist and pulled me back toward him. "So you went to him, not me?"

"He was up too. I didn't purposefully seek him out."

"No," Niero said, coming closer. "It was I who sought her."

"You . . . sought *her*. For what reason?" Ronan asked, letting me go to focus on Niero.

"Because she is agitated. Restless. Ill at ease."

"Then it was I who should have attended her," Ronan said, turning to fully face him in challenge.

Niero did not flinch. "You do not wish to fight me, Knight. No matter how . . . agitated you might feel. There is no cause for jealousy here. *No* cause."

CHAPTER
12

ANDRIANA

No?" Ronan asked, fists clenching and unclenching. "You've always been against us being together, opposed any romantic inklings. Are you sure it's not because you entertained some of your own?"

"Ronan," I tried, growing thoroughly embarrassed. "You have it all wrong." I moved between them, shoving one muscular, broad chest away from the other. "Now stop it."

"Think on it," Niero said, focusing only on Ronan. "I opposed your union at first, but not since we returned here. I was only following what the elders had directed—that you were to hold off on such feelings because it might get in the way of our mission. Now the Maker has made a way for you and Andriana, as well as Killian and Tressa."

"And yet you did not take vows with Azarel, as the elders dictated," Ronan said.

"Azarel and I have our own reasons not to take the vows. You will simply have to trust me."

The sounds of approaching footsteps finally registered in my ears, and it was then that I noticed that Niero was already pulling away. It wasn't just footsteps, I registered. Boots. Many pairs of boots approached.

"What? At this hour?" Ronan grumbled, alarmed, and pulled me slightly behind him.

They entered the hall. Two guards each holding two people in custody. I gaped at them in shock. Two Pacifican women, their gowns in tatters and shoulders bleeding, as well as two men.

"We found these Pacifican spies in the Valley!" said one Aravander guard.

"They're lucky we didn't kill them on sight," said another.

"We are not spies!" cried one of the men.

Their hands were bound, and their eyes were covered with blindfolds. The Aravander guards shoved them to their knees, and the women cried out. I winced as I felt a wave of their fear and pain. "Stop!" I cried. "There is no reason for such rough treatment!" Again, my eyes went to their shoulders. There was blood there on each of them, but not a lot.

Behind them came several of the elders, who gave us a surprised look before turning to the newcomers before them. Cornelius was among them, looking like he'd been awakened from a very deep sleep.

"They were found hiding at the mouth of the Valley, Father," said one of the guards to our elder. "Our scouts saw them and tracked them for a good distance before capturing them and bringing them to us."

Cornelius nodded. "Remove their blindfolds. And someone go and fetch Vidar and the other Remnants not already here." He gave Ronan, Niero, and me a second, curious glance, obviously wondering what we were doing here, given the hour.

"Please, we are seeking sanctuary," said one of the young men, as soon as his blindfold was removed and he blinked a few times. "May we speak to Lord Cyrus?"

"What makes you think Lord Cyrus is here?"

The young man's eyes moved from Cornelius to Ronan and me, then back again. "Because *they* are here—Andriana and Ronan of the Valley—and Lord Cyrus helped them escape."

To recognize us, know our names . . .

"You came from the *palace*?" I spit out.

But Cornelius held up a hand, shushing me, and I belatedly felt his agitation over my intrusion.

"How do you know these two are who you think they are?" the elder asked them gravely.

"Because every servant within Palace Pacifica knew them. Or at least Lady Andriana," he said, his face turning toward me. "She was at the ball on the emperor's arm. This one, here," he said, gesturing to one of the women, "attended her. Saw to her hair."

Ronan tensed beside me, jealousy rising like steam from his head, but I ignored him and came around the elders to face the girl. I studied her brown hair, now in matted tangles, but I remembered the hazel-green eyes and curvaceous body that had made Lord Maximillian stare after her in a proprietary way I hated. She wore a pretty pendant that hovered between her ample breasts. So did the other one. I'd never seen palace servants wear anything but the black leather braid across their heads. It was then that I realized Cornelius was waiting on me to confirm her story.

"What they say is true," I said. "She, at least, was assigned as my servant."

Cornelius considered this. "How did you reach the Valley from Pacifica?" he asked. But when the first man tried to speak, he shushed him, clearly waiting on the other girl to answer.

She swallowed hard and then said, "We escaped from Castle Vega. The Council brings a good number of servants with them when they retire to the palace there. We were among them, and when we four were sent to the market, we simply kept walking."

"For what purpose?" Cornelius asked, leaning toward her.

"To escape. To find freedom. To know more about the Way. That which had drawn Andriana to escape. I mean, we thought, um . . . we wondered . . . we *hoped* there was a reason. After all she had, all she was offered, for her to run away? We thought there *had* to be something mighty to pull her from the palace. That perhaps there was truth we needed to know for ourselves."

Cornelius straightened slowly, hands still behind his back. "How do we know that it's not all a ruse? That you are not spies?"

"We're not!" cried the other woman. "For weeks now we've been secretly meeting with one well-versed in the Way. Do you know of him? Father Jarad?"

We all shared a look, but clearly none of us had.

"He taught us some of the Sacred Words!" she cried. "You must believe it. The more we learned, the more we wanted to know. Until finally," she said, looking to the others, "we knew we had to come to you. To live in the Community in order to know more."

Bellona and Vidar arrived then, along with Chaza'el. Chaza'el wearily rubbed his eyes.

Vidar spread out his hands, offering his services.

Cornelius waved across the newcomers, silently asking for his spiritual appraisal.

"You say you were meeting with others of the Way?" Cornelius asked, scrutinizing them thoughtfully, with chin in hand. "In Pacifica?"

"Oh, no," said the young woman with the pendant. "We dared not there. But in Castle Vega, there are more opportunities. More distractions for the Pacifican guards."

"Distractions you took advantage of."

"Many did," she said with an earnest nod.

"I find nothing to fear in them," Vidar put in, looking to Cornelius. He shrugged. "Shadows, but from what we've witnessed, that comes with the territory these four have been inhabiting."

It was true. Any time spent near the Sheolites seemed to leave an echo of darkness. It was like dipping your hand in dye; you could wash your hands, know they were clean, but they'd still be partially stained for a while.

"Andriana?" the elder asked me, waving toward the newcomers.

I reached down to touch a woman's shoulder. "May I?"

She frowned in confusion, but nodded. I closed my eyes a moment, searching her, then shook my head. "Fear, for certain. But wouldn't we all be edgy if we were in their position? They might fear how we will receive them—or even fear that we will turn them back."

"Chaza'el?" Cornelius asked, turning to my slight brother behind him.

"I have not seen them among my visions as of yet," he said.

Kapriel arrived then, alongside Lord Cyrus, as did Tressa and Killian. They were lodging in another wing of the Citadel.

But it was at the prince that the four new arrivals all stared. I gasped, feeling their collective, stark terror at once. They fell to their faces, arms outstretched across the floor.

Automatically, I reached for my armband, wondering if I was feeling the chill of warning within it. But it was only these people, I understood then, and what they were feeling. They thought Kapriel was Keallach, his twin. They thought that, somehow, all was lost. They were defectors, not only of the emperor's service, but his empire itself. And yet the emperor haunted them.

"No, brothers and sisters, there is no need for that," Kapriel said gently, going to reach out to one and then the other. "I am not your emperor, Keallach. I am his brother, Kapriel. And while I am a prince, here in this place I am but your brother." He looked to Cornelius and Vidar, confirming what he had gathered. That they'd been vetted and were safe.

"Rise, new brothers and sisters of the Way," Kapriel said. "You are welcome among us, and I pray that you will find sanctuary and peace here. We ask that you contribute in any way that the Maker has gifted you to do so."

Gifted them to do so. I knew, inherently, that they had gifts. Just what they were, I had yet to discern.

CHAPTER 13

KEALLACH

My heart stopped as the missing servants' tracking devices suddenly ceased moving at the mouth of the Valley. The devices had clearly been discovered. We'd been watching for days, my Council jubilant that the trap they had set had been sprung. And they were growing more celebratory still, the closer the servants got to the Valley. But the ID chips had obviously been removed and destroyed.

"You'd better hope your second phase works," I grumbled when we convened the next day. But I had a hard time breathing normally as we waited for the technician to focus in on an image among the swirling gray-and-white snow on the screen before us. Gradually, the image began to take form. It was dark and grainy, but clear enough.

I sucked in my breath when I spotted Andriana, even for a moment, and grimaced when I felt sick with longing. I knew the other men had heard the childish sound emerge from me too. This made me angrier still.

But the servant girl moved too quickly, turning toward an old man again as he spoke, and her amulet necklace—with the tiny camera embedded inside—slipped partially beneath her tunic. Now all we could see was Ronan and, behind him, the one they called Raniero.

I tensed. *Ronan*. If it hadn't been for him, Dri would still be here. With me.

"See if you can get the second camera operational," Sethos said, leaning closer.

"There is no sound?" I barked.

"No," said a second man in gray, in front of the terminals, who was fiddling with several dials and keys on his board. "Not yet. For some reason, it is not transmitting. Or perhaps we are simply too distant."

"Well then, get closer to them," I commanded. "To Castle Vega. Or set up a station near the mouth of the Valley, if necessary. This information will give us everything we need to know about that Citadel and the people within the Valley, her defenses." *And bring Andriana back to me.*

"What if they take off their necklaces?" Fenris said, breaking me out of my reverie.

"They're worth a small fortune," Daivat said. "If they sell them or give them away, someone else of prominence—and access— might pick them up, wear them, and be of use too."

Fenris nodded. "But you're right, Highness. Hearing what they have to say now is key."

"Then make sure we soon establish the audio connection," I said tightly. It was the least he could do for me after everything he had messed up. "There are more people entering that Valley every day."

"Why not ignore them?" Daivat asked from the corner, where he leaned casually against a table.

"Because they are people of the Way," Maximillian said wearily, leaning the back of his head against his chair. He was still looking peaked, but day by day, he was gaining strength. "And the Way is fueled by their growth and passion. If we do not eradicate every one within those cursed mountain walls—"

"Save two," I interrupted. "Andriana and Kapriel are to be returned to me."

"Save Andriana and Kapriel," Max amended with an apologetic nod, "the rest must be destroyed. Because every one of them shall stand against us. They are a cancer that must be cut out of the Trading Union before they infiltrate every corner of it."

"They would never truly be such a threat," scoffed Fenris. "Even if we kill most of those in the Citadel, we will bring this resistance to its knees."

"You might be surprised at their . . . voracity," Maximillian said. "Isn't their presence indicative of how even one can infect many?"

"Walk with me," I said to him, after it was clear that the servants were being led down a cavernous hallway and into a dorm-like room with a hundred beds. "You there," I said to two others in gray. "Make certain you begin mapping every inch of the Citadel."

"Yes, Highness," said one.

Sethos was near them now, overseeing scouting parties to gain all the information he could about what lay outside the fortress.

Maximillian rose from his chair and shook off a servant's helpful arm, straightening his tunic before following me out the door. I took it slowly, but not too slowly. I was still angry with him, despite his injuries. He had pushed Andriana too far, too fast. If he hadn't, I thought, she would still be here with me, even if Ronan had begged her to go. There had been something between us that could not be denied. In time, I would not have had to compel her to kiss me, touch me. She would have done so of her own accord.

"I'm with you on this, Max. I want every single one of them driven from the Citadel," I said to him as we paused by a window overlooking the Great Expanse. "I want this rebellion put down, once and for all."

"It shall be done," he said.

I glanced at him and felt a momentary pang of guilt when I noticed the beads of sweat on his brow, evidence of the effort this exchange demanded of him. But anger and agitation overtook me. "It will take more than killing everyone within the Valley to stop this. For every person that girl encounters, I want a picture and a name attached. Family members, community of origin, all of it. We must not root out just these followers, but every family member and friend they have."

"Yes, Majesty."

We stood there, looking out over the green grounds that led to the woods into which they had escaped, eluding my guards and even the Sheolite trackers. Cyrus . . . Only thoughts of his betrayal made my pulse pound through my temples faster than Maximillian's foolish choices. "I want Cyrus to be brought here too," I grit out. "To die slowly."

"Yes, Majesty," Maximillian said with particular vehemence.

We stood there a moment longer before he dared, "What is it, Majesty, that you intend for Andriana?"

I could not voice what I hoped might be possible. I knew it was foolish; I didn't need his pity. "I don't know. I only know that I do not yet wish her to die."

He paused. "And your brother?"

"Again, I am uncertain. I only know that if he and Andriana die, any hope for a unified empire will go with them. No one is more powerful than a dead martyr within the people's minds. Bring them to me. And we will see what comes next."

He turned to go, awaiting my dismissal.

"Bring them to me, Max," I repeated. "Or I will be forced to go after them myself."

CHAPTER 14

RONAN

I stood beside Killian and Tressa as servants came to collect the newcomers and usher them to their quarters for the remainder of the night. As the last one passed, Tressa reached over and stayed her hand. "Sister, tell me. What happened to your shoulders? Are you in need of healing?"

"No," said the girl, shaking her head. "It was merely our Pacifican ID chip. The Aravanders . . . they do not like the chips. They fear they might be tracking devices, so they cut them out from beneath our skin."

Tressa grimaced. "That must've been painful."

"They were actually quite careful, making the smallest of cuts." She looked over her shoulder. "The blood must have spread as we walked the remainder of the way to the Citadel." She gave Tressa a reassuring smile. "It looks worse than it is."

"Well, as you get washed up, if you decide you need some stitches, feel free to ask for them tonight."

The girl gave Tressa a shy smile. "No healing prayer for such things? You are the healer among the Remnants, are you not?"

"I am," Tressa said. "But I suppose the Maker assumes we can handle such small matters without divine intervention."

The girl turned away reluctantly, following the servants. The women were heading to the female bathing quarters, and the men toward the male bathing quarters. "C'mon," Killian said to me under his breath. "Let's go take a sauna ourselves and see if we can find out more about our friends to the west."

I nodded, and when Dri looked my way, I gestured that I was going with Killian and I'd meet her at the room. She nodded too, and I could see the question in her eyes. Were we okay? Could we just move on from whatever had transpired with Niero? I turned away, not ready to respond, even silently. I wasn't sure where I stood with Niero, nor why he agitated me so much. There was still something that niggled at my memory about him, something I should remember. Earlier, I had thought I'd seen something more than brotherly love in what he shared with Dri. But it was clear to me that wasn't the reason for my agitation. It was something else.

"Hey, heading to the sauna?" Vidar called as we gathered with the Pacifican men and dismissed the servants, telling them we'd show the way ourselves.

"Yes," I said, glad when he joined us. Sometimes his humor could elicit information from newcomers like no other form of questioning could.

We went down to the Citadel's cavernous, steamy sauna chamber and then hovered above the neighboring pools, which were constantly flowing with fresh water from mountain streams that fell through a channel in the granite walls, supplying the whole fortress with what we needed. In it came, and out it went, flushing out the latrines, which kept the whole structure surprisingly clean, even with hundreds of inhabitants. I'd have to remember to check it out with Killian—the tunnels that brought in the water and took it out. I knew that the Community elders had likely thought of any vulnerability in the fortress, but I'd rest easier knowing myself how those barriers were constructed.

"This way," I said to the newcomers. We learned their names were Deshaun and Gregor, and they'd originally been from Georgii Post before finding work at Castle Vega. After training, they'd been taken to Palace Pacifica, but they always were a part of the staff that accompanied any of the Council who returned to Castle Vega because they were well versed in how the butler, Mr. Olin, liked to run the household there.

"Oh, I remember that guy," Vidar said. "He was a beast! You couldn't miss a bit of dirt with your cloth or he'd come after you."

"I'd heard you'd found work within the walls of Castle Vega," Deshaun said mischievously. "It was all the servants could talk about for weeks."

Vidar laughed. "We only lasted a day. Apparently, they didn't take kindly to Remnants in the household."

The two men shared a brief look. "You're lucky you lived to tell about it," said Gregor. "Such appearances so close to danger only fuel the stories about you. Everyone wants to know more."

"The Community, deep underground at Castle Vega, and more apparent at Georgii Post, is growing," Deshaun added. "Ever since you stayed in Georgii and helped that family escape, the numbers there swell. Many are hoping you will return. What Asher began, others have grown with the orphans and more, despite the Pacificans' efforts to crack down on them."

"When someone threatens to take something from you," Killian said, tossing us each a towel before we disrobed and went into the sauna, "you're more likely to consider the value. So the Pacificans' efforts . . ." he said, tossing his dreadlocks over his shoulder with a cheeky grin, "only aid our own."

"It's true!" said Deshaun. "The more they try and quiet talk of the Way, or squelch people from repeating some of the Sacred Words, the more others whisper of it."

We followed Killian into the sauna and took seats on the benches hewn from the cavern walls. I reached forward and dumped bucket after bucket of water on the heated rocks at the center. Steam immediately billowed up and around us. I leaned back against the wall, closing my eyes and feeling my lack of sleep catch up with me. Maybe after this bath I'd go and find Dri and apologize for that nonsense with Niero.

"So, what's with the necklaces?" Vidar asked, pointing to the nearest man's chest. We hadn't known they wore the same ones as the women had, and I hadn't noticed them coming in. "Is that a form of matrimonial symbol or something?"

"This?" said Deshaun, lifting it between thumb and forefinger and gazing down at it. "No. It's just something they gave us a week ago. Some sort of further symbol of 'solidarity' that every servant is supposed to wear. It's forged in platinum, or I would've burned it with that uniform over there," he added, gesturing with his head back to where we'd changed. I'd seen a fresh, clean stack of clothing awaiting each of them after our bath. "We're wondering if we can sell them, or melt them down and use the money to get our new start here." He let the necklace drop to his bare chest.

I rose, moving tentatively toward him. "May I?" I asked, reaching toward it.

"Sure," he said amiably as I lifted it in my hand. "Or you can have it," he said. "We owe you our lives. Perhaps it will be of some use to the Community?" He slipped the leather strap from around his neck, and I remembered one of the women offering hers to Dri as we left, and Dri slipping it over her head. I lifted it to the light, studying the gleam of polished metal and the tiny, round globe of iridescent glass at the center. It reminded me of the center of the abalone shells that some Aravander children gathered, and I marveled at the rainbow of color . . . but then stilled.

I turned my fingers a fraction. And froze.

A tiny, perfect square was visible within the iridescent dome.

A camera.

"Spies!" I smashed the necklace to the ground, ignoring the cries of the newcomers. Then I went to the other man, savagely ripping his pendant from his neck, and smashed it to the ground. Killian was already lunging toward the first, hands outstretched for his throat, all too clear about what alarmed me so. He drove Gregor to the wall.

"We . . . are . . . not . . . spies . . ." Gregor choked out, even as I grabbed Deshaun's wrist, twisting it behind him.

"We're not!" cried Deshaun. "I swear it! We had no idea! You must believe us!"

And I did. They were innocent. Pawns.

Used by players who now had likely seen the inner chasms and chambers and hallways of the Citadel, who were mapping it even now.

As they followed every person who yet wore one.

Which led me to . . . Dri.

CHAPTER 15

ANDRIANA

I stood looking out from one of the few small, northern balconies in the Citadel; the sheer face of the mountain below kept it from being a way in for intruders. *No one but Niero would be able to get through here,* I thought, *and he has wings.*

"Ah, *there* you are," Ronan said with relief when he saw me. "When I returned to our chambers and you weren't there . . ."

I gave him a coy smile over my shoulder. "There are only so many places I could go. Tonight . . . I wanted to see out. As much as I appreciate the Citadel, I like far less stone between me and what the Maker has made."

He came up behind me and wrapped his arms around my waist. I sank into his embrace, grateful that he seemed to have moved beyond the incident with Niero.

"How did it go?" I asked. "With the newcomers?"

"Fine, fine," he said, kissing the side of my head. "Dri . . ." he said, a bit too casually, "do you happen to have the pendant the Pacifican girl offered to you?"

I turned in his arms to look into his face, deeply shadowed with the torch behind him. But it did not take my eyes to sense the alarm in him. "Why?"

"Dri," he said, "the pendant. What did you do with it?"

"I . . . I threw it out there," I said, gesturing behind me to the balustrade and the steep cliff beyond with one hand, feeling the quick pulse in his arm with the other. "The girl meant it as a gift, but I couldn't help feeling that it was anything but. It reminded me too much of . . . Pacifica."

He stilled and heaved a sigh of relief. "Right. Of course you did," he said, lifting a hand to caress my cheek and smiling. "Such a wise, *wise* girl." He leaned close and kissed my nose, then turned to walk away, bent on some new mission.

"Ronan?" I said, chasing after him. "What's wrong?"

He stilled and looked back at me. "The enemy infiltrated the Citadel tonight," he said.

My stomach tightened in terror. "What?"

"Those necklaces," he said, glancing toward my chest, "they were like mini-drones. Tiny cameras, disguised in jewelry."

"*What?*" I repeated, striding toward him, with each step understanding better why I'd felt the urge to throw the pendant to the rocks below.

He rested his hands on my hips and stared into my eyes. "They've been eradicated. Every one. The other woman's. The two the men carried. The Pacificans . . . Keallach"—he shrugged slightly—"Sethos . . . who knows who is behind it. They've figured out that the power of the Way is growing. And the only way in is through those who are drawn to it."

"So they used them," I said, my eyes and thoughts distant, wandering toward the window and balustrade. "Allowed them to leave, to come here. As a method of entry. When they had no other methods."

"Yes," he said. "And now they've seen at least a portion of our fortress, our defenses."

I swallowed hard, thinking about taking that necklace, where I'd walked, what I'd done before I threw it away. "Do you think they could only see? Or might they have heard as well?"

"Why?" he said, his fingers tightening at my waist. "Did you say something that might have compromised our security?"

"No," I said, shaking my head miserably. "I didn't say anything. I just helped them see the way to our very own quarters." The thought of Sethos seeing me here, in the heart of our Citadel . . . I wrenched away and walked back to the tiny balustrade, looking out and over our Valley, so peaceful this night. So pristine. So . . . holy. Our sanctuary.

Yet, I felt invaded.

Ronan came up behind me and, sensing my tension, laid gentle hands at either hip, then waited.

After a moment, I took a deep breath and said, "You're certain they had no idea what they wore?"

"No. Vidar would've known if they were truly spies. And you would've detected something within them too, would you have not?"

I considered that, and then finally, reluctantly nodded. I realized that I wanted someone to hold accountable.

"No," I said. "I wish there was someone besides myself to blame, but there is not. Pacifica entered our gates, an invited guest for all intents and purposes. And now, we'll have to live with the consequences."

KEALLACH

I rewound the tape and stared at the footage from the necklace that had briefly been around Andriana's neck. Still no sound. Only grainy images.

But she was there. In the Citadel.

Walking down the hall to her quarters—clearly shared with Ronan, judging by the masculine sweater cast over the corner of one of their beds, and the sword tipped beside the doorway—and then to the cliff face, where she stared at the pendant for a long moment, and then cast it away.

I watched every second of the footage again and again, searching for each detail I could find, of the Citadel for certain, but moreover, of her.

She looked well. Somewhat rested. Healed. Whole. Hopeful in one step, pensive in another. Curious and wondering as she peered down at the pendant and then pulled it from around her neck. I froze the frame just before she decided to toss it away, down into the abyss below, where the camera's lens no doubt cracked into a thousand pieces. I stared at her face and recognized that look of curiosity and wondering and hope . . . until just before the moment I knew it dissolved into distaste and fear. It was a transition in her expression that I'd witnessed firsthand.

And it was one that I'd hoped to see eradicated from her memory forever.

It was wrong, so wrong, to see it in my beloved's face.

She was to know only love, and peace, and security. This was my Call, from deep within. To make certain that all of my brothers and sisters felt nothing but those things. And yet it went beyond that when it came to Andriana. And Kapriel. To them, first, was I bound.

Whoever followed us, followed.

Or did not.

Andriana and my brother were everything to me. The last, true, possible links to the One that had ushered me into life and waited to walk beside me in the future. Without them, I was alone. Yes, *yes*, surrounded by many. Always so many. But yet still alone.

I needed them. Had to have them by my side. One way or another.

It plagued me that because of something Pacifica had sent, because of something that she had received, Dri knew anything but peace and joy. She had sensed distaste and a fear that drove her to toss the pendant from the cliff. And yet, if it took some pain, some discomfort, to bring her back to me, and behind her, my brother . . .

So be it.

Maximillian appeared in my doorway, silently awaiting orders.

"Now that our plan has been discovered," I said with a sigh, "any element of surprise is lost to us."

"Yes, but the footage is of use to us, Majesty. We've mapped much of the main floor of the Citadel."

"And we know where Andriana's quarters are," I mused, reaching out to touch the screen.

"Indeed."

"You've seen that things are in order for our new plan?"

"Yes, Keallach," he said, coming to stand beside me, looking down at the screen. "All is in order."

"Good," I said, switching off the monitor. "Be ready at a moment's notice. As soon as we find an opening, we move."

CHAPTER 16

ANDRIANA

Niero and Cornelius bade us to forget what we'd learned of the pendants and the possible breach of security.

"Long has the Maker seen us here, in the Valley," said Cornelius, laying a fragile, age-spotted hand upon my shoulder, "and long has he seen our enemies rise in the west. What will come, will come," he said with shrug, willing courage to me that I felt. "We trust in his providence and what will transpire."

"Even within the walls of Zanzibar," I said, pulling one of the heavy shoulder straps of my pack up higher with one hand. As if saying it one more time would make it seem more reasonable. My eyes shifted to Tressa, who looked a bit wan, and to her grim-faced Knight, Killian. Even our handfasting and tattoos didn't make this mission anything close to a tolerable risk. The Lord of Zanzibar would want our heads. And there were many other enemies within those towering walls. But Tressa also knew there was someone there she was to heal. We were counting on one lone person to somehow make a way for us to not only survive, but to turn some of the populace of the ancient, teeming city to followers of the Way.

Every time I thought about it, I knew it to be the Maker's design. He wanted us to know that this wasn't about us and what we could do . . . but what he could do through us if we totally submitted to his will. Clearly, we'd all felt this was his will for some time. In ways, it was a relief to finally be stepping into it, rather than thinking about it and worrying about it.

"Zanzibar," he said, lifting one gray brow and quirking a sly smile. "If he sends you to such a place, then clearly those of us left behind have far less to be concerned about."

"And yet *that* is not exactly the assurance we seek, Father," Vidar cracked, walking past. "But thanks for the effort."

I kissed Mom and Dad good-bye, focusing on the pride they felt as they looked upon me, rather than on their fear. We headed out and spent that first night with Tonna, and then we carried on toward Zanzibar in the morning. There were ten of us—Ronan and me, Niero and Azarel, Killian and Tressa, Chaza'el, Vidar and Bellona, and Kapriel—but we planned to enter the city in groups of three in order to be less conspicuous. We'd discussed leaving Kapriel behind—those in power in Zanzibar might note his mirror image of Keallach, ruining our ability to hide—but in the end, we figured our time in hiding would be limited. And where the Remnants had been called, we were convinced we had to go together.

"I can't believe we're doing this," Vidar said as we neared the towering city gates. "We didn't exactly leave through the front door last time."

I swallowed hard. We were all thinking the same thing. We'd killed or injured a good twenty guards on our way out and rappelled off the far wall to escape. And this was the first place we'd ever encountered Sethos. I shivered at the memory. If Keallach could only see him as we saw him that day, fingers like talons, screeching like an unearthly animal closing in on its prey—us—might he see his trainer for who he truly was?

"I never intended to return," Tressa said. "But the Maker has different ideas."

"He usually does," Niero said, edging past her. The afternoon was drawing to a close, and people were thronging toward the gates.

I knew we could all feel the pull of whomever we were here for, just as we had from the Citadel itself, but Tressa was excited beyond measure, hope and desire twirling inside her like a small tornado. It would be she who led us to the man or woman the Maker wanted us to heal . . . if she wasn't recognized and arrested first.

We parted into our small groups, those who had never been in the wretched city divided among those of us who had. Kapriel was with Ronan and me. Chaza'el was with Niero and Azarel. Vidar and Bellona were with Killian and Tressa. We all rode mudhorses, intent on doing whatever the Maker would have us do here in this city, and then getting back to the relative safety of the Valley, even if we had to ride all night to do it. We allowed Tressa's group to take the lead, but kept them in sight. Behind us was Niero's trio. Once inside the city, the forward team would board their horses in the same stables we'd used last time and then allow us to keep them in sight as we searched for the Maker's mission here.

"Easy, Dri," Ronan murmured as we pulled to a stop, a hundred people ahead of us waiting to get past the guards at the gate. "Remember, the last thing they expect is for us to return."

I knew he was right. But this whole blasted city smelled of the underworld. My mouth was dry; my stomach roiled. I fought off the urge to touch my shoulder, where the tattoo of the city was now embedded in my skin. I wondered if it would pass inspection. I wondered if they would believe that I was Ronan's bound wife, or if—

"Hey," he said, reaching out to take my hand in his. "Look at me."

I turned to face him, his green eyes warm and reassuring. "We're together," he said with a shrug. "Sent here by the Maker. Who can come against us?"

Plenty, I wanted to say, but I knew what he was after. "No one." I swallowed. "At least no one we cannot deal with."

"That's right," he said, a tiny smile lifting the corners of his full lips. I looked down at our hands and wished we were back in the Valley with all that was familiar about us. Or in the stronghold of the Citadel. I wished our battles were over. I wished all of this was behind us, with not so much ahead, rising like a flash flood coursing down a streambed.

Andriana.

I whipped my head around, distinctly hearing Niero's voice. But when I glimpsed him, there were thirty people between us, even though he stared directly forward at me.

Do not be afraid. You are a Remnant. Born for just such a time as this.

I laughed under my breath. I'd always wondered if he could read my thoughts since he often responded to me before I'd given voice to anything that was troubling me. It made sense that he could do so—and respond to me in kind.

I will take heart, my friend, I thought, hoping he could hear me. *For you are with us, as is the Maker.* Casually, I turned in my saddle and waited until I glimpsed him again. He was smiling.

And yet hadn't Niero himself been taken captive? In Keallach's desert monastery?

And did I not escape my captors?

I huffed a laugh. It was both captivating and aggravating, this inner dialogue.

"What is it?" Ronan asked me, shooting a quizzical look.

"Oh, nothing," I said, shaking my head, as if I could dislodge Niero from my mind. "It seems I must learn some lessons, over and over again."

"Some lessons are more challenging than others," he said, "and have to be carved from stone rather than clay."

"Agreed," I said, after a moment. Ronan wasn't one to often spout such deep wisdom, but what he said had been perfectly stated. And at that moment, I chose to act on all I had learned and move forward from there, rather than to backtrack. *I want to be clay, not stone.*

I set my mind and heart to the task at hand, gazing upward to the massive red walls of the ancient city, beyond the armed guards who patrolled there, trying to use the inner eye that Vidar could so easily capture in order to see both angel and demon. I thought I glimpsed a dark presence perched at regular intervals, almost like the gargoyles on palaces of old, but I wasn't certain. When Vidar was within reach, I could more readily make such things out.

"Dri, keep your head down," Ronan said, and I immediately bowed my head, aware that I'd appear brazen for a Zanzibian bride.

"Did anyone see me?" I whispered.

"Two guards above us are together, pointing at you and talking."

A shiver of apprehension washed through me.

"They're likely just remarking on your beauty," he said, trying to ease my fear.

"With Tressa so near?" I scoffed. "I doubt that."

I could feel his soft gaze on me, but I didn't look at him, as I was unable to keep my eyes from the other guards ahead. "For as much as you understand what everyone *feels*, Wife," he murmured, "you understand surprisingly little of what everyone *thinks*."

I eyed him then, returning his soft smile. He was good at protecting me, in more ways than one.

He dismounted and then helped me down—not that I needed it. It simply was expected here. He took the reins of both of our horses, and we eased forward, funneling inward with the crowd until we finally stood between the two guards, following Kapriel.

They let the prince right through, but they slowed as they turned to us.

"Well, well," said one, looking me over from head to toe. "This is a fine piece of woman flesh," he went on, slowly trailing behind me as Ronan handed our papers to his companion. "Where do you hail from?"

I forced myself not to react or respond. It wasn't the way of the women in this city. *It's not the way, not the way, not the way.* The way for women here was utter subservience; they were as much livestock as humans to the men here.

"My *wife* and I are proud citizens of Zanzibar now," Ronan said, the muscles at his jaw twitching as his eyes flicked to the other guard who remained behind me.

The guard leaned closer to me, taking my hair in his hands as if in a sweet caress, his breath drifting over my shoulder. It was surprisingly clean. "Ah, no. I would remember this one. And you. You're a brute, aren't you? But this one . . . your bride, you say? Gods, man, how did you get so lucky?"

"I don't know," Ronan said, his jaw muscle twitching, belying his tone. "Right place, right time."

The guard's left hand brushed my hair to one side, even as his right hand fingered the neckline of my tunic. Then, ever so slowly, he pulled the scooped neckline down over my shoulder.

My breath caught. I clenched my fists. His movements were not at all the casual check of a disinterested guard perusing his thousandth Zanzibian mark of the day. It was an invasion, designed to agitate Ronan and strike fear in me.

Remain still, Niero said to me, silently. *It'll be over soon.*

I bowed my head, using everything in me to remain in place, playing my part. To not elbow the man in the belly, making him double over. To not then turn and knee him in the face.

"May we pass?" Ronan growled, taking one step toward the guard and me. The other guard stepped between us, unperturbed, looking at the papers in his hands. "We bear the city mark," Ronan said. "All we wish is to get to our quarters. *Unmolested.*"

"Easy, there," said the guard behind me as he ran his thumb over my tattoo. "It's fresh, but it's there," he said to his companion. "It's the true mark."

"He bears it too," said the other, glancing at Ronan's tattoo and then back to the papers. He suddenly turned to me and lifted my chin. "Look at me, woman." He leaned closer, still holding my chin, and said, "Where do you live in this city? Why do we not recognize you?"

I let my eyes lift to his and willed my heart away from fear and fury, transforming them into favor and protection. "We are new here. And we live along the Fifth," I said gently, as we'd rehearsed, while sending those key emotions of grace into him. "In the old Kocho building. My husband purchased it for us as a wedding gift."

His lips parted, and his eyes widened and then softened as my emotions shot through him as clearly as a sweetly poisoned arrow might. I held his gaze. A moment later, he abruptly clamped his lips shut and said, "It's true. That old Kocho place sold weeks ago. Welcome home, fellow citizens," he said, gesturing inward.

And then we were through. I was grateful to take Ronan's hip with one trembling hand and walk in the odd Zanzibian way of couples, our stride in tandem down the street, the horses trailing behind us.

Kapriel sidled beside me. "Sorry you had to go through that," he muttered, gesturing back toward the gates. "It was all I could do not to bring down a lightning bolt upon them."

I smiled. "Glad you didn't. That would have brought us some undue attention."

"How did Azarel fare?"

"They didn't give her a second glance," he said, "after seeing Niero."

I considered that and wondered what methods an angel had to change a guard's mind, or strike terror in him without saying a word.

The streets were busy, with many out to finish their errands before nightfall, and I allowed myself to reach out, absorbing the odd, dark tension that seemed to plague this city. When we finally turned the corner and reached the stables, I sighed in relief. The first group was there, and the last was right behind us. Niero slipped a gold coin in the stable boy's filthy fist, and we had a few moments alone.

"I forgot just how much I loathe this city," Vidar said, looking uncommonly grim. But I knew firsthand what birthed that response. There was a reason why a Sheolite tracker had so very nearly caught us here on our previous trip; Zanzibar was a breeding ground of evil. With men outnumbering women three to one, every female had become a commodity. And yet with every family allowing only a male heir to inherit, females were constantly killed, often as infants. Some were sold to pimps in the inner circle of the city, where we'd seen so many prostitutes, their eyes sunken and glassy, as if they'd long ago vacated their bodies. Others were sold to Pacifica to work in her mines or factories. I wondered how many girls had ended up there. The custom had begun after the Great War as a means of population control; within the walls, space was finite. And the walls had once been the main protection Zanzibians had against Drifters and rival feudal lords with growing armies and an eye on expansion. But what remained was twisted and wrong for men and women alike. Again, I wondered why the Maker would send us here. As powerful as we were together, how could we fight against such depravity? How could we reach a people who had traveled such a dark road for so long that their ears had to be deafened by lies, their eyes blinded by deceit?

We sat down in a newly cleaned stall, atop fresh hay lining the walls. Azarel handed out pieces of flatbread and dried fish. "Eat," she said. "We'll need our strength." I nodded, but I shoved the food into my pocket as she moved on to Tressa. The whole place made me feel vaguely nauseous.

I looked over at Tressa as she bit into her fish. "Did they recognize you at the front gates?"

"They didn't recognize me," she said softly. "Nor I them. Most of our lives were spent below ground, and the people we knew were from the center of the city, with the forgotten ones."

"But she still had to keep Killian from cutting one of the guard's tongues from his mouth," Bellona said, nudging Tressa's Knight.

"The man was . . . less than polite," Killian ground out.

"Someday, we shall go back to those men and teach them what it means to respect our wives," Ronan said, sharing a warrior's promise with his brother.

"There will be other guards who will remember Tressa well," Killian said to Niero.

"I know," he said, chewing on a bite of bread. "If they get in our way, we must deal with them as quickly as possible."

Meaning, they would have to die, I surmised.

"I'll be first in line to help with that endeavor," Killian said, visibly cheered.

I remembered the men who had held Tressa in chains on the palace wall. How they'd taunted her, touched her, even as those at the city gates had begun to do with me. "I understand your rage, brother," I said to him. "Your desire for vengeance for your bride, to make right all that was done wrong to her. But surely we were not called to return to this city, at this point in our journey, simply for that. There has to be a greater call within." I looked to Tressa, knowing she'd felt the pull to heal.

"Yes," Tressa said, placing her hand through the crook of one of his arms, which was wrapped around his knees. "There is someone here to be healed—perhaps many. That is the beginning of what we're to do here, at least. I'm certain of it."

Killian didn't like that I had called him out. He stared at me for a long moment as the others grew silent. At first, I could feel his resentment, almost *hear* the derogatory response on his tongue, but then there was a softening, the wash of wisdom warming him, the soothing pull of the Way. "You speak the truth, Dri. But I'm telling you now, it will be difficult to keep my anger in check." He shook his head in apology, and some of his dreadlocks fell over his shoulder.

"We're with you," Bellona said, putting a hand on his other huge forearm. "Look to us if you doubt your ability to discern between protection and retribution."

"I will," he said with a nod.

"It is imperative that we move with the Maker here, not in any way against him," Niero said, looking around at all of us. "As Tressa said, it begins with those she is to heal. So let us find that person, or people, and then see where we are led next. But now, we must move. Once it grows dark and people are indoors, our movement will be more conspicuous."

We rose, and as we did so we came together, putting our hands together in the center of our circle, each saying a short prayer. "Protect us, Maker," Niero said. "Go before us," Kapriel said. *Beside us . . . behind us . . . move within us . . . move those around us . . . show the people your power . . . call them away from the dark . . . and to the light.*

By the time we were done praying, the energy in that dark stable felt more like the warmth of a popping campfire, hours old. Pure joy and assurance surrounded us, the hallmarks of the Maker. It was true; we all knew it.

We were here on his mission. Now it was time to see it through.

CHAPTER 17

KEALLACH

Maximillian burst into the western sanctuary as I knelt on the floor, meditating. I cast aside my irritation over his interruption; I hadn't managed to focus on any sense of inner peace since the day I returned to the palace and found Andriana gone.

Seeing my silent assent, Max grinned. "They've been seen. All the Remnants are in Zanzibar."

"Zanzibar?" I said, rising, feeling my weak knees. She was there. They all were. But in *Zanzibar*? "Surely they don't think they can win over anyone there to the Way. Lord Darcel himself told me he'd have every one of their heads for daring to free a prisoner from his palace walls."

"Then perhaps Sethos and his men won't have as much to do upon their arrival," Maximillian said, grinning and crossing his arms. He held up his hands when he saw my expression. "No, no, Majesty. Lord Darcel has been informed. No harm is to come to either Lady Andriana or Prince Kapriel." He stepped closer and laid a hand on both of my shoulders. I noticed he was looking stronger today, more himself. "Perhaps this very night, it will be over. The Remnants—and their rebellion—quashed. Those you love, back where they belong, where their gifting can be . . . utilized best. It's finally happening, Keallach," he added in a cheerful whisper, using my familiar name. "All that you've dreamed of."

He dropped his hands and went to the window with a spring in his step. "We'll bring your brother here, reinstate him as sub regent to you, and you shall wed Andriana. Together, the three of you will be the face of the new Pacifica. All will willingly follow you."

My heart pounded. Could it be? Had the Maker made a way for my own plans to unfold, exactly as I had dreamed? A bit dazed, I walked to stand beside the window with Maximillian and looked over the green lawn to the sea. Andriana had loved the sea. She'd wanted to go swimming. Now she'd have the chance.

"How do you know they're in Zanzibar? Will they realize they've been recognized?"

"Easy, easy," Maximillian said, a cocky quirk to his smile. "We have spies everywhere—not among the Zanzibian guards, among the people. And it was two of them that radioed us the information."

I breathed a little easier. The Knights would've been very aware of any of the guards or Zanzibian patrols. But in a crowded city like that . . .

"There's more," Maximillian said, leaning closer as if to share a secret. "We've activated Kapriel's and Andriana's ID chips. Not only will Sethos know they're in Zanzibar, he'll know exactly where they are. I tell you, Majesty, tonight they shall be ours again, and the Remnants' cause will be something of the past."

I gaped at him. "The Aravanders took out the Pacifican servants' chips as soon as they entered the Valley! Do you think they'd allow Kapriel and Dri to walk about with them still embedded?"

"No," he said, lifting a brow. "But neither of them know they have one. Kapriel's was embedded in the center of his back when he was so terribly ill. Andriana's was embedded when she was in and out of unconsciousness, in those first days in the palace." He held up his hands again when I shot him a dark look, remembering my rage at her mistreatment. "It wasn't me. It was Sethos. And while I did not approve of his methods at the time, I have to admit, it will serve us well in the days to come."

"Where?" I grumbled. "Where did they put it on Dri?"

He steepled his fingers and looked back out to the ocean. "Directly atop her cracked rib, where she was feeling some pain already and wouldn't think about it further."

I let out a huff of a laugh and shook my head. The ID chips were incredibly tiny. And given that neither carried their chip in the traditional Pacifican location of the right shoulder . . .

I reached out and patted Maximillian on the back. "Well done, brother. Well done. Now order a transport. We will travel through the night. I want to be near Zanzibar as fast as possible. Because when this tide shifts, I want to be there to witness it firsthand."

RONAN

A large part of me thought we would be heading into the inner district, the city's dark center, where we'd encountered the prostitutes and drug dealers before, and where we'd eventually found Tressa and Killian's hiding place, deep within the sewers below. But when the Remnants urged us, as one, toward the palace, my breath caught. *Not there, Maker,* I breathed. *Anywhere but there.*

Surely he wouldn't send us where we might be most in danger. Where we could not hide. Where we'd have little chance of slipping in and then slipping out of this cursed city.

Or would he?

I took a deep breath, and Vidar caught my look of understanding, clasping me on the shoulder. "Hold on, brother," he said. "This is bound to be . . . new."

I concentrated on Dri's hand at my waist, her pace matching mine. She was with me, behind me, I reminded myself. Safe for the moment. There was not one among us who didn't understand that we were to go wherever the Maker sent us. But wariness and wonder twined in every one of our hearts.

"Do you think there are any trackers here, in the city?" she asked quietly, memories of our past experience clear in her tone. I wished I could turn and face her; I didn't like that she wasn't beside me, my partner, my equal, my love. For all to see. And I hated that she was afraid, that I couldn't protect her from the truth. "It's a distinct possibility. Pacifica will want to protect her allies from the infiltration of the Way."

"Then why does he not show himself?"

"Because *they* do not yet want to be seen."

She fell silent. But it was necessary, this warning. As readily as we'd gained entrance to this city, I knew there would be no easy exit. And there was no way that Pacifica wasn't watching every single person who entered or exited the Valley now, either. Spies were everywhere. I'd felt their eyes upon us from the moment we had left the comforting cover of the pines and had begun plodding through the damp sands of the desert, and then with increasing weight as we drew closer to Zanzibar. Regardless of what the Maker would have us do here, we had to do it quickly and return to the relative safety of the Valley as soon as we possibly could.

Niero didn't pause at a cross street that would have led us deeper into the city. He just continued, unabated, toward the palace, which loomed larger before us all the time. Vidar, just ahead of me now, with Bellona trailing behind him, wavered on occasion, and I knew he must have been seeing what we all sensed—the damnable creatures of the dark, watching, observing our trek forward. And yet no soldiers came against us; no whistles shrieked; no bells clanged in warning. I tried to ignore the admiring, lustful glances of the men we passed by, knowing that my jealousy would only increase Dri's angst. But thankfully, by walking in this manner and wearing the band of leather around her wrist that marked her as a married woman in Zanzibar, the glances were fleeting. The men knew there was one sure way to quarrel with another in this city, and that was to make a move on another man's woman.

I silently thanked the elders for acquiescing and allowing our binding, if not full marital vows. When we'd entered the city before, we'd been lucky to avoid detection for our first precious hours on the streets, no one noticing our women were missing the leather bracelets. But even Tonna hadn't offered anything but paperwork to get us through the gates that day. I knew it was all a ruse, really. No piece of jewelry or binding vows could keep Andriana fully safe. Only the Maker could. But I was fully in favor of using every element at my disposal to try. And while our binding both partially satisfied me and aggravated me because our union wasn't complete, it was something. The Maker had made a way for us to be together and to honor the Community's ways and the elders' intent. And I would choose to find satisfaction in that, over and over again.

Zanzibar was a city with curving walls and concentric circling streets inside. But the palace before us took up a good portion of the western edge of the city, and what it lacked in graceful style, it made up for in sheer size. Before, we'd managed to distract the guards that patrolled high above and scaled the walls; I doubted that trick would work again. And it appeared that Tressa was guiding Killian straight to the palace gates, despite the fact that her Knight argued furiously over his shoulder with her. *Straight to the gates?* My heart pounded, and sweat broke out on my clenched palms. What sort of madness was this? Forget the bindings, the tattoos. We might as well have just turned ourselves over to the city guards. We'd be hopelessly outnumbered in the palace.

"Take courage, Knight," Niero said, alongside of us for a moment. "We arrive here far more powerful than when we were here last."

I snorted. "But we didn't exactly enter into the lord's lair directly," I hissed. "We freed Tressa and ran, as I recall."

"The time for running is over," he said evenly, looking into my eyes. "It is time to stand and claim what belongs to the Maker. And what belongs to the Maker?"

"Everything," I said slowly, wondering over the truth of that word, even as it came from my mouth.

"Indeed," he said, giving me a hint of a smile. He and Azarel pressed forward, presumably to be closer to Killian and Tressa when we reached the palace gates. There were no beggars about as we neared it, as there were in the wealthier parts of other towns and cities. There were no handicapped children or aged men that Tressa might be called to heal. But then that made sense; the Lord of Zanzibar banished or killed anyone with any infirmity at all. Which only led me to believe that the one we were called to heal—the reason we'd been summoned to this foul city—was within.

I stifled a groan as Killian did what I'd feared and walked directly up to the palace guards, standing at the center of twelve others. Above, on the wall, there were an additional six. "We demand an audience with the Lord of Zanzibar," Killian said, his voice sounding strangled.

"Of course you do," retorted the guard, looking him up and down, as well as Tressa, then on to the rest of us. "And who are you?" He brought up his gun and leveled it at Killian's throat. We stilled. The other guards followed suit, all bringing up their weapons and aiming them at us. Above us, I could hear the crack of additional weapons coming off of safety.

"We are the prophesied Remnants," Tressa said, coming out from behind Killian. "Zanzibian-born. As well as our Knights and companions," she went on, voice high and clear, her eyes blazing with a confidence that could only come from the Maker. "There is one in this palace who ails, and I have been called to heal him."

The chief guard gaped at her. "Even if you are who you say you are, you have your information wrong, girl," he sneered, squinting at Tressa as if he recognized her. Her hair was hidden beneath a hood, or they would surely have identified her as their escaped prisoner. "The Lord of Zanzibar allows no illness outside his gates, let alone within."

"It is a child," Chaza'el said, stepping forward, only stopping when another guard's gun pressed into his chest. "A tiny babe. The lord's own son."

"The lord's heir has yet to be born," scoffed the guard, puffing out his chest. "And when he is, he shall be as whole and hale as my own."

"He was born this morning," Tressa said. "But the child's heart is weak, his life fading from him even now as we—"

The guard moved as if to strike her, and she shied away, but Killian stayed his hand.

Behind them, the gate unexpectedly opened. The chief guard scowled over his shoulder and wrenched his wrist from Killian's grip. A younger man hurried up to him, looking tentative, and whispered in his ear. The chief guard straightened, took a breath, and then turned to the other guards. "These people have been summoned within," he said gruffly, as if it was his own idea. "Relieve them of their weapons, and search them to be certain no more remain in hidden places."

We were pressed to face the walls, our hands on the rough adobe brick above our heads, the guards' hands searching and locating each sword, knife, gun, lance, whip, arrow, and axe upon us. I grit my teeth as the guard next to me took overly long with Andriana, searching the long lengths of her legs. "Get it over with, man," I spat out, "or I shall come and find you later."

"Careful," sneered my own guard, taking a handful of my hair and yanking my head back, "it's a capital crime to threaten a Zanzibian guard."

"Thankfully, I don't answer to anyone but the Maker."

The man stilled, and the other took a halting breath. Here in this city, too, the Maker's name had long been taboo. But it had the desired effect; they left Andriana alone and shared a long look, as if debating what to do in response.

"Come along," called the chief guard. "Inside with you. Stay together. Two by two. Men in formation, with your women behind." To the guards as they passed by, he said, "Never take your eyes off of them, you hear me? Trust them not for a breath of time. If they are who they say they are . . ."

We left him behind and trudged inward through lush desert gardens, full of perfectly formed cacti and palms, all set in ovals filled with white rocks. Ahead, the palace entrance loomed, with multiple balconies on either side, each covered with swooping canopies to guard those who lounged below from the sun. Though the sun had long set by now, people were on each balcony, watching us, covering their mouths as they spoke about us in undertones.

Two massive wooden doors—twice as tall as I—opened, a servant standing beside each one, at attention, and another wordlessly turning apparently to lead us on. We progressed inward across polished concrete floors, past cavernous rooms that spoke of wealth and privilege, and a shiver ran down my back as I remembered the last palace I had been in—Keallach's home. Would the Lord of Zanzibar prove as formidable a threat as our lost brother?

Perhaps more so, I thought grimly. At least Keallach was Ailith at the core of him, and was bent on winning Andriana, if not the rest of us too. This one ahead . . . Who knew what drove him?

The guards herded us up several flights of stairs and into the throne room at the end of the hall. We could see a man in a fine robe, chin in hand, staring out the window. On either side of him was a man, one younger, one older. Beyond them were women in a group, all dressed in fine gowns and huddled together, whispering behind their hands to one another as they perused every one of us from head to toe. The rest of the cavernous room was empty, save a dais and three ornately carved chairs.

We were set into a line, side by side, and then forced to kneel. It felt wrong, vulnerable—alarm bells ringing in my head as a Knight—but then I knew this was the only way. We couldn't win over the Lord of Zanzibar by physical might. The Maker had led us here. And now, unbelievably, I knew he bade me to stay on my knees.

Only when we were all kneeling did the lord turn and eye every one of us. He was younger than I expected—no older than his third decade—and handsome in a slight, refined way. His skin was smooth, but his eyes . . . his eyes were hard. They glinted as they landed on Tressa.

"*You,*" he spat out, striding toward her. His male companions—advisors, I assumed—flanked him. "You dare return to my city?" I stiffened, as I'm sure Killian did. How did he manage to stay in place when the warlord threatened his Remnant?

But Tressa didn't flinch. "We came to aid your son," she said, her voice high and clear. "The Maker has sent us."

The man's eyes, cold as granite, slid over the rest of us. "The fabled Remnants and their Knights, willingly surrendering to me?" he asked, crossing his arms. "You think I would trust you with my child? You left my city in tatters the last time you departed. Spreading lies about healing those with the Cancer when we all know it is incurable."

"They are not lies," Tressa returned, with a shake of her head. "The Maker saved many on that day. As he can save your—"

The lord slapped her savagely before any of us saw it coming. Killian growled and began to rise, but two men behind him shoved him back to his knees. I reached out and grabbed his arm, steadying him, encouraging him to remain down.

"No one speaks that name in this city," sneered the lord, leaning down toward her.

"That is unfortunate," she returned evenly. "Because it is only by *that* name that your son shall live to see tomorrow."

The lord straightened and looked down his nose at her. "How is it that you know I have a baby son? It has not been announced. Only my closest advisors and these ladies know of it, and they have been in my presence since the child was born only hours ago."

"I could have been a day's journey away, and I would have known you had a baby son with an ailing heart."

His eyebrows furrowed. "How do you know it is his heart?"

"Because the One I serve told me. He has prepared me to heal your child, if you will allow me to do so. My fellow Remnants will aid me."

"I can't allow that," he scoffed, making a face. "What rumors would that begin? That I allowed the very girl who escaped my walls, the one who refused to become one among my treasured harem, to march into the nursery to try her healing arts on my son?"

"If you wish for your heir to live, then yes," she returned.

"Are you threatening my child?" he cried, leaning closer again. I could feel Killian tense beside me.

"No, Majesty. I am *warning* you. The babe has but hours left."

"Impossible," he sneered, crossing his arms. "I have the finest physicians in the city attending him this very moment."

"And they shall not save him," she said. "There is a hole in his heart. That is what likely took your other children too."

"And how do you know of *them*?" he asked, his voice high and crazed. "It is *you*," he spat out, inches from her face. "You've cast some sort of spell upon my children! Cursed them!"

"No," Tressa said. "The only curses upon this house and this city are those that you and your father and your forefathers have welcomed in."

"She speaks lies," said one of the lord's advisors, edging forward.

"Hang them all at once, and be done with them," said the other. "Pacifica will be in our debt."

"Except for the girl the emperor seeks," said the first advisor, moving down the line until he stopped before Andriana.

It was my turn for my fists to clench. It took everything in me to remain on my knees. "Keallach will no longer be interested in Andriana," I said. "He wanted her as his wife, but she is my—"

"And this one," sniffed the other, stepping toward Kapriel and ignoring me. "The lost prince. There is a ransom upon your head, Highness, as well as the green-eyed girl. One that will be good for the coffers of Zanzibar." He laughed under his breath, his eyes holding no true mirth. "Imagine such prizes walking right through your gates, m'lord. The emperor will reward you in more ways than one if we deliver these two back to Pacifica and be done with the rest."

"You shall not do that," Tressa said, rising to her feet.

I resisted the urge to close my eyes as I waited for the lord to strike her again.

"I shall do whatever I wish," he said, incredulous, "*girl*."

"But you won't. Because you want your babe to live. To grow fat and take his first steps and giggle when you make a face at him. You want him to learn what it is to run a city and deal with politics. You want to know what it is to be a father of a living child, and not simply a father with one more tiny casket in his cemetery."

A flash of pain crossed his face as if she'd struck him.

"The Maker has healed many beyond those who have suffered from the Cancer here," Tressa said. "We have seen a crippled child's foot straightened. His grandmother and a Drifter chief, both blind, now see. We have watched a woman on the verge of dying from days of poisoning rise and walk again. On and on, this tapestry of healing has been woven until now. Today. When the Maker has chosen your son to save, so that you might know your Creator at last."

The lord gaped at her, looking pale and confused.

"There is a way out of your distress, my lord," Dri said from beside me.

"The child can live," put in Chaza'el. "I have seen it. But only if you allow Tressa to heal him."

"Dare to risk it," Vidar said. "Turn away from the dark ones who cloud your mind."

"Why would we risk entering your city?" Niero asked. "And come straight to your gates? Unless we could do as we say?"

"Silence!" cried the lord, turning away, his head between his hands. But I could hear the choking sound and knew the Remnants had struck a nerve. He cared for this child. Wanted him to live more than we might have believed. Needed his heir to live, in this city full of sons.

His advisors shared a worried look. The older one said to the guards, "Take them all to the wall, except for Prince Kapriel and the one they call Andriana. Take those two to the dungeon."

"No," I said, on my feet, trying to get between Dri and the two nearest guards. The other Knights were doing the same. One guard went to the concrete floor heavily; I thought I heard Tressa cry out. But then more guards arrived, flooding the room, over-powering us. Four men took me down, each sitting on an arm or leg. Killian was still on his feet, wildly striking out.

"What is the harm in allowing me to try?" Tressa cried, her voice pure anguish and terror as two guards dragged her from the throne room. "My lord, why not allow me to try and save your child?"

She was at the door when the lord at last raised his head. "Wait," he called, and his voice rose above the rest of our clamor.

The guards stilled, and we all gradually looked back.

His advisors turned to him, their faces awash in fear and frustration.

"I will give the girl a moment with my child," he said wearily.

"My lord . . ." began one.

But the lord raised a hand, silencing him. He looked at Tressa, and for the first time I could see the lines of strain about his eyes and mouth. "Come," he said, walking past her.

She hesitated until he looked back at her, clearly agitated and perplexed. "We are strongest together, my lord," she said, straight-ening her shoulders. "Your child will have the best chance if all the Ailith are in attendance."

His eyes hardened, and the muscle in his clenched jaw twitched. "You get one chance at this, girl. If my child dies, so will all of you. Even those the emperor wishes saved." He waved his hand over us in a dismissive manner, and muttered toward the guards as he passed, "Bring the whole lot of them. What does it matter?"

We filtered out into the hallway and down a side passage that led to rooms with a more feminine touch. Where he kept his concubines, who were undoubtedly the single biggest symbol of his wealth in this city so in need of women. In one room were five of them, circled around a table, somberly sipping tea from delicate china cups. At the end of the passage, in a room dark but for three candles, sat a woman quietly weeping as she rocked a tiny babe in her arms.

Even I could feel the love this lord had for the woman—and the ache within him. It took me aback. For all his power and wealth, he had no dominion over life and death. It made sense that it was here that the Maker would pierce his heart.

The woman stared at us in confusion and pain, tears streaming down her cheeks, as the lord came to stand beside her. She looked up at him and gave her head a small shake of apology, as if warning him that there was no hope. The babe's time was short. The child was quiet save tiny, frantic breaths. His eyes were closed; his skin fearfully gray; his lips blue. Tressa went to the woman and knelt before her. "My lady, we are the Remnants. And the Maker has sent us here to give you back your son."

The pretty woman's eyebrows knit together, and she searched Tressa's eyes, as if wondering if she could dare to believe. Then she looked to the Lord of Zanzibar in alarm. It had to be Tressa's mention of the Maker's name. But when the lord did not react, she searched the face of everyone else present and landed at last on Tressa again.

"Please," Tressa said, lifting her hands as if already cradling the babe. "May I?"

Swallowing hard, the young mother lifted the tiny boy up, kissed him on the forehead, and then set him in Tressa's arms. She sank to the floor before her. "Please. *Please*. I beg you to heal my son."

Tressa looked into her eyes. "Believe, my friend. Today, the Maker shall restore your son to you, whole." She bent her head and began praying as the lady bowed low, giving sway to deep sobs of both fear and fervent hope. The other Remnants put their hands on Tressa's shoulders and arms as she began to whisper her prayers. We Knights did the same, forming another circle, all praying that the baby would live, and in turn, that his parents would believe. There was no fear within me. The Maker had seen this, from start to finish. And he would not have brought us here, to face such danger, unless he had a plan. A plan to grant life and hope and healing.

I awaited the child's hearty cry with such anticipation that it made my skin tingle and my heart pound. Looking around, I saw that my companions smiled too, feeling the same confidence. Vidar's eyes were wide, and he scanned the room. It was then that I could feel what he so obviously could see—angels slipping between us, around us, above us. Shivers ran down my neck and over my arms, and I wasn't even ashamed of the tears that slid down my cheeks as Tressa lifted the baby upward. "You brought this child into the world, Maker. We commit his life to you. Move within him. Knit together whatever ails his tiny heart. Make him strong and whole. We claim your healing power on this child, in your name, Maker. The One who was, and is, and is to come."

"The One who was, and is, and is to come," whispered the young mother, rising to stare at Tressa, nodding again, as if accepting it as truth. Trembling, she turned to take her lord's hand, and I could see that he, too, now had tears streaming down his face.

"The One who was, and is, and is to come," he repeated, sinking to his knees. The young mother did the same beside him, looking up at their child, for the moment utterly broken, yet utterly hopeful.

"Yes," Tressa said, laughing under her breath as she wept, lowering the child back into the cradle of her arms, kissing him on the forehead, and returning him to his parents. "*That* is the One who has restored your child to you. I beg you to honor this gift, my lord and lady. Forever."

The little boy, now pink and squirming, gathered himself up for a proper cry, mewling with the strength of a healthy newborn. His parents laughed, eyebrows high in surprise, looking at each other, then to the baby, then back to us. The lord rose—wiping his wet face with the backs of his hands—and helped the mother of his child up to her feet, then reached out to Tressa.

"I am overwhelmed," he said to her, then glanced at Kapriel. "At once aghast at all I have done and failed to do. I didn't know. Could not imagine . . . My friends," he said, desperation weaving his brows together, "forgive me for wanting you dead. For any harm I did to you or yours. I did not recognize you for who you were . . . servants of . . ."

"The Most High," Kapriel said gently.

The lord nodded and then bent his head a moment. "Does your Maker . . . Is there room for one such as I among your people? Can you ever accommodate one as friend who was once your mortal enemy?"

Kapriel stepped forward, and Tressa looped her hand through the crook of his arm. They shared a smile before looking back to the lord. "There is always room in the Maker's kingdom," Kapriel said.

The lord thoughtfully took his son from the young mother's arms and knelt again before Kapriel. The woman did the same.

"From this day forward, I am in the Remnants' debt. All I am, all I have is yours to use as you wish. I, Lord Darcel, swear allegiance to you, the true Prince of Pacifica."

"As do I, Lady Shabana of Zanzibar," she said.

Kapriel smiled and laid a hand on each of their shoulders. "Allegiance to the Maker and his people is the best place to start. But that will demand some sacrifices. Are you ready to change the very face of Zanzibar? Change the laws to abide by the Maker's ways?"

The lord faltered a moment, looked down to his child, and then looked up in agreement. "I am."

"Then rise, brother. We will serve the people of the Way together."

CHAPTER
18

ANDRIANA

We have to get out of here," Ronan said in my ear. As the day of feast celebrating the safe arrival—and healing—of Lord Darcel's heir wore on, we'd thought the press of the peoples' need would wane, but it simply swelled. More and more of the ill were brought to see Tressa, and hundreds of others begged for a word or a prayer with one of us. Kapriel called upon the clouds to build and build into a terrifying, swirling mass that looked as if it might sweep us away, and then with a wave of his hand, it became awash in the colors of a rainbow and then dissolved into mist. Chaza'el shared visions of what he saw in Zanzibar's future—a great city with many towns surrounding it, living no longer in fear, but in strength. Vidar located three men and a woman beset with demons, and together, we freed them.

By evening, we were aware that pilgrims were coming to us from outside the city, summoned by the stories of miracles and hope. Only the closing gates stemmed the tide for the night.

"It's good, though, right?" I said, wading down the street, the Knights doing their best to press the people back as we made our way to the relative sanctuary of the palace. "All of these people," I said, gesturing over their heads—sending many people into gasps of hysteria, as if my mere action held some sort of miraculous power—"they will protect us, if the need arises."

"We think," Ronan said. "They're in the infancy of their faith," he went on. "And no infant is trained to go head to head with a Sheolite scout, let alone a tracker." His eyes traced the lines of the rooftops, searching for any lurking enemies, even as we spoke.

His barely disguised mention of Sethos sent a shiver down my spine. He was right. We had to go. We all knew it. It was a heady experience, being here during this time of transformation. Seeing a city change before our very eyes, between one sunset and another. Horrible laws had been abolished. Women freed. Men incarcered for abuse. People of all ages healed. The broken were forgiven. Families discovered new hope. My heart felt at once full and yet weary, as if I could not take in one more ounce of the Maker's glory, his ability to take something that was so dark and release a hidden light.

We'd lost Tressa and Killian in the crowds, but up ahead I could still see Vidar and Bellona. I noticed Vidar studying the city wall above us. No longer did the guards patrol with a stance that said they wanted to keep others out; they patrolled to keep order, as best they could, among the people that thronged the city streets. The marketplace and pubs and inns swelled with activity, and merchants left their stores at night beaming. Free trade and more traffic made for far better commerce; however, we also knew that those of the underworld had slipped in among the pilgrims, pickpocketing and robbing both the wealthy and the poor.

Still, it was a good place, this city, for the first time. It was now a whole place, not the dark shell of a town. And Darcel, the Lord of Zanzibar, and his new wife, Shabana, were the right leaders for it. They had wed almost immediately, and his harem now prepared to vacate the palace and reestablish themselves with the ample funds Darcel had gifted them.

"One more dinner here, together," I said to Ronan. "And then we shall slip away as the pilgrims sleep. Darcel has promised us two Jeeps to carry us all the way to the Valley. We'll make far better time than we had on our mudhorses. And even if Keallach's spies have told him of our presence here and they threaten to close in with force, they'd still have to be a day away, right?"

He nodded, his green eyes still clearly troubled by the unseen threat that always followed us. Again, Vidar's tight attention caught my eye. Bellona stood beside him, and they stared upward, as if looking for one particular guard. We came alongside them, and Ronan whispered, "What is it?"

"Those of the dark are with us," Bellona grunted. "We need to get the Rems into the palace." A swirl of foreboding entered my belly, and I looked up again, even as Ronan took hold of my elbow and pulled me forward.

"The angels defend us, even now," Vidar said to me with hooded eyes. "But there are more dark ones arriving by the moment." It was then that I saw Niero had disappeared. Was he up there, doing battle on our behalf?

I felt a mad impulse to turn and run for the city gates. But we had to get back to the palace, to find Tressa and Killian, Chaza'el and Kapriel, before we went. And the sun was coming down. As much as I'd proposed leaving under cover of darkness moments earlier, the thought of heading out across the desert with Sheolites in pursuit struck terror within. Images of the time we'd tried to outrun Drifters in the desert—with Niero getting shot and me getting captured—cascaded through my mind.

People began screaming ahead of us, turning in a wave and stampeding toward us. A woman fell, and Ronan helped her back on her feet so she might escape being trampled. We were pressed and pushed until we had no choice but to turn and run with the rest, before we'd seen what so alarmed them. Was it soldiers? But I knew from the chaos all around me—the particular fear in those who passed me—that it was worse. The Sheolites and their wraiths were here.

"This way!" Bellona screamed to us, dashing into a side alley as the bulk of the crowd pressed onward, along First Street, toward the main gates. She yanked Vidar behind her, and Ronan was pressing me forward, urging me to follow them. But still, I looked back. I wished we could get to the palace to be with the others. But Raniero and Azarel were with Kapriel and Chaza'el, and hopefully Tressa and Killian had joined them. They wouldn't be without defense. We simply had to find our way back to them safely.

Bellona and Vidar ran to Second and then Third, down the alleyway before taking a sharp right, where we could be out of view for a moment. We gathered together, and I knew that in the deep shadows my expression of panic must mirror what I saw on my friends' faces. "How?" I said, panting. "How could they have gotten inside once the gates were closed?" I realized I'd felt a measure of security when the gates closed at sunset, thinking any battle would be at bay until at least morning.

"Over the wall," Vidar said, pushing damp hair from his forehead. "That was why the unseen battled to make a way for them. They knew surprise was their best method of attack."

"Because they wanted us separated, yet trapped, within these dreaded walls," Bellona hissed, pacing. "To divide us is their best opportunity to capture us. We should've left this morning and gotten back to the Citadel."

"And missed what the Maker released today?" Vidar asked, shaking his head. "Never. This was exactly what we came for. To heal the babe, yes. But we also came for the people who turned to us afterward—*that* is what pleases the Maker most."

"They would have come after us anywhere, Bellona," Ronan put in, taking my hand. "Haven't you felt it building, the threat? They've been hovering near, waiting. We were not born to cower in the Citadel. We were born to move out and into the world in the Maker's name."

"Yeah, well, now we need to find our way back to the palace," Bellona groused, "so we can live to move out into the world again tomorrow."

"Agreed," Ronan said, and we set off running.

As the street opened up before us, I saw Vidar falter—heard him urge his Knight to wait—then saw Bellona abruptly dodge and roll, coming to her feet with a knife in each hand. Vidar slid, feet first, narrowly avoiding the swinging blade of a Sheolite sword. Ronan skidded to a stop, lifting his arm to protect me. "Back!" he cried. I leaned hard against him—my momentum too much to fully stop in time—but in the same movement, I turned on my m to run in the opposite direction.

But it was Ronan's turn to run into me as I came to a dead stop again.

Because two blocks away was Sethos, striding toward us with twenty Sheolite scouts behind him. In their crimson capes, they were like blood oozing from a vein, passing between the tight adobe walls that only allowed them to come toward us one man at a time. If we could hold them off, we could handle them, one at a time. If only the first didn't happen to be Sethos.

He continued his brisk, confident pace toward me, not running and well aware that we couldn't go far. Behind me, I heard another tracker's shriek and groaned, inwardly. We were surrounded.

"Come along, Andriana. Ronan. There is no need for this to become bloody," he called, lifting a hand to us as if he might be conciliatory.

"Oh, I think it will be bloody," Ronan said, stepping in front and tucking me behind him. "This city is ours now. It has been claimed for the Maker. Lord Darcel stands behind Prince Kapriel."

"A faulty decision that will be corrected shortly," Sethos said, nostrils flared.

From above, a brick came down, narrowly missing Sethos. Then another fell, striking the man behind him.

"Leave them alone!" cried a woman, tossing a third brick after pulling it from the crumbling wall before her.

"You will not have them!" cried another. More bricks rained down. Sethos stopped, cursing and pointing upward to those behind him, sending men after those who dared to defend us. Two archers began shooting at the women, whom I saw had been joined by several men and children too.

We weren't alone in this battle. And our best way out was behind us. My heart leaped, as if it had previously slowed to a deadening beat. Energy shot through me, sending my fingers splaying. I turned and ran back to Fifth, pulling out my sword from the scabbard at my waist. I heard Ronan do the same behind me. We emerged onto the wide street, and I whirled, striking the nearest Sheolite with every ounce of force I had within me, concentrating on the Maker and his mission rather than on any emotion my enemy might feel.

"Duck," Ronan grunted, and I fell low without question, hearing the whistle of a blade swing past me. As if in an intricate dance, my Knight stepped forward and stabbed my assailant under the arm, where his leather armor breastplate gapped for a moment. I rose, turned, and with one, smooth stroke, nearly severed him in half. Across from me, Bellona did the same with her adversary, wincing as blood spurted across the street. But she was immediately on the move, turning to face the tracker.

He sneered at her as the two of them circled, panting, sizing each other up. "Give it up, Knight. This is *your* last order."

A dagger came sailing through the air, blade over handle, whipping between Ronan and me, and almost pierced the tracker's throat. But he reached out and caught it, just as the point nicked his skin. He flicked it back at Vidar so fast that Vidar blinked in surprise. He bent backward at the last possible moment, and the blade passed just beyond his nose. "Man," he said, straightening and wiping his upper lip. "I have to confess I'm not feelin' a lot of the Maker's love for these guys."

But Bellona had used the tracker's momentary distraction to draw an arrow and send it through the air toward his heart. He whirled, and the arrow did little but tear through his red cape. She pressed forward, picking up a Sheolite's sword and bringing it down toward his chest. He narrowly parried in time, holding off her press with gritted teeth until he could lift a booted foot and shove her backward. Ronan drove forward, taking over as Bellona regained her footing. But just as he neared the tracker, more bricks rained down—one catching the tracker dead center on his forehead. He staggered backward, dazed, blood trickling between his eyes and along his nose. Another hit him on the shoulder, and as he wheeled about, still another hit him on the head again. He slumped to his knees.

Vidar, his sword in both hands, turned and brought his blade down across our enemy's neck, making certain he wouldn't rise to track us ever again.

I looked away, up, to see several old women and girls, bricks in hand, eyes alight with glory. "Run, Remnant!" cried a girl. "Run! We'll try and keep them from you!"

"Come on," Bellona said, taking the lead. "This way!"

We pounded over the cobblestones after her, not arguing. If Sethos had brought more than just his forward forces of Sheolites—if there were Pacifican soldiers approaching too—and if the Sheolites had gotten to Lord Darcel, we had to convince him to remain true.

CHAPTER 19

ANDRIANA

We'd wound our way through the streets—Bellona and Vidar just a block ahead of us—when an arrow pierced Bellona's shoulder. She cried out and spun to one side, and Vidar immediately turned to scan the rooftops. Another arrow narrowly missed him, and Ronan shoved me around the corner. "Take cover!" he cried.

But around that corner was Sethos, again, along with three scouts. I stared at him in horror. How on earth had he found us again? We'd taken turn upon turn.

Ronan drew his sword, as did I.

"Come now," Sethos said soothingly. "Put down your weapons, and you both shall live to see tomorrow."

"I'd rather die than return to Pacifica with you," Ronan said.

"As would I," I said.

"Oh, I'm not offering to take you back with me, Knight," Sethos said. "I'm offering you one more sunset before you are impaled in front of Zanzibar's gates. That shall make an appropriate example for your new . . . followers." With two fingers, he waved the others in to capture or kill us.

I could feel the chill throbbing in my armband and knew that the dark ones were in their company too. I imagined wraiths streaming through the city streets, circling us, choking us.

We had to make our escape. Fast.

I glanced over my shoulder and saw there were four more Sheolites who had just turned a corner and spotted us. "Ronan, we have company back there too," I muttered.

I caught a wave of despair and frustration from him as he attacked, taking down one scout in a remarkably swift move, then immediately turning to the second. I waded in with him, doing battle with the third while Sethos hung back, watching in a fairly disinterested way.

The man I battled was strong and matched every strike and swing I tried. He grinned at me, realizing my strength was failing, and drove me backward. I nearly tripped a couple of times, and he nicked my shoulder, but I held on, confident that he had orders not to kill, but to capture. But they clearly had no such orders about Ronan. The other Sheolites gathered behind me, creating a barrier that I doubted I could escape, while still more arrived and closed in around my knight.

Fear took hold of me.

I was going to lose this night.

Ronan.

My freedom.

They would take me to Pacifica and force me to marry Keallach—he could compel me through the vows—or Sethos would see me die before the gates, alongside my Knight.

Do not fear, came Niero's voice in my head. I looked around as I swung my sword wildly, but I could not see him. *The moment you begin to fear is the moment you doubt your Maker's love. Do you believe he loves you? Cares for you? That he is with you, even now?*

Was this really the time for preaching to me?

Where are you, Niero? We need you!

I grimaced and ducked, narrowly avoiding the side of the Sheolite's sword from bludgeoning my chest, then I grabbed my dagger from my calf sheath and stabbed it into the Sheolite's thigh. He screamed and staggered backward a few steps.

Behind him, Ronan fell and rolled as his own adversary struck at him, again and again, his sword narrowly missing Ronan on the stones each time.

What do you believe, Andriana?

The Sheolite I faced wrenched out the dagger from his thigh and flung it to one side. Then he came after me with renewed vengeance.

Niero. Now's not the time . . .

I blocked the next scout's first blow.

If you died this day, what would the Maker say to you? What is the truth in your heart?

Irritated, I cried out, whirled, and missed the Sheolite with my blade. I tried to concentrate, to figure out what Niero wanted me to see.

I believe I was created to serve the Maker.

Truth, indeed. What else?

I believe the Maker loves me and wants me to live through this . . . I parried a blow and then punched the Sheolite in the throat, sending him reeling back, clutching his neck, eyes bugging out. Another stepped forward to take his place, face alight with glee. And I was so tired, then. I knew my strength alone would not be enough to carry me through. Nor Ronan's.

That he is with us even now, in this desperate moment . . .

Yes, he is.

Niero dropped down from the rooftops between Ronan and the Sheolite, in a deep crouch. The surprise of his arrival gave my Knight a chance to gain his feet again. In two breaths, the scout was dead. Niero whirled, his ivory wings lifting in glorious fashion, taking down the man who threatened me too. I gasped at the glory of him, the wonder of him, as mighty and powerful as that night in the barn when Ronan was saved.

He moved past me so quickly that he was a blur and killed all four at our back flank with one perfect strike after another. My heart soared in praise for the One who had sent this one to walk alongside us, fight alongside us.

But a low, foul hiss behind me made me turn. Sethos.

The dark master's eyes were on Raniero. "You dare to unfurl your wings here, before me? A dove before the wolf? I'll have you begging for your life."

Raniero turned, panting slightly, and tossed his bloody sword to his other meaty hand. He seemed bigger than he normally did, as if he bore the strength of ten men inside his body. And perhaps he did. "You, my once-brother," he said to Sethos, "are the beggar at *life's* door. But that passage was closed to you long ago, forever."

Sethos turned, a swirl of red fabric, and I saw then the black wings emerge. I staggered backward as the two tall men came together, swords clanging, and tried to believe my eyes, yet chastised myself for not seeing it all along.

Of course. Sethos was a dark angel, just as Niero was one of the Maker's loyalists. Everything about them seemed heightened, brightened, larger, in every sense of the word. Even as I absorbed the truth of their order, I couldn't quite rectify how I knew both of them in memory with how they appeared now, before me. And I was very glad that Niero had arrived before Sethos revealed himself. Because Sethos was the most frightful creature I'd ever seen.

He was Death, personified.

Niero sent Sethos stumbling back with a fearsome strike, and turned to us. "Run," he said under his breath. "Get back to the palace. Now."

He turned to meet Sethos's next blow, his massive arms trembling under the force of it.

"But you—" Ronan began, blinking as if he could force himself to see things as they once were, not as they were now.

"Go!" Niero bit out through clenched teeth, swinging again at Sethos, once, twice, three times in rapid succession.

I took Ronan's hand and pulled him toward the alleyway again, and eventually he shook off his amazement enough to really put himself into our escape. We moved so fast we felt as if we were lifted by angels. And perhaps we were.

We made it past Third, to Second, and were almost to First when I saw them—the first of the men in red, running by on the main road. I ducked into a doorway, and Ronan pulled me close, under the crook of his arm, the two of us gasping for breath. More Sheolites ran past the open mouth of the alley, a swath of red, with three patrols of Zanzibian soldiers in pursuit.

"It's all right," I whispered, looking up at him in the deepening shadows, "they're running away. The Zanzibians—Lord Darcel has stuck to his word! They fight for us!"

Ronan closed his eyes and leaned his head back against the wall behind him, relief wafting from him into me. "We're safe for the moment. Which is good," he panted, looking down at me. "I'd rather not see another man in red this night."

"But tomorrow would be all right?" I said with a grin.

"Oh yeah, tomorrow," he returned with a huff of a laugh. "Tomorrow, we can each take on another hundred. As long as Niero's with us."

"Agreed," I said with a slight smile. Our bravado, even false, gave me a measure of comfort.

He paused a moment. "Dri . . . how long? How long have you known that Niero was . . . other? Over these last weeks . . . I think I've known all along. But didn't. Does that make sense?"

I gave his hand a squeeze. "I knew he was different the night we reached the Hoodite cave. His ability to heal . . ." I shook my head, remembering his broad back, the hundreds of scars, and how his bullet wound looked months old, rather than just days. "But he didn't fully reveal himself until the night we almost lost you after our escape from Palace Pacifica."

"He revealed himself? To everyone?"

"To me. And to you, but you weren't quite coherent. After that, it was like whatever cloak kept him hidden from Vidar's eyes was removed, and he knew too."

"How is it that Vidar didn't recognize him before? Or Sethos?"

I shrugged. "I don't know. Maybe angels have the choice whether to reveal themselves fully to those around them. Vidar knew Niero was a force of good, just as he knew Sethos was a force of evil. Just not how . . . *deep* either man delved into each side."

"You know I'm going to have to tease him about that," he said with a grin.

I grinned back. "I think that would only be appropriate."

We stilled, and Ronan pulled me closer as we heard more boots running down the street just ahead of us. But it was a patrol of twelve Zanzibian soldiers. Still, we held back. Even if they were our allies now, we weren't quite ready to trust them completely.

"Ready to try and get to the palace?" Ronan whispered, once they'd passed.

"Yes."

We took off again, slowing at the corner of First and peering in both directions. The street was dark and quiet, many of the citizens likely cowering indoors, waiting out the fighting and wondering what the morning would bring after so many changes and such a threat.

As did we.

CHAPTER 20

RONAN

We ran directly up to the palace gates. There were no guards outside, but the doors were barricaded. Six guards peered down at us, each holding a torch against the gathering dark.

"We are Ronan and Andriana of the Valley!" I called, agitated that we weren't immediately recognized and admitted. "Let us in, quickly!"

The guards looked grimly down first and conferred together for a moment, their hesitation making me want to scream. I wanted to get Dri inside, to relative safety. The Sheolites might be on the run at the moment, but . . .

"It's all clear! Let them in!" one finally called over his shoulder, down to those below on the other side of the gates.

We heard the slide of the crossbeam, and again I looked down the street, both relieved and unnerved by the total silence and emptiness of it. The guards cracked the door just enough to allow us entry and then quickly barricaded it again. We were ushered by two grim-faced soldiers inside the palace, where we found our companions in a public room near the front, clearly waiting on our arrival. Lord Darcel, Lady Shabana, and the baby were with them.

Quickly, we greeted one another.

"Where's Niero?" Vidar asked.

"He sent us on," I said to him, knowing that among all the Ailith, he'd be most likely to understand what had truly transpired. "He saved us from Sethos. As did the people of your city," I went on quickly, turning to Lord Darcel. "If it wasn't for them, raining down bricks upon the Sheolites, and your soldiers, chasing others, we might have been captured. Or worse." I cast a grim look to Dri, and she nodded, even as she accepted a goblet of water from Tressa.

"We must get you out," said Darcel. "Before the Pacifican politicians come."

"They're coming?" I asked. "You know this?"

"They've sent word," he returned. "We did not reply. I'll deal with them when they arrive at our gates. For now, we have the remaining Sheolites trapped in the southeast corner of the city. We will make sure every one of them dies this night. But we only have an hour, maybe two, before their reinforcements arrive. You must be away."

"But Niero isn't—" Bellona began.

"Niero will join us in time. He'll be all right," Vidar said to her.

"How will you hold the city against them?" Killian asked Darcel.

"Their forward forces surprised us," the young lord replied, face grim. "They won't do so again. And this city has stood for a very long time. Thanks to you, we have renewed reason to hold the gates."

We all rose, accepting packs from servants, which I assumed had water and food in them. Then we said quick farewells to Lady Shabana, holding her bundled babe, and followed the lord down the hallway to a servant's passage, then into the bowels of the palace. Behind a trapdoor, we entered a tiny, rough-cut tunnel, cold and damp and full of spiderwebs. Carrying a torch, Darcel led us all the way to the end, and after pulling an ancient key from his pocket turned it in the lock of one door and then another. Wet, slimy steps were below us, and by the smell, I knew they led to a sewage tunnel. "Forgive me," said Lord Darcel, his nose wrinkling at the foul stench. "It's the only way out of the city that I know of, without everyone knowing you've gone. And we want our enemies to think you're still here. It will buy you precious time."

It was an ancient, last-resort escape route. This was perhaps the only time it had ever been used as such. But undoubtedly every royal who'd ever inhabited the palace had known of it. I had to admire Darcel—a man who had probably never had dirty hands, let alone been ankle-deep in sludge—as he led us through one iron gate after another. At the end, he opened the fourth gate and pointed out into the inky black night. "Once away from the wall, head directly east to the river. There, you will find Drifter drivers waiting with Jeeps that will get you to the Valley before morning. They work for us and have sworn to care for any that I protect with their lives. You can trust them."

"Thank you, my lord," I said.

"Thank you, Ronan of the Valley." He took my arm and then Killian's, then said good-bye to the others. "If our enemies come against you in the Valley, we will come to your aid. We owe you our lives. Our future too."

"We're indebted to you," Tressa said.

"It is to you and yours that I owe my debt," he said, kissing her hand and holding it with no trace of the lechery that once was so evident in him. "You," he went on, his voice cracking, "have changed me. In so many ways. For as long as I live, know I will serve you and yours in any way possible."

"Serve the Maker in all things, and all will be well," she said. "Continue all that has begun! It's a new day, Lord Darcel. For you, your family, and your people."

I shook my head as we slipped out of the city, wondering at all that had transpired. Of all the people who had found new life after encountering us, the Lord of Zanzibar had to be the biggest transformation of all. And what his transformation meant, for an entire city . . . in retrospect, it made clear exactly why the Maker had sent us here. At no other time in his life had Darcel been ready to hear the truth, let alone abide by it.

"What about Niero?" Tressa asked as we all hurried toward the river.

"I imagine he'll be along shortly," I said, giving Dri's hand a squeeze.

"How?" Killian asked. "Will he sprout wings and fly?"

"He'll find a way," I managed to say, my voice strangled. I didn't know why Niero had kept his angelic secret from us for so long, but I was determined not to be the one to break such a confidence.

"If he can make it out of Wadi Qelt and arrive beside the Isle of Catal in a boat," Kapriel said, "I'm sure he can manage this as well."

"I don't like it," Killian said. "We're best when we're all together. Strongest."

But when we reached the river, relieved to wade in and wash away the stench of the foul sewer, Niero surprised us. "About time you arrived," he said. "The drivers are just over the hill."

"Niero!" Killian cried, reaching for the man's arm in the dark. "How did you—"

"I went over the wall instead of under it. The lord had told me how he intended to spirit us out of the city. I took a chance that I might find you here."

"Did you kill Sethos? Is he gone?" I asked, taking my turn to grip the man's arm. But it was . . . different, knowing what Raniero truly was. It made me feel cautious. Not in the sense that I couldn't trust him, but more like he was again new to me, like an old friend or a brother returning home after several seasons away.

"No," he said, and I could hear the bitter disappointment in his tone. "Time and again, he went after you; once he knew you were beyond his reach, he escaped me."

My head jerked upward. We could all hear the sounds of engines in the distance, as vehicles bounced over the sand dunes, making their way toward us with headlights off. We all stood and gathered together, Knights before their Remnants, Niero before Chaza'el and Kapriel.

When they pulled up before us, their faces becoming clear in the dim moonlight, I drew my sword.

Because the Drifters who had come to fetch us and take us home were familiar . . . in a very bad way.

They were the very same group that had kidnapped Dri.

The same group that had shot Niero and left him for dead.

CHAPTER 21

ANDRIANA

Had these Drifters just happened upon us before the others arrived—those that had answered Lord Darcel's call to transport his "guests" to the Valley?

"Easy there," cried one man. "I'm coming toward you, alone. Do your best to not run me through yet. I'm unarmed."

He jumped to the ground and padded toward us between the second and third vehicles, hands raised. It was Bushy, the huge, barbaric man who had so mistreated me. Left me chained in the cave while he and his people all drank themselves into a stupor. His eyes flicked over the others until they rested on me. He smiled and tilted his head in my direction. Ronan shifted, blocking his view. I moved to peek over his other shoulder, but Bushy was looking at Niero.

"'Spect I deserve this kind of greeting," he said, reaching a hand out to Niero.

Niero did not take it.

"But we're friends now, or would like to be. People of the Way, my group of Drifters are now."

"You," scoffed Killian, gesturing toward him. "Forgive me for being skeptical."

"Don't blame you," Bushy said, raising one brow and nodding. "We captured two people you had run across, a grandmother and her young grandson. They told us what had happened. At first, we didn't believe it, but the more that sprite of a goatherd and old cheesemaker yammered on about their story, the more our minds started to open." He put his hands on his hips, bowed his head, and shook it. "Takes some people a long time to put their faith in something like the Way, and others not long at all. I 'spect the Maker had been workin' on me for a good, long while. We were ready for a change." A grin spread across his lips, and I remembered well his white teeth and foul breath. "And it doesn't hurt that it lifts my skirts to do what anyone in power has forbade everyone to do . . . claim faith in the Maker."

Vidar stepped out from behind Bellona, walked right up to the giant of a man, and looked up into his face a moment. Then he grinned and offered his arm. "Welcome, brother. We are glad to have you. As well as to get a ride rather than walk for two days home."

We climbed into the Drifters' vehicles, still a bit dazed by yet another turn, yet feeling utter peace about it too. "Now this could only be of the Maker," I whispered to Kapriel as he climbed in beside me. "If you had met these people when we had . . ."

He gave me a little smile. "Don't you see it yet, Dri? The Maker is calling the worst, the farthest, the hardest to him first.

It's like folding a pastry in and in and in further, until all are included. He's long had a heart for those who have no one else, or perhaps they are the first to recognize how much they need him. Those who have power and authority? They shall be last."

"Except for the Lord of Zanzibar."

He smiled again. "Well, yes, him."

"And you, the lost Prince of Pacifica."

"I've been the Maker's subject since the day my parents first told me of him and what I had been born for. But few would say I have any power and authority."

"You bear the power and authority of the Maker," I said. "That's all any of us need." The engines rumbled to a start. I glanced over my shoulder as Ronan climbed in behind me, electing to stand beside Chaza'el. "What could be greater?"

"Perhaps that power *and* the throne of Pacifica?" Kapriel said, grinning at me.

"Well, that would be good," I said, joining in with my own conspiratorial smile.

KEALLACH

In the cramped transport, I paced back and forth in front of Sethos and two of his wounded Sheolites. He stood stiffly before me, staring straight ahead. Maximillian, Daivat, and Fenris stood behind me.

"Let me be sure I understand this," I said. "You had a hundred Sheolites at your disposal. Three of your elite trackers. A device to tell you *exactly* where my brother and Andriana were. And you *lost* them."

"We were far outnumbered, Majesty," Sethos said stiffly. "The Zanzibians turned against us, from soldier to commoner. And the city was full of the faithful. We got close—very close—to Andriana. But then the one they call Raniero intervened."

"Raniero, their captain? He is a match for you?"

"He is," Sethos said. "I'm sorry, Highness. I have failed you."

"Yes. Yes, you have," I bit out. "And now it's time to take things into my own hands." I turned and strode to the technician who had a screen before him and was overlaying a map of the city and the outlying regions. It only took a moment to see the two blinking lights indicating Kapriel and Andriana. They'd made it out of the castle, under cover of darkness. They were escaping.

Heading home, back to the Valley.

I paced back and forth, thinking, pressing the sides of my head and squinting my eyes, trying to find a way through. We could try and capture them again, out here. But we would be out-numbered if Zanzibian patrols on the wall saw us and intervened.

Deep within, I knew such an action would ruin everything. After the complete turning of Zanzibar, after such wins for the Way, they would be feeling strong, as if the Maker himself was encouraging them onward. He was, in a way. And I had to har-ness that power too . . .

No. I couldn't force Andriana and Kapriel to come back with me to Pacifica and gradually win their full support.

I had to convince them to give it to me willingly.

ANDRIANA

The sun wasn't even up yet when we arrived at the Valley mouth, with grit covering our faces and weariness making our eyes ache. But we were home and arriving victorious, in many ways. The Maker had sent us to Zanzibar, and we'd returned after claiming the city—that horrendous city—as our own.

We'd battled back Sethos and his Sheolite warriors and all survived to see another sunrise. We'd seen Lord Darcel's son restored to him and the nobles and commoners alike commit to One higher than they. The incredible sequence of events still made my heart swell with praise for the Maker and the way he had made for us. And for them.

We shook hands with our unlikely saviors—the very people who had once threatened to sell me to the Zanzibians—and tried to convince them to join us in the Valley.

"Nah," said the bushy-bearded man—Redd, I'd learned his name was—with a shrug, patting his steering wheel. "Gotta stick with these, and you Valley-dwellers don't go in much for roads. But if you need us, we won't be far. For now, we'll make sure that no one comes after you. Rest easy. You can trust that you'll get all the way to the Citadel this night." They handed us several torches and a lighter. Vidar set one torch after another aflame.

"Thank you," Kapriel said.

Redd gave him a surprisingly regal bow and rose slowly, grinning. "I await the day you ascend the throne, my prince. When the kingdom is at last in your hands again."

Kapriel spread out his arms. "The kingdom is already here. It is, and has always been, and will be forever, the Maker's own."

"The One who was . . ." said Redd.

"The One who is," said those nearest.

"The One who is to come," said everyone else, in unison.

With that, we turned to go, climbing the path inward that had become decidedly more worn with all the pilgrims and refugees who had arrived. It was wider and flatter, with more rocks dislodged. There were wheel marks from where people had pushed carts and wagons. Hoof prints from goats and sheep, herded inward. Mudhorse tracks too.

As always, the Valley felt as welcoming and reassuring to me as my mom's own arms, opened wide. But this night, there was something different. Something off. One by one, each of the Ailith slowed, recognizing it. We looked at one another, silently understanding. We were not alone. There was another nearby.

One of us.

Except every last one of the Remnants was accounted for. Unless one of our lost brothers or sisters had miraculously found their way here. My heart leaped at the thought. After all, it had been our enemy who had told me that others had been captured and murdered on the road to us. What if they had lied? What if . . .

Ronan gripped my wrist and pulled me back as I tried to surge ahead. "No, Dri, wait," he whispered, passing me by. "Let us check it out first."

I stifled a groan and followed behind him, ignoring how his whole *being* practically turned into a scowl when I refused to stay put. But how could he think I would be left behind? This was a Remnant ahead of us, or a Knight—clearly Ailith blood.

We crested a small rise in the path and looked down to a shallow clearing among the woods, the light from our torches filling it like a bowl as the rest of our party arrived. There we found a young man on his knees, dressed in an old, worn sweater and dirty pants, with only a small bag strapped across his chest. His head was bowed.

At first, I didn't recognize him and wondered why no one spoke to him. But when I looked over at the others and saw Kapriel's profile, gaping in disbelief, I knew who it was before I even saw the newcomer raise his chin.

Keallach.

CHAPTER 22

ANDRIANA

I watched it all unfold as if it was happening to someone else. Everything seemed slow. Muted. Ronan growled and pulled his sword, as did Bellona, both of them rushing toward Keallach.

I screamed. I thought I screamed, anyway, along with Tressa. I could feel my mouth open and the strain in my throat, but I couldn't seem to hear anything. Niero opened his mouth in an obvious shout as he surged after the knights.

Chaza'el stepped forward, eyes wide.

Kapriel closed his own eyes and lifted his face, fists clenched at his side, as if in agony, beseeching the Maker.

Killian, Azarel, and Niero circled us, partially crouched, looking toward the trees, preparing to defend us. They worried that Keallach was only the first of many of our adversaries. I reached up to my arm cuff and patted it, wondering if it was working correctly. Why it was neutral. Because it didn't know if Keallach was friend or foe?

Then everything clicked into real-time action. Fast. Loud. Everyone moving and shouting at once.

Keallach remained on his knees, palms open, as if surrendering. "I am unarmed!" he shouted to Ronan, as my knight lifted his sword to strike, just feet away. "I mean you no harm!" He kept his head bowed, shouting it again and again. "I mean you no harm! Mercy! I beg you for mercy!"

Ronan's mouth twisted into pure, impotent rage. I knew his loathing then. His hatred for our brother-enemy. Jealousy. A thirst for revenge. My heart wrenched in terror for Keallach. And yet I also knew enough of Ronan to realize that he would never kill a man who wasn't trying to even fight for his life. It was dishonorable.

Still, I was moving before I quite realized what I was doing. Walking calmly. Sliding between Ronan and Bellona. Then, turning to stand between them and Keallach.

Ronan's frown increased, his sword still in the air. "Dri . . ." he bit out, sweat rolling down his temples, even though it was in the cold early morning hours.

"Ronan," I said, lifting my hands to him. "Please put that away. We are in no danger here, together."

"She's right," Vidar said. "He's alone."

Still, Ronan stood there, sword hovering, as if he still had half a mind to drag me aside and murder Keallach. "You would defend him?" he raged at me. "Even after all he did to you? To us?"

"Was it him?" I cried. "Or Sethos? I swear I saw evidence that he was manipulating Keallach, making him do things, messing with his mind. Perhaps he has, all along!" I dared to glance Kapriel's way, testing my theory to see if he might agree, but he was looking to the ground, shaking his head slowly, hands now clasped together.

Niero sighed heavily and turned halfway around to lay a gentle hand on Ronan's arm. Without a word, Ronan lifted his eyes to the starless sky, heaved a breath, and then sheathed his sword. But then he shoved between Niero and me to reach Keallach. He lifted him up to his feet, both hands fisted in Keallach's shirt, and pulled his face close. "Why are you here?" he grunted. "Tell us!"

Keallach didn't look away; he only stood there, with no fight in his stance whatsoever. We were all silent, waiting. "I am here to answer the Call. I'm very late. But I had no choice. After I spent time with Dri . . ." He glanced my way, hopeful, but I only frowned back in confusion, desperately trying to get some sort of emotional foothold with him. "And nearing you all and what was unfolding in Zanzibar . . . The Maker brought it all up again for me," he rushed on. "And I knew I had to leave Pacifica behind, if necessary, in order to serve with you. Ever since . . ." He dared to look my way again, but Ronan stepped between us. "Ever since Andriana left the palace, I've been . . . *adrift*. Agitated. And I realized that it wasn't just her I was longing for. It was you. The Remnants. My Ailith kin. The Call itself. You were all in on something that everything in me longs for too."

I think we all held our breath a moment, wondering if we'd heard him correctly. Ronan let out a choking, scoffing laugh and then tossed him backward. Keallach narrowly kept his feet, but then he just stood there, chewing on his lip and clenching his fists, and yet choosing not to engage Ronan. Slowly, he looked from one to the other of us. "I know you all must be skeptical, but it's the truth. I've been called, the same as you. And I am here to answer. As well as beg you for mercy. I know I've done terrible things. That my men have—"

"Enough!" Azarel cried, nocking an arrow and aiming toward Keallach. "He lies! You cannot believe a word from his mouth!"

He looked at her again, squinted, and then said, "Az? Azarel? Is that you? It's been . . . it's been so long."

"Not long enough," she ground out, arrow still aimed at his throat.

"Azarel," Kapriel warned, pain still etched in every syllable he uttered. This was tearing him apart, seeing Keallach again.

"I agree," Bellona said, pacing back and forth, hands on hips. "I say we kill him and be done with it. His people almost killed Andriana. And her parents. And he would've let Kapriel die! This is no brother of ours! Kill him! Now!"

Keallach was shaking his head, hands still up. His misery and sorrow engulfed me.

"No," I said. I wasn't quite ready to fully defend him. But neither was I ready to see him murdered. "We can't."

I didn't have to reach far to feel the renewed rage and jealousy within Ronan.

"She's right," Tressa said.

"No, Tress—" Killian groaned.

"No, listen," she went on. "Did we not just leave the foulest city we've ever entered? And did we not just see the Lord of Zanzibar himself turn to the Way?" She looked at each of us until we met her gaze. "Can you deny such miracles? Such changes of heart? Such healing?"

Ronan turned to Kapriel. "What say you?" he asked gently. "You who have suffered at your own twin's hands?"

When he didn't respond, Ronan moved on to Vidar, his desperation growing. "Or you, brother? What do you sense in this one? Tell me his blood does not now run with the same oil as his master, Sethos!"

But Vidar remained still, staring at Keallach. After a moment, he gave his head a tiny shake. "He's neither light nor dark to me. Perhaps he isn't fully on either side yet. I want to hate this one. Deny him. But Ronan," he said, reaching out to put a hand on his shoulder, willing him to comprehend the utter neutrality we all felt, "we can't. We just can't."

"It's a trick! A spell!" Ronan spat out, shoving away Vidar's hand. "He's found a way around your gifting." He turned. "Chaza'el, tell me you have seen the truth," he said, his voice rising in desperation.

Chaza'el gazed back at him, black eyes somber and still. He bowed his head and then glanced around at all of us. "I have seen Keallach, fighting beside Bellona and Ronan," he said softly, as if he could not quite believe it either. "Not against them. But that is *all* I have seen."

Niero took a deep breath and then sheathed his curved blades on his back. "We must retire to the Citadel. We'll bring Keallach along, his hands tied. If nothing else, he might serve well as our prisoner."

"Prisoner?" Killian scoffed. "This one will bring the weight of Pacifica down upon us before we're ready to defend ourselves."

"Or with him, we might be more ready than ever," Niero said, folding his arms and inclining his head toward Keallach. "One who can move objects—a Remnant. Alongside his twin, able to control the weather itself. Between them, they could defend us against anything Pacifica brings at us."

"Yes," Keallach said, excitedly nodding. "I know I have wronged you—all of you—terribly. But I can only beg you to seek your hearts. Wouldn't the Maker be warning you if I was a true threat?"

"Oh, he's warning us," Vidar said, stepping toward him. "Don't get ahead of yourself, *brother*. We're not ready for you to nestle into our mother's bosom quite yet." He passed him, heading up the path.

"Good," Keallach said, nodding, earnest. "That's good. Right. I would expect nothing less. Give me time. Test me."

"It's a ruse," Bellona said, arms crossed, looking to Niero as he began to bind Keallach's hands behind him. "A means to get inside the Citadel."

"We will not bring him inside," Niero said. "Not until you all agree it is right to do so."

"I, for one, vote that we keep him chained up outside during the deep of Hoarfrost," Bellona sneered as she passed him, following Vidar.

Keallach nodded, and I felt the sorrow from him. "That would be just," he said sadly. I frowned. Could he truly be feeling contrition? Or was it all a trick, as Bellona said? But he couldn't manipulate minds . . . only bodies.

Bellona turned, walking backward, studying him a moment longer. Then she just shook her head, turned on her heel, and hurried on.

"What say you, brother?" Keallach said—almost shyly—to his twin.

"I have nothing to say," Kapriel said. "Other than I cannot trust you. Not after everything. What you ask is . . . impossible."

I swallowed against the gathering lump in my throat as I experienced the aching swell of his grief along with him.

But Keallach was feeling it too. For the first time, he seemed totally open to me, no walls within. Their combined emotion actually made my knees weak. All of that loss . . . all of that brokenness . . .

Keallach stared back at his twin and looked as if he might cry. Behind him, Niero finished binding his hands. "There are not enough apologies to make amends," Keallach said. "I can only beg you for mercy, brother. Mercy and mercy and more mercy on our past. And give me a chance at a future."

Kapriel stared back at him. "I don't know if I can find it within me to give you anything, past or future." But there was longing within him too, a chasm of loss, harrowingly deep. I'd never sensed it in him before, and now it came at me like it wanted to pull me in.

Separate yourself, Niero said to my inner ear. *These are their emotions; it's their tragic tale, not yours.*

But isn't it all of ours? We're all connected.

Not this part. You can't bear it all as your own, Dri. Take a deep breath, and set it aside as their pain, not yours. If you take it all on, you'll sink. We need you to swim, Dri. Stay afloat. There is much ahead of us.

I nodded as I passed him, heading toward Ronan, who awaited me ten paces up the path and still seething. Niero was right. If I took on the twins' grief and Ronan's rage and Azarel's bitterness and Bellona's distrust and whatever else everyone was feeling, it would be too much. For the first time, I thought about my ability to cast emotion into another. I was born to acknowledge emotions. Could I not use that for healing emotions, healing a person's heart, much like Tressa healed the body? If I could do that, could I not persuade Kapriel and each of the Ailith to give Keallach another chance?

If he was innocent.

But what if he isn't innocent? Niero asked me.

I scowled. *Just because you can read my thoughts doesn't mean you should.*

Agreed. But just because you can cast emotion doesn't mean you should.

He was quiet then, which suited me. I fell into step behind Ronan, who hiked up the trail with the longest strides possible, which he knew bothered me since it meant I had to practically run to keep up. After a while, I let the distance spread between us, forcing him to slow down if he wanted to stay beside me. He could be angry. I understood his frustration, his distrust. But he didn't have to take it out on me.

After a while, I caught up with him again. "I understand why you're so frustrated," I said, reaching out and casting a sense of calm into him.

He shook off my touch. "Don't do that," he said. "Not now. It feels manipulative."

"I'm not trying to manipulate you," I said. "I'm just trying to calm you down enough for us to talk." But Niero's words came back to me. Maybe he was right. It wasn't really fair for me to use my gift on a fellow Ailith.

"I want you to stay away from him, Dri. As far as possible. I just don't trust him." He looked over his shoulder, down the trail.

"I know. I will. Until we all are fully satisfied, I promise to be with him only when we're in a group. All right?"

Ronan took a deep breath and offered me his hand. "All right."

I slipped my hand into his, and we resumed our hike up the trail. It wasn't long before we knew that the Aravanders were with us, edging nearer, so stealthy that we could not yet see them. They were the perfect guardians for the Valley, able to easily get close enough to discern enemy from friend.

"Take your ease, guardians!" Bellona yelled from fifty paces ahead. "We are the Ailith, returning home. Bellona and Vidar here!"

"Killian and Tressa here, along with Chaza'el!" shouted Killian from behind them.

"Ronan and Andriana here!" Ronan called.

"Niero, Azarel, Kapriel, and our prisoner here!" Niero finished.

I frowned that he did not name Keallach and went so far as to call him a prisoner. But it was probably for the best. Keallach was no favorite among the Aravanders, particularly after their recent losses north of Pacifica. They might string him from a tree or shoot him through with arrows before we had half a breath to intervene. Thankfully, the dark of night would keep them from recognizing Kapriel's twin. It was best to wait until morning to reveal him so we could address the issue with the elders and the Community at large.

But by the time we reached the Citadel, I knew there would be no waiting until morning.

CHAPTER 23

RONAN

As soon as we got to the Citadel and I saw Dri safely to our room, I paced by the window. "Why don't we each grab a sauna or shower and a change of clothes before dinner?"

She narrowed her eyes at me. "Ronan, where are you really going?"

"I just need to see to some things," I mumbled, already turning toward the door, working on concentrating on nothing but feelings of peace and tranquility, trying to block her attempt to read me.

"See to *Keallach*, you mean," she said, moving toward me. "Let me come with you."

"No, Dri. I need to handle this alone. I want you to stay away from him. At least until we decide what is going on. Let me do some fact-finding, all right? At least for tonight. I promise I'll report everything I learn. And I promise not to harm him. Yet."

She put her hand on my chest and looked up into my eyes for a long moment. "All right," she said softly. "But please . . . don't hold anything back from me. I remain separate for your sake, and to honor your request."

"Thank you," I said, my voice coming out a little strangled. I knew Dri didn't understand why I was so angry and agitated with her, but she'd just have to wait to work things out with me. There was a fairly large part of me that wanted to beat the truth from Keallach's lips.

She tilted her head up, and I bent to give her a quick kiss. But it was clear to both of us that my mind and heart were not focused on her.

I doubled back and fairly sprinted down the hall and through the tunnel, emerging outside beside the boulders. I found them down below, Niero holding one of Keallach's elbows, Killian holding the other, and facing four of the elders. Citadel guards encircled them, all carrying torches. Four Aravander archers were at intervals too, each with an arrow nocked. It made sense that he'd chosen Killian to assist him and sent the others inside. He'd suffered the least when it came to Pacifica's *emperor*, our *brother*. My mind practically spat out the names, and Niero's dark eyes shifted to me for a moment.

"I still don't understand why you've brought him here, to our very door," Cornelius said, his voice tremulous.

"We had no choice," Niero said. "He met us on the path at the mouth of the Valley. We could either kill him, bring him along, or let him follow. We thought it best if we kept an eye on him."

"Father, I am here, begging for mercy," Keallach said. "I know I do not deserve it and—"

Cornelius lifted his age-spotted hand to stop him. He leaned close to his face. "Your words mean nothing to us, serpent-eater."

I think I took my first breath. Finally, someone was going to put a stop to this madness and send him away.

The elder circled Keallach and his captors, slowly, his watery eyes never leaving our adversary. When he had completed his circle, he clasped his hands, bowed his head, and stood silent. The other elders did the same, understanding what he was after. After a moment, he lifted his chin and looked to Niero. "What do you propose we do with him, my son?"

"Leave him out here, secured and under guard," Niero said. "I will stay too, on guard, to make certain he doesn't use any of his gifting to make his way out."

"You are immune to his sorcery?"

"It isn't sorcery—" Keallach began.

"Sethos has warped what was given to you by the Maker into something foul indeed," seethed the elder, getting nose to nose with him. "If that isn't sorcery, I know not what is."

"But that's why I'm here, Father," Keallach returned, lifting his brows, suddenly looking younger. "To seek your assistance. I want to be free of him—every bit of him. I need your prayers, the Maker's cleansing. Healing. Can you not aid me in that endeavor?"

His words brought Cornelius up short.

The old man lifted his chin and stared at Keallach, unblinking. He glanced to the other elders, silently seeking input, but they too remained silent. "Bind him, hand and foot, to the biggest tree about. Keep him under guard through the night. We shall seek the Maker's guidance in this and make our determination as to what to do come morn."

Cornelius looked to Keallach, then to the Aravander leader on his left. "Summon your people. Establish the series of new posts we discussed earlier. I don't want any further surprises."

The Aravander inclined his head, accepting the assignment, and turned on his heel, slipping into the darkness of the forest.

"We are prepared for attack, come this night or any night this Hoarfrost, or next Harvest, or the next. Tonight, we rest and seek the Maker's guidance," Cornelius repeated, and then he left the circle, the matter clearly settled for him for now.

The others followed him, leaving Keallach alone with me, Killian, Niero, eight Citadel guards, and three Aravanders. Keallach lifted one brow. "Fourteen men to guard me?"

"We are aware of what you can do," I said.

He eyed me. "Listen, Ronan. I made some mistakes with Andriana . . ."

It was the only opening I needed. I let out a growl and tackled him to the ground, tearing his arms from Killian and Niero. I managed to punch him twice before my brothers lifted me away from him. Two Citadel guards moved in to help Keallach back to his feet. He sat up, wiping blood from the corner of his lip with the back of his hand and staring at me. "I deserved that."

"That and more," I spat, trying to wrench away from Killian and Niero. But they held firm.

Keallach got to his feet and stared at me. "So this hatred boils down to my feelings for Andriana? Or something else?"

"There are many reasons that drive my hatred for you," I ground out.

"But mostly it's about Dri," he said gently. The Citadel guards began to pull him around, heading toward the old grove of trees, but he struggled against them. "Please, Niero. Ronan and I need to have this out."

The guards paused, and Niero gave a wave of assent. "Release him," he said. And at the same time, he and Killian let go of me. Again, I didn't wait. I charged, driving into Keallach, finding satisfaction in hearing his soft groan as my shoulder met his belly. We went to the ground, and again I pelted him across the mouth, and again, until I saw his hands were raised on either side of his head in a position of surrender. I paused, my fist hovering midair, panting as I fought to make out his words. "Mercy, brother, mercy," he was repeating. His teeth were ghoulish, stained red, and I hated him—hated him with everything in me—but I couldn't continue to beat him if he didn't come back at me.

I grimaced and groaned before grabbing hold of his shirt and lifting him to his feet. Then I drove him back into the nearest tree, slamming him into it. His head whipped back and forward, and his eyelids lowered, hooding the orbs so hauntingly like Kapriel's. "What . . . is . . . your . . . game?" I grit out, my face almost upon his.

His eyes cleared, and he looked back to me. "There is no game, brother. It is as I've said. I shall bring no further harm to you and yours. I only aim to help you."

My fists twisted in the fabric of his shirt, and I lifted him to his toes.

"Ronan," Niero said, warning in his tone. But I ignored him.

"Brother," Keallach said, swallowing hard, struggling for air.

"Stop calling me that," I cried, throwing him to one side.

He skidded through pine needles and cones and underbrush, took a deep breath, and then lifted himself up and turned to sit, remaining down. He'd hit a rock or something. There was a new gash on his cheek, streaming red blood, and for the first time I felt a pang of regret. *But Andriana,* I reminded myself. *Think of all he did—and tried to do—with Andriana!*

"Think on the Maker's ways, Ronan," Niero said. "Not on our own ways. Not on Keallach's ways."

"Stay out of my head, Niero," I said.

I stared hard at Keallach. "Andriana is mine now. A bound bride. We shared our handfasting vows on the first full moon of Hoarfrost."

Keallach stilled, clearly stunned. "But you . . . you are not—"

"The elders gave us permission," I said, knowing he was going to take issue with the traditional age. "In order to honor what was in our hearts, as well as to protect her from men like you who might choose to try and take advantage of an unclaimed woman."

His eyes shifted back and forth, measuring me, thinking. He swallowed hard. "It was a wise choice." He cocked his head. "And your full matrimonial vows are yet ahead of you?"

I squinted, wondering if I'd misheard him or if there was a note of challenge in his question.

"She is yours, brother," Keallach quickly amended, again lifting hands of surrender to me, as if surprised that I would take offense at the question. "I will not endeavor to do anything to break you apart. I was merely curious."

"Yes," I said. "When we reach our second decade, we intend to exchange our full matrimonial vows."

He nodded, as if this was glad news. News he'd hoped for. "She loves you," he said. "She's always loved you. I am glad the elders blessed your binding."

I put my hands on my hips, still panting from my exertion, and looked to the ground. I had to admit that if I had just met this man today I would not be able to grant him anything but favor, grace. Could it be? Could he truly be changed? Our brother, restored? The elders had searched him and allowed him the night. So had our fellow Ailith. He was right. What drove me was petty jealousy. Fury over boundaries that I felt were mine to hold, and that had been breached. They were human feelings; base, not holy. And I was called to serve a higher power than myself.

I turned partially away, rubbing my neck and closing my eyes, feeling the deep weariness of the last weeks and months suddenly, as if someone had tossed me one of the nearby boulders to bear.

A hand slipped over my shoulder, and I winced but remained where I was. Niero. "Isn't that enough for one night," he stated, more than asked. "Go and rest with Andriana. We shall face this conundrum together, tomorrow."

I eyed him. "You won't leave him? He has the power to—"

"I know, brother. Trust me," he said. And I thought that out of everyone about us, Niero could keep watch on the one I distrusted most.

I nodded, swallowed, and with one more glance at Keallach— beaten and bloody but looking as peaceful as Kapriel—left the circle of light and climbed toward the Citadel.

His expression haunted me. Outwardly, he appeared as innocent as his brother. And that called me to accept him as another of the Ailith . . . long away, now returned home.

But something just wouldn't let me rest.

There wasn't anything specific that I could put my finger on. Only a subtle knowledge that Keallach had somehow, in some way, just won.

CHAPTER 24

KEALLACH

I watched the Knight fade away into the dark, knowing he doubted me, as did the others. But it had all gone as well as I could've possibly hoped.

I was in. Or nearly in.

I had them thinking, wondering if my story could be true.

They were angry, but they'd wanted to believe it. Even my brother . . .

A pang of sorrow went through me. I hated that I was going to hurt Kapriel again, especially since he hadn't immediately turned from me, as I had expected. But he and the others of the Way threatened everything we had worked so long to build.

We'd seen enough from the hidden necklace cameras the defectors carried before they were discovered. Learned enough from bits and pieces of their conversations when the audio worked. Seen firsthand what could happen when a city like

Zanzibar fell. The power among the people of the Way was exploding, and as Sethos put it, the only way to stop them was to destroy them, from the outside in as well as from the inside out.

And now I hovered, just on the edge of breaking inside.

It would be tricky, mastering my emotions so that Dri and Vidar continued to read only what I wanted them to read from me. And to convince Dri of my desire to fully embrace my Call as a Remnant, I had to open my heart fully to these lost brothers and sisters that I knew still drew me from a different angle. As much as I endangered them, they also threatened me, making me truly want to be one with them, forever. I honestly did feel the Call. I did not have to lie when I apologized for ignoring it for so long. It felt exquisitely right to be here, among them.

It just wasn't possible to stay.

And so I would remain, I decided, tied up, with guards all around me. I would balance on this high wire until I could see a way to quell the rebellion and make as many of us as possible one within the empire.

If I could do this—just manage to convince them to fully take me into their fold—I might escape with much more than I had ever lost.

ANDRIANA

I think I spent half the night trying to think my way through the Keallach situation. But I tried to remain still and not toss and turn, fearful that I'd awaken my finally dozing husband. Ronan's arm was flopped over the side of his cot, but his lips were together, rather than slack, telling me that he was asleep, but barely. I stared over at him, at the way his dark hair draped over one brow and waved across his ears and neck, and how the candle he'd insisted we kept lit this night caused the angles of his cheek and jaw to cast deep shadows on the far wall. I loved him. With everything in me, I loved him. I would never let anything—or anyone—get between us. Didn't he know that?

I closed my eyes and willed assurance into Ronan. Love. Affection. Dedication. Loyalty. Commitment. I prayed he would dream of me, feeling all of those good, solid feelings. Moments later, his breath became deeper, more rhythmic and settled. It soothed me, too, to think on such things, and gradually I settled into slumber at last.

It seemed just moments later that the alarm bells began ringing.

Ronan and I sat up, together, flinging back our blankets and blinking heavily as we heard shouts from far away and boots running down the corridors. "Everyone! To your positions and fully armed! Attack! We are under attack! This is not a drill!" yelled a boy as he ran by, repeating it over and over, his voice growing dim as he receded down the hall.

Someone rapped at our door. "Dri? Ronan?" Bellona cried.

"Coming!" I shouted, pulling on my boots as Ronan pulled a sweater over his head. "Meet you outside!"

"Got it!" she called.

Hurriedly, we finished dressing and took up our weapons, running out the door, not bothering to shut it. We ran down the corridor, to the main hallway, and down the tunnel, making our way outdoors.

In the early hours of morning, it seemed like utter chaos outside. Torches streamed by, held by groups of Aravanders and Drifters and Valley-dwellers alike. Everyone surged west, toward the mouth of the Valley. I realized that they all had stations, positions they were to occupy. But where were we to go? Where were the other Ailith?

Ronan seemed to wonder the same thing at the same time. He reached out to stop a passing Aravander female, fearsomely tall and strong. "Where are you going?"

"To stop the interlopers," she said, pulling up the strap of her quiver. "They drove us from our land, but we will stop them here."

I heard the curious sound, then, in the distance. A *chop-chop-chop* rending the air, like we'd never heard before. "Ronan, what is that?"

"Ronan! Dri!" Bellona called, and we saw her then on an outcropping to our left with most of the others with her. Ronan took my hand, and we climbed upward until we found ourselves in a small clearing with a defensible rim of stone all around, three Citadel guards peering outward over their guns, as if they might be able to see through the near-dark.

"Where is Keallach?" Ronan cried when we saw that he wasn't with Killian and Niero.

"Still tied below!" Niero muttered, dismissing his concern. "We have bigger issues at the moment."

Ronan bit his lip, and I knew his wariness as my own. But he said nothing further.

Niero bent and drew in the dirt at our feet. "This is the Valley," he said, hurriedly drawing two lines that widened where we were and narrowed at the far end, near the Desert. "Last night, Pacificans cut down a couple hundred pilgrims from Zanzibar who were following us home, and infiltrated the Valley. We've lost our front two guard posts, and the Aravanders have all fallen back to about here," he said, drawing two lines about halfway up the Valley.

I sucked in my breath, trying to get my mind around his words. They'd "cut down" pilgrims? Meaning, they'd killed them? In the distance, I heard that odd sound again.

Niero met my gaze. "That's the sound of a helicopter."

I gaped at him. A helicopter hadn't been flown since the days of the Great War, at least that we knew of.

"That's what they used to kill all those people," Chaza'el said, eyes wide and haunted. "Shot them from above. They're dead. So many dead . . . men, women, and children," he said, the last word emerging as a whisper. He rubbed his hands down his face, leaving his fingers over his mouth, as if wishing he could forget what he had seen.

"Set that aside for now," Niero said, taking Chaza'el's shoulders in his big hands. "Have you seen anything else? Anything else we can do to turn them back?"

Chaza'el paused, as if searching his mind, but then he shook his head.

Niero turned to Vidar. "What about you? What do you sense? Are these just Pacificans coming our way, or are they Sheolite too?"

"Sheolites among them, for sure," Vidar said grimly. "And more . . ."

He glanced my way, and I knew. Trackers. Wraiths. I took a deep breath, steeling myself.

Together, we ran down the trail. Niero shouted over his shoulder, "Stay together! Fight together! Remember that you are strongest together!"

I looked back, noticing that every alcove among the rocks was now filled with armed men and women ready to defend the Citadel. I knew that inside they were rolling the heavy stones across and barricading the tunnel, making it impossible for anyone from the outside to enter without assistance. This both heartened me—the hundreds inside would remain safe, regardless of what we faced—and terrified me. It felt like we were locked out of the only secure place I knew.

Under the wing of the Maker is your strongest place to be, Niero silently said to me. *We are not alone.*

Agreed, I responded ruefully. He was right, of course. Why did I always resort to fear and trembling? I had to be strong in the One who had formed me. . . who had marked me as Ailith . . . who had known this day was coming from the start. Praise. Praise was what always got my head and heart in order when I started to crumble.

I thanked the Maker that we were together. I thought on Niero's words—together, we were a pretty potent force. And then I thanked the Maker that dawn was breaking, that we didn't have to combat our enemy in the dark of night. But it was early yet. The shadows were deep. My ears pulsed as I tried to hear anything, sense anything ahead of us. But all I heard were our footfalls, our combined labored breathing, and in the near distance now, the helicopter.

We passed Keallach, on his feet and straining against the ropes that held him. "Let me come with you! I can help!"

"Help?" Ronan cried over his shoulder. "You are the one who brought them here!"

"I didn't! Don't you see? Sethos and the Council now count me as a traitor!" he called, but we didn't respond. I knew it was probably unfair to put the blame entirely upon him, that our enemies were here because of our success in Zanzibar—we were getting too strong, drawing too many to our side—but I remained silent.

Farther down the path, we passed people heading toward the Citadel, already carrying wounded across their shoulders back toward safety. *The injured from the front posts.* Tressa moved among them, praying healing over each of them. Killian pulled arrows from the shoulders of two and bent to dig out a bullet from one man's thigh with the tip of his knife, then set to bandaging it. I tensed. We were clearly getting closer. Two groups of Aravanders met up with us: one with eight fighters and another with twelve. We paused to catch our breath and hear their reports.

"They're at least a hundred strong," said Jezre, the Aravander queen's husband. "They've fanned out in groups of three, flushing everyone inward to the Citadel, thwarting our efforts to get around them and trap them between us. That helicopter," he said, tilting his head toward the Valley mouth, "accompanies them, sweeping from one edge of the Valley to the next. We are doing our best to kill the people manning the guns aboard her but have failed so far. Those guns—they're more powerful than anything even the Drifters have. And they appear to have endless rounds of ammunition."

"Give me a shot," Vidar said, pulling his machine gun around his side. "I will take them out."

"Or me," Kapriel said, stepping forward. Azarel was with him. He closed his eyes and bowed his head, his hands in fists. At each side of the Valley, over the mountains, I saw clouds beginning to swirl and felt the first tug of real hope. Sethos thought he had the advantage, with his flying machine, but we had the means to take it down, one way or another.

A group of Drifters came over the hill before us, hauling wounded between them and over their shoulders. There was blood, so much blood, everywhere. Tressa moved toward them, touching every one she could, and we watched each of them regain consciousness, blinking heavily. But after so much blood loss, they'd need more time to recover. "Take them toward the Citadel," Niero said. "The passage is closed, but we'll want to get them inside as soon as it's safe to open it again."

"They'll be upon you soon," a Drifter grunted, picking up his friend again. "Take defensive positions!"

We looked about. "There!" Niero said, pointing to an out-cropping of rock that would give us protection on three sides. "Half of you there, and the rest among the trees to the far side. If it feels like we cannot push them back, retreat to the boulders beside the Citadel. Do you understand me?"

We all nodded, already in motion. We knew that if we had to we could get to the Citadel and climb ropes that those above would cast down for us. But that would be our very last resort. Without a good lead, they'd simply shoot us as we climbed.

Kapriel went to the outcropping with Vidar and Bellona, Azarel, Killian, and Tressa. Niero, Chaza'el, Ronan, and I moved out together, our task to flush groups from the trees toward the others, where they could take them down.

Niero was moving toward the right when Chaza'el whispered hoarsely, "Not over there," and I could see his eyes were wide and dilated. "That will be deadly. This way."

We followed him, partially hunched over, readying ourselves to roll left or right to avoid any arrows or bullets coming our way. We could hear the helicopter, its ominous sound edging closer and closer from our right. Above the trees, the clouds were building, deepening, darkening, and swirling. Lightning flashed. Thunder rumbled. If we could just buy Kapriel a bit more time, the helicopter would be no match for him.

The bullets strafed our path, coming right between Ronan and me, an inch away from my boot. I rolled left and Ronan came with me, deeper into the trees. Niero and Chaza'el went right, just as the helicopter emerged above us. My eyes searched the dense underbrush, looking for a telltale sign of red or gray among the dark green. The man had said the helicopter was providing cover for the fighters moving inward, so they had to be here. Had to be. Why couldn't I see them? Sense them?

We dodged around a huge tree and under the sheltering leaves of a massive patch of giant fern, praying it would shield us from the helicopter moving slowly above us. The gusts cast down from the helicopter's blades sent the tree branches swaying, as well as the leaves above us. Belatedly, we saw we would be exposed, if we hadn't been already.

"Move, Dri!" Ronan cried, just as gunfire rained down on us from above. He grabbed my hand and fairly wrenched me around the trunk of the tree as bullets pelted the other side, landing in the soft, fleshy wood. Another gun sounded—likely Vidar's—and the helicopter rotated to return fire. We heard the thrum of bowstrings—perhaps ten at once—and saw a volley of arrows fly toward the open space of the helicopter. We heard a shout, and the pilot tried to move away. I knew at least some arrows had entered the compartment. And then Vidar opened fire again.

"Dri," Ronan growled. I looked his way and followed his gaze. Two Sheolites were on our left and two to our right. At the center were two more.

Niero and Chaza'el charged the two Sheolites on the right flank, and we went after those on the left, pulling our swords as we went, glad they didn't appear to be armed with guns. But we knew the Pacificans would be, and they couldn't be far behind. Ronan reached the men before me, driving back the closest with a roar and strike of his sword then trying to plunge a dagger in the belly of the second. He missed, but I was right on top of him, managing to nick the Sheolite's shoulder with my sword as he spun away. Thunder cracked, making me wince. Winds swirled around us, now from the clouds above as much as from the helicopter, which had moved off and appeared to be solely focused on our companions at the rocky outcropping. Swords clanged as Ronan and his opponent engaged, and steps away, a second Sheolite stepped toward him, and I knew he was in for a serious battle. Chaza'el and Niero engaged their own adversaries. But I stayed focused on the one before me, circling, making sure I had a secure footing before I moved, desperate not to fall. The man was about my size, and strong. He moved in, faster than I anticipated, striking once, twice, three times. I narrowly blocked each blow and waited for my opportunity.

He continued to try and make me circle, hoping that I would trip or give him my own open flank, but I refused him. I feinted left, then left again, then right, and spotted my opportunity. He brought up his sword just a moment late as I brought my own down across his neck, dealing him a blow that would kill him in seconds. I leaped away and dared to glance about, wondering whom I would encounter next and how Ronan fared, when a blinding bolt of lightning came down and struck the helicopter.

I ducked and rotated to my left, sprinting away after seeing the helicopter tilting sideways, the engine faltering. It sounded like it was falling.

It took about five paces before I realized I couldn't see anything, that I was crashing through the brush, blind. *The lightning.*

I cried out, blinking, seeing nothing but white light as the hair on the back of my neck and arms stood on end. "Ronan!" I shouted, reaching out toward where I thought he'd been last. But my shout was lost among the fierce, howling wind and roar of the helicopter, clearly struggling to stay aloft. I crouched, feeling the welcoming ferns and praying that I was somewhat shielded by trees. If my enemies knew I was weakened so . . .

Awful sounds of crunching metal and splintering wood filled my ears. I heard men cry out and scream, from above and below, and covered the back of my neck with my hands, wondering if the helicopter was coming down directly on top of me. I braced for impact. On and on it went, metal sounding as if it was bending, breaking, the *whump-whump-whump* of the blades slowing, cracking against trees. Finally, I heard the machine hit the forest floor and come to a rest. After the cacophony of noise, even the fierce wind sounded like silence.

I held my breath. Seconds later, there was the sound of battle resuming, at least in three locations. Shouts, grunts, and swearing. I blinked and blinked again, praying desperately that my vision would return. Half of me waited for a sword to slice through my neck or belly, or an arrow to pierce my heart. I crouched down, never having felt as vulnerable as this in my entire life. Even when I'd been taken captive by Sethos and Keallach . . . to not be able to see . . .

I squinted, praying the Maker's name over and over, desperately trying to think of his wing covering me. I kept holding my breath, trying to listen, to be able to anticipate and protect myself from others who might be coming after me. This inevitably led me to hyperventilating. Where was Ronan? I didn't dare cry out, in case my enemies were closer than my Knight. But where was he? How far was he from me?

I got even lower, splaying my hands out, reaching, and finding fern stalk after fern stalk. Apparently, I was below the giant fronds, which was probably why I still lived. I vacillated between continuing to move or staying still, praying that no one would come across me, hidden among the forest's deep undergrowth.

Bullets riddled the air, and I put my cheek to the damp soil, listening, listening. I thought of other ways we listened, saw and remembered seeing angels alongside Vidar, as well as demons, wraiths. I dug my fingers into the loamy earth, reaching for a connection with Vidar, desperate to see what he could. For a moment, I could see nothing but the ghostly white blur that had filled my eyes since the lightning struck, but then shapes began to take form . . . all dark.

I held my breath, nearly passing out as one black form after another flashed before my blind eyes. At first I thought them all Sheolite, or wraiths, or demons in human form. But gradually, I began to note nuances between them. There were angels and demons among the forest for certain—I could see them all in fuzzy silhouette—but those of the Dark had grotesque growths along their necks and upper backs, like mushrooms growing among the crevices of trees. When they turned, battling the angelic beings that now ringed me, protecting me, I could clearly make them out.

Gunfire sounded; men cried out. Maybe one woman too? I prayed Vidar was getting closer to me, noting the presence of heavenly forces here. Wouldn't he be drawn to them? A shiver ran across my shoulders, and I fought the urge to stand up, to edge closer to the heavenly soldiers that battled for my safety. But I knew I had to stay engaged in the here and now, the present, the earthly.

Because my earthly adversaries were still numerous.

The trouble was, as I remained hidden from my adversaries, I also remained hidden from my friends. Would the Ailith be able to feel their way toward me?

A roar sounded over the ridge, and I bit my lip until it bled, refusing to cry out, no matter how great my fear. The Pacificans and Sheolites surged as one, their black allies among them. In seconds, I would be overcome.

"Dri!" I heard Ronan call. But he was far away. So far away . . .

I dared not respond.

"Andriana," whispered someone much closer to me. Within ten paces.

"Andriana," he repeated, and then I knew him, both by presence and voice.

"Ke-Keallach?" I choked out in a whisper.

"Over here, behind the tree," he said, his voice barely reaching me. "Come this way."

I paused, considering. Was it a trap? Some trick of the mind?

"I can't," I said, clenching new fistfuls of soil in my palms. "I can't see."

"You can't *see*?"

"The lightning—the helicopter," I whispered. "I'm blind!"

KEALLACH

I paused. *Blind*. She couldn't see. For the moment, a warrior, but completely vulnerable.

I could take her, now. Lead her away from all of this. To safety. I wouldn't have my brother, but at least I'd have Dri. And maybe in time there'd be an opportunity to encourage Kapriel to join us.

Was this it? Truly my only chance to win one of them?

No. It was too soon. And there were things here, among them . . . things of the Ailith and the Community that I so wanted to know.

I stopped short. Things I wanted to know for the good of the empire? Or for me?

The Way was powerful. Being here, among them . . . as much as I wanted Dri, I had to admit, I wanted to be in the Community more. Fully accepted. To know what it meant to be a bonded Remnant, with the ceremonial cuff on my arm . . . and my gifting in full force. I wanted to know what it was to use my gifts as high gifts, rather than the low gifts that Sethos had trained me to use. To know power, as part of the larger Body, rather than in mine alone.

My eyes focused on Dri again, among the ferns. To do this, I'd have to think of her only as my sister, not my love.

My sister. My *sister*.

ANDRIANA

"Keallach?" I whispered, terrified that he'd left me. But I thought I sensed him nearby. Why was he hesitating?

We fell silent. Not ten paces away, men surged past us, closing in on my Ailith kin in the protected alcove. Startled, I found that while I could see nothing else, I seemed to be able to see those of the light and those of the dark, at least in silhouette. *Ironic*, I thought. *In blindness, I see fully for the first time.* Was this what it was like to be Vidar? To have his second sight?

Two turned my way, as if they'd sensed me. I froze.

The two shook their heads and moved on, chasing after the others before them. Had Keallach compelled them onward, away from me?

Sounds of gunfire rattled in the distance. For a moment, the forest grew quiet about us.

Keallach reached me at last, falling to his knees. "Dri?" He took my hand. "Can you really not see?"

"Keallach," I said, confusion warring in my heart. It was such a relief to not be alone, but of all the people who might've come to my aid— "How did you get free?"

"We have bigger things to worry about," he said, squeezing my hand harder. I heard him turn, as if looking about and scouting an escape route.

"Tell me!" I insisted in a frantic whisper. "How did you get free?"

I felt his agitation, then his anger at me questioning him. "I willed a guard to do so. When I saw the helicopter come down, yet heard the ongoing battle, I couldn't bear it any longer. I had to come to your aid. All of you," he added hurriedly.

"And yet it is me you are with," I said dully.

"I found you first. And you're alone. The others have one another."

"And Ronan?" I asked tightly.

"He's alive. Searching for you. But Niero dragged him off, narrowly keeping him from becoming surrounded."

"Can you help get me back to the others? There will be more Pacificans and Sheolites coming this way. If we can find Tressa, maybe she can heal me." Again, I waited and wondered if this would be when he confessed, told me the truth—that this was all a ruse and he was dragging me back to Palace Pacifica.

"We'll find her, Dri," he said, his tone bearing an oath.

I swallowed my surprise.

"Come," he said, gripping my hand, helping me rise. "It's good timing now. Hurry."

I hesitated.

"Dri? Come on! We have to move!"

Still, I waited. And I felt like everything came to a standstill about me.

As if this was a moment of decision I'd remember forever.

"Keallach . . ." I said breathlessly, looking up and about at the angels with their backs to us and then to this . . . brother. They'd *let* him in. Let him come beside me. "The truth. You must tell me the truth." I covered his hand with my other, focusing everything on reading him. "Did you really come to answer the Call? After all this time? Have you really turned away from everything—and everyone—in Pacifica?" A shiver ran down my neck remembering Lord Jala, Fenris, and the others.

He took a deep breath. His grip changed as his hand settled more fully between mine, and then he laid his other on top. "Search me, Dri," he said urgently. "*Know* me. You tell me if I am your brother or your enemy."

I did, then. I reached out, and in that moment, it was as if we were in the old days and I could give him an X-ray, from head to toe, and see his emotions on that film. And what I saw was commitment. Connection. Love. Hope. Passion.

I took another breath. And then I squeezed his hand.

"Get me to Tressa, Keallach," I said.

"I will," he promised.

CHAPTER 25

ANDRIANA

The storm was still swirling overhead. I could smell the mingled aroma of rain and lightning on the wind, but no rain fell. The winds were fierce, though, threatening at times to tear Keallach and me apart and making it hard to breathe. Clearly, Kapriel was using it as a weapon against those who closed in on the Ailith at the outcropping, sending gales in every direction. When I fell for the third time, Keallach grabbed hold of me and pulled me close, shouting in my ear. "It's no use! We can't get to them this way! We have to go around!"

I nodded and followed him, glad to be able to take a breath when we gained some distance. "Can you get me to Ronan, at least?" I asked. "He'll endanger himself looking for me."

Keallach hesitated. "Do you sense that, over there where they are? That's them, isn't it?"

I turned and looked over my shoulder. I still could only see a pearlescent landscape, a blank page, with no bodies—angelic or demonic—in view. But that wasn't what he meant. He meant I could sense the Ailith, as he could too. And he was right. In one direction was a fierce concentration of them—likely Kapriel and the rest—and in the other was likely Ronan, Niero, and Chaza'el. The trouble was that there were also strong numbers of our adversaries in both directions.

"I know that you came out here to fight," Keallach said, pushing hair back from my face.

I stiffened at his touch, and he dropped his hand.

"But Ronan would want you safe. And to trudge into either of those battles would do nothing but endanger you. You bear a weakness in feeling everyone's emotions as your own—you've learned to deal with that. But are you really ready to go in blind?"

"I don't know," I whispered, utterly confused as to what was wise.

Just thinking about nearing our enemies felt foolish and paralyzing. I'd come so close to being killed in the woods. If it hadn't been for Keallach . . .

"You're trembling," he said, his voice tender. Compassion swirled through him, and sensing that in him made me want to cry. "Come here," he said, pulling me close.

I entered the circle of his arms reluctantly, stiffly, but gradually relaxed. He stood with his back to the full force of the wind, and we leaned against a tree. Protected on two sides, I felt the first measure of hope I'd felt in some time.

"Are you cold?" he asked, rubbing my back a little.

"No," I said, pulling a little away and rubbing my eyes. "It's only this blindness. It's terrifying." I turned and looked outward, willing my vision to return, praying that the Maker would restore it.

I can't fight without sight, Maker.

You are blind? Raniero's voice cut into my mind like a burst of sunlight entering a dark cave. I'd forgotten! Since the accident, I'd forgotten one of the best tools the Maker had given us—this means to communicate.

You have what you need within you, Andriana. It has nothing to do with what your body can or cannot do. Where are you? We'll come to you.

My first thought was panic. Defense. If Niero and Ronan found Keallach with me . . . *I'm safe. I can't see, but I have . . . a guide. Tell Ronan I'm safe. I will meet you at the Citadel.*

Stay where you are. Kapriel is turning the Pacificans back. Together, we are sending the Sheolites away. We'll come for you if you can just remain hidden for a bit longer.

No. I must be away. Someone is with me. He'll get me safely to the Citadel.

He was then silent. Because he was busy killing Sheolites and demons? Dark angels? Were all trackers really dark angels in disguise? Something told me that Sethos would have used his skills of persuasion to bring others along his dark path, and I shivered again.

Keallach moved closer, wrapping me more tightly in his arms. "Dri—"

I squirmed away. "Don't do that. It's too . . . intimate."

I felt his irritation, his frustration, even without touching him.

"I only meant to keep you warm. To comfort you," he said.

"Well . . . don't. Just get me back to the Citadel alive, will you? It's the best thing you can do for me. I think Niero will get Tressa and all the rest of the Ailith back to the fortress as soon as he can."

He paused. He knew what I also knew, that to return was to face judgment for his escape. He would have to admit he had used his gifting—limited as it might be—to bring down his guards in order to do so. Even though he'd used the opportunity to come to our aid, how would the elders react? How would the Ailith respond?

"Come," he said, lacing his fingers around mine. "The faster we can get away from this place, the better. Can you see anything? Anything at all?"

"The spiritual realm, nothing more." I winced, feeling a chill enter my armband.

Keallach paused, contemplating. "That won't help you avoid rocks on the path."

"No, it won't," I said, my heart beginning to pound as I recognized this particular degree of cold.

"Will it help you escape a tracker?" asked a man from above and behind me, startling us both. Keallach whirled, and I could hear the sound of a sword exit its sheath, even as Keallach shoved me behind him.

"Dri, give me your sword," Keallach hissed. "I am unarmed."

"What about two trackers?" asked an idle voice, again, behind and above me.

My heart stopped. I'd know the silky undertones of that voice anywhere.

Sethos.

I could imagine his dark wings, massive and wide, as he descended. His dark eyes, squinting as they focused on me.

Maker! Raniero! Help us! Sethos is here!

I could hear the crack of branches and cones as both dark beings alighted.

"She communicates with our enemy," Sethos sneered. "Stop her from doing so again, would you, my brother? I will address the emperor."

"Get back," Keallach said. "I am no longer one with you. I will not return!"

"Silly boy," Sethos said, clearly advancing upon him from the front. "I ought to kill you for betraying me."

A hand snaked out and grabbed my wrist, wrenching me away from Keallach. It was the other dark one. I screamed. Such frigid cold entered my arms where he gripped me. This was the source of my shivers . . . not terror, not my blindness! The Maker had been trying to warn me, sending my arm cuff into warning chills. The power in Sethos's companion was lethal. I felt as if I was choking, my very insides turning to ice, my lungs crystallizing bit by bit . . .

Dimly, I heard the *whoosh* and *thunk* of a big arrow, then another, and felt my adversary shudder. He'd been hit. But still he held me. Black rage flooded from him, engulfing us both, further choking me. And yet in that moment, I felt the old doorway open. That space that held so much curiosity for me. The space I'd come close to before. Could I dominate it now? Conquer it? I felt dizzy with the rush of promise the thought brought to me.

In my mind, I edged closer to the doorway, feeling the flutter of wings entering and exiting. The darkness was pulling at me, enticing me, wrapping tendrils around my neck, my arms, my back.

I needed no breath. I was beyond breath. Above breath.

I needed no warmth. In this space before me, in the cold, was peace and security. Constancy. Had we had it wrong all this time?

Whispers filled my ears. From far away, I felt my body lurch, hold, and lurch again, but it was as if it was happening to someone else.

This way, this way, this way . . .

Come inside. Come with us. Come. Come. Come.

No, Andriana! Break free. Break free of him! You are nearing the door of death! Turn away, sister. Dig deep. Remember the truth. The truth, Andriana!

Come . . . sister. You are so weary. You've fought for so long. Lay down your sword. Know the security we can offer you.

Truth. Niero's word came back to me. I circled it in my mind, as if it was spelled out in giant, stone letters, and I could run my hands over the T, the R, the U . . .

That is not the way, said the voices, so soothing, so welcoming. Filling my ears. Blocking Niero's. *This way . . .*

But my mind kept turning back to the word that gripped me, as if I were a ship chained to an anchor that both held me captive and kept me safely moored in the harbor. I ran my hands over the next letter in the word I needed . . . desperately needed for some reason. The final T. The H . . . I envisioned *truth* engraved upon rock. Rock. Stone. So much like . . . what? Memory tugged at me and then eluded me, over and over. What was it that I was supposed to remember?

This way. Enter in, sister. This is where you belong. This is where you all belong . . .

It came to me then.

Stone . . . like the Citadel's granite.

The Citadel.

The Community.

The Way.

The *Maker.*

Power surged through me. I turned, took hold of the tracker's wrists, got a foot up against his thigh, then the other against his belly. I bent him in half and then launched him backward, away from me, cutting off his foul, dark funnel and his link to my soul.

I gasped, feeling as if I'd just narrowly escaped drowning and crawling across the forest floor, anxious to put any inch of space I could between me and the dark angel who had almost conquered me. Pinpricks of heat began to poke across the skin of my arms, bringing life back to limbs that felt dead.

Andriana, Niero's thoughts fairly screamed at me. *Chaza'el has seen. Vidar knows. We are coming.*

CHAPTER 26

KEALLACH

I watched with some amazement as the tracker fell to the ground, away from Dri, and she turned and crawled away, her face horribly pale. But she was alive and away from him, which brought me a huge measure of relief.

With Dri a safe distance away, Aravander arrows rained down from the branches above, piercing the tracker's chest again and again, driving him backward, farther away from Dri. But he still managed to keep his feet. And no arrow came in Sethos's direction. Because of me? Was I in the way? Or had Sethos erected some sort of shield of protection around himself that he hadn't thought to offer his companion?

We circled, my old trainer and I. The one who had taught me to wield a sword for the first time. To feint and strike, pierce and block. I'd long been a decent sparring partner for him. But I'd never bested him. We'd parried and practiced for years. We'd even practiced this particular play, preparing to accomplish what we both wanted. And yet . . . now . . . I wasn't sure it was what I wanted at all.

The first arrow struck near him, sticking into a huge pine, bouncing from the reverberation of impact.

Sethos lifted a hand without looking, closed all five fingers around a single point in the air, and then flicked his fingers to one side. An Aravander cried out, rotating several times in the air before landing just steps away from Andriana.

"Come now, Majesty," Sethos said soothingly, playing the part, doing nothing but protecting himself from my wavering sword. "This folly is over," he said. "You tried to join the Remnants and found out what I told you all along—they won't accept you. They left you in chains, vulnerable, even as we swept in, did they not? We can make amends after we put down this Union rebellion together. Look. Andriana is within reach even now. We'll take her with us."

I shivered, feeling the pull of his promises, promises that preyed upon my own desperate hopes. *My sister,* I reminded myself. *My sister.* What would I do for my true sister? What might I have done for my twin? What would that relationship be like now, if I'd chosen a different path long ago and not listened to Sethos? I struck out with renewed vigor, irritated that this rehearsed play now felt desperately wrong. "I am done with you! Done with Pacifica! I am where I belong! I will prove myself to them in time." The words came easily . . . as if I meant them.

His eyes narrowed, and he blocked my fourth strike and turned, easily avoiding my fifth. "Look," he said, nodding over to Andriana, who scrambled through the drifts of rust-colored needles, as if looking for something. "Just say the word, and I shall pick her up and get you both back to safety. All can be as we imagined. With you two united, the entire country is ours. These battles, these deaths, and those to come? They will be over. You can save your precious Remnants—and more."

His words infiltrated my mind, and my heart swayed again, to the other side. Andriana. Together with me. Safety for the rest. Peace. That had been the plan all along. Why must this cursed Call confuse me so much? I wanted to drop my sword and press my hands to the sides of my head.

"I am not going anywhere with you," Andriana said, lifting a bow, one lone arrow nocked across the string. She was trembling, her eyes clearly still blinded, but she cannily pointed it directly at Sethos.

His eyes narrowed as he stared at her. "I thought you could not see," he sniffed.

"My earthly eyes are blinded," she said, "but I can clearly see those of the light . . . as well as those of the dark."

She let loose the arrow.

I agreed with her. We wouldn't go with him. We belonged here. Here.

But neither could I let Sethos die.

I lifted a hand and shoved the arrow from its track through the air, and it swerved to sail beside my trainer's head and past us.

A tiny smile edged the corners of his lips, his thanks silent.

My savage anger returned, and I heaved my sword and struck at him three times in quick succession, driving him backward.

He held my last strike, our blades crossed above our heads. "Are you becoming confused, Majesty?" he whispered, concern knitting his brow. "It was bound to happen, spending time with so many of the enemy these last hours."

His fatherly tone grated against me like tiny pebbles biting into my skin. "Stop it!" I hissed, whirling and striking again, this time with an edge. "Quit working your spell upon me."

"Spell?" he said, pushing away my blade and striking back at me for the first time, squinting at me. "There is nothing happening here that you do not want," he growled so that only I could hear.

"What I want? Or what *you* want?" I whispered back.

He paused. "Remember our plan, Keallach. Stay true. It is for you that I do this. It is you I serve." There was pain, now, in his eyes. That edge of betrayal again, making me falter. Was I born to disappoint everyone around me?

I pushed Dri's next arrow aside as well.

"Keallach!" she cried. "Did you do that?"

"I will take care of him," I grunted, driving Sethos backward. His red cape got tangled between his legs, and he narrowly kept from falling by dodging right, pushing off a tree, and wheeling to my other side.

"She can be your bride," Sethos said lowly, his soothing tone back in place. "Isn't that what you've wanted most? One of the Remnants at your side, forever?"

How many times had he placated me, persuaded me, with that tone?

"She is Ronan's bride." I said half-heartedly. But in saying it, I found a bit of strength. And as I moved forward, against him, more strength welled up within me. Surged within me. This was the right way.

He had confused me. Mastered me. But the Maker was fighting back . . . reclaiming me. Power ran through every muscle and sinew of my body. I was faster than ever before. Stronger.

"Majesty," Sethos bit out when I nicked his neck. His eyes narrowed. "*Majesty* . . ."

But never had my feet felt more grounded. Never had my energy remained true. Never had my eyes been more quick, my movements more fluid. Was this what it felt like to fight for the One who had created me?

"She is not to be mine, Sethos," I said, striking again and again. "She is my Remnant sister, nothing more."

Sethos let out an unearthly screech, breaking up my holy rhythm. He seized upon my momentary confusion to leap forward, pressing me backward until my boot heel caught on a log and I stumbled. He leaped and sent me sprawling, my sword flying from my hand. He grabbed hold of my collar and twisted it until I couldn't breathe. "You *fool*," he said. "She is handfasted, not bound by forever vows. I doubt they've even——"

An arrow thrust through his back, the bloody tip exiting his chest. Then another. His face turned into a frightening grimace, then pure rage, and he flung me back to the ground and straightened, breaking the tip off the first arrow as he did so, then wrenching it through as he turned. I gaped at his strength, his tenacity, even wounded. And I faltered, wondering if I'd ever escape him, ever be free of the many bindings he had around my mind and my heart.

He was heading toward Dri. And while she should have turned and run, she kept drawing one arrow after another, driving them into Sethos.

But then I saw the others had arrived. Raniero, fully revealed in angelic form, landed to Dri's left, sword in hand. Another man, equally as strong and regal, stood on her right. Still others appeared, and interspersed between them all were the Remnants and their Knights of the Last Order.

Sneering, Sethos turned slowly, still on his feet with more than eight arrows through his chest. I looked for the other tracker, suddenly terrified that he neared me or one of my Ailith kin, but he'd disappeared.

When Sethos completed his turn, he stared straight at Raniero.

"This is not over."

"No!" Niero cried, racing toward him, all sinew and bulging muscle and wide wing.

But by the time he reached the center of the circle, Sethos was gone, leaving only his red robe behind.

CHAPTER 27

ANDRIANA

I could feel the collective awe among my fellow Ailith as we watched one of Raniero's angelic companions shoot into the sky, chasing after Sethos. I could see both as streaks above me, flying faster than any bird or drone or even the helicopter.

"Whoa," Vidar said beside me, "if you could've seen that . . ."

"I did," I said, turning toward him. He was but a light silhouette to me, but I knew him, clearly.

"You saw that?" he said. "Two streaks in the sky?"

"Yes! It's all I *can* see right now. Is that the kind of thing you see all the time?"

"All the time. Lately, it seems like whenever I close my eyes, I see everyone as either light or dark."

"Vidar," I said, reaching out to touch his arm. Knowing he wasn't understanding yet. "That's what I see too."

"You do?"

I nodded.

He quieted as the others gathered, all talking at once. "So tell me, Dri," he said. "What do you see when you look toward Keallach?"

I turned and gazed in Keallach's direction, where he was facing off with Killian and Ronan. "His silhouette is light but not nearly as bright as yours, or any of the Ailith."

"Right," Vidar muttered, taking me by the hand. "That's what I'd call spiritual confusion. The guy isn't fully swayed, one way or another, despite what he says. But maybe he can't be if we don't welcome him in? I mean, how can a man join a family if the family keeps him standing outside in the rain?"

I thought about that. "It could be."

"So what happened to your eyes?"

"The lightning," I said. "When it struck the helicopter, I was very close and staring right up at it."

Tressa was there, then, reaching up to touch my face. "Dri?"

"Tressa," I breathed out in relief, hope rising within me. Vidar stepped aside so Tressa could begin her work. She helped me sit and then tilted my head up, clearly examining me, then she bent her head, as if listening. I felt the quickening of her pulse and the pleasure that shot through her as she heard from her Maker, and I had no choice but to smile along with her. But if she heard something audible from him, I couldn't make that out.

"So . . ." I said hesitantly, willing myself not to cry. "How bad is it? Am I to be healed?"

"He's already begun his good work," she said, laying gentle fingertips across my eyelids a moment and praying aloud. "Now come back to the Citadel. I'll see to you further, and you should rest. Come morning, we'll pray your vision is back to normal."

"That's a prayer I'd welcome, again and again," I said, accepting her hand and rising. She tucked my hand through the crook of her elbow, and Ronan returned to my other side.

"I could carry you," he half-offered, gruff and irritated. It didn't take my empathic skills to know that it was Keallach's presence that agitated him.

"I don't think you need to bear that particular burden," I said, taking his hand. "Just go slowly."

"Ahh, Dri, you know I would if I had to," he said quietly, pulling me closer for a quick kiss to the side of my head. "I'm so relieved you are all right. That you weren't hurt more in the fight. Or from that helicopter . . ."

"Thanks to Keallach," I said. "He saved me, Ronan."

I felt the tightening in the muscles of his arm. "I'm aware of that."

"He could have forced me away, if that was what he was after," I said. "Between him and Sethos, I wouldn't have had a chance." I pulled him closer. "I think this is the real thing. I think he's been called home at last and he's turning toward the light. But Ronan, Vidar wondered that if we don't *welcome* him, he can only come so far. He's behind us, in so many ways. Think of what our trainer taught us and showed us over the years. Now think of what Sethos taught Keallach. We need to start training his mind . . . and his heart. And the only way to do that is to give him a chance."

"A chance," Ronan repeated, heaving a breath. "Please, let's just get you back to the Citadel. We can deal with *him* tomorrow." With that, he took my arm and turned, swinging me neatly onto his back with my legs wrapped around his waist and my arms across his shoulders. I shrieked at first but then settled in, feeling the great weariness of our battle settle down upon me at last. I realized that, in carrying me, Ronan felt joy and contentment and pride. Security, in certain measure.

I'd let him carry me, I decided, if it only brought out good feelings like that. After the night we'd had, we needed all the good we could gather.

RONAN

I found him the next night in one of the Citadel lookout alcoves. Usually, these carved balconies in the rock face held armed guards. But tonight it was only Keallach, his arms outstretched along the short wall before him, looking over a moonlit valley.

It irritated me that the elders had agreed to let him in, citing his defense of Andriana and his battle against Sethos as evidence enough of his intent.

He'd been quiet and moody all day as the Community tended their wounded and burned their dead. Even now, the acrid scent of charred flesh filled the air.

We'd lost more than forty brothers and sisters. Two of them had been children. The elders had moved everyone into the Citadel, flooding it with people. Only four bands of Aravanders and Drifters remained along the Valley floor, committed to remaining as forward guards and scouts to sound the alarm if our enemies invaded again.

The halls and corridors were packed with hundreds and hundreds of people. It had made me feel claustrophobic as I made my way through the Citadel looking for Keallach. But somehow now, even when I was outside in the relative quiet, I felt equally as pressed—short of breath, confused. My eyes narrowed at Keallach's back. Was it him, somehow manipulating me?

But he glanced over his shoulder, as if sensing my presence, and seemed genuinely surprised. "Ronan," he said, edging to his right, making room for me. "I was just admiring the view."

I stepped forward and looked out over the Valley with him. It was beautiful. A three-quarter moon in a cloudless sky made the river below us a glittering, waving ribbon. Even in the relative dark, I could make out the deep umber and fading gold of trees steadily preparing to molt their leaves. A cold breeze that more than hinted at Hoarfrost rushed through the trees, and I closed my eyes to let the whooshing sound seep into me, reassuring me. It was the song of home, of the Maker on the move, of a hope and a future.

After the day we'd had, it was what I needed most. *Thank you, Maker,* I prayed.

"There is much joy here," Keallach said, eyeing me sidelong for a moment before looking out again. "Even after all you— we—have experienced of late. It's joy that I sense the most. And it seems both oddly timed and yet perfect too, in the midst of everything."

He seemed mystified by this, and I had to think it over a moment before I could respond. Dri's words came back to me. *He's so far behind.* "It's the Community," I said. "Even in sorrow, we have one another. We know morning comes after the night. And we know the Maker has not abandoned us. In those things alone, we have cause to celebrate, to find hope and joy, regardless of what we face."

Keallach was silent for a while, then asked, "How does Andriana fare?"

"She is resting again," I said, trying not to betray how his question rankled me. "Tressa prayed over her and set new poultices across her eyes. She thinks Dri will be much better after another night's rest—she thinks the Maker wants her to rest, and this is how he's seeing it done." I paused, trying to gather myself together to say what I must. "Listen, Keallach, I wanted to thank you. If you hadn't been there, when she was so vulnerable . . ." My voice cracked, and I coughed, embarrassed.

"It's what I would've done for any of you," he said earnestly, "and what I hope, in time, you all would do for me."

When I didn't respond, he turned away and stared back out to the Valley. "I suspect you didn't seek me out to simply express your thanks," he led.

"No."

I took a deep breath. "I suppose I am seeking confirmation. Reassurance that you are here to stay with us. That your time with Sethos last night didn't sway you."

"Weaken my resolve, you mean, to join you."

"That too. Andriana . . ." I paused to choose my words. "After her encounters with Sethos, she's been . . . susceptible, in a way. It's as if he leaves a trapdoor in her mind and heart that can be utilized by the dark long after he leaves."

Keallach nodded. "I know of what you speak. And perhaps it is what leaves me with this lingering sense of separation. It's as if I know I am to be with the Community, but I cannot fully engage. Something holds me back." He paused, looking out to the Valley, thoughtful. "*Sethos* holds me back. I hear his words in my head. Old words, whispered to me over the years, and new words too."

"My trainer always told me that the adversary had no sway in our minds and hearts that we did not allow. My current experiences validate that thought," I said.

Keallach let out a hollow laugh. "Sounds easy. But it is harder than that."

I nodded. "It *is* hard. But it is also simple."

He crossed his arms and turned to look me full in the face. "Explain."

"It is hard, because it essentially means submission to the Maker. As a man, as a Knight, I think we resist this submission. We want to conquer our adversary ourselves. Beat him down." I gestured to the water below us. "Consider the river. If you were a part of it, you could choose to make your own way, on the edges, fighting through rocks and dirt and trees to create your own current. Or you could enter deeper into the center of flow that has already found its path, and follow where it leads. It's working with the current, absorbing and utilizing its power, that makes the difference."

Keallach studied me and nodded. And I didn't need Andriana's gift in order to feel his gratitude, his relief, in comprehending what I was saying. "So simple . . . so terribly simple," he muttered, looking back to the river. "But hard." He let out another half laugh. "I've spent my whole life on the edges of the river. Making my own way. Forcing my own way. Or Sethos's."

"Maybe it's time you give sway to the Maker and discover what peace and joy truly mean. It doesn't mean we don't encounter our share of rapids and waterfalls. But we're always in the river, surrounded by him. And that makes all the difference."

He nodded, smiling with me—and in that moment, I wondered what I was doing, doubted what I was doing—but soon, his eyes narrowed. "Why are you helping me, Ronan?"

I shrugged and shoved my cold hands into my pockets, wondering the same. But after a few seconds, the answer came to me. "Because I am the last one you would have expected, right?"

"Well . . . Kapriel or Azarel and Bellona might have been close."

I smiled at that. "True. But I'm well aware that I have my own unique complaints against you. The Community is only as close as the two farthest individuals allow it to be, and I never wish to be a hindrance to the Community." I glanced in his direction. "And yet there are a couple of things that make me hesitate. As Dri's protector and husband, I want to know you're true to your word, Keallach. That you've left Pacifica and your dreams for her—and *you*— behind. That you can hold to this new path and not be swayed by the nets you still feel bind you—Sethos's nets. But as your brother, I also feel pressed to reach out a hand. To pull you into the current before the moment has passed and you are too far behind to catch up. No matter how much I, as a man, wouldn't mind if you were far in the distance, as far as Dri is concerned."

Keallach laughed, and this time the sound was genuine. "I never expected to hear something so eloquent out of you, Knight."

I grinned. "Believe me, they are not my words. They come from my trainer and the elders of the Citadel, and those who came before them. But I am a good listener, and I am glad to pass along wisdom to another."

Keallach nodded. "You are a good man, Ronan. I'm telling you here and now that I'm here to stay. I will prove myself in time—to you, to Dri, to the other Ailith. The Maker has called me anew."

"Good," I said, measuring him carefully. "But I must know what you feel now for my *wife*, Andriana, specifically."

He eyed me and straightened. "You said it yourself, Ronan. You've won her. You are handfasted and to be formally betrothed five seasons hence. I've put my feelings for her aside. I am now nothing but her brother and she my sister. I swear it to you."

His words seemed true, but there was just a hint of something else beneath them. "You attempted to . . . win such a vow yourself," I said. "From Andriana. Back in Pacifica. You abducted her, held her captive, and then attempted to make her fall in love with you."

"Because of Sethos's insistence." He took a deep breath and rubbed his forehead. "I was not in my right mind. I believe that

Sethos held me spellbound, or something. Pressed me to use my gifting against her, rather than for or with her. It shames me to this day." He gave me a raw, open look, as if he desperately wanted nothing but forgiveness and acceptance.

I felt my resolve and suspicion crumble a bit. "But yesterday . . . Keallach, I heard Sethos mention Dri. What did he say?"

He waved me off. "Idle attempts to lure me to return," he said, grimacing. "He was using everything he could. He knew he was losing me. That I was turning my back on him." He shrugged and shook his head.

"But in mentioning Dri—"

"Look, Ronan," he interrupted, lifting a hand. "Andriana is beautiful, inside and out. I'd be a liar if I didn't admit to finding her attractive. But she is *yours*. She always has been. Even in the palace, when we had time to be alone, I knew it was you she longed for. Never me. The Maker put you two together for more than serving the Way. I will honor that."

I studied him for a long moment. He seemed completely earnest. "So I will ask this of you but once. You are not here to try and get close to her again?"

He tilted his head a bit. "Only as a brother longs for a sister's company. No more than I long for Tressa's. I swear it." He reached out an arm to me and waited.

And after a long moment I took it, accepting his pledge and, in doing so, allowing him past my defense, deeper into the Remnants' circle at last.

KEALLACH

Andriana's Knight left me, and I turned back to the view again, inhaling a deep draught of fresh, Valley air. A tiny grin tugged at the corners of my lips.

They would cave, the Ailith, one by one. Give in to my persistence. Allow me full access in time. I knew it was true.

My mind raced as I thought about Ronan's analogy of the river, because, truly, I felt like I was getting closer and closer to the center's pull. And yet I could not deny the desire to lead a portion of the water away, to forge my own river, to carve new territory from the earth, bring forth new growth, and explore farther, rather than be trapped in an old, tired path not of my own making. Standing here, I felt like I approached a split in the river, and it gave me power to know I had the ability to choose. And that power made me feel stronger than I had in some time.

This wasn't about what the Remnants wanted.

This wasn't about what the Maker wanted.

This wasn't about what Sethos wanted.

This wasn't about Pacifica, or the Trading Union.

This was about me. What I wanted. Solely me.

It niggled at me that I hadn't told anybody how Sethos had so easily found Andriana in Zanzibar, and now here, in the Valley. Of the tracking devices still pinging away like homing devices within her and Kapriel. For the time being, I wanted to know that I could use them myself, if necessary. And as far as we'd planned, Sethos was to leave me for a week or more, to infiltrate deeper. So he and Pacifica would not be an imminent threat, which gave me full sway. I knew I'd given him cause to wonder, the way I'd acted, the things I'd said. But I wagered he'd think he could win me back on a moment's notice.

But he'd be surprised if he tried.

Because this is about me, and what I want now, I repeated to myself. *About how I fully come into my own. Into my own power. Me.*

CHAPTER 28

KEALLACH

The next morning, I finished my breakfast, ignoring the fact that no one spoke to me or sat beside me, then I watched as the Ailith rose to follow Niero, never looking in my direction. I followed Andriana with my eyes for but a moment—just long enough to tell that her vision seemed perfectly normal now— then looked away before Ronan could catch my wondering glance. At the doorway, Niero turned and watched them file past, then stared over at me. He grabbed Kapriel's arm, said something in his ear, and I saw my brother hesitate and then nod once.

I wiped my mouth and returned Niero's gaze, trying not to blink. He'd been revealed as both man and angel. Could he discern my inner thoughts?

I concentrated on what I knew he'd approve of within me, what I honestly felt anyway. I wanted to be one with the Ailith. To take my place among the Remnants. To know what it was to be in the Community—fully a part of it. Maybe it was even more than I dreamed. Maybe it was all I needed, deep within. Who knew? Maybe it'd be enough for me to turn away from Pacifica forever. I was open-minded enough to consider it.

I just needed a chance. A chance to see. A chance to try.

Others around me had fallen silent, waiting and watching.

Give me a chance, Niero. Just one.

I wanted to will him to obey me, as I willed others to act. But since the night of the attack, I had not used my lower gift. I'd sworn to Niero that I wouldn't. *"Not until the day you or a trainer or another teaches me how to make it a higher gift again,"* I'd promised.

His lips parted, and I held my breath. The moment was finally here. I exalted in it.

But then Niero clamped his lips shut and turned away, disappearing through the arched doorway.

Stubbornly, I grabbed my plate, took it to the dish bin, tossed it in—ignoring the cracking sound—and followed him out. *No one left me behind. No one refused me. I was the—*

I caught myself at the doorway. Grabbed hold of it, as if to physically restrain myself.

Here in the Valley, I was nothing more than anyone in the room. I glanced over my shoulder and saw that many stared after me. Some mocked, some appeared like they felt sorry for me, and others looked upon me in open distaste. I supposed that made sense; many blamed me for the pain they suffered. I was the scapegoat for their hatred.

I wrenched away and strode down the hall toward my quarters, turned the corner at the far end, and came up short.

Kapriel was leaning against the wall, head down as if praying, arms folded.

I stepped closer to him, and he winced.

I stilled, waiting.

Slowly, my brother opened his eyes and looked into mine. "He said it was up to me. Whether or not I let you train with us today."

His hesitation told me all I needed to know. "Don't worry about it," I said, starting to walk again. "I already know the answer. This place is full of hypocrites," I said, throwing up my hands. "They say they believe in the ways of the Maker, of the Way itself. Of love, and peace, and forgiveness, but do I see any of that?"

He followed behind me, eventually catching my stride. "You and your people have kidnapped and enslaved and oppressed and dominated ours for years," he said. "Did you really think you could just come in here and all would be well? They're wary. We're all wary! And for good reason."

I turned and faced him. "For how long, Kapriel? We're in the middle of a battle with Pacifica, a battle about to become a war, and I've just switched sides. Thrown it all over to be a part of this," I said, gesturing at the rock walls. I took a deep breath and pinched the bridge of my nose, then put my hands on my hips and looked him in the eye again. "I threw it all away, Kapriel, so I could be a part of *your* life again. Part of the family that is the Ailith. I know I made horrific decisions, made terrible mistakes," I said. "But I was only a kid. Please," I said, reaching out to him, but he edged away from my touch. "Please. Niero's right. It's your place to decide if I should be officially allowed in or escorted to the desert to be abandoned there. Of all people, it's your place. But Kapriel . . . I'm begging you to forgive me."

I swallowed hard, remembering the day our parents died. The day our Knights died. The numbing horror of death upon death of people we loved most. The cascading sensation of it all falling away from me, spinning out of control. I pressed the palm of my hand to my head and closed my eyes, wanting to block the memories but now unable to stop them.

It was all there. Present. More vivid. Like I'd never fully remembered it before.

Had I?

Had I?

Mom. Dad. Their blood spreading across the marble floor, their eyes wide yet unseeing.

Kapriel, being led away, his hands tied behind his back. Beseeching me with his eyes that saw all. Trying to make sense of everything that was transpiring around us.

"Not my brother too—"

"It's the only way," Sethos had said. *"The only way for you to rule a kingdom of peace and prosperity."*

But had I known a day of peace since then?

Had I ever appreciated a single portion of the wealth granted me?

It was all so empty . . . so empty.

"Oh, Kapriel," I uttered, sinking to my knees, my legs suddenly weak and wobbly. "What did I do that day? How could I have given up all that mattered?"

It wasn't until I felt his hands on my shoulders and his forehead touching mine that I recognized that tears flowed unabated down my cheeks.

I hadn't cried since the day before it all changed. The day that Sethos found me, weeping in my room, frustrated about my brother's favor with my parents and crying over some injustice. Sethos had grabbed that as a foundation and had built upon it every day forward.

Kapriel's own tears fell upon my cheeks, mingled with mine, and ran down my cheeks and neck. Then he straightened, wiped his eyes and nose, and helped me rise.

Giving me one last, searching look, he uttered a simple sentence. "Come, join your Ailith kin, brother."

I saw them then, gathered at the end of the hall. Every one of the Ailith. Waiting.

My cheeks burned. Had it been their combined power that broke through my walls of false protection and partial memory? My steps weren't as sure now as I walked toward them. I felt weak, vulnerable, exposed. Yet the looks on their faces were more open, cautiously approving, and welcoming than ever before.

As I joined them to leave the Citadel for the day's training, all I could think was, *What just happened to me?*

But all I could feel was brilliant, blinding hope.

ANDRIANA

I was both surprised and utterly moved when Ronan finally told me what he'd done three nights past, as we walked to the dining hall for supper. We were among throngs of people, so his words were brief, but I understood the magnitude of what had occurred, given his fluctuating feelings of caution, elation, and lingering fear. I imagined that if we were to allow Keallach complete access, we'd all be feeling that way for a while. I shook my head, wondering over it. How had the Maker made such a thing possible? And why was I continually surprised by his might and reach?

Niero caught up to us, moving to my other side. "We have new arrivals in the Citadel," he murmured.

"New arrivals?" Ronan squawked, glancing Niero's way as we got jostled about. The passageway was packed with people, all excitedly talking and laughing or grumbling at once. "Where will we put them?"

"Believe it or not, there's still room in the south quadrant. The elders planned this fortress well."

"Thank the Maker," Ronan said. "Where are the new ones from?"

Niero's dark eyes twinkled, and his lips twitched with a smile. "I think I'll let you discover that yourselves."

We finally reached the dining hall, and I took a deep breath, appreciating the cavernous space after the cramped nature of the hallway. Before us were lines of tables and benches and people already busily helping themselves from platters full of food. My eyes widened as I noted chunks of meat on each platter, which people were merrily slicing and serving to others at their tables. By the color and texture, I knew it wasn't mudhorse. And we hadn't had meat in the Community since we arrived home. It was a rare treat before; with so many people here now, it seemed impossible.

We made our way to the front of the room, where we'd become accustomed to eating alongside the elders, all dressed in white. My eyes fell greedily upon the quickly disappearing meat at the center of the table, and my stomach rumbled. It smelled delicious. "Venison?" I asked, finally putting a name to what I'd seen and eaten only once, with Chaza'el's people north of Pacifica.

"Yes," Niero said, eyes sparkling. "Our visitors brought it with them—along with an entire herd of deer. Zulema and her grandson are now discussing with Dagan how they shall encourage breeding and expansion of the herd." He inclined his head toward a table to our right, and I saw the farmer and goatherds excitedly talking while busily stuffing their mouths with food. We also had rice on our table—a rarity we'd only periodically had access to. But we'd learned that Dagan had planted seeds upon his arrival, taking advantage of the last of Harvest's warmth and our wetlands to coax a small crop before snow fell. I let the kernels shift in my mouth before chewing, enjoying the nutty taste.

Vidar and Bellona joined us across the table, and he hooted, eyes wide, as he discovered what was before us. When Niero shared the news with them too, as Ronan cut them both a generous slice, Vidar said, "Who are these newcomers? I believe I must kiss them all on the mouth."

"Not that they'd appreciate that," Bellona said, shoving a bite between her lips.

"I don't know if you can judge such things. You've never kissed me," he said, pretending hurt. "Your own bound husband."

"Nor shall I ever."

"So you say, now. I keep telling you that our handfasting could be so much more."

"Vidar," she growled.

Ronan squeezed my knee under the table, and I shared an intimate smile with him. As much as Bellona and Vidar were bound for protection only, our own promise held the hope of so much more. I couldn't wait for the day when I could give myself to him, holding nothing back. But both of us wanted to wait. To honor the Community's customs and the elders' request that we remain chaste.

Just five seasons away, I thought wistfully, with an inward sigh. I inhaled and caught the scent of Ronan, all clean soap and pine and leather. *That's not helping, Dri,* I told myself, forcing my thoughts to other things.

We had a war to win first. A war to survive. I looked around the table at all the faces I loved most—every one of the Remnants, the Knights, the elders, and at the far end, my parents. If any of them died . . .

That thought snapped me out of any romantic notions.

My eyes slipped back to Keallach, in halting, uneasy conversation with his brother. They were making headway together, but it was painfully slow and awkward. And I didn't blame Kapriel for his caution. As loving and giving as he was inclined to be, his twin had hurt him in horrific ways. Had robbed him of his parents. His throne. His future.

But Keallach was trying so hard. And his total breakdown in the hallway that pivotal day seemed to signal the turning tide or the beginning of something much bigger.

Moreover, it was their mirrored emotion that made me think that the twins might eventually find their way back to each other. *Hope* peeked out from behind the shadowy curtains of fear. That was the chief emotion I sensed from both of them, and that built hope within me too.

A commotion at the entrance gradually drew the attention of everyone in the hall. Eight large men, looking larger in their fur vests, entered the room in pairs. In the back was a couple I didn't know, about my parents' own age.

"Dri," Ronan said, voice strangled, half rising. "*Dri.*"

My eyes focused on the first man's face. The beard had made me pass him over on my first glance, but there was no hiding his identity the second time I saw him. I let out a cry and scrambled off the bench, rounding the table and hurtling myself down the aisle, launching myself into his arms, laughing, laughing so hard I was crying.

He'd bent, arms open, and lifted me, turning me around in a circle as I kissed his cheek and he kissed mine.

It was our trainer.

The man responsible for preparing Ronan and me for all we'd endured and encountered. The man responsible for saving our lives, time and time again.

Ronan grinned and clasped arms with him, but then moved past him. Puzzled, I watched as he went to the couple at the end of the line. The woman put her hand to her mouth, and her eyes streamed with tears.

"His parents," my trainer said, nodding after him. His arm was draped around my shoulders, warm and reassuring, and his joy equaled mine. After my parents and Ronan, and now the Ailith, there was no one more important to me than this man. And I'd been so afraid he'd been killed the night of our Call, the night when our parents and guardians and trainers were supposed to slip away to new communities, in case the Sheolites tracked us to their doors. His arm fell from my shoulders, and he squeezed my hand. "Go to them," he urged me lowly. "I know you must. There will be time enough for us to catch up."

I looked up at his grizzled face. He wasn't handsome. His skin was pockmarked around the new beard, his hair receding. But he was beautiful to me. Always a perfect mix of challenge and encouragement, sometimes pressing me on when necessary, sometimes holding me close and shoring me up. I couldn't wait to find out what these last months had been like for him. But he was right—my place was with Ronan. Meeting my new kin. As part of our safety precautions, I'd never met them, and he'd never met mine until the night he came to claim me.

Feeling unaccountably shy, I eased toward the trio. His father caught sight of me first, and Ronan and his mother parted slightly to welcome me.

"Mother, Father," Ronan said proudly, "I'd like you to meet my Remnant, as well as my handfasted bride, Andriana of the Valley."

His mother sucked in her breath over his words, then hurriedly smiled, as if embarrassed over what might be perceived as a slight. I knew she couldn't be truly pleased over our early vows—she hadn't been here to witness what had necessitated it. So I set it aside as she took my hand in both of hers, raised it to her lips to kiss it, then cupped my cheek. "A daughter," she breathed. "And so beautiful," she said, glancing over her shoulder at Ronan. "Clearly, you have much to tell us."

His father was moving in to greet me too when we heard the first alarm bells. It took a moment to register what we were hearing. Men and women were rising and running to the door before it became clear.

"Attack!" shouted a man at the door. "Attack! Everyone to their stations!"

Ronan took my hand and said to his parents and our trainer, now at his elbow, "Follow me!"

We heard a blast and then felt the repercussion down the passageway as we ran, pausing to reach out and steady ourselves as gravel and dust filtered down around us. Then another blast rang out.

"They're trying to destroy the cavern entrance!" Ronan ground out. He paused to put his parents in our room. "As soon as Dri's parents arrive, close this door and bolt it, understand? It will withstand much," he said, patting the iron door. All the Remnants had reinforced doors to their rooms, which at first I'd thought was overkill. Now, with the enemy potentially at our door, I thought it exceedingly wise.

"What about you?" his mother cried, clinging to his hand.

"We must go to the others," he said. He pulled her close, kissed both her cheeks, and drew away.

"We'll be back," I found myself promising, even though I knew I had no business doing so. "Our reunion has only just begun," I added, forcing a grin. Perhaps a lie was what we both needed in the moment.

"Come, Dri," Ronan urged, pulling me away.

"Wait for my parents before you bar the door!" I cried. "They know to come here!"

His mother and father nodded just as Ronan pulled me around the corner. We met with our trainer in the passage, with the rest of his men hovering over his shoulder. "What is the protocol?" he barked, hearkening me back to countless drills with him in the forest.

"We are to convene with the other Ailith on the third level."

Our trainer turned to his men. "Two of you remain here at the door. See that it is sealed, with all their parents inside, before you leave it. Then go to support those at the Citadel entrance." He turned back to Ronan. "Lead us on."

We ran up circular stairs to the next level, and then the next, pressing our backs to the wall to allow men carrying an injured woman, pierced by bullets to her shoulder and belly, pass us by. Tressa ran after them, with Killian just behind. "We'll meet you there if we can," he called over his shoulder.

As we got nearer to the alcoves that allowed Citadel defenders to fight off attackers, we could hear the thrum of a helicopter—or two?—the constant drum of gunfire, and the dull sound of bullets against stone. My arm cuff sent waves of cold and heat through me. We passed the first alcove and glimpsed men and women hiding behind stone barriers, waiting for the gunfire to abate so they could return fire. I felt their terror and prayed for safety for us all. *Maker. Shield us!*

I wanted to curse the helicopters for the unfair advantage they seemed to give our attackers, the insurmountable strength it felt like they leveraged from it.

In times of stress, rely on what you know to be true, not what you feel, I reminded myself before Niero could when we found him alongside the others. He gave me the slightest nod, clearly approving, and I smiled, feeling ridiculously proud of myself at a moment when I needed to be thinking forward, not back.

But you are thinking forward, he silently whispered to me. *What we learn from the past influences our future.*

Right, I returned, focusing on Keallach and Kapriel, who were laying out a plan on the ground, sketching and taking turns talking. It was wondrous, watching them excitedly work together, their minds seeming to click faster than ours could. Each built upon the other's last thought, forming a plan of counterattack. I tried to swallow, my mouth dry. I felt the growing silence all around among the Ailith, our trainer and his men, and the few elders who had congregated here so far.

Because what we were witnessing was what the Maker had clearly ordained.

Twins, meant to work together. Brothers, meant to rule together.

Because together, they were stronger. Each at his best.

Gradually, they came to the end of their planning and became aware of all of us, looking on in silence. I could read them both, so clearly. Keallach looked up and around at each of us, a tad defensive, as if bracing for reprimands. Kapriel was experiencing an odd mix of excitement, pleasure, and embarrassment. Because his brother proved useful? Because he allowed him in?

Keallach rose slowly and waited for Kapriel to do the same. "Is it a good plan then, brother?" he asked, reaching out an arm.

Kapriel paused. "It's a good plan," he said, pausing for a telling moment before taking his arm. "I mean, if all the rest of the Ailith agree," he added belatedly.

But I knew what my brothers and sisters knew—as Niero knew—that we were destined to follow them, together. As they explained where the helicopters were—two on the broad face of the Citadel wall, one over by the entrance, shooting anything that moved—we agreed that we would once again have to find a way to take them down. I groaned, inwardly. Undoubtedly, that would involve encountering some pretty scary heights. I prayed my part could be played out with my feet on solid ground at all times.

I needn't have worried.

We were heading out, our plan to begin with Kapriel taking down the helicopters by calling upon the wind again, when two bombs entered through two alcoves, one on either side of us. The force of their explosions sent me flying, and I rammed into a wall, my shoulder and temple hitting with such force that I couldn't breathe for long moments after I opened my eyes and fought to see anything in the dust-filled cavern.

The candles had been snuffed out with the explosion. The only light was the dim remains of the day, shining in streams from the alcoves. I could make out bodies. So many bodies.

And then I felt the chill of my arm cuff. The hair on the back of my neck rose.

Sheolites. *Trackers*, I amended in my mind, feeling the pinch of ice-cold that could only mean that dark ones on the level of Sethos and his companions approached.

Some of our Knights were struggling to their feet. Ronan unsheathed his sword, alongside our trainer. Niero already stood, moving forward, a curved blade in either hand. Vidar and Bellona were still trying to rise.

There were sounds of gunfire, but it seemed like it was from a great distance. Or as if I had mounds of gauze in my ears, plugging them up.

"Dri," Keallach said, pulling at my arm and lifting me. "Come on. We have to move."

I allowed him to help me, watching as Kapriel did the same with Chaza'el. There was more machine gunfire. The constant *rat-a-tat-tat* that sounded more like *buh-uh-buh-buh* now in my ears. *The explosion*, I understood dreamily. It had hurt my ears. Muffled them. And my head . . .

"Ow!" Kapriel said as we passed him. He reached for his arm cuff just as I felt the wincing cold too. His wide eyes met mine.

It was worse than it had been in the tunnels of Pacifica. I turned, fumbling for my sword and struggling with the sheath strap that held it in place. My fingers didn't seem to work as terror seized me.

"He's coming," I said to Kapriel.

Keallach paused. "Who?"

Without the arm cuff, he didn't know what we knew. Our enemies had infiltrated the Citadel. They were here. And close. I was sure of it. "Sethos," I said. "And other trackers."

Right then, we saw the light before us cut off repeatedly and heard new gunfire. An arrow shot past us, against the back wall, and splintered. Then another.

"Ronan!" I cried, intending to go after him.

"Dri!" Keallach grabbed hold of my shoulder, stepping before me, protecting me, and trying to see what was happening without putting himself in the line of fire. We heard the clang of swords. The grunts and muttered words of men in battle. My hearing was returning, but with it a terrible ringing . . . and an ache so fierce I fought the urge to sit down and cradle my head between my hands.

Keallach stiffened, and he hurriedly grabbed my elbow, turning me in the other direction as he reached for his brother. "This way!" he cried. Vidar and Bellona were beside us. I looked over my shoulder for Ronan and began to pull back to wait for him when I saw what had alarmed Keallach. Two figures in red cloaks exited the first alcove tunnel, following four Sheolite scouts who glanced down at the devices in their hands and looked our way. I recognized one of the tall figures as a tracker from the Pacifica tunnels. The other was clearly of similar stature. How had they gotten past Ronan and our trainer? Niero?

We all drew our swords. Vidar pulled out his guns and began firing, but both trackers pulled shields from their backs, which seemed to repel his bullets, and continued their advance. Behind them now, the four Sheolites followed.

Kapriel and Keallach moved out together, attacking with such efficiency that it again struck me that they were exactly where they belonged. Together, they were stronger than any of us, even paired with our Knights. Together, they pressed back one tracker until he fell to his back, then they quickly dispatched the second. Keallach sliced him across the belly, and when he bent, Kapriel took off his head.

I gaped at them.

But they weren't done. They circled the first tracker, who had leaped to his feet in a spookily inhuman move and now had a sword in both hands. His eyes shifted back and forth, waiting for one or both of them to make a move. Bellona and Vidar had taken on the four scouts, and I knew Chaza'el and I had to come to their aid. But I was still fuzzy-headed, barely able to put one foot in front of the other, and overwhelmed by the incessant cold radiating from my arm cuff . . .

Incessant cold.

"Andriana," Chaza'el whispered, turning to me with eyes wide, pupils dilated. He grabbed hold of my hand and yanked me downward, just as a sword came past that would have cut me in two. Chaza'el rammed his dagger into Sethos's calf and reached up to meet the other tracker mid-tackle. They rolled across the floor, Chaza'el half the tracker's size—yet still somehow ending up on top. He sprang away, tossing another dagger with deadly accuracy, which the tracker only narrowly caught before it pierced his neck. The tracker advanced on him again.

My eyes tore back to Sethos, and I chastised myself that I hadn't been watching the viper all the while. My head truly wasn't quite right. He spat blood and wiped his lips with a gloved hand, narrowing his gaze at me. I looked away before our eyes locked, aware that he used that connection to somehow gain entrance to my mind and heart. *Maker, give me strength,* I prayed, unsheathing my sword at last and preparing to meet his advance. I knew he was far stronger, but the One who had made me was stronger yet.

His first strike made my whole body feel like it was ringing in response. But he didn't stop there. Again and again, he struck, and clearly knew as well as I did that, with each blow, I weakened. I gave up one foothold after another, my desperation growing at the same pace as his glee.

This was not a man who wished to preserve me for his emperor.

This was a dark angel who wished me disposed of, before I destroyed everything he'd built.

When I felt the cool stone at my back, I lifted my sword to block his next strike. He pressed his own sword downward, and our blades got closer and closer to my neck. The metallic slide sent shivers down my arms. "You," he hissed, "have caused me much trial. *You* have threatened all I've worked for." Then he pressed inward, and with a wave of fear, I knew he intended to slice my throat with my own blade.

The weight of it choked me.

Wind began to blow around us, driving out the dust, making me blink constantly in an effort to see. Then Sethos's eyes widened, even as he continued to stare at me. He still pressed inward, but now I was able to press back.

"Majesty . . ." he ground out, sounding only spiteful.

"Let her go, Sethos!" Keallach cried, reaching his hands out to him. He was using his gift to move Sethos the tiniest amount—every smidgen of which I was grateful for because it granted me that much more oxygen.

"Yes, let her go!" Kapriel echoed, but with his command he sent a burst of air that made Sethos careen two steps to the side, away from me.

I gasped for air, aware for the first time that sweat streamed down my face and neck. Vidar shouted and drove forward, blade high—his bullets likely gone—bringing his sword down on Sethos from behind when Sethos rammed a short sword backward, through my Ailith brother's belly.

"Vidar!" I screamed, feeling as if his name spread out over minutes, not seconds.

Kapriel sent another burst of air in Sethos's direction, nearly succeeding in forcing him from his feet.

Sethos gave him a long, steely look, then turned and fled down the alcove passageway. Ronan and our trainer tore past us in pursuit, but my eyes were on Vidar. I grabbed hold of him as he crumpled to his knees. But he was heavy, and he fell partially atop me. Still, I held on to him, easing him to the side and to his back, pressing down on his wound with both hands. I grimaced as blood seeped between my fingers, staining them as red as the Sheolite cloaks. "Go find Tressa!" I urged Kapriel and Keallach, hovering above me.

It was then I saw Chaza'el, his head still, eyes wide. At first I thought he was having another vision, lying there so still. But with a gasp, I knew that he was dead.

"No," I muttered, tears springing to my eyes. "No, no, no!" I looked to the twins again, already turning. "Hurry! Please hurry!" I sobbed. Perhaps, if she was in time, we could pray—pray all together—and bring Chaza'el back to us. We couldn't lose both of them. I forced myself to concentrate on Vidar. Even in the dim light, I could see he was fading to a ghastly shade of gray.

"Tell Bell," he grunted, his voice terrifying with gurgles, "that I always knew she secretly loved me."

"Shut up," I said, fury washing through me. "You use your energy to *fight* this, Vidar. You hear me? *Fight* this."

"It's bad, Dri," he said, and I felt the terror within him, the giving up.

"Yeah? So was Ronan! So was Killian! Tressa and Niero . . . they healed them! You just stay still and stay quiet, and pray the Maker doesn't take you home yet. Do you hear me?"

"Dri? You're shouting."

"Oh, Vidar," I sighed, half laughing, half crying.

Bellona cried out behind me and rushed in our direction, sliding to her knees beside us. "Vidar," she began. "What happened?"

"Don't make him talk," I said, fear rising in me as the blood continued to seep between my fingers and spread out across Vidar's tunic in a widening pool. "We need a medic. And Tressa. Tressa, most of all."

"Where is she?" Bellona said, rising.

"No, Bellona—the twins went after Tressa. They'll be back soon. See if you can find some gauze, or something to help stanch this blood."

"Two pretty girls, looking . . . after . . . me," Vidar quipped, but his tone had none of the lightness of his words. I looked in alarm to his eyes as they rolled backward.

"Vidar!" I grunted, pressing harder, as if I could will the wound to seal itself.

Ronan, Niero, and our trainer came into view, and my heart leaped, hoping that Niero might again intervene on our behalf. On Vidar's behalf, I thought, looking upon my brother with every ounce of hope in me.

"We need Tressa!" Bellona cried, fury carefully masking her panic as she placed her fingers over mine.

"Keallach and Kapriel are looking for her," I explained to the others. "But we don't have much time."

Niero moved to the torch on the wall and drew a long, thick dagger from his belt, placing the tip of it directly in the flame.

"What are you doing, Niero?" I asked shakily, well aware of his intent, but hoping he would resort to his . . . other methods. "Tressa is coming!"

"If she does not reach us in the next moment or two, you know what I must do."

I can save him with human methods, he willed into my mind, meeting my gaze. *He can survive this.*

He intended to seal Vidar's wound shut with a searing blade.

The horror of it sickened me. "Niero . . ."

"It is the Maker's way, to show us the means to accomplish his task," he said, turning back to the flame.

I winced and stared back at Vidar's terrible wound. "We don't even know if there's more damage inside," I muttered.

"If there is, only Tressa's prayers can heal him. And those will work regardless of whether the skin is sealed or not. Right now, we must stop the bleeding, or we will lose two Remnants this day instead of one."

Tears welled in my eyes as I again looked to Chaza'el, so terribly still.

"Lift his tunic," Niero said a moment later. "Ronan . . . Dri."

Ronan took hold of my shoulders and gently eased me back. "No," I cried, watching as Vidar's blood continued to spill faster when my pressure lifted. But still Ronan pulled, clearing a space for them to do what they must.

"Try and bring the skin together," Niero directed Bellona.

She pressed from either side, leaving enough room for his blade to cauterize the skin together. She turned her face, and after looking to the empty doorway, said, "Do it."

Niero pressed down with the hot blade without pause. My stomach roiled as the peculiar odor of hot blood and seared flesh filled the air, wafting upward in steam. I turned away, pressing my face into Ronan's chest. He stroked my hair with one hand and held me tight with his other arm.

Vidar came to with a scream, and Bellona shoved his shoulders down. "Look at me! Look at me!" she cried, forcing him to concentrate. "You are not alone. We are with you!" But by then, it was over. Niero lifted the blade and flung it toward the wall, bending to take one of Vidar's hands in both of his. "Forgive me, brother. It had to be done. You were going to bleed out."

Vidar nodded, silent, lips parted in desperate pants that were partly tears. Sweat ran down his temples, and his eyes were wide and round. Once Bellona captured his attention, he closed his eyes and clenched his teeth so hard I could see the muscles in his jaw and neck pulse with the effort. Blessedly, he blanched and passed out again a moment later. I think we all breathed a sigh of relief.

Niero laid his broad palm on Vidar's chest and bent his head, closing his eyes as if in prayer. I knew he was searching my brother to find out just how bad his wounds might be. After a moment, he looked toward us, face grim, which made my heart pound in fear. "Go and see if you can find Tressa— see what keeps her and the others. We will bring Vidar to the meeting room. Gather every elder you see and tell them to go there, along with the Ailith. We must decide on how we shall proceed."

Ronan and I immediately did as he asked, running out the tunnel and to the stairs. But when we got to the lower levels, horror overtook us. This was why the others hadn't returned with Tressa and Killian. Everywhere we looked, there were dead or dying people.

Men, women, and children, some infants, lying beside their parents.

Worse were children weeping, clinging to mothers and fathers who were long dead.

There were murdered elders too. I glimpsed one, slumped against a wall, his eyes wide, as if in shock, as if he couldn't believe that this was how it would end. Another lay twisted on the floor, as if she had been writhing in pain when she died.

The stone floors were covered in blood. We almost slipped several times because of it. The walls were streaked with it, reminding me of my home after the Sheolites came and took my parents. I had been so afraid . . .

"My parents," I said, gripping Ronan's arm. "*Our* parents."

"They should be safe," he said, not sounding entirely sure. "I doubt our enemies took the time to break through that reinforced door. But we'll go to them."

I nodded, my stomach twisting as I saw yet another dead child in the arms of a wailing, wounded mother. There were survivors, and that was a blessing. But their combined emotion—terror, grief, agony—made me turn and vomit.

Ronan's hand covered my shoulder until my belly was emptied.

"I'm sorry," I said, wiping my mouth with the back of my hand. It was the last thing he needed to deal with.

"It's understandable, Dri. I know . . . I know this must be a lot for you. Feeling everything. Everyone."

An armed guard came trotting through from the direction of the front gate. Ronan stopped him. "Have you repelled them all?"

"For now," spat the young man, probably only a season younger than Ronan and me. "But we're trying to re-form in case they return."

"How many dead outside?"

"Only a few. Most retreated inside before the stones were rolled into place after the helicopters arrived."

"How'd they get through?" Ronan asked, his tone tight and high, as if he still couldn't believe it. We thought we were invincible within the castle cut from the cliff.

"They blasted through. They had missiles on those helicopters." He turned his face and shook his head. "*Missiles.*

Some say that they had dynamite too, at the gates. How are we to fight against such a well-armed enemy?" He shook his head again. "The explosions killed some. And then the cursed Sheolites swept through while we were still trying to regain our feet, killing everyone in their path. If there hadn't been guards deeper in the Citadel to repel them, they might still be here, murdering all who remain."

I swallowed hard at the thought. Worse, I knew that they'd been after us—the Ailith. How many had died, standing between our enemy and us?

Ronan reached a hand out to cover the young man's shoulder in encouragement as we prepared to move on. "The Maker shall sustain us," he said. "He will show us the way. Do not lose heart. Share that with everyone you see, all right?"

The guard nodded and moved on. I clung to Ronan's words too.

We turned a corner and at last saw Tressa and Killian. He had an arm around her waist, and she looked beyond weary, her task clearly taxing her strength. I'd been so afraid that the reason they didn't return to us was because they'd been killed. Blood completely covered both their shirts, and I knew it had to be from a combination of repelling our enemies and tending to the wounded.

"There are so many . . ." Tressa said, pushing the back of her hand to her brow and meeting my gaze. She knew I felt the collective pain in a way that even she could not. It bonded us.

I reached out and took her other hand. "The Maker will sustain us all," I said, realizing I'd adopted Ronan's comforting words. It was what we all needed. To focus on our one, true, eternal hope. Anything else, as today had so vividly shown us, was temporal. "We're to meet. They're bringing Vidar. Niero seems to think . . ." I paused, my voice cracking.

"It's bad," Ronan said. "Vidar needs you, Tress."

Killian nodded, pulling Tressa along, but it wasn't long before she knelt beside an unconscious man. "We'll be right there," she said, looking up at us. "I know we're to go to Vidar. But the Maker calls me to heal this man first."

Ronan looked at me in desperation. We were close to the passageway that led to our quarters, where our parents were. While Tressa prayed over the man, we might have just enough time. Wordlessly, we agreed, practically running now. If anything had happened to our parents, if they'd come out to try and help defend the others . . .

But then, there they were, outside the reinforced door, working together to aid those around them—bandaging, bringing water. Ronan's mom had a child on one hip, his face covered in tears and snot and misery. Ronan went to them, and I to my parents, hugging them and directing them to the meeting place. "We have to hurry," I said. Mom and I led the way, with Dad behind and Ronan and his parents following.

We were halfway there, relieved to see that this quadrant of the Citadel seemed to be fairly untouched by the destructive path of the Sheolites, when my arm cuff began to chill. "Mom," I said, reaching out to grip her wrist, frowning, turning, trying to ascertain where the threat was coming from, even as I saw Ronan press toward us. But by then, they were there—two Sheolite scouts who had been left behind.

Or had remained behind, hoping for just such a moment as this.

They both struck at me at once.

If Mom hadn't managed to block one's blow and drive her dagger into his neck, I would've surely died. The other was fierce enough—seemingly as strong as Sethos in his manic drive toward me—that he almost cut both my belly and neck by the time Ronan and Dad intervened and made sure he never rose again. Only as my cuff began to warm did I begin to breathe normally again. Then, I looked around at our parents with pride in my heart. All four held both sword and dagger or shield in their hands. Somehow, I thought that if Ronan and I hadn't had our trainer, these four would've done their best to prepare us to survive.

"Why?" Ronan asked, panting. "Why is it always *you* that they're after? You that they find?"

"Those two weren't out to capture me," I said, my voice trembling a little. "They wanted me dead. Come," I urged as Tressa and Killian caught up to us, wide-eyed as we wiped our blades of blood. "We need to get to the meeting hall."

We set out again, this time with Ronan and Dad taking the lead and me paying special attention to any warning the Maker might be sending me through the arm cuff. But I only felt growing warmth.

When we reached the hive-like room, I wanted to weep at the sight of all the bloody and hastily bandaged elders, and at how many of their seats were empty. I stopped when I saw where the oracle had once sat—the ancient woman who was blind and yet could see more clearly than others. Tyree was here without Clennan, grief etched into his face, and when Tressa saw him, she let out a cry, knowing what it meant right away. Her foster father—the only father she'd ever known— was now gone. Tyree took her into his arms, and they cried together. It was as if the Sheolites had come in with a special focus on killing every elder and Ailith possible, but the carnage they left behind told me they'd had instructions to kill anyone in their path.

Mentally, I breathed a sigh of relief as each of my brothers and sisters—Azarel, Cyrus, Asher, Niero, and the others—arrived. But Vidar was still unconscious, and when Azarel and Asher helped Keallach and Kapriel carry in Chaza'el, lifeless, I cried out and went to them. I choked out a sob, looking at his black eyes—eyes that would never see our future again. I closed my own, tears coming fast then, and heard others around me. But Niero put his hand on my shoulder. "Come, sister. Pray with us for a brother we might yet be able to save."

I tore myself from Chaza'el and entered the circle around Vidar, joining hands with the others. Bellona was on one side of him, Tressa on the other. He was still terribly pale, his skin an odd gray, as if chilled to the bone, but he was sweating at the same time. Tressa had both palms on his chest, head bowed, praying. And quietly, we all echoed her words. "Maker of all, we commit our brothers Chaza'el and Vidar into your care. Chaza'el has gone ahead of us, but we beg you to spare Vidar. Bring him back to us, Maker. Knit together his wound from the inside out." Gently, she moved her fingers to hover over his wound—fiercely red around the cauterization. "Just as you knit him together in his mother's womb, Maker, knit him together again. Keep his heart steady, his breathing sure. Bring him back to us in the name of the One who was, and is, and is to come."

"In the name of the One who was, and is, and is to come," we repeated, over and over.

"You are Shammah, ever-present, Maker," Tressa prayed, and I could hear the tears that threatened to choke her as she invoked strange, ancient names for the One who spoke us into life. Had an elder dared to share them with her? My heart thrilled to the names that I felt I should've known all my life.

"You are Nissi, our banner. You are Raah, our Shepherd. You are Tisdkenu, our righteousness." Even with my eyes closed, I could see the room was growing brighter, the torch flames rising. Heat flooded through my arm cuff. The presence of the Maker was so tangible that I could barely breathe.

"Maker, you are Rapha," Tressa whispered. "Our *healer*. Holy and mighty, holding all our lives in your very hands. Bring Vidar back to us now. We ask this in your name, above all names."

And then it was done.

Tressa was silent. We were silent.

But Vidar did not respond.

And still did not respond . . .

I opened my eyes just as Vidar blinked slowly and then focused on each of us. "Finally . . ." he mumbled, barely able to form the words, "I'm the center of attention."

I huffed a laugh, sinking to my knees, and the entire chamber exploded in applause and cheers, even from those who ailed.

On the edge of our circle, I saw Keallach sink to his knees too, mouth slack with wonder.

Bellona closed her eyes and lifted her chin, her face so open in gratitude for a moment that it took me aback. She was beautiful as her usual fierce self, but she was even more so when she allowed herself to be vulnerable. "Thank you, Maker," she breathed.

"See? You do . . . love me," Vidar said, closing his eyes and wincing slightly.

"Does it hurt?" Tressa asked him. Killian had come around Vidar to kneel at Tressa's side, his arm again around her waist.

"Only a lot," he said, giving her a rueful grin. "It feels like I've been in the worst battle of my life."

"You have," Niero said. "In more ways than one."

The way he said it, I knew that we'd almost lost Vidar. By the look on his face, Niero had felt Vidar's life slipping away. Perhaps as an angel, he could sense it in a different dimension than we had. I looked over my shoulder to where Chaza'el's body lay, aching that we could not have saved him too. Ronan put his hand on my shoulder, and I welcomed his wordless reassurance.

"So what shall we do now?" Kapriel said, turning to speak to the rest in the chamber, as well as to us. "The enemy has shown us that we are vulnerable, even here."

"They've declared war," Killian said, helping Tressa to a bench and wrapping a blanket around her shoulders.

"We need to leave the Citadel," Keallach put in, lifting one hand up and away. "To remain here is to invite them to continue to come after us. We need to divide and hide, as the Drifters and Aravanders do, making it harder for them to find us and destroy so many of us at once."

"They would not have been able to harm us here," said our trainer, rising to his feet, "had they not had the helicopters and missiles. Both their arsenal and such distinctive weapons must be removed if we are to have a hope in this battle."

"Ivar speaks with wisdom, as does Keallach," said an elder.

As surprised as I was at praise for Keallach, the use of our trainer's true name struck me even more. Ronan and I shared a glance. We'd long tried to guess his name as children, but he never told us if we were right or wrong. His identity was hidden for his safety, and that meant going so far as to not use his name. I never knew where he lived, just as I never knew where Ronan lived, or his parents. But the elders knew him. They'd likely commissioned him on the day my parents and Ronan's arrived with us in their arms.

"We could go east and north, deeper into the cold, to my people," Barrett said, from halfway up the chamber. "They would welcome you, and the Pacificans would find it a hardship to bear further cold and wet, especially with Hoarfrost upon us. You could spend the season among us, allowing the wounded to heal and welcoming more who seek the Way. We could send out guerrilla parties to destroy the enemy's helicopters and missiles, assuring a fairer fight come next Harvest."

"That is what they will expect of you," Keallach said. "*Us*," he quickly amended. "They will assume we will flee. What if we make it look like that's what we are doing, but catch them by surprise?" He began to pace, drawing each person he looked toward into his words, and I glimpsed the charisma that made him a natural leader. "They expect us to run, but the Maker did not call us to do so. He called us to fight for what is right and true. He called us to fight for what is his—his people."

I stared at him, his words resonating in a new, impossible way inside me. His people. His children.

"It is true that the Maker calls us as such," Ivar said gravely, studying the young man from under bushy brows. "But discerning his timing is key. We must not rush to respond to our own agenda or vendetta but, rather, to follow his lead."

Keallach nodded, accepting the subtle challenge with good grace. He was growing, maturing, before my very eyes, I thought. Maybe we all were.

"There are people here and about us who are called to the Way," I said, surprised to find myself speaking, but unable to stop. "Everywhere we go, they come to us. Others come to us who have never met us. Some of you came to the Valley that way. But there are others, behind the Wall, who have been imprisoned and enslaved. Even now, whispers of our presence might have reached them, perhaps giving them hope of rescue. Many of them are children, and many will not survive another Hoarfrost, even in Pacifica's more temperate zone. If we are to take the fight outward, I can't help but think that saving those children is a part of the Maker's mission for us."

"You propose that we march into Pacifica?" Lord Cyrus asked, sitting with his new bride, Justina, up on the left. I was relieved to see them both alive.

"We are still many, even after the carnage of this day," I said.

"And we shall grow, exponentially," Kapriel said, nodding.

"There *are* many more," Azarel said. "In and around the Great Expanse. And word has reached us that Georgii Post is ripe for a turn in command. If we were to stop there en route, I'm confident we could take that city first and free her people to follow us into Pacifica."

"Those helicopters would not have reached the Citadel had Keallach been in full command of his gifting," Kapriel said gently, steadily looking at his brother. "Between us, if Keallach were granted his full gifting—"

"You can't be serious," Ronan barked, frowning at Keallach. "It is too soon."

Others around him, including Azarel and Bellona, agreed.

"If I advocate for him," Kapriel said, turning slowly to look at one face after another, drawing them in, "who can truly argue? Keallach's choices have been the source of much pain in this room, but I suspect that no one has suffered more because of them than I."

Keallach's head dropped to his chest, and he closed his eyes, as if trying to bear the weight of his guilt again.

"But this is a new man before us," Kapriel went on, stepping forward to put one hand on his brother's shoulder. "The man that the Maker breathed into life on the morning he breathed life into the rest of the Ailith."

The room grew silent, and Keallach's chin slowly rose again.

"Kapriel, are you certain?" Azarel asked, so quietly that only a few of us heard.

He nodded, staring at his brother.

"I myself am not certain," Keallach whispered.

"Sometimes it takes a vote of confidence from another to push us over the edge of indecision," Kapriel said. "I see you, brother. I know there still is a struggle within you. But there is not one of us here who is purely good, is there?" He looked around to Vidar, Tressa, and me. To the Knights. "If the Community had forced any of us to wait until there was no trace of darkness within us, no self-serving impulse, no desire to have our own way, would we have our armbands yet?"

I swallowed hard. It was true.

"If he has found it in his heart to forgive Keallach, how can we not?" Azarel said, her voice uncommonly soft, as if half present, half in the past. She'd been there, with them. "I say bless him, grant him his armband, and ask the Maker to bestow his full gifting at last. With the two of them together"—she paused to wave at the twins—"we *could* take the battle to Pacifica."

Ronan clamped his mouth shut, and I knew the agitation and trepidation within him. But I also understood the truth of her words. If Keallach could press people to act in a certain way—as well as physically move objects simply with a thought—and Kapriel commanded the skies, then helicopters and missiles ceased to be a concern.

Cyrus rose. "Pacifica is in a weakened, volatile position," he said. "The Council of Six is down to four, with Broderick dead and me here. The emperor himself is absent from his throne," he went on, walking down the steps, gesturing toward Keallach. "Sethos has undoubtedly tried to keep that quiet, but Keallach has been with us for some time now. I'd wager the rumors are fierce among the nobility by now."

"Sethos will have no choice but to seize the throne for himself," Keallach said, nodding in agreement. "Some will take no issue with it. Others will."

"There will be much vying among the nobility to fill those two places on the Council," Cyrus said, steepling his fingers, thinking as he paced. "And that will put families in power at odds."

"And yet those who remain—Fenris, Kendric, Daivat, and Jala—will resist any newcomers to the Council."

"Leaving the inner circle on defense," Cyrus concluded. "Pacifica will begin to crumble from within, even as the Way continues to chip away at every inch of the Wall."

The room seemed to absorb this information. Pacifica, vulnerable?

"What do you say, Vidar?" I asked, edging nearer to him, inclining my head toward the twins. "You are the one who discerns dark from light. What do you sense in our brother today?" Together, we looked toward Keallach. I rubbed my arm cuff and, with relief, felt no cold edge of warning.

Vidar paused and concentrated, never blinking.

Keallach turned to him and squared his shoulders, turning his palms slightly toward him, as if welcoming his internal search. "I have done much to harm many of you and those you loved in my years as leader of Pacifica. But I beg you to finally forgive me and welcome me into your fold for good. Free me to aid you and do my best to atone for my past sins." As he finished speaking, he looked at his brother. "Or if we must wait, I understand. I submit to you, my brothers and sisters. I submit to you."

Kapriel held his gaze for a long moment. His arms were folded, and he bent his head as if thinking, second-guessing himself. The rest of us were silent, waiting for his decision first. Azarel was right. If he could forgive his brother, who were we to stand against him?

Kapriel lifted his chin and let his arms fall to his side. He stepped toward Keallach, as did the rest of the Remnants, almost as if we were of one mind. When he reached Keallach, he put his hands on his shoulders. Vidar put a hand on his arm. Tressa, too, a hand. I reached out and touched his other arm, closing my eyes to search him for any emotion that might betray evil intent. The Knights and Azarel and Niero all came around us.

"Maker, show them," Niero prayed. "Make it clear."

"Show us," Tressa whispered. And the rest of us repeated the words.

The air felt supercharged, the room utterly silent, except for the pulsing in my ears.

I concentrated only on Keallach, searched, delved deep within him, half hopeful, half terrified at what I would find. I couldn't bear more disappointment or sorrow this day.

And there *was* an edge of darkness. Pride, chiefly, as he struggled to find true humility at the center of our circle. But there it was. A thirst for power.

Yet it was with some relief that I decided the presiding emotions within him were longing, love, and hope.

The same emotions that had first drawn me to him.

When I opened my eyes, I looked to Vidar, and he shook his head slightly, eyes rounded, as if surprised. "There are echoes of the darkness within him," he said, barely louder than a whisper, "but not much more than I sensed in Dri, after Sethos wormed his way into her heart."

I felt my cheeks burn a bit at this memory but looked to Keallach, feeling renewed camaraderie with him because of this shared failure. "Sethos is strong, but the Maker is stronger," I said. "Among us, we can help Keallach learn ways to keep the dark one from his mind and heart."

"Be certain, Ailith," Niero warned from over my shoulder. "You all must be of like mind. What you propose could unleash either a true guardian of the Way or a very serious enemy with gifting that equals Kapriel's."

"We are certain," Kapriel said, his tone more confident after our prayer.

"We are certain," Tressa said.

"We are," Vidar said.

"Yes," I breathed in wonder, tears coming to my eyes as hope surged within Keallach, steady and true. "We are."

CHAPTER 29

KEALLACH

I struggled as I knelt, my bare arm extending toward Raniero to place a hand on his shoulder, preparing to receive the ceremonial cuff. The Ailith knelt in a circle with me, placing their hands on the shoulder of either Remnant or Knight beside them, and there, in that moment, I felt their combined power anew. Part of me wished to confess my original intent in coming here, my desire to infiltrate them. And yet to do so now would mean breaking this momentum, perhaps making them rethink their blessing over me at all. Besides, I had been deeply changed over these days with them. My heart was changed. I no longer wanted to break them apart and take Dri and Kapriel away. I wanted them *all* with me, forever, whatever that took. Was that not what it meant to be one with them? Was that not all the rationale I needed to serve the Maker alongside of them?

I guessed that Sethos now knew of my change of heart. That was why he had sent Sheolites to kill Dri during the raid, rather than capture her. He wanted to shake me up, remind me of his power. Call me back to him in a fit of rage, if necessary. But I was not going back. Not to him. Not yet.

An elder opened a box and extended it to Cornelius. The room was full, but silent, everyone eager to witness what many had only heard rumors of—a dedication ceremony for a Remnant. I knew I was the last one. Sethos had seen to it that the others were killed.

But mine would. This day. My heart swelled as Cornelius took the hinged cuff from atop the others in the box and turned to me, looking me in the eyes.

"You were once our sworn enemy, Keallach. Your people have murdered our own and made slaves of others. Do you confess those sins?"

"I confess them," I said, sorrow penetrating my very bones. If I had known, if I had only made myself more aware rather than looking away. If I had pressed in, seen the truth behind Sethos's lies . . . "I confess it," I repeated, "and I wish I had the power to make it right."

"Only the Maker has that power," Cornelius said. "But he washes you clean in your confession and takes pleasure in your desire to do right in the future. Do you desire to do right? To serve alongside your Ailith kin, to serve the Maker in all things, setting aside your own agenda in order to serve the Community?"

"I do," I said, staring at him earnestly. "In every way possible."

"Do you pledge to stand against the Dark and serve the Light in all ways?"

"I do, with the Maker's aid."

"You were born to be one with your brothers and sisters," Cornelius said, looking around to the others. "And the moment has come at last. Prince Keallach," he said, leaning closer, "with this cuff you become one with the Ailith and enter into the full breadth of your gifting. May you use that gifting to serve the One who was . . ."

"The One who is . . ." joined in the Ailith.

"And the One who is to come," thundered everyone in the room.

In that moment, Cornelius shut the cuff around my upper arm, and an explosion of heat ran through it and then through my body, making my head spin for a moment. But as it stilled, energy seemed to fill and part from my fingertips and toes, too much within me to be contained. But it wasn't pure energy, I finally identified, it was pure joy. I shouted out, in exaltation, pulling Kapriel into my arms for a hug, then Niero, despite his reluctance, then the others, ending with Cornelius, whom I pulled close to kiss both cheeks. "Thank you, Father Cornelius. Thank you."

"Don't thank me," he said with a low-timbre laugh. "Thank your Maker."

"Oh, I do! I will! Forever!"

Entering the Remnants' fold in full, breathing in the entire blessing of the Maker for the first time ever, feeling the pulsing warmth from the cuff, being surrounded by Ailith . . . Such pure joy, I thought, such a sense of *completion*. I blinked back sudden tears in embarrassment. And yet I hadn't felt such emotion, such pure gladness, such glory, since I'd been a boy.

It was like coming home.

And I'd almost missed it. Never known this peace, this security. This was where I'd belonged all along, in the Community. I felt their embrace, the wash of forgiveness flow around and through me. Hadn't even the Maker blessed my presence with the searing of the cuff to my skin?

When all had shared their congratulations, even Andriana and Ronan—with a bit more of a stilted hug and arm clasp than the others—Niero circled around and looked at me and my brother.

"It's time," Niero said.

"Time?" I repeated blankly.

"I will spend some time with the two of you now. You both have been without a trainer—a *blessed* trainer—for many years. I would like to gauge where you are and what is needed, both within and without."

I swallowed hard. Sethos and I had ceased our daily training sessions the night of the Call to the Ailith. After that day, when I'd ignored the holy summoning and knew that Sethos had sent his Sheolites out after my brothers and sisters, I simply couldn't abide training any longer. It felt wrong every time we sparred, every time he tried to work with me on a more primal, emotional, mental, or spiritual front. I supposed now, as we walked, leaving the Citadel, that it had been the Maker continuing to agitate me. To nudge me into acknowledging what I'd known all along. That I belonged here, with my holy kin, rather than in the West, as a pawn of the enemy.

I gave my twin a shy smile and patted him on the back as we walked. It troubled me, the lack of muscle and bulk there, where I had it; his strong but gaunt frame was a daily reminder of what he had endured—because of me. And yet he responded to my touch with nothing but trust and joy in his eyes. "It reassures me, brother," I said, inclining my head toward Niero, who led us, "to have you with me in this. And what is to come."

"It is my joy," he said, eyes soft and warm, "that we are reunited, in body and spirit. All is as it should be."

I paused, wondering if I had the courage to ask what I needed to ask next. "Kapriel," I began. "Can you truly forgive me for all I've done against you? How I harmed you and the people we loved?" My voice cracked as I uttered the last word, remembering our mother. Our father. That terrible day that Sethos struck them both down.

I'd spent every season since then trying to forget that day. Repeating to myself, over and over, that it was necessary, all of it. Their deaths. Kapriel's imprisonment.

Kapriel stopped in the passageway and turned to me, putting a hand on each shoulder. "Brother, it was as if you were reborn the day you came to the Valley and joined us. Everything before is forgotten. Don't you see? The Maker has made a way for all things to be new between us." His grip tightened. "All things. I forgive you. Let us make our way forward. I believe . . ." He paused and looked after Niero, who waited for us now, ahead. "I believe," he resumed, looking me in the eye again, "that Mother and Father would have wanted nothing less for us. Let's move forward with that thought, as if they had given us their blessing this day. To you, as well as to me. All right?"

I swallowed hard and gripped his shoulder when he tried to leave. "But you forgive me? Kapriel," I whispered, "I must hear it from you."

His eyes searched mine. "I've already forgiven you," he said. And then he pulled me into a fierce embrace.

We left then, me once again wiping tears from my eyes with the back of my hands, as if I was a boy, not a man. Never had I thought it truly possible. Complete acceptance. Complete reunion with my twin. Sharing this Ailith bond in full, as well as our blood bond. Truly, it was as holy an experience for me as receiving my armband. Maybe it was because of the cuff, I considered, that I could now feel it in full.

Niero led us out and around the boulders, waving to scouts and armed guards who gave us the all-clear sign but watched our progress with curiosity heavy in their eyes, as if they longed to follow us. Ivar, Ronan and Dri's trainer, emerged on the path ahead, as if he'd been waiting there. Stupidly, I realized that he had—that he was here at Niero's invitation and would be a part of our training. I shoved away a surge of defensiveness, as if the man would be inclined to be against me. The Ailith had a holy bond with me, which was reason to offer me uncommon acceptance, but would all followers of the Way feel the same? I would just have to prove myself to those who found it harder, I resolved. I'd show them all, in time, that they hadn't made a mistake. That it had been a good choice, to allow me to be one with them.

In time, we passed through a small grove of aspens that were about to lose the last of their golden leaves, and then through a shallow valley of pines, emerging in a small meadow full of dormant, brown grass that reached our knees. Ivar removed his backpack and tossed me a wooden sparring sword and Kapriel another. Then he pulled out two for Niero, one for each hand. He unstrapped a wooden staff from his back, apparently his customary weapon. But this one didn't have a blade on one end and a metal-fortified end on the other, as was customary. It was a sparring staff.

Ivar saw me eyeing it. "You want this or a sword?" he asked.

"The staff is what I am most accustomed to," I said. "But I can use either."

His gaze deadly calm, he handed over the staff, as if unworried about what I could do with it. Niero watched. He knew Sethos often carried a double-tipped staff. Did he judge me for favoring a similar weapon?

Niero faced off with me, and Ivar with Kapriel. "Ordinary mortal rules at first," Niero said with the glint of a smile while weaving two sparring swords in the air, as if getting used to their weight. "Then we shall allow you to bring in your gifting."

"And you?" I tossed out to him as our wooden weapons met between us. "Will you keep to ordinary *mortal* rules?"

"The best I can," he said, smiling slightly. He lifted his chin. "Whenever you are ready, *prince*."

He hadn't even uttered his last word when I struck, surprising him a bit, I think. But he quickly rallied, and we set into an earnest session of sparring, which grew in intensity the longer it went on. We were well matched. Niero was bigger and stronger than I, but I was quicker and lither. I drove him, bit by bit, toward a rock I'd spotted behind him. With a well-timed block, whirl, and drive, he stepped against it, and I surprised him by driving forward, throwing him off balance and using the staff to trip him at just the right moment. He fell to his back, eyes widening in surprise, as my sparring staff pointed toward his throat.

"And so now you shall kill me?" he asked.

"Of course," I began, but that was when I felt his boots on either side of my ankle. With a quick move, it was my turn to land on my back.

He managed to knock the wind out of me and rolled atop, pinning my chest with his knee, one practice sword at my neck. "Pride goeth before the fall," he quipped. "A proverb especially important for the highborn to note."

"Noted," I gasped.

He let me up and offered a hand, but I ignored it, my ego truly stinging a bit. I looked to my twin as I rose. He wasn't doing much better—lifting his hands in surrender as Ivar brought the broad side of his sword against his belly.

Frustration and anger roiled within me. We were better than this! Why shouldn't we unleash all the Maker had granted us if this was a true practice session for battle?

"Because you are not to call upon your gifting in frustration and anger," Niero said, putting the tip of one wooden sword to the ground and the other to his shoulder.

I looked to him in surprise.

"Yes, I can read the Remnants' thoughts. On occasion," he said, lifting one brow.

I can also do this, when the Maker allows it.

"When the Maker allows it?" I asked, blinking in surprise as his words rang in my ears. "When would he not allow it? Why?"

He lifted his chin, pleased at my ability to hear. "No one ever knows why he does what he does. We can only trust in the goodness of his will."

I considered that and then went back to what he'd said. "You say I should not call upon my gifting in anger and frustration."

"Correct, because that centers on you. That is what made your gift a low gift, in Pacifica. But here, you will transform it into what it was meant to be—a high gift. You are not to call upon it out of your own desire to accomplish something you alone want," he said. "You are to call upon it out of a desire to serve the Community or, at the very least, your fellow Ailith. Otherwise, it is nothing more than a parlor trick, right? A spell, of sorts. A sorcerer's spell."

We stared at each other. I knew he spoke of Sethos. Of his means of manipulating me.

"He used your gifting for his own purposes," Niero said quietly. "Didn't he? By convincing you to use them for *your* gain."

I grimaced, remembering Andriana. How he'd made me . . . I turned my face away from Niero in shame.

"If you do not operate out of pride," Niero said, "but out of total service to and trust of the Maker, Sethos shall not be able to infiltrate your armor again. He is strong, but the One we serve is stronger. Always remember that."

I nodded, and we squared up again for another round of sparring. When I succeeded in a mock-death strike against his throat, he gave me a calm look. "Good. Now practice calling upon your gifting. Not for you. But out of a desire to serve your new-found Ailith kin."

I narrowed my gaze. "But I could kill you."

One side of his mouth quirked into a mocking smile. "I have been called as a guardian of the Remnants. I do not fear your gifts. Simply practice calling upon it, as if I were your enemy, threatening your new brothers and sisters."

I thought of Andriana. Ronan too, I quickly added in my head. I thought also of Tressa and Killian, Bellona and Vidar, Chaza'el . . . and paused.

Sorrow is all right, Niero coached within. *It's an emblem of compassion. The opposite of pride.*

I thought about how I was sorry I'd never truly known Chaza'el. Never seen his gifting in action. I turned toward Kapriel, as he bent over laughing with Ivar on the ground. I hadn't heard him laugh in some time, and the sound of it brought a swirl of joy to my heart. A surge of love and a desire to be fully restored with my brother for years to come. To be one with the Ailith until the end of my days . . . My arm cuff began to warm, and I breathed in, feeling as if my lungs were expanding, my muscles doubling in size. It was such a pure sensation that I actually lifted and looked at my arms, expecting them to be bigger. They weren't, but it was then that I realized that this was a holy strength I sensed, my gifting coming to fruition. Sethos had always told me I was gifted, but he'd bound me in ways I had not recognized.

"Pretend I am he. Pretend I am Sethos," Niero grunted.

I lifted my hands to the pines that bordered our meadow, and then waved toward the angel who dared to spar with me. A thousand pinecones came pelting toward him.

I lifted my hand at the last second, and the wave of them hovered midair, then dropped to the ground. I stared in surprise. Never in my whole life had I had such control. Short bursts, yes. But sustained? Nothing like that. I lifted my hands, staring at them, wondering over the odd force that seemed to be heating them even now.

"Excellent control," Niero said, a smile lifting his lips, "for one so new to his gifting. But don't fear for me. The Maker will not allow me to die here, in this. Show us what you can do, Keallach. Explore it." He gestured toward Kapriel and Ivar, and the two took cover near a boulder, watching us intently.

I turned back to the trees. I thought about the Ailith, about needing to make a path. About the desire, so deep within, to lead them. To someplace good. Someplace safe. I lifted my hands straight out from my body then separated them.

There was a cacophony of noise as six giant trees fell, pulling up massive root balls as they went, a neat line between them. *A path,* I thought, eyes wide in wonder.

Pretend I am coming up behind you, Niero said, within.

I looked to an old fallen log ten paces ahead, and with a wave I sent it over my shoulder, barely ducking. I could smell the scent of rot and wet decay from the dirt that fell as it passed me. I brushed the dirt off my shoulder. Belatedly, I worried about Niero and turned, but I saw that he was halfway across the field, that I'd completely missed him.

You're slow, he taunted. *I'm Sethos, remember?*

My eyes narrowed. I stared at him, pretending he was Sethos and bent on killing my brothers and sisters.

I brought down the trees behind him.

Again, my heart pounded as the branches shook, settling in a giant swath of green.

"Not bad," Niero said in my ear.

My head whipped to the side. "It's fortunate for you that you are not of this world."

"Indeed," he agreed. "But I believe it will take both you *and* your brother to trap another who shares some of my own angelic gifting." He waved Kapriel over to us and explained his thinking to him and Ivar.

And then we set to work, contemplating various scenarios and practicing execution. By the end of our session, I was so weary I contemplated lying down right there in the meadow and sleeping the night away. Kapriel looked the same, wavering on his feet so much that Ivar pulled one of my brother's arms across his shoulders and wrapped a supporting, strong arm about his waist. "I think it's time to call it a day," he said.

"Agreed," Niero said. "But we return at dawn."

"At dawn?" I croaked.

"There is no time to dawdle, Keallach," Ivar said. "Because Sethos and his ilk might be the ones to wake *us* at dawn. You and Kapriel must build upon your gifting. For the good of the Remnants, as well as the Community. We're all depending upon you."

"And you were born to serve together," Niero said. "So newly reunited, it is best for you to spend every waking moment contemplating that thought and practicing, in big and small ways, how that connection might be best utilized. Understood?"

"Understood," Kapriel said.

"Understood," I echoed. But as I walked beside my twin on the way back to the Citadel, I was plagued by the thought of the chip inside him, and inside Dri too. Even now, I could imagine Sethos or Jala watching the blinking emblem on a screen and knowing that Kapriel was outside of the Citadel. Vulnerable.

I glanced nervously to the skies and listened for the warning *chomp-chomp-chomp* of a helicopter blade. And yet for the first time, I knew I had the capacity to truly fight back in a way that would help all the Ailith, as well as my new people.

If Sethos wanted to come, let him come.

But somehow, some way, I had to find a way to keep him from Kapriel and Dri.

CHAPTER 30

ANDRIANA

It didn't take long for the twins to ease into sharing leadership of the Ailith and, within days, of the people. Keallach worked hard at deferring to Kapriel, building him up, encouraging him to assume ultimate command, knowing we would be troubled by anything else. He accepted Kapriel's decision almost every time when they disagreed, or he came up with a compromise. He did not act as an emperor, but rather as a co-regent, as they were born to be. Gradually, the elders began to defer to them, seeking their counsel and direction on strategic decisions, as if it had been divinely ordained. Niero and Cyrus spent late nights with them both, talking politics and devising plans that might bring us to the swiftest victory.

It was as if Kapriel had been waiting for Keallach to return to him before assuming his rightful position. Before he'd been rather reserved and careful in sharing his opinion. Day by day, he became more forthright. More princely. And we all admired him.

It was Kapriel who decided we would have a formal funeral service for Chaza'el and the rest who had died. As we said tearful good-byes to our dead on funeral pyres in the same sacred field in which Ronan and I had taken our vows, our scouts kept an eye to the skies, but we had newfound confidence in facing the powerful helicopters, knowing that, with the twins at our side, we would have our fair chance in battle.

We stood beside the wrapped form of Chaza'el, who had been placed on a short funeral pyre, serving as his family, much like other families gathered around their dead on the field, each waiting to set torch to dry tinder. Three women with long, metal tubes this time, instead of triangles, stood beside Cornelius at the center.

"From dust we came, and to dust we shall return," Cornelius said.

The women hit their deep bells, sending a somber sound that matched our mood out across the field. Once, twice, thrice.

"They are dead to us, but very much alive in the Maker's presence," Cornelius said. "When we join them, we shall be reunited. Grieve for them now, dear ones. But rejoice in the promise of our future reunion."

Again, the bells sounded.

As was our tradition, that was all that was said. Niero lowered the torch to the tinder, and fire rapidly spread around the perimeter of the wood, soon licking up the dried branches beneath Chaza'el's body. The heat was intense, and Ronan pulled me back a step, wrapping me in his arms as I wept. For as much as Chaza'el had seen, beyond what we could see, I reveled in what he might be witnessing now, in the afterlife. I was happy for him, but the sorrow I felt in his loss went to the very marrow of my bones. We hadn't been close, but he'd been family to me, my brother in every sense of the word. And to send him off now, before our mission was complete, seemed wrong.

It made me feel vulnerable, as if part of our protection was gone. And it made me feel weak, as if part of the structure that made us Remnants had disintegrated. What might we have been, in time, if our lost brother and sister had managed to join us? I glanced over to Cyrus, who had sorrowfully confessed to us that it was Pacificans who had brought them down. Murdered them. How powerful might we have been with them beside us? And how much loss could we withstand and still face the battle ahead? My eyes shifted to Tressa, weeping beneath Killian's arm. To Vidar, wiping away a tear with the back of his hand, his customary smile and quip absent from his lips. Then to the twins, standing stoically together, Keallach with his hand on a staff, Kapriel's on the hilt of his sword. Keallach appeared shaken. Was he feeling this jolt of familial loss as we were?

The fire fully engulfed the pyre, as it did the countless other pyres across the field. The women began ringing their bells in a rhythmic toll, beginning slowly and gradually gaining speed until the pyres collapsed in on themselves, wood falling on top of the bodies as if claiming them again, welcoming them back to the earth.

The bells tolled in swift succession, their somber sounds filling my ears and seeming to somehow echo the black smoke that rose to the cloudy sky and then disappeared.

Then, all at once, the bells ceased, their last notes hovering in the air.

Only the crackle of the super-hot fires, the sniffling of men and women, the quiet weeping of the bereaved, now filled our ears.

It was over. We turned and processed in silence down the hill, through the smoke that drifted across the dried grass.

My tears spent, I heaved a sigh and was thankful for the quiet skies, that it was the ceremonial bells we heard, not Aravander alarm bells. Zanzibar had moved out in full force from the city and had mobilized as many of their Drifter minions as possible to erect a desert post, guarding the mouth of the Valley over the last week. Apparently, that had set Sethos back a bit to consider strategy. Whatever drove him to leave us alone, I thanked the Maker for it. We needed this time to grieve Chaza'el. To come together in his honor. And somehow, the thought made me think he'd seen this brief respite coming, which made me smile.

Ronan and I walked a few paces behind Keallach and Kapriel. I thought I'd feel more wary of Keallach, more watchful around him, worried that he might abuse his newfound power. They appeared as princes now, wearing thick, white capes trimmed in animal fur. The capes had been a gift from the elders two nights ago—a costly gift, but we all liked it. Visually, it united the brothers and presented a stark contrast to the blood-red capes the Sheolites and trackers favored.

The two were in earnest conversation, and at one point Kapriel lifted his chin and smiled at his brother, placing a hand on his shoulder as they walked.

"It's as if they'd never parted," Ronan said, face a bit skewed in wonder. Fat snowflakes were now falling from the dark clouds above us, and I pulled my own thick Aravander cape more tightly around me. "As if there was never bad blood between them."

"It's as it was always meant to be," I said, glad for it with every measure within me. "The power of the Maker to make wrong, right."

"Indeed," Ronan agreed.

When we reached the Citadel, we saw twelve men and women return to their task of trying to leverage a boulder to one side, helping to create a renewed barrier at the entrance. The missiles and Sheolite dynamite had created a small crater that had once been a field of boulders, blocking any direct, mass attack. Together, the group hung on and pressed down on the thick post they used as lever, but after a moment, it cracked, as if in outright refusal to budge the belligerent stone. Several of the workers let out sounds of disgust, and I saw there were several other beams that had also broken.

"Allow my brother to do this," Kapriel said, gesturing toward Keallach.

Keallach's eyebrows curved together in surprise. "Are you certain?"

"Why not?" Kapriel asked. "The gifts of the Maker are almost better used to serve the Community than they are to repel our enemies."

"Agreed," Keallach said. "Please, friends," he said to the workers. "Stand aside."

They scrambled over the ledge and closer to us, their combined curiosity making me want to burst with hope and excitement. Keallach bent his head in prayer and then lifted his hands, as if holding the boulder in the distance. Then he turned his cupped hands, as if turning the boulder itself, and the giant stone began to move. People gasped and shouted as the crowds caught up in time to see what the newest Remnant could do.

And what he could do was impressive. Over and over, the boulder rolled, across smaller rocks, all the way to the left side of the entrance. "About there?" he asked the man in charge of the task, a smile quirking the corners of his mouth.

"That'll do, Prince Keallach," said the man with a nod.

"Anything else?" Keallach asked.

Surprise made the man's eyes widen and then narrow in consideration. "Well, if it's not too taxing, if you could move this"—he went over to another massive boulder, bigger than the last—"next to the first one. We hope to create another rolling stone barrier."

"Done," Keallach said, bending his head again. Then he repeated the actions.

We all watched in wonder as Keallach mentally rearranged the stone debris to reconstruct the gateway, increasing its defensibility and strength even beyond what we'd had before. When he was done, sweat poured down his face, and his shirt clung to his damp chest, but he'd refused to stop. The workers turned and applauded him, and so did we.

"Rather convenient to have such gifts on our side, don't you think?" Vidar quipped from my side. Kapriel was turning snow in the air, grinning as the people exclaimed while he cast the streams of white in an elegant coil upward.

"That is what Sethos longed to control," Ronan said. "Both the twins, on his side, rather than on ours."

"It was a clever plan," I said. "Even when Keallach was with him, it kept Kapriel from all he was meant to be." I gestured toward him. "It was if he'd been hobbled. Now . . ."

Now we could both see. When we'd been called, we'd had no idea that the twins might be a part of our divinely appointed circle. And with them both gaining full command of their gifting and our people, it felt like we had a hundred helicopters at our disposal.

We entered the Citadel and made our way to the gathering hall for a meeting that Kapriel and Keallach had called. Joining us were the elders in the first few rows, those in our inner circles above them, and then as many others as the room could hold. I was a bit surprised at how crowded it was, but many were anxious to know what was next and how we planned on responding to the threat of more attacks.

When the twins stood, the room grew silent.

Kapriel stepped forward, his face grim, as Keallach took a seat. "Brothers and sisters, thank you for meeting with us today. Niero, Keallach, and I have been talking at length over these last days, as we grieved our dead and started to rebuild. No one knows what Sethos, the Council, and Pacifica are capable of better than Keallach and Cyrus. And what they have shared with me is frightening. Not only does Pacifica plan to dominate the Trading Union—usurp her into the empire—but they also plan on eradicating every one of the faithful within those new borders. They shall not take us prisoner or enslave our children—their mission is simply to murder every one of us and anyone associated with us, in an attempt to eradicate people of the Way, now and forever."

He paused and swallowed hard as many people in the room either gasped or shouted in outrage. "We've seen it here, ourselves," he went on, gesturing toward the passageways. "They did not spare our children. Their goal is genocide. They have finally figured out that you might outlaw naming or worshiping the Maker, but you cannot stop it from happening inside us." He put his hand on his chest. "The faithful will remain forever faithful, because persecution only sends us into deeper, more hidden territory where we can be free to worship and live as our hearts demand."

He lifted his chin and looked slowly around the room. "Brothers and sisters, Keallach and I feel it is time to come out from hiding. To cease running. To reclaim what we were born to govern—Pacifica herself. We believe it is not wise to remain here, awaiting the next attack. We believe it is time to take the fight to our enemies and destroy those that threaten our goal to return life, in its fullest, to every person, in every land we can touch."

I stared at him as I absorbed the collective mix of surprise, chagrin, and pride that swirled about the room. We Ailith knew what was coming; what we didn't know was how our people might react. Everyone began to speak and shout at once. I saw Azarel and Asher share a troubled look, as if this wasn't what they expected out of Kapriel. I supposed they'd spent years trying to rescue their prince from the prison in Pacifica; the last thing they'd imagined was his returning to that land. But Niero stood behind the brothers, in full support.

It was then that I saw it. Kapriel and Keallach thought of themselves as superior. Born to be co-regents, with undeniably the strongest gifts among us.

I checked myself. Was I jealous? Was I being petty, because I somehow felt left out or less-than? Was this simply another echo of the evil that Sethos had planted in my heart, coming out at a critical juncture when the twins most needed my support?

No, Niero said to me silently. *It's simply a shift in the dynamics of the Ailith. Stay together, as close as possible. Refuse anything that divides you.*

Tressa rose from her seat, and I looked to her in surprise. She rarely spoke in larger groups, unless pressed. "The Way is a path of peace," she said, her voice high and clear. "The Way is a path of healing and joy. It is one thing to defend ourselves from the enemy; it is quite another to attack." She looked to our brothers. "But the Maker has led us to this place. Given us the opportunity to free those our enemies have enslaved and protect ourselves from the coming slaughter. I fully stand behind this plan. We will enter Pacifica, and in time there will be others there who come to know the gifts the Way brings."

"There is nothing that surprises the Maker," Kapriel said. "And we believe," he said, pausing to look at his brother, "that he plans to use us all to usher in a time of peace. Of hope, for a weary world on the brink. Are we not an example of what could be, here in the Citadel?" He looked up and around the room. "Even after we've suffered terrible losses?"

People nodded and murmured their assent.

"It is one thing to win over people who have nothing to lose," said a Drifter, rising to his feet. "It is another thing to win people who have everything they need."

More sounds of assent rose around the room.

"But they *don't* have everything they need," Kapriel put in. "They worship nothing but themselves. Their women make up their faces, as if to say they are above death. Immortal. And yet they are plagued by infertility, when they each long for new life above all else. Children of their own."

"And so they steal ours!" called out a woman from Georgii Post.

Keallach took a deep breath and looked to me. "It is true. Pacificans are in as dire need of the Way as any others. And if we were to lead them, if we had their resources at our fingertips, there would be plenty for all in the Trading Union."

"At what cost to them?" I asked. "Are you so certain that the people of Pacifica would agree to share, if it meant they had less?" I'd seen them firsthand. Witnessed their wealth. And was not at all certain they would give way to generosity.

"Not with Sethos and the Council leading them," Keallach responded. "We cannot win over the people of Pacifica if her dark guardians block our path or, worse, succeed in their goal of killing us. They have to be eradicated. It's us or them."

The room erupted with applause and shouts. We were weary of being the hunted. Power surged in and through us. Was this truly our time?

I swallowed hard, remembering the sheer, dark hate in Sethos's eyes, in Lord Jala's too. And how they'd sent those Sheolites into the Citadel, bent on tracking me down, killing me. They'd murdered Chaza'el. Tried to kill Vidar.

Keallach's eyes sparkled when he saw that he'd managed to give me something significant to consider. "You know it's true. More than any other here, Andriana, because you've seen it yourself. They shall be relentless in their pursuit of us. You think the last attack was the worst they can bring us?" He waved upward. "Despite our gifting, they will continue to find ways to surprise us, murdering us one by one, as they did Chaza'el. They will not be planning just a few more attacks upon us here, hoping to take one Remnant each time. They will plan on *waves* of attacks." Cyrus nodded, behind him.

"So what do you propose?" Vidar asked. "Lay a trap for the dragon and cut off his head?"

Bellona said, "We could lay waste to the aqueduct feeding their cities. And when they come to repair it . . ." She lifted a brow as others loudly agreed around her.

"Except Sethos is far too clever for that," Keallach said, lifting his hands to settle them, his tone reasonable, not condescending. "And his intention is to focus on offense, rather than defense. He'll know that the losses of our people will galvanize us. That it will press us to become more vigilant in our defenses. I believe it is only because Zanzibar has come to our aid, setting up a defensive force in the desert even this day, that they have not yet come again. But they *will* come. They will send countless Pacificans to their deaths in relentless fighting, hoping that, in time, they'll be lucky and kill one or two of the Ailith and elders here, another couple there, until every leader you have is gone and our various tribes again scatter." His eyes narrowed, and his jaw muscles flexed as he looked about the room. "They are determined—as I once was with them—to eradicate the faithful and all who follow or support us. Because they want *domination*."

"Am I not the perfect example of that?" Kapriel said softly, stepping forward. His words hung in the air. "Sethos hoped I would die in that island prison, or turn from the Way. Next time, he won't wait."

Keallach turned to me. "Andriana can testify to it too. What Sethos and the Council are like. The lengths they're willing to go to press their way."

Startled at him calling me out, I stared back into his eyes. They covered me: warm, concerned, apologetic . . . and oddly intimate. I felt Ronan tense beside me. I frowned at Keallach in confusion. But the people all looked to me now, waiting for me to speak.

I rose on trembling legs. "I do know the enemy we face, from firsthand experience. Sethos will not stop until he sees his vision complete. They were willing to kill my mother and father before my eyes in order to make me . . ." I paused, looking again to Keallach and feeling Ronan's tension rise. "In order to force me to do what they wanted. They cannot be allowed to continue to rule. We must take back the Pacifican throne for the people of the Way. It was the Maker's desire to see Keallach and Kapriel on the throne there, not Sethos. But first," I said, looking to each of the other Ailith, "I think there's one more outpost that needs to be claimed for the Trading Union. They will help support us and lend us people for the fight to come."

Every one of them returned my gaze, with understanding. If we were stronger because of Zanzibar's support, what would we be if we took Georgii Post?

Kapriel looked to Keallach in wonder. "She's right. She's absolutely right."

Kapriel's expression of brotherly love and admiration as he turned back to me made me smile. But Keallach . . . his expression took me back to Palace Pacifica, when he was in full pursuit of me. I blushed and glanced at Ronan in confusion.

Thankfully, the room was a mass of chatter and cheering and debate.

Except for my husband. Only he looked dark and frustrated in the midst of the swelling joy about us.

CHAPTER 31

RONAN

Keallach met my gaze as he exited, clearly inviting me into the discussion he knew we had to have. "Wait here for me, Dri," I said. "I'll return for you."

I didn't wait for her assent, only followed him out the door and down the hall to a secluded alcove. He turned around, and I studied his face in the dancing light and deep shadows of the torch behind me. "You are angry that I made Dri speak?" he asked.

"No! Well, yes! More how you were looking at her in there," I said in a harsh whisper, shaking my head. "What was *that* about, Keallach?

He frowned and looked genuinely surprised. "What do you mean?"

"You were looking at her like you did in Wadi Qelt. Like I'm sure you did in Palace Pacifica," I said, edging closer to him. "Like you *wanted* her. She felt it too."

He lifted his brows in shock and then frowned. "There are things that Dri experienced in Pacifica that only she and I remember, because she and I were the only ones who experienced them." He cocked his head. "I'm sorry, brother, if I looked upon her with anything but sisterly affection. Memories of those days bring up old feelings for me. And seeing her speak so boldly ... Perhaps you were only sensing my old admiration?"

I clenched my fists. His words and tone were innocent and apologetic, but there was something beneath them. Did he toy with me? "Perhaps," I said shortly. "But in that place, in those memories, lies a danger. For both of you."

He nodded, as if letting my words sink in. I frowned.

"Dangerous, yes," he said. Was that a tiny quirk of a smile?

"There is no need to bait him, Keallach," Niero said, surprising us both.

Keallach turned his head sharply, as did I. The man was sitting on the edge of the wall, casually leaning back against the cliff, as if giving no care to the precipitous drop on the other side. But given that he was an angel ...

"This is between us, Niero," I said.

"I thought it best if there was a third present," he said to us. "You two have done remarkably well together. I want to see it continue."

"It matters not to me who listens," Keallach said with a slight shrug. "I have nothing to hide." He had regained his innocent expression, but I couldn't help feeling that there was something just below the surface.

"I think there is something yet that you hide," I said.

He didn't move as I got closer to him with each word. "I think that as you have gradually come into power of a sort again, it brings back feelings and thoughts of Andriana by your side as a mate. But she is *my* wife, Keallach."

"Your handfasted wife," he said casually, running his fingertips over the stone. "As I understand it," he said carefully, "you have not yet become . . . of one flesh. Nor shall you until your second decade."

My eyes narrowed. "Are you threatening to intervene?" I asked, taking fistfuls of his tunic in my hands.

"Ronan," Niero said.

With a sigh, I dropped my hands from Keallach.

"I am simply clarifying facts," Keallach said, crossing his arms. "And while you seem to imply that I am overstepping my claim in taking any form of power in leading the Remnants, perhaps you yourself have made undue claims upon Andriana's future. There is a reason the Community urges us to wait until our second decade to exchange our vows, right? It gives us all time to really weigh our decisions. Consider other . . . options."

Niero was beside us then, sensing my gathering rage, even while Keallach looked as if he'd barely noticed it, going on and on in his irritatingly reasonable tone.

"In the eyes of the Maker," Niero said, "Ronan and Andriana are one. Their vows were spoken from the heart and will be consummated upon their second decade, in keeping with the Valley custom."

I narrowed my eyes at Keallach. "Our vows are something that only Dri and I can truly remember, because in that moment, it was as if we were the only two present. Just as we will be present again, five seasons hence."

"Clearly, you share an enviable love," Keallach said, ignoring my jibe. He let out a huff of a laugh and stepped away from me, brushing out his tunic and pulling his robe back over his shoulders. "Come now, brother, let's get past that, shall we? You won the girl, and I'll admit it chafes at me once in a while, but I'll get over it. We have bigger things to worry about."

I crossed my arms. "Yes, we do. But I am Andriana's protector. And if you are thinking about pursuing her again, manipulating her—"

"*Manipulating* her?" he cried, offended. Then realization struck him. "You mean as I did in Pacifica, using the low gifts."

I drew in a breath and pulled up short. "Yes."

"Ronan," he said, "I was not in my right mind when that happened. I had allowed Sethos . . ." He looked to the night-covered valley again, as if recalling a troubling memory. "I was far from the path," he went on, looking to me again, and then to Niero. "But I am no longer. Thanks to the Ailith, I am where I belong, and I will not lead Andriana—or anyone else—anywhere I don't truly think they should go."

I took a breath, relieved that he seemed to be coming back to himself, the Keallach we'd accepted as brother. But still I stared at him, taking his measure, within, thinking over his words. *Anywhere I don't truly think they should go . . .* But what if he thought Andriana should go with him, to Pacifica?

But surely he was beyond that. Well beyond that.

"I admit it, brother. I wronged you and Andriana," he went on. "But I don't intend to repeat that in the future. I swear it." He reached out an arm. "Now can we set this behind us, once and for all?"

"If you agree to not pursue Andriana as anything but a friend, this won't be an issue again."

"Agreed," he said, and I took his arm.

"Good. Thank you." He glanced at us both. "So we're good? Nothing else to resolve?"

"For now," Niero said, dark eyes sliding over him.

"All right. Good night." He turned and left us.

"Good night," Niero said. I remained silent. A farewell felt . . . too kind.

I walked to the wall and leaned heavily against it, looking out. Niero remained, waiting me out. "It is one thing," he said, setting one foot to swinging casually, "to allow Keallach into the Ailith fold." He looked to me. "It is another to allow a brother to enter one's heart."

I sighed and turned to lean my back against an archway, folding my arms again. "Is it the guardian in me that keeps me from doing so? I confess that I seem to be struggling with letting past sins stay in the past, when the others seem to have accepted him wholeheartedly. Even Kapriel. And I know that is the Maker's way."

"It is," he said gently, then peered upward. "But the Maker still intends for us to be wise. And the Remnant with the gift of wisdom never made it to our fold."

I considered his words. "What would you advise, then?"

"Take Keallach at face value now. He was made new the day he turned from Sethos, took his vows, and accepted the cuff. We must treat him as such. But . . ." His words faded as he frowned.

"But?"

"But just as Dri's window to the soul was once open to the dark, so was Keallach's, for a far greater length of time. We shall watch him, together, with eyes and hearts that refuse ignorance."

I nodded. "Agreed. Though I don't anticipate it being easy."

"Nothing worthwhile ever is, Knight," he said. He hopped off of the wall and paused beside me to put a hand on my shoulder. "Rest easy about Dri, though. She is yours, through and through. She loves you. She always has. Don't let jealousy cloud that."

CHAPTER
32

ANDRIANA

So, we head to Georgii Post," Tressa said the next morning, looking around at the rest of us. We had all been fairly quiet around the table, even as the rest of the dining hall remained boisterous and loud with laughter and bickering and cheers and jeers alike. Dimly, I realized I'd become accustomed to the din. It comforted me, especially when facing such dark ideas as wading into an unfriendly city again.

"We were sent to Zanzibar," Killian said, taking a swig from his ceramic cup. "It couldn't be any worse than that."

We all nodded, knowing he spoke the truth. If the Maker sent us, we would go. And he'd planted this new goal in each of our minds at the same time, even if I'd been the one to voice it. But we'd lost Chaza'el since we went to Zanzibar, and nearly lost Vidar too. We knew we were divinely appointed, but not immortal. And the last time we'd been at Georgii Post, there had been Sheolites and Pacifican guards in every direction. It didn't exactly bring up fond memories.

"The Maker gives you not a spirit of fear," Ivar said from his seat across the table from me. "Only hope. Only confidence."

Again, we all nodded.

There was a commotion at the dining hall doorway as some newcomers arrived. Sesille, the once-blind Drifter chief, was at the front of them. They approached us, he and four others, with excitement on each of their faces.

"Sesille, my friend," Kapriel said, turning to take his arm in greeting. "What word do you bring us?"

"We've been to Castle Vega and back, my prince," said the barrel-chested man. "And the gates to the city were closed. Word about the castle is that there is chaos within because of what is happening in Pacifica herself."

"And that is . . ." Keallach led, stepping beside his brother.

"There is infighting as bad as in any Drifter tribe," he said, with some satisfaction. "Noble against noble. Citizen against citizen. Some have called for Keallach to be reinstated, and they were immediately killed. Those who try and leave Pacifica, to come to the Trading Union, cannot go without special papers now. The Pacificans are fully occupied with maintaining peace at home."

"Which is why they haven't returned to come after us," Keallach said, chin in hand.

"They are crumbling from within," Azarel said, eyes round with amazement.

"Indeed," Keallach said, taking a couple of steps and then turning, excitement practically sparking from him. "So we know we are to begin in Georgii Post, but why stop there when the enemy is weak? Why not go from there to Castle Vega?"

We all turned to look at him.

"If we are successful at Georgii Post, we could build on our momentum," he said. "People would follow us, help us."

Vidar was the first to speak. "If Pacifican soldiers were measured in grains of sand, the number in Georgii Post would represent enough to chafe in the shoe, but Castle Vega would represent an entire dune. It's practically Pacifica itself."

"Which would be a good place to declare ourselves," Kapriel said quietly, rising. "Pacifica, and yet not." His eyes sparkled. He'd gained some weight and more color in his cheeks over these last weeks, looking more and more like his twin.

"Or the worst place possible," Niero said. "Do not go unless the Maker calls you to it, because as much as it would be a symbolic triumph for people of the Way, it could become a death trap for you. Only the Maker can lead you to such a decision."

"But if he *did*," Keallach said, eyes glinting, "then it would be an excellent stepping stone into Pacifica. What Sesille describes is civil unrest. The people are afraid, confused. What I want to spark is spiritual unrest."

Niero frowned. "Meaning?"

"Unrest for all the right reasons," Keallach said, lifting his hands. "I know people in Castle Vega. Many people. If we were able to persuade some in the castle to abandon the trappings of their lives and join us, if they never returned, more behind the Wall in Pacifica would hear of it and begin to wonder what we offer that Sethos cannot. Don't you see? They would contemplate their own lives, their present, their future, possibly for the very first time, allowing the Maker to begin to work."

Kapriel nodded, moving toward his chair, his excitement palpable. "They are a people, long asleep. It's our chance to shake them awake."

"If the Maker calls us to it," Ronan reminded them, his brow furrowed.

"Of course," Keallach said, nodding reassuringly. "If he calls."

"But it would make sense," Kapriel pressed. "Would it not?"

"Possibly," Niero said. "But wait on him. Do not press your own way in this, understood? We are on his path, working in his timing. If we make this more about us than him, then we leave the path. For now, you've mutually agreed upon his call to Georgii Post. Right?"

"Right," we all murmured, trepidation swirling about us, even as a steady assurance filled each of our minds and hearts.

There was surely more than one battle ahead.

Soon, there would be outright war.

CHAPTER
33

ANDRIANA

We approached Georgii Post with hundreds of armed people alongside us. But when we reached the first part of the curving canyon that descended downward between soaring red cliffs, our four scouts rode back to us, eyes wide.

"You're not going to believe this," said Barrett.

"They seem to be welcoming us!" finished his younger, Aravander companion.

Keallach and Kapriel shared a long look. "How so?" Kapriel asked.

"A Georgii guard met us, waving a white flag," said Barrett, giving the second a warning look about interrupting him again. "The Pacificans heard we approached, and since they felt their support within the city had slowly been eroding, they elected to vacate the city rather than oppose us. They didn't want another Zanzibar experience. They decided to cut their losses and retreat to Castle Vega."

"To Castle Vega!" repeated the second gleefully, unabashed by his superior's sour look.

"Do you think it might be a trap?" Ronan asked, lifting a hand. We'd assembled as a circle, we Remnants and Knights, as well as other key leaders, Cyrus and Sesille among them.

Barrett studied Ronan for a moment, and his lips twitched. "Could be. Hard for me to believe the Pacificans would simply abandon such a fruitful city within the Union. But the people assemble, clearly ready to welcome the crown princes." His dark eyes moved to Kapriel and Keallach.

"Which means it could be an even more elaborate trap," Kapriel said, looking to his brother. Keallach, arms crossed, nodded once.

"What do you sense? See?" Niero asked Vidar.

"You mean, besides a warm bed beneath a roof tonight, I assume," Vidar said, moving past him to look down the serpentine canyon, as if he could see the city gates themselves.

"Besides that," Niero returned. We'd all inwardly groaned when the cold, pelting rain of Hoarfrost greeted us the moment we'd left the Valley mouth. Some had outright wondered if it was a sign we should return home.

Vidar wiped his wet face and took a few more steps to the edge of the cliff, where we had been awaiting our scouts before descending deeper into the canyon, in order to avoid an increased chance of attack from above. After several long moments, he turned and shook his head, looking perplexed. "I think it's only the lingering stench of our enemies. It feels safe to me." He nodded upward, to the canyon rim. "And we are not alone."

I shivered, recognizing at once the truth of his words. Our unseen guardians had not left us since the attack on the

Citadel. Every day, they went before us, beside us, behind us, and there were days I didn't remember to reach out, to see if I could sense them. And then I was surprised when someone—usually Vidar—reminded me. Silently, I apologized to the Maker. How much he did for me—for us—day in and day out. How much he watched over us, led us, and protected us! And yet how much I forgot.

Make me a daughter of memory, Maker. Don't let me forget to honor you. Help me to make you first and foremost through every hour.

The young husband and wife we'd rescued from Georgii Post approached Ronan and me as we resumed our progress down the canyon on mudhorses. "Everything all right?" the man asked, casting a suspicious glance down the road before us. We'd left their child in my parents' care, aware that their experience and knowledge of the city would be valuable to us all. Bravely, they'd agreed. They'd been as clearly called to join us on this mission as they had been called to come to us in the Citadel, a week past. Azarel and Asher were with us too, given their experience and connections in Georgii Post, but also because they seemed to be an integral part of our team now, just as Cyrus was. And due to Azarel's gifts with the bow and Asher's ability to connect with others, they were becoming invaluable to us. Especially without Chaza'el . . .

A pang of sorrow went through me at the memory of him, dead in the Citadel. He had been as serene in death as he had been in life, almost as if he'd been asleep, rather than having moved on to the afterlife. Perhaps it had been a part of his gifting—flowing with life rather than butting heads with it over and over again allowed him to "see" forward, on occasion. I glanced at Ronan and reached over to take his hand in mine.

He cast me a curious look, but I said nothing, just squeezed his fingers and looked forward. Whatever was ahead of us, I would do my best to take in stride. There'd been so much battle in our lives. Perhaps here, now, the Maker meant us to simply be with him. Perhaps he had already won any victory necessary.

Niero was the first to hear the singing as we edged ever closer to the city entrance. He pulled up short and lifted a fist, signaling that we were all to stop. And that's when we heard it too. Thousands of voices, some deep and resonant, others high and melodious, all singing the same song I'd heard as a child but forgotten.

Ronan's face broke out in a smile, eyes wide in recognition, and he began to mouth the words with them. Asher wasn't mouthing the words, he was belting them out, one hand thumping his chest, the other lifting up to the sky, tears streaming down his cheeks. Azarel looked similarly stricken, her face uncustomarily soft and reverent, like I hadn't seen it since that day in the Hoodite cave. And then I thought of it. Was this a song they had taught their precious orphans? In their school before the children had been taken? Some to be adopted, and others to work the cursed mines?

Was it possible? I felt like we were dreaming as we moved again as one, now singing what we could remember of a song that our ancestors once knew well. We rounded the corner, and the song became loud enough to cover the noise of our horses and clanking swords and the rough purr of engines. I wanted to stop, just then and there, to absorb it. The hundreds, if not thousands, of people. The waving of their arms, the undeniable swell of joy within them all.

Before us, the crowd parted, and we passed through, many reaching out to touch us, faces wet, others kneeling in reverence of the Maker's Way, so visible in our arrival. We had expected battle. Bloodshed. But all we received here, now, was love. Adulation. Praise. Welcome.

It was little wonder the Maker had called us here. He wanted to remind us that we were his people and we were not alone on this journey. We'd suffered. Taken terrible losses. But here there were more to stand against the tide.

We all recognized this truth. Not one of our faces was dry, even Killian's, I noted with a giggle. His usual stern expression was broken by utter surprise and joy as the crowd moved into another song, one I knew him to hum on occasion, but for which I had never known the words.

We finally came to a stop at the chief magistrate's sprawling home, where apparently the city's people expected us to stay. There was no gray uniform in sight, no Pacifican perusing the Georgiians as if they were Pacifican subjects rather than citizens of an independent town of the Trading Union. Servants bowed and welcomed us, offering to show us to our rooms after we ate. But first, there was a banquet table that they wanted us to see.

We were led into room after room of tables, laden with food like I hadn't seen since I'd fled Palace Pacifica. Fruit—dried and fresh—along with cured meats and fresh bread and jugs of wine and five different kinds of cheese. Most sat down at the first empty spots they reached, but we Ailith carried on until we entered a larger room, with a huge, circular table.

"This is where you belong," said the head servant, a tall, thin, angular man with a pinched look to his face but eyes and heart full of nothing but relief. "This is where you have always belonged, I wager," he added with a solemn nod.

We spread out along the edge, and I took a seat between Keallach and Ronan, not willing to find another simply to spare Ronan's feelings. Not in this moment. It was all so right, and there was such an intense feeling of homecoming that I didn't want to obey any spirit of hesitation, nor entertain any thought that might mar it. This was what my mom meant about home being anyplace in which one met like hearts. It didn't matter that we weren't in the Valley. Or in the Citadel. It only mattered that we were with fellow people of the Way.

Almost every seat in the huge circle was filled. Vidar poured a goblet of wine and lifted it up. We followed his gesture and did the same, waiting on him. "To a battle won, that we didn't have to fight," he said.

"Hear hear," we all said, drinking to his toast.

"I submit," said our servant-host, who had introduced himself as Clancy, "that you have been battling for some time, in ways that we haven't seen ourselves, but that have borne beautiful results. To the unseen battle and the spoils of war," he said, lifting his goblet.

"Hear, hear to *spoils*," Vidar said, and we repeated his reply with smiles and soft laughter. Niero was right. Our responsibility was to go where the Maker led us, to do what he asked, and trust him with what we could not control. Was this not evidence of that fact?

Ronan cut a slab of oddly pale meat and put it on my plate, eyes twinkling at the bounty. We hadn't eaten since breakfast, and my stomach rumbled in anticipation.

Keallach turned partially toward me, as if he'd heard. There was half a loaf of bread in his hand, and he bit a chunk off, chewing the crusty delicacy with emphasis as he watched me cut a bite of meat and place it in my mouth. I closed my eyes, wondering over the taste of lemon and rosemary on a delicate, white meat.

"Chicken," he informed me conspiratorially. "And very well prepared."

Chicken, I repeated silently in my head, eagerly taking another bite and another, until my whole portion was gone. I eyed the table platter, wondering if I could be so bold as to take another piece before even my fruit and vegetables and bread was gone. Ronan was distracted, talking and laughing with Vidar on his other side.

"Go on," Keallach chided. "This is the first of many feasts, and you've gone without long enough."

It was true. How much had I missed over the years? Sacrificed? Wasn't I worthy of abundance, for once? Even when I'd been in the palace before, I'd felt half sick. I'd not been in any position to truly enjoy the bounty. Here, now, for the first time in my entire life . . .

The thought brought me up short. *For the first time in my entire life.* While others were outside, still never having had the chance. I stuffed a bite of bread in my mouth, chewing on both it and the thoughts roiling about in my head. What were we doing in here with such bounty? Who were we to separate ourselves?

I was rising before I fully recognized what I was doing.

"Andriana," Keallach said in a hush, "what is it?"

"Dri?" Ronan asked, finally turning my way again as I shoved my chair back and waited for others to see me. Gradually, the room grew quiet.

"Are not all invited to the Maker's feast?" I asked carefully. "And yet here we sit, as if we were conquerors. As if we deserve more than our brothers and sisters, some of them new to the faith today. Let us take our fill, but not beyond, and then take the rest to the others."

"No," Tressa said rising, reaching for another platter. "Your first impulse was right, sister. Let us take it now, before we even take our fill. To those who can't even reach the gates of this mansion. To the sick, the weak, the hungry . . ."

Keallach and Vidar made half-hearted attempts to sway us, but we ignored them. As one, we knew this was the next, right step, and all of us gathered up every smidgen of food and all the jugs of wine and carried them out, past the others in the next rooms who gaped at us and then gradually followed suit. Together, we moved outward to the street and divided naturally along the labyrinthine avenues and alleyways, handing out plums and apples and bananas and slices of meat and chunks of bread. Ronan was with me for a time and then he was not, but I wasn't worried. I sensed only pleasure and peace among the people. Joy and praise. Excitement. Gratitude.

And as I continued to hand out all I had, I realized I was no longer hungry. Feeding others fed a deeper part of me. Finally, my platter was empty except for one last slice of cheese and one chunk of bread. I set the silver platter on a low wall and smiled as a little boy tentatively grabbed hold of it. "Go on," I said. I knew he'd just finished the apple I'd given him. "Take that platter. Sell it and use the proceeds to help you buy food for yourself and others over the coming weeks. Agreed?"

He nodded excitedly. I scooped up the bread and cheese before he made off with it too, and then looked around, wondering whom the Maker would have me feed next. This alley was deep in shadow, and yet I knew I was where I was supposed to be. I took a few tentative steps, smiling as people passed by the mouth of the alley singing and laughing. It was so vastly different than the last time we'd run through this way, battling back such horrific evil, with Sheolites kidnapping children and trackers who hunted us. Now the streets were awash in peace. I took a few more steps and saw her . . . a small child, curled up in a ball against a gap in the wall, her knees pressed against her chest and her dress much too light in the face of a night that, even now, whispered of Hoarfrost snowflakes.

I knelt before her. "Hello, little sister. My name is Andriana. What is yours?"

"Dolla," she said through chattering teeth.

"Are you sick, Dolla?" I asked.

"No," she said. "Only cold."

"Why are you not with the others?" I asked. "Have you not heard the singing? The celebration?"

"I, my, I . . . can't. I am not one of them. I have no family."

"Hmm," I said. My first instinct was to reach for my cape and give it to her, but I realized I'd left it inside. I glanced around, toward a sputtering street torch in one direction and into the gathering dark in the other, but the child and I were momentarily alone. Feeling nothing but the urge to ward off the obvious chill the trembling child felt, I pulled my sweater off and then pulled it over her head, helping her to press her tiny arms through the long arms until her small, grubby hands peeked out the ends. In one hand, I placed my last chunk of bread, and in the other, my last slice of cheese. "You do have a family, Dolla. You are one of the Way, if you claim the Maker as your own. He sees you and loves you, little one, as a treasured daughter. Always remember that, whatever comes."

She nodded, her big, brown eyes intent upon me, even as she bit hungrily into the cheese. Her mouth fell open, and she chewed more slowly, as if exploring the new taste of it. As if she never wanted to forget it.

I sat down beside her. "Did you ever meet a man named Asher here, who once ran a school?"

Her face whipped up toward me, half of her searching me, as if to see if I might be playing some sort of cruel joke, and half of her alight with hope. "Asher! Is he here?"

"Yes," I said with a smile. "He has returned, along with his friend, Azarel."

"Azarel!" she squeaked. "It is true, then," she said, scrambling to her feet. "The time for the people of the Way has come! I was so scared! Last time, when people of the Way came . . ."

"It ended poorly," I said soberly, looking up at her. In the meager light cast from the street torch, the bones of her face stuck out in stark contrast to what the normal swell of childhood's bounty should be. I reached out and took her empty hand, not wanting her to fear for her bread. "But the Maker is ushering in a new day, a new time for the Way, Dolla. Do not be afraid to serve him."

She nodded eagerly. "Can I go to him? To Asher?"

"Of course," I said, rising. "I will take you to . . ." But she was already sprinting away, my sweater's edge dangling around her calves. I laughed and wondered if she would be able to find him, but I figured the Maker would show her the way.

I rubbed the back of my neck, shivering a little in my T-shirt and realizing that the crowds had departed for their homes, leaving this section of town very quiet. That was when I saw him. As Dolla passed by, his silhouette was clear with the street torch behind him.

"Keallach," I said, stepping toward him, feeling an odd lurch of my heart. He swept off his fur-lined cape and began to wrap it around my shoulders, but I blocked him. "No, it's okay. I'll be warm enough until I get back."

"Don't be foolish," he insisted, pulling the cape around my shoulders again and tying it at my neck. "You are shivering nearly as much as that little girl was."

My hands dropped, almost as if they were beyond my will, and I realized he spoke the truth. I hadn't felt the chill of the night as I served others. But I did now. And his cape, so thick and soft, still warm from his own body, readily warded off the cold. He took an inordinate amount of time tying the knot. Maybe it was because he was staring at me, as if silently begging me to look into his eyes.

"Keallach," I began, slow alarm building within me, and yet I felt frozen, unable to say anything more. I was distantly shocked as he cupped his warm palm against my cheek, urging me to look upon him again. And when I at last met his gaze, my pulse quickened.

"That," he said, inclining his head toward the spot where Dolla had been, "was the most selfless, beautiful thing I've ever witnessed."

He leaned in then, kissing me softly. It wasn't like the last time we'd kissed in the palace. This was a longing, a hunger that my heart noted and, in turn, wanted to assuage. There was a fire building within me as his kiss deepened.

It was the chill of my armband that snapped me out of my dreamlike reverie and brought me back to myself with a start as he pressed my back against the wall, even as he pulled me closer.

"No," I said, finally finding my voice and the sudden strength to push him away. "Keallach, *no*. What is going on here? What are we doing?" I cried.

He staggered back from me, looking dazed and startled himself, then his brow lowered. "Dri, I'm sorry. It was the wine tonight, the joy of the day. I—"

"No!" I said, fumbling at the knot of his cape, suddenly desperate to get him—anything of him—off of me. How had

I allowed . . . But I hadn't allowed it. Not really. My arms had been—

"Keep it, Dri, keep it! Wear it back to the mansion," he muttered, closing his eyes, deep regret wafting through him.

Regret, I registered. *Sorrow. Fear.* And as those emotions emerged from him, I also noted that my arm cuff was warming. He looked at me with his beautiful eyes, nothing but pain in them, and fear that he'd just destroyed everything he'd so carefully built.

"Keallach, what *was* that?" I spat out, still angry with him, even as I felt for him over his pain and confusion. "Did you just compel me?"

"It was nothing," he said, shaking his head in agitation. "Echoes of my old feelings for you."

"Old feelings," I said. "Feelings you aren't to allow to reign any longer, now that I am Ronan's wife. And you, my sworn Remnant *brother*."

He let out a hollow laugh. "You, of all people, should know that *feelings* are a hard thing to master." He straightened slowly, looking into my eyes. "Andriana. You were the first one, you know. The first one who made me remember . . . called me back to the Way I thought was lost to me. If it wasn't for you . . . I'm so grateful for you, Dri. So grateful."

I swallowed hard, recognizing the growing heat rising between us, the spark in the air that I found tantalizingly hard to ignore. And in turn, the returning chill of my armband.

I grit my teeth. "This is the remains of Sethos's spell, nothing more."

"But Dri, I need to—" he began, his voice heavy with agony.

"*No.* Don't say it," I said, putting up one hand, and with the other, finally managing to untie the knot and free the cape from my shoulders. I handed it over to him as the drizzle became a drenching, icy rain, but he would not accept it. His guilt shifted to anger.

"Take a moment to search *yourself*, Dri," he said, water dripping down the chiseled lines of his cheekbones and jawline, down his neck, which had such an attractive hollow just there . . . "You feel it too. This pull between us. This pull that is more than the spell that Sethos wove. Any *compelling* that you may wish to blame." He reached out to take hold of my waist again. To pull me toward him.

"Maker," I breathed. And with the last of my strength, I took hold of his wrist, turned, bent, and yanked him over my hip and to his back on the cobblestones.

I put a knee on his chest and leaned down so I could look him in the face. He heaved for breath, looking partially stunned and partially like this was exactly what he wanted to happen. Like he knew he deserved it. "This ends here," I panted. "Never again," I said, watching as rain dripped from me and onto him. And yet I found it oddly tantalizing, as if the weather itself was weaving us together, one raindrop after another streaming down my face and onto him. "Never again," I bit out.

"Never again," he said slowly, each word an agony. "You're right, of course. So, so right . . ." I watched as raindrops ran across his lips, until I was leaning closer, thinking how much I wanted just one last kiss from him. To be certain. Sure that this was right. That *he* wasn't the one that my heart wanted most . . .

Until I was kissing him, and he was wrapping his hand in my wet hair and then rolling me over onto my back, kissing me deeper. "Andriana," he moaned between kisses. "How I've longed for you, Dri."

"No," I said, feeling the chill of my armband, remembering myself again and now sick at heart, trying to press him away but finding I had no strength. "No, Keallach, no," I said, moving my head as his lips moved to my ear and down my neck. "Please, stop," I whimpered, feeling unaccountably weak, unable to move other than to allow him more space for his sweet kisses along my neck. "Keallach. *Keallach*."

"Andriana, don't stop this," he said, his arm wrapping around my lower back, pulling me closer, up to match the arc of his own body.

"Stop," I said. "Please, stop. I am Ronan's," I said, my voice gaining strength. "Ronan's."

"In name only," he soothed, his lips moving along the soft flesh beneath my jaw. "You have not yet consummated your vows. There is time to make another choice. Many seasons yet, to see what might unfold."

"No," I said. "It is done. I have made my choice. Keallach, please."

"Please, Andriana, don't back away now," he said, wrapping his fingers through mine, pressing my hands above my head, to the cold stones.

Of Georgii Post.

A city belonging to the people. People of the Way.

The Way . . . The Way . . .

"Maker," I breathed. "Maker!" I called. "Give me strength!"

A hand reached down and yanked Keallach bodily from me.

I blinked against the rain, feeling both the cold shock of it—without Keallach's body or his cape shielding me from it— as well as the heat of my arm cuff. I knew, then, that we were surrounded by angels.

But Niero was the only one I could plainly see. He shoved Keallach back until he was against the wall, his huge hand at the prince's neck, strangling him. "What are you doing to her?" Niero ground out, his jaw muscles pulsing, the veins in his arm sticking out. "What have you done?" His wings unfurled. I felt his righteous fury. I knew then his deadly intent.

I rose, rushed to them, and grabbed Niero's arm with both hands, trying to pull it away as Keallach gasped for breath. "No, Niero! No!"

"He carries with him the stench of Sethos still. He is not free of his old master. He was using his low gifting against you again!"

"Yes!" I agreed, panic rising. "But when I've succumbed to the dark, you've granted me grace, time and again, have you not?"

I felt him falter a bit, then press harder, choking Keallach.

"Niero!" I cried. "Let him speak. Don't you see? He is not fighting you! Yes, he used his low gifting. But he isn't using his higher gifting now, is he? I feel his sorrow, his anger at himself." I was angry at him too. But if he died here, now. . . "Niero, we need him. With us. To battle what is to come."

"You and Dri are both the strength of the Remnants, and the weakest links," Niero gritted out, his face an inch from Keallach's.

"Yes," Keallach gasped. "Help us. Help . . . me."

His words made Niero's breath catch and then his eyes narrowed to slits. He took Keallach's throat with both hands, lifting him up until he was on his tiptoes.

"Niero," I wept, "don't do this. Is the Maker really . . . is he really calling you to end Keallach's life?" I choked out, unable to stand straight, feeling the weight of my terror and sorrow.

Niero held Keallach up against the wall, wriggling, desperate for seconds that seemed like hours. And then he let him fall, his hands swooshing out in an arc, as if he were washing him away. Keallach fell heavily, gasping for breath. He reached for me, but Niero took hold of my arm and yanked me away from him and down the street.

When we'd turned the corner by the next torch, he swung me around to face him, a hand on either of my arms. "Andriana," he whispered, a tone I found more frightening than when he shouted, "you must find it within you . . . how to discern what is truth, and what is a lie."

"I know," I whispered in return, half crying. "I know," I repeated, the tears now flowing. "But I can't. Back there . . . with him . . . it was as if I lost myself."

"You *did* lose yourself," he said, shaking me a little, staring down at me with fierce consternation. "Everything about you that was true and righteous. You allowed yourself to be sucked into what was primal and sinful. You are more than that, Dri." He released me, and I shuddered as I felt his disappointment. "Over and over again, we go through this," he said, pacing back and forth before me. "When it comes to battle, you must rely on what you know, not what you feel. The enemy will continue to use all that is good in you"—he paused to put his finger to my chest—"a gifting the Maker gave you himself, as his own, righteous weapon. But you can choose not to allow the enemy to use it."

"How?" I shook my head slightly. "I don't know. Tell me."

"You *know*. You've always known. You simply must *choose*," he said sharply.

My head whipped toward his, his words sifting through my mind again. *Choose, Andriana. Choose for right. Choose the Way. Choose strength. Choose wisdom. Choose a love that never fails, not a love the flesh pretends.*

I closed my eyes and lifted my face to the cold, stinging rain. The Maker would never leave me without the weapons I needed to fight these lingering evil spells of Sethos that haunted both me and Keallach. He had given me Ronan, whom my heart loved. The man whom I desired. A man I wanted to share my bed with, when the blessing ceremony occurred at the right time, in the right season. Surrounded by family, both blood and spiritual kin.

Not give myself to another on a city street, as if I knew no sense of value, hope, or strength within. He'd tried to warn me. Called to my heart, sent a chill through my armband. But I'd ignored it, choosing to give into old, intriguing desires.

My teeth clenched, and I straightened, my hands in fists as I turned to face Niero. "I have failed my Maker and my vows for the last time. My enemy will never use me for his gain again Help me, Niero. Help me find the armor I need for my heart and this battle to come. To see it through to the end."

He stared at me for a long moment. Then a slow smile spread across his face. With gentle hands, he took hold of my cheeks and bent my head for a single, benediction kiss on the forehead. "Consider it done, daughter of the Way."

CHAPTER 34

ANDRIANA

I knew what I needed to do. As soon as Niero released me, I turned and ran back to the mansion. I passed scores of people, reaching out, calling to me, but I was single-minded.

Vidar and Bellona looked up as I passed. "There you are," Vidar said. "Ronan was looking for you."

"Where is he?"

"Niero told him to wait for you in the receiving room."

I thought about that as I ran through the corridor to the sprawling receiving room that had held scores of people when we arrived, but now was empty. Save for Ronan. He was pacing back and forth in the corner of the first alcove, rubbing his hands together. I pulled up short, heartsick over what was to come.

"Oh, thank the Maker," he said, rushing toward me, taking my elbows and pulling me in for a hug, wet as I was. "I lost you in the crowds. It felt safe, but . . . I'm sorry. I should not have let the moment distract me from looking after you. Look at you. You're soaked through. Let me—"

"No, I owe you an apology, Ronan," I said, gently squirming out from his embrace. I tried to swallow but found that my mouth was dry. He stood there before me, brows lowered, concerned. "I was out there," I began, gesturing toward the door, "distributing the last of my food, when I saw a tiny girl. She was barely clothed, and you know how cold it is out tonight."

His green-brown eyes shifted over me, across the bare skin of my arms, covered in goose bumps. "So you gave her your sweater . . ."

"Yes."

"You are so generous, Dri. It's part of what I—"

"No," I said, putting up my hand to stop him as he moved toward me. I knew if I didn't get this out, I might never tell him. And if I didn't, Niero would. He would demand it. "I mean, yes. I gave the child my sweater, and the last of the food. But when I rose to follow her back, I saw that I wasn't alone."

His brow lowered farther but he lifted his chin, lips clamped shut, waiting.

"Keallach was there," I said.

I saw the muscles of his neck and jaw tighten.

"And at first he didn't do anything but give me his cape."

"A proper thing to do," Ronan said tightly. "But then?"

"But then he kissed me."

Ronan stared at me as I held my breath. "And then?"

"And then I flipped him on his back," I said, proud of myself for a moment.

He watched me, and I knew that my emotions must have been playing across my face. He reached out and tucked a strand of my hair behind my ear, his movement measured, deliberate. "And then?" he whispered.

I turned halfway from him, folding my arms in front of me. I blinked rapidly, as if watching it play out again in memory. "And then I was . . . pulled in. We kissed again."

"He compelled you," Ronan said bitterly.

"Yes," I said, nodding. "And no," I added, shaking my head in misery. "Honestly, Ronan. There is a draw between me and Keallach. There always has been. And tonight . . . It was all mixed up. I can't blame him entirely."

"But there wouldn't have been anyone to blame if he hadn't *compelled* you," he said, lifting my chin. "Everyone struggles with sinful desires, momentary thoughts along dark paths, Dri. But if someone else forces you to keep that path open, rather than dismissing it . . ." He shook his head. "How did you stop it?"

"I called upon the Maker and Niero arrived, yanking us apart. He . . . he almost strangled Keallach."

"Good," Ronan sneered, pacing away, then back to me, his movements now stiff. "Good!" he repeated, angrier now. He put his hands on his hips and closed his eyes, obviously seeking a measure of control.

"I'm so sorry, Ronan. I have no excuse. There is something between us that . . . something dark that emerges now and then . . ."

"Please," he said, lifting a hand and closing his eyes against the pain my words had caused him. "No more. I don't want to know more except for this: He *did* compel you, as he did before? Right?"

I remembered how my hands had remained at my side for so long and how I was surprised by my own willingness to return his passion. How Niero accused him of using low gifting. "Yes," I whispered.

I shook my head and closed my eyes, rubbing my palms into them for a moment before looking at him. "I promised Niero today—and I promise you now—that it will never overtake me again. The Maker warned me of it, used my arm cuff to sound the alarm. But I was slow to recognize it. I won't be next time. I promise you." I took his hands in mine and moved closer to him. "Please, beloved. Forgive me. With the aid of the Maker, it shall not happen again."

He considered me, and though there was a measure of pain and betrayal, there was a larger measure of love and forgiveness within him. He pulled me into his arms. "With the aid of the Maker, the aid of your handfasted husband, and the help of Niero to back us up, I think you have a good chance of honoring that promise."

I nodded, tears welling in my eyes. Then I shook my head. "I do not deserve your forgiveness."

"Hey," he said, lifting my chin. "It is the hallmark of the Community, yes? We all falter and fail one another. But if our intent is to change our ways, to strive to do better the next time, how can we keep from offering what the Maker himself gives us?"

"But this has cost you," I said. "I can see it."

He gave me a gentle smile. "It is only pride that makes this hurt," he said solemnly. "And you, wife, are worth any price I have to pay. Any price."

I swallowed hard and then pulled him close, wrapping my arms around him, laying my cheek against his chest. "You are such a fine man, Ronan. So unbelievably good to me."

"I only give what you are due."

His words confirmed what my heart had pledged. I loved this man, through and through. He was my best friend. My husband, for all intents and purposes. My future lover. My only future lover. Someday, the father of any children we might bear. The Maker had brought him to me and kept him beside me, despite such hard truths.

I would not fail him again.

KEALLACH

I was still struggling for breath when Dri left Niero's side and the mighty man returned to face me again, with nothing but rage and suspicion in his eyes. He lifted me roughly to my feet, keeping one hand on my shoulder. "You shall be held accountable by the Ailith. The Maker will lead them in the way of wisdom. The dark still lives in you, and it is much stronger than it's ever been with Andriana—testimony to your many seasons with Sethos by your side."

"But is the Maker not stronger yet?" I said, angry that he was so ready to believe the worst of me. I belonged here, with them. I knew I did. I reached up to rub my forehead, trying to figure out what had happened between Dri and me. "I don't know what happened, Niero. Honestly. I've been committed to the fact that I must uphold and honor the vows that Dri and Ronan have taken, regardless of how I feel drawn to her. And then . . . it was only for a moment . . ."

"Save your words for your Ailith kin," he said, turning me around and dragging me along beside him. My legs moved reluctantly, seeming to know what I was just coming to figure out—I was to face a sort of moral trial. Similar to when they all voted to allow me to accept my cuff.

My cuff, I thought with alarm, fighting the urge to reach up and rub it. It had become precious to me, granting me more power than ever before, warning me of danger—a danger signal I had ignored with Dri. Would they . . . could they take it? It seemed impossible. But if the Maker had a way to fuse it to my skin, I knew he must have a way to remove it too.

Or maybe they would elect to try to kill me. I swallowed hard as we turned the corner. *Let them try. They are strong, but my gift is stronger. Niero is only fortunate that I held back or—*

"Such dark thoughts, my prince," Niero muttered. "Trust me, even with your impressive gifting, you do not want to take on an angel of the Maker's dominion."

I frowned. I hated that his power allowed him to know what I was thinking. "I am merely preparing myself for what is to come. Thinking it through. Not intent on acting on every thought."

"See that you don't," he bit out, "because you will find that the Remnants will have me backing them as well."

We reached the front entry of the mansion and rushed past several gaping men and women, eyes full of curiosity over what had us in such a rush. Kapriel was the first to spy us, and a pang of guilt rang through me for a new reason. He would see my actions not only as a disappointment as a Remnant brother, but as my twin also. I knew he felt especially responsible for my acceptance among them. Had it not been for him and Dri speaking up for me . . .

"All is not lost," Niero said, as he left me to walk the remainder of the way with my brother following behind. "You simply must face the truth with humility and then confidently trust the outcome. It is the Way."

I stared at him over my shoulder. He offered me hope? After all that righteous rage?

He waved me off, as if reluctant to have even offered that.

"What is he talking about, Keallach?" Kapriel said, looking over my soaked clothes and the crumpled, soggy cape in my hands. "What has happened?"

I clamped my lips shut, my eyes slipping to Dri and Ronan in the corner of the receiving room. I paused in the doorway a moment, chagrined to find fear in my heart, knowing that Dri would easily read it in me. Such emotion shamed me. Sethos had drilled me and drilled me to face my fear and conquer it. I winced and cocked my head, feeling shame anew. Of all times, this was not the right time to summon memories of my old trainer and his dark ways.

Ronan was striding toward me, Dri hurrying after him, and yet she didn't catch up until he had his fists full of my tunic, pulling my face close to his. I met his gaze, not fighting back. "I failed you, brother," I said miserably. "And our sister too. Please. Forgive me."

He lifted his chin, measuring me through slit eyes. "Do you sense any genuine contrition within him, Dri?" he said over his shoulder, never looking away from me.

"I do," she said softly.

His breathing came out in heavy huffs, but after a moment, he released me and let his hands drop to his sides. "Then I suppose," he said, leaning in until our faces were an inch apart, "I must forgive him."

"Yes," she whispered.

He nodded thoughtfully, taking a deep breath. "I forgive you, Keallach. I do. But if you ever touch my wife again," he said, twisting partially away, "I shall have to do more than *this* . . ."

I saw his fist too late. I think a part of me felt I deserved it, almost leaning into it, offering the full breadth of my cheek. Still, the impact sent me reeling across the stone floor, landing heavily on my side, knocking the breath from me. My jaw screamed with pain, and my vision swam. I looked back to see Andriana covering her mouth with both hands and Ronan cradling his right fist in his left. Kapriel stepped toward me, his movements oddly slow, as if time itself were stopping.

When my head cleared and Kapriel helped me sit up, I noted that the other Ailith had arrived. "Help me rise," I muttered to Kapriel.

"Are you certain?" he whispered. "Maybe you should stay down."

I grimaced, half because of a throbbing pain in my head and half because of what this revelation might do to our newly reformed relationship. Fear tightened its grip around my heart. Had I just destroyed every important bond in my life? Would I be cast out as quickly as I'd been taken in? What would I do then?

Face the truth with humility, Niero had said. *And confidently trust the outcome.*

"So," Vidar said, looking from me to Ronan and back again, "I take it you two aren't getting along."

"You could say that," Ronan said. "Or weren't getting along. I think we've both made ourselves clear now."

"But this brother has ignored the vows he took to uphold the ways of the Maker and of the Ailith mission," Raniero said formally as he closed the doors behind Tressa and Killian, who were the last to enter. They all formed a loose semicircle around me and Kapriel, who stood just behind my left shoulder.

"What has he done?" Kapriel said.

Niero looked to Andriana. "He has compromised your sister, calling upon the low gifts to compel her when she resisted."

Kapriel gaped at me with horror in his eyes.

"He . . . kissed me," Dri said softly, a blush rising on her pretty cheeks and down her neck—a neck that, Maker help me, I still longed to kiss. "Perhaps compelled me to kiss him in return. I cannot be certain," she rushed on, glancing guiltily toward Ronan, "if it was my own darkness or a darkness within him, or both."

"What say you?" Niero barked to me.

"It's true," I said, hating the quaver to my voice. "I gave into my lower gifting, out of an old desire to have Andriana as my own. I have failed her, Ronan, and the rest of the Ailith," I said quickly, lifting both hands in beseeching fashion. "I beg for your forgiveness, all of you. Trust me. No one wants this . . . untoward desire to disappear more than I."

Vidar's smile had faded, and he crossed his arms, chin in one hand, nodding thoughtfully. He glanced over at his peers, both Remnant and Knight. "We knew when we accepted him that there was a risk of the dark rising in him again. And if a kiss is the worst it gets . . ." He quirked a brow and tilted a toothy grin, looking for humorous agreement, right and left. Finding none, he quickly sobered. "Honestly? I sense no more darkness in this brother than I do in any of the rest of us. It's just like it is in Andriana—a kite that seems to catch wind once in a while, threatening to rip away from its string."

"Or is he merely more adept at keeping it hidden?" Killian asked, edging closer, as if he could make out the word *guilty* written across my damp, chilled skin. "After all those years in Sethos's care?"

"If we begin doubting everyone because of what we cannot sense, rather than what we can," Tressa said, "then the enemy will bind us without ever touching us! Wouldn't that be a lovely trick of Sethos's? Planting doubt everywhere, rather than trust. Come, let us arrive at a quick decision and move on. There are people

I must see before we leave this place this night, good people we are to heal so they might serve the Way. I say that Keallach has confessed his shortcomings, his sin." She moved past Killian and peered up at my face, toward what must be a bruise, now, on my jaw. "And from the looks of it, Ronan has exacted his own manner of punishment." She straightened, not offering to lend me her healing touch—choosing to let me suffer—and stepped away again.

"Tressa speaks the truth," Niero said. "You cannot let such things tie you in knots for long. You must press through this. It is as important for Keallach as it is for the rest of you. Search yourself for wisdom."

Kapriel had begun to pace, hands behind his back, cheeks red. It was as if he felt my sin as his own. "Have him kneel," he said.

I did as he asked before Niero could shove me down. I shook my head. This was it. "I swear I will never harm any of you—or knowingly cause any of you to falter—again."

"Gather around and place your hands on him," Kapriel said, ignoring me. They drew closer, each placing a hand on my head or shoulders or back, as instructed. As they did so, my arm cuff began to warm as it hadn't in some time. "Search deep within for the Maker's wisdom, as Niero instructed," Kapriel said.

"Please," I whispered, my heart thundering in panic. This was where I belonged. Where I had been called. "Brothers. Sisters. I was wrong. Please don't cast me out because of my mistake."

No one responded. They were silent, closing their eyes, as if listening, searching me as thoroughly as Andriana could, paying attention to their arm cuffs, but more than that too. I kept my head bowed, submitting, as I'd not done since the night of my acceptance into their fold. *Face the truth with humility. Remain confident in the outcome.*

Please, Maker. Let me stay. Let me stay, let me stay, let me stay . . . I was wrong. So wrong. Help me to avoid such action in the future. I am yours. Theirs . . .

"He is genuine in his apology," Dri said to the others, her voice little more than a reverent whisper.

"Or is he genuine in his desire to remain here, with us?" Ronan returned.

Silence resumed as new guilt shot through me. The Knight was correct in his assumption. What did motivate me more? My desire to stay with them or my contrite heart? I focused in on what had led me to Andriana, how I'd let passion and desire and an overwhelming impulse to control her, own her, claim her, be my guide. I felt the lifting of her hand, as she knew this within me too.

Stick with that line of thinking, Niero said silently to me. *If you dare to clean out the dark oils that Sethos left behind, you may find healing. Freedom.*

I did as he asked, pressing in when much of me wished to withdraw. Being a Remnant demanded I find new ways to express the courage that the Maker had planted in me.

Since the moment he knit you together in your mother's womb.

I swallowed hard. *Mother.* I could see her, in memory. So soft. Eyes alight with knowledge and hope. Until she was dead on the floor, bleeding out. *Mother.*

Father. So firm and strong, but with a propensity toward playing little jokes on Kapriel and me. Presenting us with riddles. Laughing. Laughing so hard that his whole body shook and his face became red, tears streaming down his cheeks. *Father.*

I was weeping. It made me angry that they pressed me so, my supposed Ailith kin. I fought the urge to send them all flying back, ramming against the far walls, and barely contained it in time.

I heard Vidar gasp, and then Dri. But I contained it, focusing on how their goal was my good, our good, not my downfall. They sought not to control me but to free me of the dark choices I had made, both in the distant and near past.

"Hold on to him," Vidar said, and I felt Dri's hand return to my back. "You are ours, brother," he said to me, leaning down to whisper in my ear. "No longer the enemy's." I heard it and recognized his words, but it felt like I was a good distance away, twisting, turning, and trying to figure out which route I was supposed to take.

"We claim this one as the son of the One who was, and is, and is to come," Vidar said. "A child of the Light. Darkness has no place here." I felt power flow through me, pushing through me, as if driving out another. I felt sick to my stomach and feared that all I'd eaten for supper was soon to spew outward.

"You are a *Remnant*," Tressa said, her small hands lifting my face. Feeling wild, I fought to focus on her blue, steady gaze, her words ringing with wisdom. "You were a Remnant from the beginning, and you are a Remnant to the end. Do not allow anyone else to claim that power, brother. You chose us once. Choose us now, forever."

I registered her words as the healing balm I needed. Invitation. Direction. Hope.

Life. Abundant life.

"I choose life," I said, reaching out to grasp her hands in mine and looking around at the rest. "I choose you, brothers and sisters."

Killian put a hand on top of mine. "We choose you," he said solemnly.

"We forgive you," Vidar said, setting his hand atop Killian's.

"We forgive you," Bellona repeated, setting hers atop Vidar's.

In turn, the rest repeated those words—the very last being Dri and Ronan—and as I closed my eyes, I likened it to Dagan, shoveling layer upon layer of dark, moist, earth atop my pleading seed, allowing it to rest, then to sprout and blossom.

And praying that it didn't get lost among the weeds.

CHAPTER
35

ANDRIANA

I said the words along with my brothers and sisters, reclaiming Keallach from the dark that threatened to pull him away from us. I still wanted him with us, regardless of what had transpired, because I was certain it was the Maker's desire. But with my hand on his back, I knew the wrestling within him. The concern. The doubt. It made my mouth dry and my palms sweat, all at once. And yet as he gripped arms with the men and hugged the women, he seemed settled, once again ours in total.

I couldn't really hold him accountable for something that I, too, wrestled with periodically. Once you'd dabbled with the dark, it left windows open in the soul that the dark ones loved to visit, trying to gain deeper access. Only time, Asher had once told me, would help me seal those windows for good. "But they'll always have slightly weaker locks than others," he'd said, giving me a squeeze of the hand and a look with his brown eyes that made me feel completely seen and understood and loved.

Ronan sidled closer to me, folding his arms and looking toward Keallach, who was embracing his brother and looking even more repentant. "It's okay?" he whispered to me. "With him," he added, jutting out his chin. "He's feeling what he says he's feeling."

"Yes," I said. "I think."

He cocked a brow, and his hand slid into mine. "You *think*? Now Andriana, are you using your head instead of your heart?"

"On occasion," I said, bumping him with my hip and smiling at his gentle teasing. "I've been told once or twice I should use both."

"Ahh, yes." His smile deepened. "And you have such a pretty head . . . and neck . . . and . . ." His eyes drifted downward.

"*Ronan,*" I said, feeling a blush rush to my cheeks. It wasn't our way to talk about such things. Was it knowing that Keallach had pressed his way with me that made him start thinking in such a manner too?

"What?" he said, casting an innocent brow upward. "A husband is allowed to admire his wife, isn't he?"

"Yes," I whispered, "for things the Community would admire. Peacefulness, patience, loving-kindness . . ."

"Ah, well, you have those too, of course. I just also like what it's all wrapped up in," he said, finishing the last of his words in a conspiratorial whisper to my ear.

I ducked my head, as his breath sent a shiver down my neck. And then I looked around quickly, both worried that someone had seen and irritated that I was worried. He was my husband, after all.

I thought I caught a glance from Keallach. But when I looked back, he was turning to leave with Kapriel, as if I was the last person he could possibly be thinking about. And I thought, *Is this his darkness we're wrestling with, or mine?*

There was no debate among us. We departed for Castle Vega as the sun was just rising, feeling buoyed in spirit by our warm reception at Georgii Post. And yet as we drew closer to the castle in the Drifter vehicles and trader trucks, I could feel the tension between my shoulders draw them tighter and tighter. Awkwardly, I moved forward in the truck, reaching out to steady myself with one handhold after another, until I could stand and hold a cross-beam beside Vidar and Bellona. I'd noticed him stand up earlier, and I could tell from his stance that he was feeling a warning too.

"What is it?" I asked loudly, the wind blowing my hair from my face. "What are you sensing?"

He gave me a half shrug, "Nothing definitive yet. Just a vague foreboding. You too?"

I nodded and looked with him and his Knight to the horizon, where Castle Vega had just come into view. From this distance, it hardly looked imposing, but we all remembered it well. What it represented. The dark arts that were practiced there in the streets. The prostitutes. The fortune-telling. A shiver ran down my back.

"This won't be another Georgii Post experience," Vidar said to me, no trace of humor in his eyes, only warning. He'd become more certain in the few moments I'd stood beside him. "We need to prepare ourselves for a real battle here."

I nodded and found myself absently reaching for my arm cuff. He was right, of course. Already, there was a hint of chill in the metal fused to my skin that had nothing to do with the cool morning wind blowing in our faces. And yet there was nothing in me that said anything but *forward*. Nor did I sense anything contrary among the Ailith.

The caravan pulled to a stop outside the towering gates of Castle Vega, which were shut up tight. Ronan hopped down off the truck bed and reached for my hand. "It appears they're expecting us."

"There's no way they want what happened at Georgii Post to happen here," Kapriel said. "It's Pacifica's last outpost within the Union. If word got out that the Pacificans had been so easily ousted there, Pacifica might be ours without a fight."

We approached the others. Keallach and Niero were in deep conversation, both with arms crossed, gesturing on occasion to the gates. Last time we were here, there had been guards at the gates and we had to present papers to enter. Now, clearly, no one was going in *or* out.

An Aravander returned to us after going to the gates and speaking to a sentry. "It's as you supposed. The city gates are closed. Indefinitely."

Keallach let out a scoffing laugh. "They so fear us?" he asked, arching one brow and looking down the line of us.

We were no more than two hundred in number. Hardly an army. We were here more for what we hoped to convey as emissaries of the Way, with strength beside and behind them. We were strong—a force to be certain—but not a threat.

"I will gain us entrance," Keallach muttered.

He walked on without waiting for our agreement. My spirit agreed with the agitation among my fellow Ailith—he really should have conferred with us before making a move—and yet my soul kept me from speaking since I supposed it would keep the rest of them quiet too . . . because we were *supposed* to be here. We all felt the whiplash nature of it. The Maker's pull was directing us inward, and yet the growing chill of our armbands made us want to run away. Here, at Castle Vega, we were certain to encounter our first real battle in weeks.

My heart stilled. Just who was inside?

"We need every Remnant on point," Niero growled as we got closer, following behind Keallach. "Dig deep. Seek out the Maker to determine how he wants you to utilize your gifting here."

We stopped, ten paces from the massive gates that were inset between the towering limestone block walls, and looked upward, side by side, with our throng of compatriots behind us.

"I am Keallach, crown prince of Pacifica and emperor of the West," our brother said, his voice echoing upward to the guards who peered down at us, their faces in deep shadow. "I demand that you open these gates at once and welcome your ruler and his friends, as you have sworn to do."

There was a prolonged silence. I was wondering if they'd elected not to say anything in response when a man finally called down to us. "You were once our emperor, Keallach of Pacifica, but now you are no more than a rebel prince like your brother, Kapriel. We answer to the Council, not to you. And the Council has ordered us to bar your entry."

Keallach's jaw muscles tensed, and his hands folded into fists at his side. "Even as a private citizen of Castle Vega, I should be granted entry. The palace itself is my private property, built by our father." He looked over to Kapriel. "Her servants are paid from our personal treasury, not Pacifica's."

"It has been seized and made an official embassy of Pacifica," returned the guard, perhaps the captain, since he was the only one who spoke. "You have been divested of every possession and property you once had, Keallach, as the result of your defection to the enemy. You are penniless." We could all hear the glee in his voice.

"You might have seized every coin I had, but I am rich beyond measure," retorted Keallach. "I have discovered wealth that my former brothers in Pacifica will likely never know."

"Oh?" said the guard. "Was there gold in the rock of the Citadel that you favor? Perhaps the Council's soldiers will return to mine it further." We could hear the chortles of his fellow guards. Clearly, he was gaining confidence.

Keallach took a deep breath to speak again, but Kapriel took a step to stand beside him, setting a calming hand on his arm. We all realized that Keallach wasn't used to being thwarted; I knew that an inner rage built within him because of it.

"There is a gold that cannot be carried in the pocket," Kapriel said up to them. "A wealth that can be mined but not measured in the ways we are used to. It's only found in the peace and security of following the Maker's Way. And the Maker has brought us here, to you, and has asked us to enter this city."

"And *we* are asking you to turn around and go away," said the captain wryly. "We shall not fall to your wiles as Zanzibar has."

"I'm afraid we cannot. Open the gates, and no harm shall come to you," Kapriel said carefully. It was then that I saw the gathering clouds above the castle.

"We do not fear you, rebel prince," sneered the captain. "You have what? Bows and arrows? A few guns among you? That will not gain you entry."

"No," he said, "but the Maker shall." He lifted his hands to the skies, and the clouds grew darker, building into a fearsome bank that spoke of hail and wind and lightning.

I could feel the electricity in the air, the promise of unworldly strength on the wind, and my pulse quickened. Vidar fell to his knees, lifting his arms. When I did as well, I could see glimpses of angels, moving so fast that it was like they were there a moment, and with a blink, they were gone—as if the veil between our world and theirs lifted and dropped, over and over again. But they were clearly amassing, and their presence made me feel a hundred times stronger. They would help us face down the chilling presence of what awaited us inside. It, too, grew in strength.

The wind whipped past us, pulling tendrils of hair from my band. Tressa fell to her knees beside me, gripping my hand in half terror, half glory. Because witnessing the Maker on the move, through us, was always that way. So beyond us, yet part of us too. Tears dripped down my face. Such honor. Such power.

May we be worthy of it, Maker, I prayed. *May we use it for your glory, not our own. Open these gates before us. Help us capture this city and put down your enemies.*

Thunder rumbled so loudly it reverberated in our chests, and the dark clouds above the city roiled in a slow circle, as if a tornado was developing directly above it. I thought I might have heard screams and cries from inside the walls, but I knew that would be impossible over the howl of wind. Then it occurred to me that, with my knees on the ground, I was feeling the combined emotions of those inside. The terror. The regret. The anger. The fear. The wild hope.

I looked up into the eye of a storm unlike anything we'd seen before. And it was magnificent, really. The lead-colored sky flashed with constant lightning, bolts of it cracking down toward the city in a terrifying display. The air smelled of ozone, and our hair began to rise—on our arms, on our heads—warning us of what was to come. "To the ground, people of the Way," Kapriel muttered, still standing with his hands cupped, lifting and swaying to a divine rhythm we could only sense as a whisper.

As we fell flat to the sandy soil, we heard the lightning hit its mark, the sound so loud that, afterward, we were partially deafened. Ronan took my elbow, urging me to my feet again, and I saw that the gates had been essentially blown ajar. As we began to move forward, I knew that it had been the crossbeam that was blasted away. Keallach was raising his hands now, leading us with his brother at the front of our V-shaped gathering, lifting and flinging wide the gates, which I remembered oxen pulling open before, all with a single wave of his hands.

"Those princes . . ." Vidar said, panting as we ran. "Not just pretty faces, are they?"

"No," I said with a huff of a laugh. "No, they're not."

But my tickled humor was short-lived as we entered through the city gates, right behind Kapriel and Keallach. Pacifican soldiers were gathering themselves even as they retreated into the recesses of the city, firing at us with guns and arrows. Even a small metal disc came sailing through the air, heading straight for my face. Ronan had grabbed my wrist but would've been too late to save me had Keallach not lifted a hand and sent the devious weapon swerving into a terrace post at my side. It pierced the wood and vibrated upon impact, its curved prongs making me swallow hard.

I looked to thank Keallach, but he'd moved on. As I watched, he saved Bellona from an arrow and sent a soldier, who had been set to pierce Killian from behind, flying toward a far wall. Kapriel was busy too—bringing a lightning bolt down in the center of the road before us, scattering a small force of soldiers who had regrouped to take a stand.

Still, even with the impressive power of the princes, bullets and arrows continued to rain down upon us. There were many, many soldiers within the outpost. Ronan grabbed my hand, and together we ran to a small alcove where the guards above us couldn't get a good angle. Belatedly, we discovered two lithe Pacifican soldiers, their faces chiseled in fury and desperation, a lethal combination. One was already striking with his sword, and I barely twisted out of the way in time. The other was upon Ronan.

The first advanced upon me, driving me out into the open courtyard, where once again bullets and arrows came perilously close. But I couldn't think about those, only about the man with the maniacal look in his eyes who struck at me again and again with his sword. I parried, repeatedly, but it wasn't long until I knew he was stronger than I.

Vidar and Bellona were in skirmishes of their own just a few paces away, fighting off three soldiers—one of whom was a giant of a man, one a lithe woman who possessed a wicked talent with her thin sword. That was all I could gather in a couple of glimpses. My opponent, sweating and grinning a little as he sensed my waning strength, kept driving me outward, away from the rest. Kapriel's wind sent garbage and hay swirling around us, making our battle's canvas an unworldly backdrop.

I bumped into a wagon and spun, just as his sword came down, splintering wood that a second before would've been my shoulder. He growled, wrenched the sword free, and whirled, clearly intent on slicing me in half. I brought up my sword and blocked him, but the impact sent a shudder through my arm that proceeded all the way up my neck and down my back. I felt my hand release my sword, as if it had in its own mind to stop such nonsense. But my enemy didn't pause when he saw this new opening. He swung wide, giving his strike added strength as he brought it down at me. I could do nothing but cradle my throbbing wrist and watch it come, knowing that this might very well be the end for me. *Maker*, I breathed.

Ronan's body hurtled against my side, sending me sprawling. I looked back, and he had blocked the man's strike with one hand while plunging a dagger into his belly with the other. The man staggered backward, dropping his sword and looking down at the dagger as if he couldn't quite comprehend it. Then he fell heavily to his rear, legs straight out before him. His eyes rolled back in his head, and he slumped into a wave of dead flesh.

Ronan reached for me, and together, we hunkered down behind the wagon, watching as the last of those who had dared to stand against us were waylaid by the princes, our fellow Ailith, and the many soldiers who had followed us in. When all was silent, we slowly rose, finding the sudden stillness eerie.

"They've retreated!" someone called.

We gathered together at one edge of the courtyard, beneath a terrace in case any other soldiers still roamed the walls. I had heard Niero earlier send twelve Aravanders to search the walls and remove anyone who did not immediately surrender, then keep watch from there to see how they might aid us as we delved deeper into the city. Taking stock, we found we'd only sustained superficial wounds.

"Not a one of us who entered the gates has been mortally wounded," Tressa said in wonder, walking past each and every person present.

"The Maker be praised," Niero said.

"The Maker be praised," many of us echoed.

"It is he who brought us here," Kapriel said, "and he who will see us through."

Asher edged closer, his hands on the hilt of his sword, the tip resting on the ground. "And now do we try and coax the innocent from their homes? Those who likely huddle in corners, fearing for their lives?"

"No," Kapriel said soberly. "We must root out the evil that still abides here, and that will protect the few 'innocents' that remain."

Again, my hand moved to my arm cuff. The chill was growing. And yet, for once, I knew it wasn't just a warning of approaching attack. It was leading us *toward* those that we were to drive out.

Because this was a city the Maker either wanted to reclaim . . . or destroy.

CHAPTER 36

ANDRIANA

Niero divided our company into three groups, assigning a small group of Aravanders and Drifters to move ahead of us and serve as scouts, ferreting out any remaining soldiers who dared to stand against us. We Ailith stayed together, well aware that while our power had grown to an impressive level, we would remain the main target for our enemy to destroy. And as we wound deeper into the city, it didn't take our arm cuffs to know there were still many enemies present.

A wail ahead of us had brought our scout party to a halt, but Niero waved them on. As we got closer, we heard the screech of a woman. Her fine linen fortune-teller's tent was now in shreds from the wind, and the sound of her voice was both a wail of despair and battle cry of fury. "Be gone from here, people of the Way! Be gone! We do not want you here! It is our city! *Ours!*"

Kapriel did not pause at the remains of her doorway; he plunged right in. My breath caught, but I was moving before I thought about it. And so were the other Ailith, until we all stood in the woman's tent, surrounding her. She moved, crab-like, her eyes and hair wild. "No!" she keened. "No! Be away from me! You are not wanted here!"

From several paces away, Tressa kneeled before her with her hands on her thighs. "We are here to help and heal. Not to destroy."

Vidar kneeled beside her and gazed at the woman, brow furrowed with concern. "Long has this city been heavy with the weight of the dark, woman. You yourself bear the burden of many demons. But we have come to bring the light." He lifted his hands to the woman, as did Tressa. The rest of us laid a hand on Tressa and Vidar's shoulders or did the same as they had, raising our hands toward the fortune-teller as if covering her, blessing her.

"No!" screamed the woman, falling back as if our action brought her physical pain. And I glimpsed the bent, grotesque forms of many, clinging to her back, her neck, her side. "No!" she cried again, writhing now on the ground, tearing at her clothes. "Leave us!"

"We have come to claim you," Vidar continued. "To destroy those who hold you captive."

"To set you free," Tressa whispered, her face and tone reverent. "In the name of the One who was, and is, and is to come."

"In the name of the One who was, and is, and is to come," we repeated.

The woman gasped, grew rigid, every limb and digit stretched taut. Then she convulsed, ramming up and down until I feared she'd render herself unconscious. Tressa scrambled forward to cradle her head—keeping her from injuring herself—praying all the while. The rest of us prayed too, each in our own way. *Free her, Maker. Make her yours. Drive away these dark ones. Fill her with your light.*

And then she abruptly relaxed, every bit of her body calming. I felt the darkness recede and slide out the door, like an inky tide. The woman blinked heavily, her brown eyes gradually clearing. Vidar was grinning and reached for her hand. "Rise, sister. You are free of the dark ones who have ruled you for far too long."

She looked up at him, and I knew the swelling wonder and gratitude within her as my own. Tears fell down my cheeks as she took Vidar's hand and rose. When we had entered, we'd seen a haggard and wild woman. Now she was serene, not beautiful in an outward sense, but so clearly beautiful from a that it took my breath away. *This* was true beauty, I thought. Light indwelling what was once a dark shell. *This* was life.

"Use this mouth," Vidar said gently, lightly touching her lips in a blessing, "to speak of what has transformed you. Use these hands," he said, lifting hers in his, "to help others. You are the Maker's, and he is yours. You will find continued life and light by remaining in relationship with him."

She nodded, tears streaming down her cheeks. "Thank you," she whispered, looking at him and Tressa and the rest of us. "Bless you."

"May the Maker bless and keep you," Niero said and then turned to go, expecting the rest of us to follow. Reluctantly, we did. Much in me wanted to remain, to know more of this woman and why the Maker wanted her freed. I knew from our last visit that this city held hundreds like her, and I wondered why she was set apart. But the answer would have to wait for another day.

As we ran down the street, we noticed many of the city's people had begun to gather alongside the road, kneeling in submission. Some begged forgiveness. Others praised our arrival. Many had tears on their faces. But we didn't have long to tarry. We knew we had to get to the castle for some reason, and quickly. We passed by the people who had surrendered—tenfold our own number—touching heads and hands, praying for them as we moved on. Later, we could divide up and reach them all, but now, the tension gathering in all of us told us one thing: *do not let your guard down*. I likened the urge to a crazy itch, or the desire to scrub away some dark spot from an otherwise pristine, white surface. An infection needed cleansing in order for it to heal.

We rounded the last corner, and there it was before us. The towering castle, with its elegant turrets and windows. I think we expected Sethos and the Pacifican guards to begin firing at us from their assigned positions above. My armband had grown colder, and the Maker was definitely leading us inward, but what we discovered confused us.

There was no one on guard.

The doors were wide open.

Behind us, some of the city's people had followed—more than fifty, many of them very young. Niero turned and growled at them. "Be away from here! It is dangerous!"

Some scattered immediately. Others backed away a bit but hovered, curiosity beating out any sense of risk. We knew well what captivated their interest, regardless of the danger. Why would the palace be open? It felt like a trap. And yet this was exactly where we had to be.

"Gather around," Niero said. We pulled into a tight circle, heads huddled together. "You know what is ahead, just as I do. Within those castle gates, we are bound to encounter new ways for the enemy to challenge us. It is the reason they leave the gates open—they're confident they can bring us down if they can just get us inside. This is a battle we must fight, but we must do it alongside the Maker, not on our own. Do you understand me?" He paused to look around, lingering on Keallach and me. "Do not let your gift lead you—let the Maker lead you. Call upon him constantly. Put him first, not yourselves. We will stay together whatever comes, because together, we are strongest. And Knights, do not get separated from your Remnants. Kapriel and Keallach, Azarel and I will be by your side without fail."

We all nodded and straightened. Wordlessly, Keallach took the lead. He, of all of us, knew the castle best. We had some experience with the kitchens and large meeting spaces and hallways, but something told me we wouldn't find our enemies there. They were pulling us in, deeper. Kapriel was a step behind Keallach, to his right. Azarel was beside him. Niero was on Keallach's left.

Five paces from the door, curved sword in hand, Niero bade us to stop while he went ahead, cautiously approaching the open doorway and peering inward. When he had cleared it, he gestured for the rest of us to follow.

As soon as we entered and paused, we heard it—someone singing, from far away. The tune sounded familiar, but I could not make out the words from this distance. My skin prickled, as again, we saw no one. Only heard the haunting voice, carried along the marble floors and plastered walls to our ears.

We passed the grand reception rooms, then the sprawling dining room where I had first encountered Maximillian Jala. And it was in passing that room, seeing the sun glint through the windows, that I remembered where I had first heard the song that was being sung ahead of us. We could make out some of the words now, and I knew that the girl had been singing for some time. Her voice was clearly strained, hoarse, giving out through some phrases.

Even before we turned the last corner to see her halfway down the hallway, I knew who it would be.

The same girl who had been singing in the courtyard the first time we were here.

The one who seemed to be singing to me, aware of my arrival when no one else had known yet. I'd gone to the castle windows as if called by her voice, and she had looked right up at me as she sang.

> "And upon the field, and upon the plain,
> The Ailith rose where they were slain,
> And forevermore, whene're she sang,
> He wept and wept and wept again."

When she saw us, her eyes widened with a combination of terror and yet also relief. Her voice faltered, and her next lyric trailed away. A man stood beside her, a sword tip held to her throat.

Lord Maximillian Jala.

I'd tried to kill him. I must have nearly been successful—there'd been so much blood that day in the palace. And yet now he stood before us, and he knew I'd tried to kill him.

"Welcome," he said, with his smooth, handsome grin. "Come in, my friends. This singer has a fresh refrain to her song that she wishes to share with you." He pressed the tip of his sword a bit deeper, and a trickle of blood began winding its way down the girl's throat and through her cleavage. "Go on, my darling," he crooned to her, as if she was a songbird to be coaxed with silvered words, rather than a woman held captive. When she remained silent, he turned toward her, stroked her cheek with his free hand, and then let his fingers drift through her blood, smearing it across her chest. "Now," he growled, no measure of cajoling remaining in his tone. "From the beginning."

She began to warble as he turned back toward us, watching us approach, his eyes mostly on Keallach and then me. When our eyes met, he rubbed his bloody fingers together and lifted them to his nostrils to inhale. I knew what he was doing—reminding me of the moment when we'd been captured in this castle. The moment he had actually tasted my blood and looked like he wanted more. My pulse quickened as bile rose in the back of my throat.

But could it be that we were merely to hear this song and face this lone man? It seemed impossible that we were called here for this. Was it just a distraction? We all looked about, wondering about hidden passageways, possibly full of our enemies, ready to pour out around us. We stopped, giving each other enough room to move in case that happened. And yet we remained rooted to the spot, listening to the song as the pale girl—sweat dripping down her face and neck, mingling with her blood—finished her task.

> "For once the king loved, and once he called,
> But weakened, he fell upon the wall.
> Even as Knight and Remnant, one by one,
> Breathed their last and knew the gall."

Knew the gall. The gall of what? As the last note hung in the air, Maximillian dropped his sword, and the girl slumped in a dead faint. Niero only narrowly caught her before her head hit the marble tiles. But Lord Jala had grabbed hold of

Keallach's wrist and swung him wide, ramming him into one wall. I heard the crack of a bone—his collarbone? Shoulder?—and Keallach gasped. I did too, reeling from the surprise and anger and pain I felt from him, ten paces away.

But Maximillian didn't relent; he dragged Keallach back to where the girl had been singing, where the floor had now collapsed into an open trapdoor.

"No!" I cried, knowing we were too late, even as we charged forward. Both disappeared below.

The floor-tile doorway clicked shut just as Azarel reached it, a second too late. Madly, she felt the perimeter of it. She looked up to Kapriel. "Where does this lead?"

He looked stunned, face blank. "I don't know," he stammered. "I don't remember that being there at all."

Azarel rose, face grim as she looked to Niero then back to Kapriel. "*Think*, Kapriel. Do you know how to get below? Is there a dungeon below? There has to be a foundation level to this massive structure, at least."

"I was only here as a child," he said, frowning and shaking his head, as if trying to reach for a memory. "And I don't think I was ever below this floor."

"That's where they lie in wait for us," Niero said grimly. "Why we can sense them but cannot see them. They mean to do battle with us in the depths."

I swallowed hard. The whole castle above—with all its beauty—reeked of evil in my nostrils, the place always sending shivers of warning skittering across my skin. But going below, to her very foundation?

I steeled myself. I was with Ronan. The rest of the Ailith. Our friends. And the Maker. He had called us here.

Together, we would see it through.

CHAPTER 37

KEALLACH

They shoved a hood over my head and dragged me forward, yanking at my injured arm until I saw bright spots of color, even in the dark. I tried to summon the strength to cast them aside, but they seemed to know my injury weakened me in other ways. With the constant pressure on my arm I could barely get a full breath, let alone move them from me.

A man cruelly pulled my wrists together behind me and swiftly chained them, then pressed me forward, a hand on my shoulder in an excruciating hold that made me eager to do anything he asked of me. Indeed, I tried to anticipate his direction before we turned corners in order to not add any extra pressure at all.

I knew from the earthy, damp smell that we were beneath the castle, near the dungeons, but heading farther west, to the vast underground storehouse that held inky space and soaring arches and crate upon crate of supplies.

It had been a place where Sethos had favored bringing me during our long training sessions. But it had been my least favorite spot in all of Castle Vega. I could smell the tang of torch oil and glimpsed patches of light behind my hood. I knew there were hundreds of places for our enemies to hide, lying in wait for my brothers and sisters, who would undoubtedly come after me.

I was yanked to a halt and heard the clank of another chain, then I gasped again as my wrists were lifted and the chain grew taut above me. I cried out, in spite of myself, pain shooting through my shoulder and seeming to pierce my temple like an arrow, over and over. I fell to my knees with my arms wrenched at a sharp angle behind me, lifted until a man growled, "Enough."

He pulled the hood from my head, and I blinked as my vision swam.

I'd expected Sethos—had felt the chill of my arm cuff become ice—but it was Max, backed by the remainder of my Council. "Welcome home, *Highness*," he sneered, bending to pat my cheek. He straightened, hands on hips, as I surveyed the rest. Two sat on crates behind him, Fenris tearing off a stray nail, Daivat leaning back against another crate, leg casually swinging beneath him. Kendric leaned against a pillar, arms crossed.

"Release me," I panted, blinking as a bead of sweat dripped into my eyes. "I command it."

"Command it?" Max scoffed. "Your days of commanding anyone are over, *Majesty*. You were supposed to infiltrate them and bring home Kapriel and your bride. Sethos was quite clear."

"And I attempted it," I said, my mind racing, trying to buy time. "But my efforts were thwarted. In time, I came to peace about it. Because I found another way. And has that way not brought both Kapriel and Andriana right here?"

Max let out a scoff. "You found another *Way*, all right. You became the head of the enemy's party! Zanzibar? Georgii Post? Now Castle Vega? To us, it seems like you've been conquered, swallowing the story of your fairy tale birthright hook, line, and sinker."

"It is not a false tale," I ground out. "It is living truth. Release me, and I shall tell you."

"No," he sniffed. "We are well aware of your gifting. Sethos believes that in this posture that gift can be controlled. You need your hands before you." He nodded, and a guard beside me wrenched cruelly upward on the chains again. I thought my wrists would break. I fought for breath as sweat ran down my brow and into my eyes.

"I am your *emperor*," I seethed, reaching hard to try and make them remember the power I once wielded.

Max leaned down. "Until you convince us otherwise, you are nothing more than a prisoner."

I took a deep breath, trying to gather my thoughts into a believable tale—some way to win them over to get out of their cruel hold. "When I arrived at the Citadel, it became clear that I wouldn't be able to convince Kapriel to leave. He is too ingrained with the rest, and the others were too protective for me to get him alone. Instead, I focused on rebuilding our brotherly trust, and I was fairly successful at that."

"Kapriel forgave you for . . . everything?" he said, his voice dripping with doubt. "The Isle of Catal? Leaving him to languish? Your parents?"

I stared back at him, remembering how I had once loved him as my best friend. I now hated him and wished I could send him sprawling with a wave of my hand. "My brother has a greater capacity for forgiveness than I ever shall have," I spat out.

"And the lovely Andriana? What came of your efforts with her?"

I glowered at him and turned my face away. Just remembering my move on her the night before—my *efforts*, as he put it—made me despise myself. I had done as Sethos and the Council had demanded, even though I knew it was wrong. With Kapriel and with her. And yet it was all confused in my mind, because I wanted both of them. Wanted a deeper relationship, wanted access. Wanted control . . . Oh, how I wanted to control both of them. To own them. To know they served me.

I winced and moved my head slowly, feeling the dark pull again, capturing me, weaving tendrils around my mind and heart, confusing my holy want with my human desire.

Maker . . .

"You came close to victory, didn't you?" Max whispered, turning a small circle around me. "But then they managed to turn you for their own goals. You abandoned us," he said. "Betrayed us."

"No," I whispered back, confusion swirling my thoughts. "No."

"Yes. Yes, you did," Daivat said, coming closer, arms crossed. "We trusted you to do this, Keallach. Believed in you."

Believed in me.

Niero's words came back to me. *Trust in the Maker, not your own gifting.*

This is not about any of you. But him. The Maker.

Maker, I thought again. *Maker. Help me. You reclaimed me. Help me now.*

Max stumbled backward as if I'd hit him, as did Fenris. The others were on their feet, edging closer, two of them drawing swords, as if I'd drawn my own. And perhaps I had.

Max advanced on me, digging his fingers across my head, as if he wished to will his own thoughts into mine.

I cried out, a shameful, unmanly cry that I could not keep from escaping my lips.

"Stop it," he hissed. "You are ours, not theirs. Ours!"

My heart lurched, swelled, and then felt as if it were being torn in two. As if I was being torn in two, straight down the middle, the dark on one side and the light on the other. "Maker," I gasped.

"Shut up!" Max cried, leaning away to backhand me across the cheek.

My resulting swing to the left wrenched my injured shoulder again, and my vision swam, making me dizzy.

Max leaned in and pulled me close. "Are we losing you, Keallach? Ah, well. As you give into unconsciousness, think back on your promises and the call of the one who made you all you were meant to be." His tone dropped. "Who *is* that, Keallach? Who made you who you are, not in legend, but in real life?"

The Maker, was what came to mind first. But soon after, *Sethos*. He was the one who had stood beside me for so many years. The one who had helped me usher Pacifica into an era of wealth and prosperity and relative health. The one who had placed me on the throne.

Sethos. My master. I'd failed him. Fell to weakness, surrounded by the Ailith. *Failed. Failed, failed, failed* . . .

Max smiled and patted my cheek. "There you are!" he said cheerfully.

Even that tiny motion set my shoulder on fire. And then the room was spinning again and, blessedly, I succumbed at last to unconsciousness.

CHAPTER 38

RONAN

"In Palace Pacifica," Dri said, taking my hand, "we got down to the dungeons via the servants' staircase. Think it's the same here?"

"It's a good guess," Niero said. "Anyone go below, last time we were here?"

Everyone shook their head. "Only up," Vidar said.

"Let's try it," Niero said, already running down the hallway. We all followed behind, nervously checking every doorway as we went. I kept Dri to the center of the hallway, ready to yank her away from trouble if someone came from the opposite side and protect her from my side too. But I grimly admitted to myself that we were just going deeper into the trap.

"Wait!" I called, and Niero and Azarel pulled up, looking back at us.

"I don't like it," I said, shaking my head, feeling my cheeks heat as I wondered if they'd think I was a coward. "We're just getting farther from any escape route down there. What if we wait for them to approach us upstairs?"

Niero frowned and looked to Vidar. "What say you?"

Vidar shifted and glanced my way, then to Niero. "I don't like it either," he said with a shrug. "Our enemy is ahead. But so is our brother. And if we don't go after him now, he might be dead or lost to us. Somehow, they've curtailed his gifting, captured him. I think it's his hands, Niero. Somehow, he needs his hands to be free in order to use his gift. And they've figured that out."

I swallowed hard. It was true. And we needed Keallach and his gifting if we were to win this war and honor what the Maker had put into motion.

Niero looked each of us in the eyes. "All right, I think we're in agreement. But stay together. Do you understand me? We work *together*. Keallach is our example—if they get you alone, they can expose a weakness. Those who are not Ailith, spread out along the perimeter once inside, and work your way inward. Be ready for my call. Those who are Ailith, stay together. Defend one another."

His instructions were passed backward. I felt like we were a powerful, tremendous force, but having to enter through a solitary doorway only big enough for one man or woman at a time sent alarms ringing in my head. "Stay close, Dri," I hissed. She nodded and squeezed my hand, following behind me as we entered the dark, musty hall.

Ahead of us were two huge Aravanders, plus Niero, Azarel, and Kapriel. Tressa, Killian, Vidar, and Bellona were behind us. Every protective fiber in me rose at the thought of Keallach, swiped from our very grasp. The fact that they were able to accomplish such a feat burned, and I inwardly vowed that neither Dri nor Kapriel would be taken away from me in similar fashion. Not while I was still living.

We walked between two banks of cells, and I was chagrined to see people wasting away within them. Some came to the iron bars, reaching out grimy hands to beseech us to save them. If the Maker would smile upon us over the next hour, perhaps we could come back this way and find a way to free them. Even as we passed, Tressa hurriedly went to the well and took the full bucket that sat there taunting them, and passed it to the nearest cell for the prisoners to share.

"Bless you, lady, bless you," the prisoners murmured.

But our attention was on what was before us. A line of torches lit up the cavernous room beyond that spread the entire width of the castle, from side to side, and was braced by huge stone arches that climbed three stories above us. It was a foundation level, providing the strength to shore up the weight of the impressive towers and rooms above. It was an architectural triumph, really, something I'd read about in the construction of castles of old, but had never seen for myself. Palace Pacifica likely had something similar, but there I had focused on getting up above, to Andriana, rather than beyond the dungeons that once held me.

I pulled her a bit closer as my arm cuff grew Hoarfrost-cold. Grimly, I recognized we were heading right where we were supposed to go. To face our enemies. What form would they take this time? I was glad for the additional troops, spreading now around the massive hall's perimeter. They would flush out any enemy hiding among the crates and bales of supplies. We walked and walked and finally saw Keallach, hanging by a chain with his arms cruelly pinned behind him, on his knees, clearly unconscious.

Rage set my heart to pounding, even if it was Keallach. He was our brother. Our kin. They would pay for his mistreatment.

"Together, Ailith," Niero said, drawing both curved blades out as the Council stepped into view, each carrying his own weapon. "Work together. Do not let them separate you."

"Niero," Kapriel whispered, belatedly understanding as he stared in horror at his twin. "Down here . . . without reach of the sky . . ."

We all comprehended his meaning at once. This was why they'd divided the twins. Why they had kept Keallach from lifting his hands before him, and separated Kapriel from the weather he could command. And without the twins' full gifting at our disposal, this would be a more challenging fight than we'd even imagined. We'd lost our two chief weapons. My hold tightened on my sword. Killian, Bellona, and Dri tensed around me. Azarel drew back on her bow, arrow notched, and Vidar's fingers danced over the triggers of two pistols. Tressa—bless her—shouldered a shield; I knew she had several daggers at her belt, but her most significant weapon would be to pray protection for all of us at the front—and for healing over those who fell.

"Welcome, welcome," Maximillian said from behind Keallach's shadowed form, lifting his hands and flashing us a grin, as if we joined him at a banquet table instead of this dank pit. "How I've longed for this day." With those words, he brought his hands together and smiled over at us. "Undoubtedly, you thought you'd seen the last of me," he said, moving around Keallach's inert form. "Thankfully, Pacifica boasts some fine physicians, and they were able to save me from death's fearsome clutches. I regret to say, however, that none of those healers are here, in Castle Vega. So as each of you"—he paused to look down the line of us—"lies dying here, your blood seeping between the blocks of this wonderful castle, know this—*no one* will come to save you."

"It is you who are in mortal danger," Niero said. "You are surrounded, our soldiers moving closer even now!" He shouted the last of his words, and they echoed through the massive chamber, giving those with us the signal to move in. Then he turned back to Lord Jala with a narrowed gaze. "Surrender now, and we shall not kill you. We will set you free with enough water and food to cross the Great Expanse on foot and see where the Maker's will leaves you."

"Well," Lord Jala sniffed, "I don't much care for the sound of that. Your own journey brought you close to death, did it not? Before you reached the emperor's sanctuary?" He glanced down at Keallach, as if our brother was sitting on a throne instead of in chains and unconscious. In that moment, I saw the glint of madness in his eyes and knew that our last battle had not only done damage to his body, but also to his mind. He'd always hovered at the edge of it. "No," he said. "I don't believe that's my chosen end." He drew out his sword and stared straight at me.

Sethos chose that moment to enter the circle of light cast by the torches, his red cape swirling about his legs as he stopped. I felt Andriana shrink back a bit, farther behind me. "So there shall be blood," he said, looking at Niero. "Or we shall take Keallach, Kapriel, and Andriana and depart, leaving you and your precious Ailith whole."

"Never," Niero ground out, his ivory wings peeking up over his shoulders.

"Never say never," Sethos said, dark wings unfurling. "Attack!"

The two rose in a streak above us, staff and curved blades clanging as crates all about us opened, the men hidden inside letting loose a battle cry. My momentary hope that we outnumbered our enemy fell away like grim, dry flakes, and I turned to counter Lord Jala's first strike.

He was surprisingly strong, given his grave injuries just weeks before. I remembered him bleeding out across the intricate, beautiful flooring of Palace Pacifica and wished I had finished him then so he wasn't here today.

"No, Ronan." Dri's quiet voice reached my ears. "We won't beat them in a battle of hate, only love. Reach for it."

I frowned, frustrated at her confusing words. Irritated by them. Could she not see that I battled to save her? To save us and all we believed in? And yet her words niggled at me as I turned, sinking against Lord Jala's third and fourth strikes, driving him backward on the fifth. *It is true,* I thought. *The enemy deals us lies, and I am accepting every card.*

Dri followed us, lifting her hands, whispering a prayer for me . . . and, unexpectedly, for Maximillian Jala. I swallowed hard as I heard her utter his name, battling between wanting her to cease and wanting her to continue. Because in her words, I sensed the balm of the Maker's sweet call, his guidance, his leading. My love was following where the Maker led her. And my best path was to follow her along the Way. In that vein, I became stronger with each strike.

"Stop it," Lord Jala seethed, trying to strike at her, but I blocked him. "Tell her to *stop it,*" he said, jutting out his chin.

I grabbed his wrist, turned, and yanked him over my shoulder, throwing him to the floor. "I do not correct my wife when the Maker has called her to do something. Nor should you," I said, setting the tip of my sword at the hollow of his collarbone.

He lifted his hands in surrender, letting his sword drop from his fingers with a clang to the stone beside him. I battled between ending his life and giving in to the call to mercy, to love, to all that Dri was praying for right now. Even for an enemy such as this. Had not the Lord of Zanzibar turned to the Way too? Dri was praying that Max would turn, see the light, know the Way that was true.

Sweat drifted down my brow as my sword hovered.

"What, Knight?" Jala goaded, eyes narrowing. "Can you not do it? Is it not within you?"

Such hate wafted in his eyes, such malice, that it was all I could do to not end him there and then. Above us, Sethos and Niero still wrangled. In a circle, all about us, soldiers fell to wounds or deathly blows. I had no time for this. I had to move on to aid the others! But still, Jala's gray-green eyes held me.

He grew still, curious, and I knew then that Dri had knelt and laid a hand on his arm, still praying. But his eyes were on me, distant, cold, as if waiting for my deathblow. But there was also a spark of wonder, curiosity, and hope kindling behind them.

I paused, sucking in my breath.

This was what it felt like to be the Maker.

To hold life and death in your hands.

To decide.

Half of me wanted to destroy this man, who had wreaked havoc upon my wife, Keallach, Kapriel, my friends, my community.

Half of me wanted to save him.

Maker, not me, but you. What would you have me do?

And the Maker stayed my hand. I'd swear it . . . he physically kept me from piercing the throat I longed to run through. He reached for Max. Reached for him. Even him.

Slowly, I knelt and set my sword carefully to one side. Then I took Lord Jala's tunic in my hands and raised him up to my face, until there was but an inch between our faces. "Know this, Maximillian Jala. I wanted nothing more than to end your life this day, but the Maker has chosen to offer you one last chance."

He blinked and shifted his gaze, considering my words. For a moment, there was hope—wild hope—within him, which I could feel as clearly as if I had Dri's own gifting. But then it was gone. His eyes grew hard, and he laughed. "Fool," he said, waving an arm.

I sensed the incoming strike too late. It hit me partway back on my skull, sending me reeling from Max, over and over. In the distance, I heard Dri scream and Lord Jala shout. But I was fighting unconsciousness. My vision steadied a moment, and I lifted myself with one arm. Then my head spun so wildly, I collapsed.

ANDRIANA

We had been so close.

I'd felt Max falter. I had a vision of what Keallach and Kapriel and he could do together, leading a whole new Pacifica in partnership with—not domination of—the Trading Union. Freeing the innocents who toiled in the mines, ceasing the kidnappings, and more. And beyond that, I had felt the hope flicker within him of something more, something beyond himself. A connection, brief as it was, with the Maker who had given him his first breath.

But just as quickly as he'd recognized the Maker, he denied him. And that action, though I should've expected it, hurt me as much as if he'd driven a sword through my belly. I ached over it, felt the sheer, heart-stopping folly of it. To deny the One who formed you and invited you into a relationship with him? To deny the One? I couldn't get my head and heart around the idea. The only way I came close was to think of myself as a god too. How else did you not bow down to the One who ruled the beginning and the end, when forced to face him at last?

I cried out as a Pacifican dealt Ronan a terrible blow, and he faltered and then fell unconscious. I picked up my sword and ran to keep his attacker from killing him as he lay there, vulnerable, narrowly blocking our enemy from decapitating him with his first strike and eviscerating him with the second.

I leaned closer to the young Pacifican, noting his skin covered in pimples. "Turn away from Lord Jala," I said, "or he shall destroy your future."

"I follow the master!" he sneered back. "Not a bit of a girl."

"But I am a Remnant," I said, lifting my brows. "Do not tempt me, or I shall loose the full weight of my gifting upon you."

"I know who you are," he said, shoving me backward and bringing his sword up between us. "What threat are you, Andriana of the Valley? Shall you kill me with *love*?" he taunted, eyeing me head to toe and back again. "Perhaps that's the way I would wish to die," he said, mouth twisting.

His words angered me at first, and then I considered them more fully. Flinging aside my sword, I leaped at him, grasping hold of his neck and arm and willing nothing but love and mercy and compassion into him.

At first he struggled, but it was only seconds before he was gazing at me with rapture in his eyes, tearing up, looking at me as if he wanted to cradle me in his arms and never let go. But it wasn't love or lust for me, it was gratitude, in its purest form. For the One who had brought him into life and seen it through. And in sharing it with him, my anger and frustration with him—every bit in me that marked him as enemy—turned to love and compassion, making me want to weep.

"This love," I whispered in his ear as he slackened in my arms, "is born of the Maker. Go and serve him. Fight those who fight against him. Let it be known that you are his soldier and no longer his enemy. Tell them why. Because you know love—the purest love of the Maker—for the very first time. And you will never go back."

He gaped at me, tears streaming down his face. "How could I? How could I ever turn away from this?"

I smiled. "Go and serve him. And fight those who deny him."

"Yes," he murmured, looking around the room, a sea of fighting men and women. "Yes."

I released him and turned to the next man who advanced on me, hope sparking in my heart. Could it be so simple? To awaken the Maker's love in each man or woman I met? Show them who they should be fighting for? Remind them of who gave them life from the very start? My heart swelled with the knowledge that this was a latent part of my gifting that I had never tapped into. A way to fight, to break, in a manner that made sense to the soul. I had known I could will emotion into others, of course. But I'd never thought to push people into facing the realities of their Maker's love. Not to brainwash or change their minds, but to open the door that so many had firmly shut and locked behind them.

This made me think of Lord Jala. I saw him, rising now, wiping his sweating forehead with the sleeve of his tunic. Ronan had come close to slaying him. I'd felt Max falter, had almost visually seen his defenses down. And then he had chosen against the Maker. Could I help him cross the bridge he was so adamantly opposed to crossing? I moved toward him, electing not to draw my dagger or pick up my sword. For this battle, I would use only the gifting my Maker had bestowed on me.

I knelt and prayed over a Pacifican, unconscious on the floor. Then I went to Vidar, who struggled with another, the enemy's sword nearly at his neck. I reached out and laid both hands on our enemy's shoulders.

"What . . . are . . . you . . . doing, Dri?" Vidar choked out, face straining and sweating while keeping the larger man at bay.

But I didn't answer. I only prayed that the Maker would show this man—once a little boy—what it meant to be loved through and through, not for what you've done, but for who you are . . . and who you were made to serve.

I felt him physically falter. A moment later, the man cried out and dropped his sword. Both he and Vidar gaped at me, but I continued on, touching a Pacifican woman who had shot her last arrow, gripping her arm even as she thrashed— until she knew. She *knew*. I felt the knowledge flow over and through her with all the relief of a cooling bucket of water after several long, dusty days on the road. Her eyes rounded as she whispered, "Thank you."

I grinned and looked around, silently asking the Maker who was next, who I might safely reach, when my gaze landed again on Lord Jala. But my actions had stirred our Sheolite enemies, and several scouts advanced on me from all sides. Even Sethos, high above us, still battling Niero, looked down at me with hatred in his eyes.

Azarel took on two of the Sheolites; Vidar and Bellona the others.

But I knew what I was to do.

Maximillian stared at me, wondering at my lack of weapon. My palms opened to him as I approached. If I could just reach *him*, show him what he was missing, turn him to our side, then the rest of the Council was bound to fall.

"Do you surrender?" Maximillian asked, stepping toward me.

"Yes," I said nodding, smiling. "Yes." As he got closer and took hold of my wrists, I looked up into his face. "I surrender to the One who was, and is, and is to come!"

He released me as if I'd burned him, but it was my turn to grab hold of his wrists. "You knew him once, Maximillian Jala. The One who brought you into the world . . . before the one who seeks to master this world mastered you. But you were born to serve your Creator, Max. Born for more. Not more things, not more power, not more control, but to serve the Eternal One. Isn't that what you seek? Eternal power? And yet there is only One who holds that in his hands, and it is not Sethos or the dark."

He grew desperate, trying to pry my fingers from his arm, looking as if he was considering biting me in order to make me stop. I could feel the cold pressing in, more Sheolites approaching . . . the *whoosh* of Sethos's wings landing nearby, then Niero's.

But I bent my head and laid my life in the Maker's hands—along with Max's—knowing that this was a critical juncture, not just for me and our cause, but for this man before me, so hateful and yet redeemable still. *Maker, open his heart. Open his mind. Let him feel your vast love and forgiveness—*

I didn't see the sword coming, but I felt the impact at my side. I crumpled to the ground, more fearful of losing my grip on Maximillian than death. But I could only relinquish to gravity's pull. I went down heavily, feeling the ripping of flesh and muscle and sinew. Only then did I lift my hand to my side and feel the warm wet of blood, far too much blood.

I blinked quickly as my vision tunneled, fighting to stay true to those I was with. Across the room, I saw Ronan, dreadfully still—dead? *Please, Maker, let him live.* And at my side, I saw Niero land, blocking a Sheolite scout's next blow across my chest, then Sethos's attack too. As if from far away, I felt the tickle of the feathers from his wings across my cheeks and felt as if they were stroking my face, encouraging me to remain, to not give in to death.

You serve the One who breathed life into you, Dri. Cling to him.

I will.

Stay with us. In this life.

I'm trying.

I could feel my heart pounding in my chest, as if it aimed to generate more blood to replace what I was losing. I reached out red-stained fingers to touch the tip of Niero's wing, dancing before me as he defended me from Sethos and others, and frowned as I noticed I was leaving crimson stains on the pristine, ivory feathers.

And then I felt horror emanate from our angel-protector, the first clear glimpse of emotion I'd ever felt from him. I managed to turn my face upward, and his horror became my own.

Because Sethos's sword had pierced him through.

Its bloody point was above me, at Niero's back, glistening in the torchlight.

He held his second curved blade to block Sethos's next blow, but he was clearly faltering.

The feathers from his wings were shimmering, almost becoming translucent.

"Niero!" Azarel screamed, the name hovering in the echoing chamber, even above all the shouts and groans and cries about us. She was swooping in—an angel too, I saw now, observing it not with shock but with dim recognition of something, again, that I should have known as fact. *Azarel is an angel.*

One of her arrows hit Sethos in the shoulder, but he merely grimaced, twisted it from his flesh, and flung it away.

Niero fell to his knees, his hands trembling, fighting to hold on to his blade but clearly unable to lift it.

I tried to rise. And knew it was hopeless.

I am sorry, sister. I will meet you again in—

He never finished that last sentence, that last whisper inside my head and heart.

Because it was then that Sethos cut off his head.

I heard the sickening crack of bone on stone as it rolled nearby and swallowed back vomit as I felt the spray of blood cover my cheek. I refused to look, staring instead at his wings as he fell to his side before me, the feathers shimmering then fading into parchment-like matte and then disintegrating into dust.

Sethos stepped through what had once been Niero, the dust spreading in small clouds beneath his sandals. He leaned down and grabbed hold of my tunic, lifting me partway up as I cried out, my side an agony of pain.

"And now, dear Remnant," he whispered, taking a deep breath, as if loving the scent of Niero's blood on me, as if he wanted to lick it from my face as Lord Jala had once tasted my own. "You are ours."

CHAPTER 39

RONAN

I came to just as Sethos dealt Niero the final blow.

And when our captain died, the fight seemed to leave us all, separating us like seeds from the cottonwood come spring, spinning and swirling on the wind.

I fought to find my center, the One who had called us here and who would call us out. Fought to forget that Niero, Raniero, our captain, our ever-present core, was gone. Gone. *Gone.*

I steeled myself and fought to take a deep breath. *Maker, help me.* They'd figured out how to keep both Keallach and Kapriel from using their gifts. Andriana was injured, maybe worse. I couldn't take in more than that. I threw myself into the fight, but I knew, deep within, that this wasn't a battle we could win.

Vidar and we Knights kept at it for a little while longer, along with our Drifter and Aravander friends . . . and Azarel. But we had to surrender. We were faltering, weakening.

To not give in was to give up the chance to win another day.

With one look to Killian and Bellona, I knew they had come to the same conclusion. We laid down our swords and lifted our hands, shouting our bitter surrender before a Sheolite or Pacifican took another of our Remnants down.

And then I moved toward Sethos, who held Dri's unconscious form triumphantly in his arms. I still had my hands up, but it took everything in me not to attack. I hated the smug look on his face, the way his eyes squinted and his mouth quirked in pleasure. I wanted to beat him into unconsciousness.

I made the mistake of looking where Niero had fallen and felt sudden, hot tears in my eyes. Azarel was there, where he had last lain, weeping, a Sheolite on either side of her.

"You thought him invincible," Sethos said, sounding irritatingly compassionate as he set Dri down on the ground and allowed me to approach her. "I understand. He was a mighty and worthy foe."

I didn't give him the satisfaction of an answer. Instead, I knelt by Dri and placed a hand on her side, trying to stanch the blood. I looked back to where Tressa was and saw that she and Killian were each held back by two Sheolites. "I need our healer," I bit out, "or she will die."

"Perhaps I'll let her die," he sniffed, crossing his arms and looking down his nose at me. "She's been nothing but trouble. I wanted her as a figurehead, an empress for our emperor," he said, gesturing over at Keallach, who now writhed anew against his chains. "But you got in the way of those plans, didn't you, Knight? Becoming handfasted mates? No," he said, shaking his head and pursing his lips. "Since she cannot be wed to Keallach, it will be best for me if Andriana of the Valley follows your dear Raniero into the afterworld." He turned to walk away from me, gesturing to the nearest men. "Bring any of the Ailith and all those who serve them—including those traitors who defected to their side after Andriana touched them—to the prison. Execute the injured. Except for the emperor. Send him to the physician."

Execute the injured. I looked down at Andriana. Sethos seemed decided. And she was dying, right there in front of me. "No. You cannot," I cried, as two men lifted me bodily from her. "You cannot!" I repeated, my shout echoing. She was bleeding out, her skin becoming a ghastly gray. "You must save her!"

Sethos eyed me over his shoulder. "Why? What good is she to me?"

I fought to think. He had only wanted her for Keallach, as a bride. "The Remnants are stronger together," I tried.

"I have the strength I need, with Keallach soon back on the throne. Tressa's skills might prove useful to me," he said, looking over at her, "but I have yet to decide what I shall do with Kapriel, you Knights, Vidar, and *this* one," he said, pausing by Azarel, who was now so heavily chained that she knelt under the weight. She spat at him, and he backhanded her, sending her reeling to her side.

"No," he said, looking back at me. "Perhaps I'll keep this clean and execute you all, save the healer. She is beautiful," he said, striding over to her and ignoring Killian, who was straining to break free of the captors beside him. Sethos reached out and fingered a coil of Tressa's auburn hair, then ran long fingers along her jawline until he forced her chin upward. He pursed his lips. "She would make as suitable a bride for the emperor as Andriana. And yet perhaps more . . . malleable than Andriana proved to be."

"Tressa is my wife," Killian said ferociously. "We have taken our vows."

"But you have not consummated them yet," Sethos said, almost blasé in his tone. "Isn't that the custom of the Valley dwellers? To wait until your second decade?"

Killian's brow lowered, and he glanced at Tressa, as if about to divulge a secret. "We were not born in the Valley. Tressa is my wife . . . in every sense of the word."

It was Sethos's turn to frown. He *tsked* through his teeth. "How unfortunate. We cannot have any question about who the father is should the girl turn up pregnant," he said. "So we are back to Andriana as the only choice."

I looked back at Dri. What nonsense was this? Could he not plainly see she was dying? How much longer did she have? I wanted to scream in desperation.

Keallach was brought toward Sethos then, his arms still chained behind his back. "I want Andriana," he said to his old master. "Send the healer to her. Save her. She will become my bride."

I gaped at him, trying to make sense of his words. He refused to look my way. Was this a ploy? A way to save her?

Or . . . had we been played all along?

"And my brother," Keallach said, tossing his chin in Kapriel's direction. His own captors had just brought his twin near. "Save him too. We are stronger together."

Sethos studied the brothers, looking irritated, and then fully faced Keallach. "I am not given to granting you your every wish, Keallach, particularly now. You did not do as I asked while among them," he said, gesturing toward Kapriel and the Ailith. "We have much to discuss before the Council will even reinstate you to the throne, let alone grant you your heart's desire when it comes to a choice of mate. The right Pacifican girl might—"

"I want *her*," Keallach ground out, sweat running down his cheek, "and my brother back in safe custody in Pacifica. Nor will you kill the others. Imprison them if you must, but do not put them to death. See to it, Sethos, or I will not help you bring Pacifica back into line."

Sethos lifted his chin, black eyes tracing every nuance of Keallach's face.

"Yes," Keallach said. "We've heard about the unrest in Pacifica. You actually *need* a union between Andriana and me. You need Kapriel alive too, more than ever, with things as they are out here, as well as at home. And I have received my gifting in full. Give me what I ask, and there will be none who dare come against us."

Sethos said nothing. Then he turned to me. "Did you bed your wife, Knight? Tell me the truth. The emperor's bloodline must be true, without question."

I glanced over at Dri, so still. It was the only way to save her.

"No," I said. "She is still a virgin. Only her heart is mine."

A small grin teased the corners of Sethos's lips, seeing what this admission cost me. "That is most fortunate for her, Knight. And most unfortunate for you." He turned to the guards holding Tressa. "Release her. See if she can do anything to stop Andriana from departing this world for the next. I guess," he said, folding his arms, "what comes next is truly in the hands of your precious *Maker.*"

CHAPTER 40

RONAN

"Place the rest in the dungeon cells. Prince Kapriel too."

The guards dragged me past Lord Daivat, who smiled lazily at me. "Don't worry, Knight. We'll see your handfasting dissolved before we leave the Trading Union, so all is in proper order. Keallach will enjoy every bit of what you missed."

I bit the inside of my cheek, tasting blood and trying not to let them see more of my anguish than was necessary. What had I done? What had I *done*? And yet, hadn't I needed to do anything possible to save Dri?

"Didn't you ever wonder how we found you and your precious Remnant in every town to which you ventured? Knew you were coming here?" Daivat continued to taunt me, following us as we were dragged down to the cells. "You're such idiots," he said. "Never stopped to think that Kapriel and Andriana had both been implanted with a chip, did you? Did you really think we wouldn't use everything we had to come after you? And you made it easy."

"Daivat!" Lord Kendric shouted, holding Tressa from one side. "Enough! Come."

I frowned, and my breath came in uneven pants. An ID chip. Of course. That was how the Sheolites had found us in the Citadel . . . how Sethos had found us in Zanzibar . . . A chip. The same chips that had given them plenty of warning that we were coming to Castle Vega, gave them time to prepare a trap that would keep the twins from using their gifts against them.

My heart raged and then sank in grief. *Raniero.*

We were thrown into the foul, stinking cells, crammed in with other prisoners who had languished there for weeks or months. There was no place to sit and barely room to stand. And yet I knew that, even if there was, I'd do nothing but pace, awaiting news. I gripped the rough bars and leaned my forehead toward them, feeling the cool temperature that almost echoed that of my armband. *Maker,* I prayed, *Maker. Show me the way out of this. Help us!*

I felt sick, on the edge of despair. Niero was gone. Dri might be dying even now. And if she lived, she might very well be wrenched away from me. I gripped the bars more tightly, thinking of her with Keallach. Again, my mind roiled. Had it all been a trick? A way for him to get what he wanted? Or was he playing Sethos, trying to make a way to save Dri the only way he could, just as I was trying to do? I bumped my head against the bars as if I might be able to beat the truth into my brain.

What is it, Maker? Which is it? Show me, show me, show me.

"Ronan," came a woman's voice.

I looked in the direction I'd heard it, perhaps two cells down and across from me. "Bellona?"

"Over here," she said. I saw her then, face pressed to the bars as mine was.

"Tell me," I said, hating the misery in my own voice, my fingers clenching the prickly metal bars. "Did Keallach play us?"

"I don't know," she said, her own anguish matching my own. "I just don't know."

The sound of boots atop stone turned our attention to those approaching. I strained to see to the left, down to the corridor that joined the stairs with the vast basement where we'd battled.

Four men carried Andriana, deadly still, on a stretcher. Two others held Tressa between them, her hands and dress bloody, dragging her forward.

"Tressa!" I cried.

"She lives!" she called to me, looking over her shoulder. "Ronan, she—"

"Quiet!" the guard said, pushing her face to one side. And then they were past us.

"Tressa!" Killian's voice called out, sounding muffled from several cells away, as if he might've been deeper than at the bars. "Tressa!"

They moved on, up toward the stairs. Clearly, they were not leaving Tressa with us. She was being taken upstairs, to where Sethos and the Council undoubtedly took their leisure now, celebrating their victory. They had the girls. There would be no reason to keep Vidar or any of us Knights alive. We only posed a danger to them. And they could make much of a public execution.

I let out a cry of rage, pushing and pulling on the bars as if I could break through them.

And then I sank to my knees, weeping.

Maker, you made me strong, but I am weak. You made me a protector, but I have failed to protect. You made me a husband, but I am about to lose the wife I love. I am nothing. You are all. Do something. Please, please do something.

CHAPTER
41

ANDRIANA

I awakened in a sumptuous room, atop fine sheets like I hadn't seen since . . .

I gasped and sat up with a start, eyes wide. And then I cried out, feeling the piercing pain at my side. I fell back to the feather pillows and blinked, willing myself not to pass out as a black wave crossed my eyes, nausea roiled through my stomach, and then again, threatening . . .

"Dri?" Tressa said, coming over to me with a hushed voice. "Shhh," she soothed. "Shhh. Don't say anything. It's best they not know you are awake."

I heard the creak of a door on its hinges and hurriedly shut my eyes.

"Is everything all right? I thought I heard a cry," said a man.

"Uh-huh," Tressa said. "I just tripped. Stubbed my toe. I'm sorry to bother you."

"Hmph," he said. "Has the empress-elect awakened?"

"No. Not yet," she said, moving, and I guessed she was trying to intercept him. "She has been to death's door. Sometimes it takes a while to regain consciousness when one has hovered so close to the afterworld."

"I see," he said, and it was then that I recognized his voice. Lord Fenris. "Well, come to me at once. I am just across the hall. As soon as she wakes. You understand?"

"Yes, Lord Fenris. I will do as you have asked."

He paused a moment and then turned on his heel, slipping through the creaking door again. Tressa moved back to me, and I watched her through slit eyes. She was in the traditional ivory Pacifican dress. I tilted my head back, rolled as if still sound asleep, then looked over at her. "What has happened?" I whispered.

She moved over to me, kneeling by my bed. She gripped my hand in hers, and I steeled myself for the worst. "You almost died. The Maker healed you, but you still are far from completely well." Her blue eyes welled with tears. "Niero died, Dri."

I shut my eyes, remembering his head, rolling. His wings, disappearing.

"I know," I whispered raggedly, blinking back hot tears. I looked at her again, my grip on hers tightening. Somehow, in sharing the aching chasm of loss, we partially filled it.

"The Remnants . . . the Knights . . ." Her voice broke. She gathered herself and then continued. "They are still in the dungeon."

I felt the devastation in her, the yawning divide she experienced in her separation from Killian. The fear there. "But still, you stayed," I whispered.

She nodded slowly. "For you. For Keallach. He's some-where near, but I haven't seen him since we were put here."

"Here?" I breathed. "We're in Castle Vega still?" There were many hours in my memory that were lost to unconsciousness.

"Yes. The last I saw the Knights . . . Sethos . . . The Council . . . They made no promises." Fear yawned wide in her eyes.

"And Ronan?"

She looked away to the window, then back. "He was there, last I saw him. But . . ." She bit her lip.

"But?"

She hesitated, as if trying to find the words. "Dri, they know. You were handfasted to Ronan, but you haven't con-summated your vows. Keallach . . ."

She looked away again.

"Tress. *Keallach* . . ." I led.

She looked to me for a moment, her blue eyes sober and steady. "He offered for you, Dri. Said he wanted you. It was the only reason Sethos allowed me near you. To heal you for . . . him." She bowed her pretty head, shaking it slowly. "Had he not, you would surely be dead."

My heart was pounding, my mind whirling. "But . . . Tressa. What do you think? Did he do it as a . . . as a brother? To save me? Or for another reason?"

She took my other hand, so that we held both fists, cross-armed together. "I don't know," she said, her blue eyes meld-ing into mine. I felt her hope, her encouragement. "But you are alive. And had he not acted, had Ronan not relinquished you—you would surely be dead."

"Relinquished," I repeated, my brow furrowing.

Hers did too. "Ronan was forced to admit that while you are handfasted, you have not yet consummated your vows."

My mouth was dry. "But why? Why should that matter?"

"It matters that Keallach still could claim marital rights of his own. And if you bear a child, there would be no question as to who was the father. It is how he convinced Sethos to allow me to try and save you."

My mouth grew drier. "So . . ." I couldn't bear to go on.

"So, he has laid formal claim on you." Her lips closed for a moment, as if she had to will herself to continue. "He intends you to be his empress."

I leaned back against the pillow. I saw it, then. That it had been Keallach's only way to save me. And yet . . .

"Let us go from there, shall we? Hoping for the best, in all?" Tressa said. "Isn't that what the Maker asks of us?"

I nodded, but I knew my heart was far more jaded than hers. I'd experienced, firsthand, the depravity and the glory of the human heart.

And I had no idea exactly where Keallach was on that spectrum now.

CHAPTER 42

RONAN

"What is happening?" I whispered to the servant girl who drew fresh water from the well and passed it from cell to cell. "What news have you?"

She looked furtively to the guards at the end of the cellblock and didn't answer me, moving back to the well, dropping the bucket, and pulling it upward again, each crank of the wheel seeming to take an eternity. She moved to the cell next to us, and I shoved men aside, ignoring their cries, so that I could get closer to her.

"Please," I said. "I'm a Knight of the Last Order. I need to know. Does Andriana live? What do they plan to do with us?"

Her dark eyes shifted my way, weighing me to see if I told the truth. "Later," she whispered out of the corner of her mouth, her lips barely moving.

I swallowed my desire to continue to harangue her. She would bring me word if she could, somehow. I had to find the patience to wait. But it was dreadfully hard. With no more than two square feet to stand in, the combined stink of us was enough to send a grown man into a dead faint if one breathed through his nose, and more than two days without much sleep or a chance to sit down . . . I both wanted to collapse and fight my way out, all at once.

Some had resorted to crying, on and off. Kapriel had led prayers every few hours, and I supposed his own years of captivity made him more resilient than I to this new torture. The Drifters and Aravanders were more given to screaming their frustration while rattling the bars of their doors. They were used to freedom and wide, open spaces. As I waited through the hours for the servant girl to return, I wondered for the thousandth time if we'd misread our call to this foul city, if we'd been more influenced by Keallach than the call in our own hearts. The Remnants had seemed so certain, so clear that Castle Vega was next. And it had been logical, given that it was the last bastion of Pacifica outside the Wall. But had we allowed pride to rush us? Had it truly been the Maker who called us here, or our brother who just made it seem that way?

But then, hadn't Vidar said that we were not alone, that angels accompanied us?

I shook my head, arguing with myself. If it had been just Keallach . . . I had my doubts about him, especially now. He'd been so ready to jump in, to offer for Andriana. Yes, it was a means to save her. But wasn't it somewhat convenient, given what happened at Georgii Post?

A sound from the hall brought my head up, and it didn't take long to know that many soldiers were approaching. As they came into sight, with a ring of keys in the first man's hand, people began to cry out, half in fear, half in hope of release. There were rumors that we were all to be executed. Some said they'd shoot us each through the head. Others said we'd be hanged. Still more thought we'd be impaled, so that our deaths would be as excruciating as possible. "Make an example of us, that's what they'll aim for," said a Drifter.

The soldiers stopped in the center of the cellblock. "Where is Prince Kapriel? And Ronan of the Valley?"

"Here," I said, coughing.

Kapriel identified himself, several cells down. Both of our doors were opened, and we stumbled out. I gaped at the others as the soldiers stuffed them back in, even as I took my first full breath in days. I could barely move, my legs partially asleep, and the guards roughly took my arms. I looked for the others.

I spied Vidar first. "Are we alone?" I asked him as we passed. "Are any of our *friends* about?"

He gave his head a brief shake. "Not since Niero . . ."

I contemplated that. So we could count on no heavenly intervention.

They put a hood over Kapriel's head and bound his hands behind his back. Would that be enough to keep him from commanding the skies? I racked my brain for memory of him doing so, but every one involved his hands. Still, could not Dri read another's emotion, even if she wasn't touching the person? And Vidar could see without even opening his eyes.

A sick feeling went through me when another thought came to me. Perhaps we were heading for our executions first. The prince who might threaten his brother's rule. And Andriana's guardian and handfasted husband. Were we not the two most threatening of the Ailith? To kill us first might bring the rest low. But if that's what they thought, they were wrong. Killian and Tressa, Bellona and Vidar . . . they would find a way to fight back.

I squinted and winced as we reached the top of the stairs, the daylight nearly blinding me. The guards at my side hastened me forward, making me stumble.

"Watch it," grumbled the one on my right. They pulled Kapriel and me down the hallway and took a left, then down another hallway. We emerged onto the patio, where there was a pool, fountain, and luscious green plants.

Sethos, Keallach, and the Council were awaiting us. A shiver ran down my back. All were in their traditional Pacifican clothes in various shades of ivory, except for Sethos, who was in his crimson cape. But unlike the last time we were here, no women paraded about, serving the men drinks and food. My eyes narrowed as I saw that there was another dressed in a red robe. I did a double take. It was Zulon, the monk we'd encountered at Wadi Qelt.

I thought there was a small smile behind his eyes, which did not bode well for what was to come. We had not parted as friends.

Keallach rose, one arm in a sling and the other bound behind his back. The Council reluctantly followed suit. Sethos stood behind him. We drew closer, and Keallach approached his brother. "Kapriel, I am here," he said, leaning toward his twin. "If we remove your hood and free you, do you swear that you shall not use your gifting against us?"

"I swear it," Kapriel said after a moment's hesitation.

Keallach nodded, and a guard stepped forward and pulled the hood from Kapriel's head. When he pulled a decorative dagger from his belt and went around Kapriel to cut him loose, Lord Jala interceded. "Not quite yet with that," he said. "Let us keep some safeguard, shall we? It's one thing to let him see; it's another to allow him use of his hands."

Keallach grew rigid, as if upset by this intervention, but he said nothing as the guard sheathed the dagger.

Kapriel blinked slowly, his hair in disarray, as he gradually focused on his brother and the others behind him. "What is it you want?" he said, his voice sandy.

"We need your help," Keallach said. "I need your help."

I searched his eyes, his gestures, anything that could tell me that he was playing a part, pretending in order to give us some edge, but I could detect nothing. My angst grew.

"We have brought you forth," Lord Jala said, stepping up beside Keallach to face Kapriel, "to give you one final chance, my lord prince. Keallach has told us that, over these last weeks, you two have been able to bridge past pain and that you were able to forgive him for the . . . injustices you feel may have occurred."

"Injustices," Kapriel repeated benignly. "Such as murdering our parents?"

Keallach inhaled sharply and closed his eyes, as if suffering over the mere mention of their deaths.

Lord Jala stared back at him dolefully. "For one, yes," he sniffed.

"Or imprisoning me for years?"

"Yes, for that too." Lord Jala glanced at Keallach and took a step toward Kapriel. "It was our understanding that you might be ready to set your past behind you and rule together with your brother."

Kapriel lifted his chin and stared straight back at his twin. "I was ready to rule with him when I thought he had left his dark past behind him. Clearly," he said, bitterness and betrayal lacing his tone, "I was wrong."

Lord Jala looked to Keallach. "You told me you had him in hand. That he would capitulate."

"I told you I thought he would work with us. If you would give me a moment to speak to him alone, I—"

"No," Sethos said, stepping forward. "This is not a negotiation," he said, turning back to Kapriel. "This is a simple offer. Rule with your brother or die. There will be no more martyred prince, languishing in a prison. We will kill you and be done with it."

Kapriel's face twisted. "It is not an offer. It is a trap. Just like everything you've always 'offered.' It's a means for you and the

378

Council to control us, use us. So to your offer, I have one answer," he said, leaning forward. "No."

"Kapriel," Keallach began.

Sethos lifted a hand to him, and he fell silent. It was clear that any power Keallach had once enjoyed was gone. So then, what was his game? What did he hope to accomplish in their fold? I watched him, hoping he would look my way.

Lord Jala abruptly turned to face me. He lifted his hands to my filthy tunic and straightened it, patting my chest in an overly familiar way. I fought to stay where I was. "I suppose that leads us to you, Ronan of the Valley." He looked up into my face. "You see, we have two routes to resolve this tiresome dispute with the Trading Union and quell the unrest at home. A throne shared by the twins," he said, with a wave between them, "or what you most fear."

I swallowed hard, my lips clenched.

"Marriage between Keallach and Andriana," he went on. "It wouldn't be quite the same, not nearly as strong, and we had hoped that our wayward princes would let bygones be bygones, but . . ." He took a deep, dramatic breath with his hand on his belly. "It appears Kapriel has made up his mind, leaving us only one choice. You must dissolve your handfasting with Andriana, and she shall wed Keallach this very night. You were very brave in relinquishing. It had never occurred to me," he said, leaning in, "that any man would be able to keep himself from bedding his bride at the first opportunity."

"Maximillian," Keallach barked as the rest of the Council chortled and hid their smiles. My face burned, and I longed to wrench free of my ropes and throttle the pretty man's neck.

"It was selfless," Lord Jala went on, straightening. "And had you not acted on your heroic impulse, she would have bled out on the stones yesterday. So you should take that as a comfort, Ronan."

He patted my chest again, and I closed my eyes, refusing to flinch. He would like to see that he had power to agitate me. He took a slow turn around me. "We will bring Andriana to us now. The monk from Wadi Qelt will perform the ceremony to dissolve your handfasting. And then you shall stand here to bear witness as she exchanges her vows with Keallach."

"No," Kapriel erupted, his guards holding him back. "Keallach, you can't."

Keallach was staring at the ground. My heart pounded. Was this what he really wanted? Deep down? And wasn't it a bit *convenient* that he could blame Sethos and his Council for forcing him to do this?

"Keallach!" Kapriel shouted, straining to escape again. "What are you doing? What's happened to you?"

"Enough, enough," Lord Jala said wearily. "Be silent now, or we shall gag you." He looked to me. "You know it must be done, don't you? Release her willingly, or we shall make her watch you die so that your handfasting vows will be dissolved in the clearest way possible."

"Give me the night," I said, trying to buy time. "Let me consider it."

"I'm afraid that's impossible," he said, waving behind me. I turned with Kapriel to look to the women who approached. First Tressa. Then Andriana, dressed in finery like I'd never seen. Her gown was high-necked and tight across the arms and down her torso, hugging every curve in a sheath of dark blue. There was a teardrop cutout giving a peek at her cleavage, and everything else was covered, but obvious. She was barefoot, and her hair fell in dark curls about her shoulders. Her eyes and lips had been made up, making her impossibly beautiful.

I gaped at her, my belly a mix of agony and glory. My best friend. My soulmate. My wife. My future lover.

And yet my wife for not much longer. No longer my future lover.

Keallach's.

I whipped my head toward him. He stood, enraptured at the sight of her too. Full lips parted. Eyes wide. Brows curved in wonder.

He loved her. He honestly loved her too. And as a Remnant, he had twice the reason to care for her, protect her. Was this the Maker's way? To save her? Perhaps to work through the two of them to see justice restored to Pacifica? I remembered how she had argued for Keallach, how she'd wished to reach him, turn him back to us. How it had seemed to work.

But had it? Had it? I searched my mind and heart to discover the truth of it. Was Keallach ours? Or had he been playing us all along?

He dragged his eyes to me then, with apology and pain clear in them. "Forgive me, brother. It's the only way," he said.

"Is it?" I asked.

"It is. Please," he said, dropping his tone so Dri couldn't hear. "Don't make this any harder on her than it has to be."

"Keallach . . ." Kapriel said, his voice pleading now. "Let us sit down and talk."

Keallach ignored him. He didn't look away from me. "They'll kill you," he whispered. "It is not an idle threat. You saw what it did to her, losing Niero. Don't make her watch your death too. Not if you can help it. They will use such darkness in her," he whispered, leaning in, "against us."

"Keallach!" Sethos barked, clearly displeased by his whispers.

But our eyes were locked, a silent promise being made. Keallach was still with us. Warning me of their plans. They hoped I would fight, hoped they would have reason to kill me. Hoped it would throw open the door within Andriana that she always fought, the door that allowed the dark to wreak havoc within her.

I nodded once and then bowed my head, unable to watch as Dri was led toward me. I forced myself to look at her as my hands were cut free and the small monk approached us. Then the Council encircled us, with Tressa and Kapriel standing on either side of me, bearing silent witness.

"Ronan," Dri whispered.

"Trust me," I whispered back, tears welling in my eyes too. I knew she felt my pain, the agony within me over this. I hoped she would recognize my surety in this action too. It was the only way. For us to survive. To fight another day.

"Take her hand, Ronan of the Valley," Zulon said.

I did as he asked, wondering if I would ever feel her long, strong fingers in mine again. I felt like I was being strangled.

The monk took a long silk strip from his shoulder and wound it around our hands, over and under, just as the elder in the Valley had done. He paused a moment, then looked to me. "Say the words," he said.

I took a breath and then closed my mouth, unable to force them from my lips.

She stared at me, openly crying now.

It was then that I felt the point of a dagger at my lower back, pressing in toward my kidney. "Say them," Lord Jala hissed.

I took another deep breath, my eyes searching her face, wanting to memorize every bit of her—her smell, the way she looked, even weeping.

"You will always hold my heart, Andriana," I whispered. The dagger pressed in harder.

"And you mine, Ronan," she whispered back.

"Enough," Lord Jala bit out. "Do what you must."

It was as if I distanced myself at that moment. As if I wasn't there, in this tight circle, holding the hand of the one I loved most. I was far away, doing the hard thing that had to be done, watching my lips move as if I was someone else entirely. "I release you," I said. "I release you. I release you."

And with a slip of the silk strip from our joined hands, it was done.

CHAPTER 43

ANDRIANA

I felt the searing pain in him, even as I recognized my own. I knew what drove him to do it. Fierce protection. Sacrificial love.

"Take him back to the dungeon," Lord Jala said to the guards. "Kapriel too. We shall decide what we will do with them later."

"No," Keallach said, turning toward me. "It is best if they are both here to witness this."

I gaped at him, wondering over his cruelty. Could he not see the sorrow that both Ronan and I felt? Did he not know what witnessing our vows would do to him?

The monk looked to me and then to Keallach, still bound. "His hands must be free," he said to Sethos. "It is part of the vows."

Keallach stared up at Sethos. "You either trust me or you do not. But the monk is right. Without us holding hands, the vows will not be binding."

Sethos's eyes narrowed.

"Sethos," Keallach said, "my sword-bearing arm is likely broken and—"

"It is not the idea of you lifting a *sword* that bothers me," he said, coming down the two stairs to stand beside us. "But you are correct. I either trust you or I do not." He considered him thoughtfully.

"Have I not done all you have asked?" Keallach said. "Did I not deliver the Ailith into your very hands?"

"At an obviously great personal cost," Sethos said, as if that was a negative thing rather than a positive. He inclined his head to a guard beside Keallach. "Free him."

I shivered as my arm cuff sent an agonizing chill down to my elbow and wrist, but then I felt warmth too, a curious back and forth.

Keallach offered me both hands, even the one that was red and swollen. Trying not to hurt his injured arm, I accepted both, doing my best to ignore Sethos beside us and to concentrate solely on my brother before me, desperate to discern if he was doing all of this for his own good, or for all of ours. Keallach stared into my eyes, and in such close proximity, touching him, I knew then what I needed to know most. In him, I read love and loyalty and hope.

For me as a sister.

Not as a bride.

He smiled a little, as if knowing I must have received his message by the look in my eyes.

"Get on with it," Sethos barked at Zulon.

The sun was setting, and clouds were building in the west as if a thunderstorm brewed. I shivered, even under the heavy fabric of my gown. My armband continued to alternate between bursts of cold and heat, recognizing both enemy and Ailith kin, as confused as I was at what was transpiring around us.

Zulon stepped closer, the small man reaching only my shoulder in height. But I remembered that he was a wicked fighter. "Who stands for these two, wishing to share their marital vows?"

"We do," the Council said as one, making me start at the volume of their combined voices. It sent me to trembling. Was this happening? Regardless of what Keallach intended, was I about to become his bride?

Keallach squeezed my hand with his good one. *Trust me*, his eyes seemed to say.

"Present the bride and groom," said the monk.

Lord Jala stepped forward. "I present Emperor Keallach of Pacifica, who wishes to wed this woman."

A long silence followed, until Lord Fenris drew his sword and lifted it to Tressa's chin, forcing her to speak. "I present Andriana of the Valley, who . . ." The sword pressed harder against her throat. "Who wishes to wed this man?"

Even without looking at her, I knew she hated every word she uttered. But Keallach held me captive with his blue-green eyes.

Such love as this, I hadn't felt outside of Ronan's own.

I gaped at him, frightened, even if his chief emotion was a desire to serve, honor, protect. I couldn't quite trust that the dark one wasn't using him to trick me into this.

I centered in, willing him to focus on those ways that served the Maker's cause. He was clearly in a battle, and I was the prize.

It was a battle the Maker and I had to win.

Call on the Maker, not your own gifting, Niero had said to me.

"Maker," I prayed aloud. "Keallach is yours. No longer theirs. Pull him back!"

Sethos was on me in an instant, clenching my throat. "You dare . . . to invoke . . . that name . . . among us?" he seethed.

Keallach lifted a hand and sent Sethos reeling away from me, slamming him against the wall. Then he did the same to the nearest guards.

Others around us surged into motion. Ronan wrenched free, taking down one captor and then another and cutting Kapriel loose.

"No!" Sethos screamed, stumbling back toward us. "Guards! Sheolites, to me!"

Kapriel lifted his hands to the skies, already thick with swirling, sunset clouds that looked like the beginnings of a vase atop a pottery wheel, just taking shape into a funnel.

I turned to Tressa. "Go to the dungeon. Find your way through," I said, reaching out to will courage into her. "Free them all. Send them to us."

She tore away, and I bent and grabbed a fallen guard's sword, just in time to block Lord Fenris's first savage strike.

CHAPTER 44

KEALLACH

Lords Kendric and Daivat fell quickly, facing Ronan, Kapriel, Dri, and me.

But Max and Fenris remained, with Sethos between them and Sheolites closing in from every side. Sethos was lifting his hands to me, fingers curved, a shriek coming from his mouth that deafened me and seemed to block me from my gifting.

I ended up near Dri, back to back. More than anything, I wanted Dri to live. *I want her to live, Maker. Take me if it has to be one of us,* I thought, the first time I'd ever thought or wished or prayed such a thing. And it felt good. Right.

Holy.

I returned Maximillian's first strikes with fervor. In all of my life, had I ever felt such a thing? Claimed? Holy?

Only the ceremony in which I'd received my armband compared. And in the Ailith's circle at Georgii Post. Surrounded by my brothers and sisters. Shoulder to shoulder along the Way. That is what I felt in this moment again.

It was like a slap across the face.

I'd been in a reverie. A dream state, casting between one realm and another. Even if I'd decided to remain true to my Ailith kin, I knew what frightened Dri. Sethos's dark power pulled me back to my old life and ways, again and again.

But I was called to the new. To the Remnants. To my Call, as deeply a part of me as the blood coursing through my veins. To the Maker.

It was he who had brought me into the world, and it was he who would usher me out.

I centered in on the thought, closing my eyes, willing away all the other forces that had a call on my mind and my heart. *Maker.*

The One who had made me one with sisters and brothers, a holy force, each with their own gift to lend to the cause . . . or forsake it.

I opened my eyes, watching as Dri caught a Sheolite guard's strike, turned, and sent his sword flying.

I swore under my breath. She was lovely.

Beyond anything I could dream of as my own.

And in love—forever in love—with another.

Ronan.

I let out a growl of complaint, finally understanding it for the last time. She wasn't mine.

She was my brother's.

My brother's. Not the brother formed in tandem in my mother's womb. But just as surely my brother's.

I turned to two guards who had just entered the fray, sending their swords skittering across the stones. They stared at me in stark terror as I approached and looked them in the eye. "Go below to the dungeons, and free the prisoners. Quickly!"

Their eyes dilated, and they turned on their heels to run and do as I bid.

I could feel my enemy's eyes on the back of my neck, his hatred, even before my armband told me he was advancing.

Sethos. My once-savior.

My utter downfall.

He carried the dead Kendric's sword in his hand and came at me, nostrils flared with rage. I blocked his strike, and our swords crossed above our heads. "I trusted you," I said, panting from my exertion at holding him back.

"As I did you," he spat, whirling to strike again.

But I could tell he wasn't certain—wasn't sure that I was wholly the Maker's yet. Because I knew there was far more power behind his strike than he had just now brought against me. And I was using my weaker hand. He was wondering if there was still an opportunity, a way in.

"It is over, Sethos," I said, our swords cutting a vibrating sound in our ears as we slid apart again. "You did your best. But this day belongs to the Maker."

With that word, he advanced on me with a vengeance, granting me no quarter, no edge. I frowned, trying to set up blocks with my gifting, but failed. I needed time to concentrate, I decided. A breath of time. But onward he came, until I was backed against a wall.

If Vidar and Bellona hadn't arrived then to aid me, each with a sword tip at his neck, I would likely have died.

Sethos stilled.

"Seems the rats have escaped their dungeon," Vidar quipped. "Shall this be a swift or drawn-out death, Lord Sethos?" he asked. Behind him, I saw Killian take down a Sheolite guard, nearly cutting him in half.

"Oh," Sethos sneered, dark eyes shifting left and right, "let's draw it out. But it will be your deaths I shall relish, not my own."

Vidar's eyes danced. "As you wish," he said, sliding his sword in a shallow groove across Sethos's chest. Bellona thrust her sword forward, aiming for his jugular, but Sethos twisted in a frighteningly inhuman move, and her sword met only air.

"You shall pay for that," Sethos seethed toward Vidar, putting a hand to his chest. He grabbed for me next, but Bellona was already pulling me out of harm's way, and I found myself side by side with Ronan, who had just brought down a Sheolite. Together, we looked around. And found whom we sought.

Andriana.

"You go to her," I grunted. "I must finish Sethos."

"Wait!" Tressa said, running toward me, Killian beside her, and placing her healing hands on my injured arm. "Just give me a moment..."

ANDRIANA

Two Sheolites moved in on me, one from either side, and I shifted back and forth. The sword was awkward in my hand, too big for my grip. And my cursed dress, so tight all along my body, made it feel like I was fighting with my legs tied together. It wasn't long before one Sheolite disarmed me, sending my sword clanging to the stones.

I glanced around for anything I could grab to protect myself, while still more Sheolites arrived to fight the prisoners who had escaped and followed the Ailith to aid us. I reached for a silver tray just as my attacker brought his sword toward me, and managed to block his strike. The tray folded around his weapon, hitting my shoulder, and I wrenched it away, letting out a humorless laugh at the look on his face. Apparently, he'd never attacked a Remnant armed with a tray. But once again, he advanced on me, pulling two daggers from his belt. I edged away, putting a table and then a chair between us.

With a roar, Ronan came after him, swiftly taking him down. Once again, I grabbed a sword from the ground and stood, back-to-back with Ronan, as the next came at us. "This cursed dress," I said to him. "I can barely move."

"Stay beside me," he grunted, blocking his next adversary's blow.

He needn't have said it. I was determined not to be separated from him again. We used long-practiced moves and quiet words of warning to deal with the two upon us, and then a third after them. Which was good, because clearly the Sheolites no longer had orders to spare me. They were bent on killing us both.

Weariness settled over me like a net. We couldn't keep this up for long. We needed the Remnants in full force. *Maker, show us the way.*

It was then that I felt the warmth in my arm cuff, the presence of the Maker and his angels. Vidar was grinning as he advanced on a Sheolite before him, waggling his eyebrows at me as I caught his glance. I saw Killian, protecting Kapriel as he lifted his hands to the sky, the wind and rain now just beginning to hit us. Azarel and Asher were there, each firing arrows into our enemies. Lord Cyrus now fought Lord Jala.

Still more allies flooded onto the terrace. Drifter and Aravander and Georgiian, and even some Pacificans, all going after our enemies. In the sky, the clouds—alight with coral sunset hues—swirled, the funnel building in response to Kapriel's call to arms. Those enemies in front of us found themselves fighting on two sides, and we began winnowing away their number. Wind began whipping around us.

Keallach was advancing on Sethos, palms out before him, face taut with deadly intent. Sethos staggered and tried to lift his sword, but it was as if it weighed a thousand pounds. "Stop it!" he shouted at Keallach. "You are mine!"

"No," Keallach said, shaking his head a little, grief in his eyes. "You tried to make me yours, but I have always belonged to the Maker."

One of Azarel's arrows pierced Sethos's shoulder.

He sneered at her as she drew another arrow across her bow, his wings unfolding behind him. But he looked again to Keallach. "You think the Maker shall forgive all you have done to harm him and his cause? He shall send you to join me, one way or another."

"No," I said, moving closer. "He shall not."

I could feel Keallach weakening, doubting in the face of the enemy's lies, and I placed my hand on his shoulder. Vidar came up too, putting his hand on the other shoulder. Together, we drove toward Sethos, knowing our Knights would protect our backs. Our battle was here, against the darkest one we'd ever met. Tressa came behind us, putting her hands on Vidar and me, and I felt the surge of power move through us into Keallach.

Sethos dropped his sword and continued to move backward. "You think this ends here?" he spat.

"Yes, it ends here," Kapriel said, coming to stand beside his brother and bringing down the heart of the funnel cloud around us. It sealed us off from the others. Every time someone tried to approach us, they were tossed aside. It was like we stood in the eye of a tornado.

Sethos hit a marble column and looked wildly about. His wings were unfurled, as if he was poised to fly, but with our combined power, we kept him in place.

Azarel approached him, drawing an arrow across her bowstring.

"For every one of the Maker's beloved you have murdered, for the harm you have wrought upon this world, I will send you to the underworld, never to return."

"You, little angel?" he sneered. "You truly think one such as you can take *me* down? Did you not see how I destroyed your beloved Raniero?"

He dodged her next arrow and advanced upon her. Azarel let her wings unfurl, and in a blur of motion drew Sethos to one side.

Allowing Ronan's sword to cut into his back.

And Killian's sword to pierce him through the belly as he arched.

And Bellona's dagger to drive into his neck.

He fell to his knees as Killian withdrew his sword, gurgling, choking on his own blood, and letting his staff fall.

"May you rot in the dark, thinking about all you once had . . . and lost," Azarel said, lifting his staff in her small, strong hand. "This is for Raniero," she bit out, and then pierced him through the heart with his own weapon.

"And this is for everyone else," Killian said, bringing his blade down across Sethos's neck in a killing arc that vanquished our enemy.

Forever.

CHAPTER 45

ANDRIANA

The wind ceased, and the sudden silence sounded like its own form of sound. It was like everyone on the crowded terrace held their breath. But as we slowly turned to see our friends, the Maker's own, standing with our foes at their feet, a cheer rose into the air. Men and women raised fists, shouting, smiling, hooting their praise, and then pressed in toward us, lifting us, dancing, and singing.

We had done it. Or rather, the people had done it, I thought. The Remnants had merely been the catalysts. All along, the Way was much stronger than anything we held as our own gifts. *Together, we are strongest,* I thought, relaxing, exulting in the sensation of being held by hundreds, passed along above them as they sang and danced, carried out of the palace and into the streets where bonfires had been lit and thousands more seemed to congregate. It was there in a large plaza that I was finally set upon my feet, and soon, Keallach and Kapriel, Ronan, Bellona, Vidar, Tressa, Killian, and Azarel were set beside me.

I caught Vidar's furrowed brow as he looked to an alleyway and spied some people, with bundles upon their backs or at the sides of mudhorses, moving away from us, down the street. I cupped his cheek and gave him an understanding look. "This is the Maker's city now," I said. "People accept it or they do not. It is their choice."

"But why?" He shook his head, hands on his hips. "Why would they not choose this?" he said, throwing his hands up and gesturing around, his grin returning. The people did not allow us to continue our conversation, but wrapped us into a dance in which you placed your right arm around the shoulder of the person next to you and your left arm around the hip of the other. To my left was Ronan, and he smiled down at me with such love and glory that I thought I might burst with how it filled me.

He helped me keep my feet, seeing anew how the gown bound me, and when the song finally waned, he pulled me aside, bending down with his knife to split the skirt from knee to ankle. I sighed with relief. Even though the bodice was still tight, being able to move freely was just the aid I sought. He sheathed his knife and then pulled me into his arms, cradling my head and stroking my back. "Dri, I am so glad . . . for all that's been accomplished, but most of all, that you are safe."

"As I am, you," I said, pulling him closer. "We might not be handfasted anymore, but I never want to be out of arm's reach from you again."

"Never," he growled, and bent to capture my lips with his own. When our kiss ended, he looked down at me, admiring me. "You're in the gown. Shall we take our vows this night?"

I smiled and gave him a sad grin. "You know as well as I do the right answer to that."

He groaned, stroking my cheek. "Yes," he said with an agonized sigh. "I do. But I shall be counting the days, Andriana of the Valley, until we celebrate the first full moon of Hoarfrost of our second decade."

"As will I," I said, smiling back at him. "But first . . ."

"Yes, yes," he said, pulling me back into his arms and kissing my head. "Pacifica, right? My Rem won't rest until every innocent is freed."

EPILOGUE

ANDRIANA

Pacifica gave way soon after. Without the Council or Sethos, they couldn't stand against the swelling forces of the Trading Union for long. And when the brothers offered to retake the throne, they were welcomed. Over the seasons that followed, many thronged to our cause. The Wall was taken down and new roads were built, binding the empire into one. One empire governed by Remnant princes, led by the Way. The factories and mines that held captive children were emptied, and people went to work in them for a fair wage. Emissaries were sent off to reach new lands with word of who now controlled our lands—twin brothers, sharing the throne in the West, honoring the One who had placed them there.

But while we often went to see our brothers, Asher, and Azarel in the West, Ronan and I mostly stayed in the Valley, where we staked out land and built cozy cottages in a new village that eventually housed each of the Ailith. Bellona became a lead hunter. Vidar became a blacksmith, but spent more time chasing the Aravander gunner-girl than at his anvil. Tressa and Killian set up a small hospital, while Ronan and I took to learning the ways of farming from Dagan. Over the next two Harvests, the Ailith set out together for a few weeks, each time called to reach a new land, to tell new people about the Way and the Maker. But we were always most content at home.

And on a perfectly still, clear Hoarfrost night, the sky alight with stars and a full moon making the snow around us glitter, Ronan and I exchanged our forever vows, surrounded by our friends and family, including grandparents and aunts and uncles and cousins that we were just getting to know, finally reunited. But even with all that family around us—blood kin and Ailith kin—I had eyes for one man alone. And that man took me home that night and made me his, in ways we had longed for, season upon season.

I awoke the next morning and found his side of the bed cold. Frowning, I wrapped my blanket around my bare shoulders and padded out to the sitting room, where I found him watching the sunrise through the window. I sat down on his lap, and he nuzzled my neck, pushing aside my hair and wrapping his arms about me. I smiled and looked out with him, watching as the sun made the clouds change from purple to deep pink to a delicate rose. It was like watching the Maker at work, blessing our day, our lives, and our love.

And at last, my heart was at rest.

"What now?" Ronan whispered. "After all we've been through, all we've seen, all we've experienced, is this to be our lives now? Waking together, working together." He shrugged. "It's wonderful, but it's all a bit . . . tame, isn't it?"

"For now," I said, turning to caress his face, the lines of a nose that had been broken a few times, the stubble on his chin. "Something tells me we'll face other battles ahead. Who knows what next year's Harvest shall bring? But for now, let's just make the most of this season of peace, shall we?"

He nodded, a grin on his lips, and he moved in to kiss me. "I have to say . . . If this is peace," he said, rising, lifting me in his arms, and carrying me out of the room, "I'm all for it."

"As am I, Husband," I said with a laugh. "As am I."